APPLAUSE

(MARGARET 'MARGOT'
THE SECOND OF THE DUDLEY SISTERS)

MADALYN MORGAN

Applause @ 2014 by Madalyn Morgan
Published worldwide 2014 @ Madalyn Morgan

All rights reserved in all media. No part of this book may be reproduced or transmitted in any form by any means, electronic or mechanical (including but not limited to: the Internet, photocopying, recording or by any information storage and retrieval system), without prior permission in writing from the author.

The moral right of Madalyn Morgan as the author of the work has been asserted by her in accordance with the Copyright, Designs and Patents Act 1988.

All characters in this publication are fictitious and any resemblance to real persons, living or dead, is purely coincidental.

A catalogue record for this book is available from the British Library.

ISBN: 978-1497449664

Book Jacket Designed by Cathy Helms
www.avalongraphics.org

Proofreading by Alison Thompson, The Proof Fairy
www.theprooffairy.com

Formatting by Rebecca Emin
www.rebeccaemin.co.uk

Author Photograph: Dianne Ashton

ACKNOWLEDGEMENTS

I thank my mentor Dr Roger Wood for his help and encouragement. Jane Goddard for the photograph of her mother Pamela, aged eight, and Getty Images for the photograph of the three young women. Author friends, Elizabeth Ducie and Jayne Curtis. Pauline Barclay and the authors of Famous Five Plus for their support. Amy McBean-Dennis and the ladies at Oh Lovely in Lutterworth, Joff Gainey and Becky at The BookStop Café Lincoln and Kelvin Hunt of Hunts Independent Bookshop in Rugby for selling my novels. I would also like to thank my soul sister Dianna Cavender, and friends Valerie Rowe and Hilda Clarke – whose faith in me has never wavered.

Applause is dedicated to the memory of
my lovely mum and dad, Ena and Jack Smith.

*

I also dedicate Applause to the brave servicemen and women of the British, Commonwealth and American armed forces. The home guard, air-raid wardens, nurses, doctors, hospital auxiliaries, volunteers, ambulance drivers, men and women of the fire brigade, factory workers, farmers, land army girls and wartime correspondents.

To the theatre owners and managers who kept the theatres open. Backstage and front of house staff who kept the theatres running, and the artists who risked their lives to keep the public entertained. To the composers, songwriters and playwrights. The entertainers who worked with ENSA and other entertainment organisations, professional and amateur.

Last, but by no means least, the mothers, daughters, sisters and wives who kept the home fires burning, so our heroes had a home to come back to.

CHAPTER ONE

'Look out! Stop!'

Margaret didn't look. She didn't stop until she was pushed into a doorway. 'What--?' was all she had time to say before her body slammed into the door. With the wind knocked out of her, Margaret gasped for breath. She struggled beneath the body of a man twice her size until she found a pocket of air, and inhaled deeply. A combination of sweat and brick dust filled her nostrils. Her mouth snatched for air and she began to choke. Her captor didn't relax his grip. He held her tightly as tiles from the roof of the once quaint Jardin Café on Maiden Lane, in London's Covent Garden, crashed onto the pavement where Margaret had been standing seconds before.

The cracking, splintering sound of snapping slates gave way to a heavier, duller sound like rolling thunder. With a vice-like grip, the man shielding Margaret took hold of her wrist and threw himself at the door they were leaning on. The door groaned, and the wood splintered at the side of the antiquated brass keyhole, but it didn't give way. Still holding her, the man lunged again. This time there was a loud crack and the lock buckled beneath his powerful body. The door burst open, propelling Margaret through its gaping entrance as the chimney from the café's roof crashed to the ground, missing them by inches.

Frightened for her life, Margaret stumbled into the darkness, lost her footing, and slid bottom-first down a flight of stone steps. The strap on her handbag snapped and the bag flew through the air, scattering its contents over the ancient flagstones. With the cardboard box of her gas mask digging into her ribs,

Margaret came to a halt beneath a huge wooden cross.

Dazed and bruised, she looked around. She could see by the beam of daylight shining into the small vestibule that she was in the entrance of a church. She could hardly believe her eyes. She had walked down Maiden Lane a dozen times before; she'd had tea in the café, bought postcards from the bookshop opposite to send home, but she had never seen a church. Now she was sitting at the bottom of a flight of steps looking up at a soulful figure of Jesus Christ on the Cross.

'Have you had enough of life, young woman?' the burly workman bellowed from inside the door at the top of the steps.

'What do you mean?' Margaret said, coughing and spluttering.

'That was a bloody stupid thing to do.'

'You're the stupid one, for pushing me down these stairs. I could have broken my neck.' She put her hand up to shield her eyes and peered at him through swirling brick dust. Because the light was behind the man she wasn't able to see his face, but she could see he was wearing workman's clothes.

'Didn't you see that bloody great big sign sayin' No Entry?'

'I didn't have time to look.' Margaret put on her best voice, emphasising the aitch in have. 'I was on my way to an important job interview and didn't want to be late,' she said, in an attempt to justify her stupidity, while biting back her tears.

'You could've been killed, never mind late!' the
man hollered, and he stormed off.

'I'm sorry!' Margaret shouted after him, but he had gone. She could have been killed, and so could he. The workman had put his life at risk to save her and she hadn't even thanked him. As the reality of the danger she'd put them both in hit her, tears welled up in her eyes. She looked up at the figure of Jesus on the Cross. Engraved above his head were the letters INRI – Jesus of Nazareth, King of the Jews. At his feet was a brass plaque with the words Welcome to the Church of St. Saviour. Margaret burst into tears.

On grazed hands and knees, Margaret picked up her comb, lipstick and powder compact, which now had a cracked mirror and was covered in brick dust. Returning them to her handbag, she sat back on her heels and looked at her hands. How can I go to a job interview looking like this? she thought. But if I don't go, the builder who saved my life would have risked his life for nothing. And what would Anton Goldman say? I've pestered him to get me the interview for more than six months.

'Anyone would think you don't want this job in the theatre,' she said to herself. She did want it. She wanted it badly. Getting a job as an usherette was only the beginning. One day she was going to be an actress and sing and dance in a West End show. It was what she had dreamed of all her life. She was going to be famous and she wasn't going to let a bit of muck, or a few cuts and bruises, stop her.

With renewed commitment, Margaret took a handkerchief from her handbag. She spat on it and wiped the streaks of dirt – a combination of tears and brick dust – from her face. She took out the compact. The powder puff was dusty too, but after blowing it and flicking it about, she pressed on the circular gauze and patted her face. Carefully she dabbed extra powder under her eyes to hide the red blotches made by her tears. She then put a dot of lipstick on each cheek and gently rubbed it in to give the appearance of a healthy glow, before applying the cherry red stick to her lips.

She made her mouth wide, then pressed her lips together, rubbing top against bottom until the colour was spread evenly. Satisfied with what she saw in the small mirror, she dropped it back into her bag. She then took off her stockings, gave them a shake, and put them on back to front. The holes, made when her knees met the stone steps of the vestibule, were now at the back of her legs and were less noticeable. 'Ouch!' As she twisted her body to check that the lines she'd drawn with her eyebrow pencil on the back of her legs that morning had not rubbed off, an acute pain stabbed at her side, reminding her that she had fallen on her gas mask. Turning again, but slowly, Margaret could see the lines that pretended to be seams were still there.

Before leaving the church, Margaret took off her jacket and gave it a shake. Minute specks of brick dust swirled through the air. Caught in the beam of light shining through the open door, the particles looked like snowflakes in a Christmas dome.

She looked at her wristwatch. If she was going to the interview she needed to leave now. Ignoring the pain in her side, Margaret bent down, took hold of the strap of her gas mask and put it over her shoulder before picking up her handbag. Stooping, she made her way to the top of the steps and the door. In the doorway she took a deep breath and slowly stood up straight. With her head held high, she stepped out into the September sunshine.

The soot-stained chimney that had almost killed her lay on the pavement in front of the door. Although it was partially hidden by broken roof slates, cracked guttering, and lumps of plaster, Margaret could see it was two chimneys cemented together. Her legs felt like blancmange. She put out her hand and held on to the doorframe to steady herself. It would definitely have killed her if the workman, who she wouldn't recognise now if she tried, hadn't pushed her out of the way. She blinked back her tears and started to step over the debris. Then she stopped. The chimney was too high to climb over, especially in shoes with high heels, and there was so much rubble on either side of it she wasn't able to go round. She rolled her eyes skyward in exasperation and froze. Half a dozen workmen on the roof opposite were watching her. She hated to admit defeat, but she had no choice. Smiling thinly, she shrugged her shoulders and walked back the way she had come.

She could still hear them laughing at the corner of Maiden Lane and Southampton Street. Without looking back, Margaret half limped, half ran along the Strand to the Prince Albert Theatre.

Bursting through the theatre's main entrance and out of breath, Margaret approached a young man sitting behind the window of the Box Office. 'I'm here to see the front of house manager, Miss Lesley. My name is Margaret Burrell.'

The man lifted his head from the book he was reading and looked Margaret up and down. 'If you'd like to take a seat,' he said, and went back to his book.

'I have an appointment!' Margaret said, somewhat put out by his lack of interest.

'I'll let Miss Lesley know you're here.'

Margaret walked across to a maroon-coloured seat that ran the length of the wall on the far side of the foyer and sat down. Looking around, she was hardly able to contain her excitement. The wallpaper was maroon with gold stripes. Regency, it was called. It was like the wallpaper advertised in her magazine – and it was expensive. The paper Dad put up in the living room at home was one and tuppence a roll. This wallpaper, Margaret decided on closer inspection, would be three shillings a roll, if not more. The curtains at the windows and doors were velvet, the same colour as the seat she was sitting on. Running her hands over the seat's smooth fabric, Margaret saw how dirty they were.

'Excuse me?' she called to the man in the box office. 'Is there somewhere where I can wash my hands?'

He lifted his head from his book and looked at her as if she'd asked to borrow a fiver. 'Through the door to the Stalls, along the corridor on the right.'

Margaret nodded her thanks and began to follow his directions. But as she reached for the handle, the Stalls doors opened.

'Mrs Burrell?'

'Yes!' Margaret stepped back in surprise and a lock of hair fell onto her face. She pushed the offending strand behind her ear and put out her hand.

'Pamela Lesley. How do you do?' she said, shaking Margaret's grubby hand.

'Sorry!' Margaret felt the blush of embarrassment creep up her neck. 'Perhaps,' she said rummaging in her handbag, finding her handkerchief and offering it to Miss Lesley, 'you could…?'

'Thank you, but there's no need. If you'd like to follow me.' Looking over her shoulder, the front of house manager smiled her thanks to a now attentive-looking man in the Box Office. Not a book in sight, Margaret noticed.

Miss Lesley led the way through the door with

Stalls written on it in gold lettering. When Bill took Margaret to the Hippodrome in Coventry they always sat in the stalls. She followed Miss Lesley down a carpeted corridor that was the same colour as the front of house furniture. There was a border between the carpet and the skirting that was painted cream like the walls. Margaret looked up and caught her breath. The walls were covered in photographs: Gertrude Lawrence, Jack Buchanan, Beatrice Lillie, Jessie Matthews and Stanley Holloway – all in gilt frames.

There were film posters of William Powell and Myrna Loy in *Double Wedding*. Clark Gable and Jean Harlow in *Saratoga*. And the new Twentieth Century-Fox film *Hollywood Cavalcade* starring Alice Faye and Don Ameche, which Bill had promised to take her to see.

On the opposite wall, Charles Laughton in *Alibi* and Richard Herne in *Wild Rose* looked down on her. She began to hum the Jerome Kern song *Look for the Silver Lining* and walked into the back of Miss Lesley.

'Oh! I'm, I'm so sorry,' Margaret stuttered. 'I didn't know you'd-- I was looking at the photographs and--'

Miss Lesley looked over the top of her glasses, opened the door on her right, which said Front of House Manager, and motioned Margaret to go in.

Margaret whispered, 'Thank you,' and entered.

'Take a seat, Mrs Burrell.'

'Thank you,' Margaret said again, sitting on a straight-backed chair in front of a big walnut desk.

Pamela Lesley, in a smart navy-blue skirt and jacket, sat behind the desk. She was a tall woman, but the chair's high brass-buttoned back almost dwarfed her. Behind her were more posters and more photographs. The posters looked older than the ones in the corridor. Most had faded and some were brownish-yellow in colour, but the photographs looked as if they'd been taken recently. They were clear and well-defined, and the people in them were dressed in modern clothes.

'Tell me about yourself, Margaret,' Miss Lesley said suddenly, making Margaret jump. 'Where are you from?'

'A small village called Woodcote, near Lowarth, on the borders of Warwickshire and Leicestershire.' Miss Lesley nodded, but said nothing. 'My father was a groom on a country estate.' Margaret sat up straight, which she always did when she was trying to impress. 'Head groom actually, at Foxden Hall, until the war. I was born on the estate. I've got three sisters, one older and two younger, and an older brother.'

'And what about school? Did you like school?'

'Oh yes! I loved it!' A slight exaggeration. 'I went to the C of E junior school in the village until I was eleven, then to the Central School in Lowarth until I was fourteen.' Margaret wondered whether she should tell Miss Lesley that she'd passed the Eleven Plus. She wanted to, but if she did the front of house manager was sure to ask why she hadn't gone to the Grammar. So, because she didn't want to admit her family couldn't afford the uniform, she said nothing.

'And have you worked since leaving school?'

'Yes!' Margaret was surprised that Miss Lesley could think it possible that she hadn't worked in six years. 'My first job was as a clerical assistant in the office of a factory in Lowarth. When I married Bill last year... Oh, it was a lovely day. The newspapers said that July the first 1939 was the hottest day since records began. Oh!' she said, suddenly aware that her chatter wasn't relevant to the conversation. She cleared her throat. 'When I married Bill, I moved to live with him at his mum and dad's house in Coventry. The company I worked for didn't want to lose me, so they gave me a job in the wages office of their aircraft factory.'

'And what brings you to London?'

'My Bill had been poorly when he was little and didn't pass any of the armed forces medicals, so he couldn't join up. He was really upset that he couldn't fight for his country, so Dad had a word with Lord Foxden.'

'Lord Foxden?'

'Yes, who Dad worked for before the war. Lord Foxden's something high up in the Ministry of Defence--' Margaret stopped abruptly. 'Bill said it's all very hush-hush. *Walls Have Ears*,' she whispered. 'I hope it doesn't matter me telling you.'

Miss Lesley smiled. 'I promise not to tell anyone.'

'Well, Bill went to see Lord Foxden and his Lordship said that because Bill could ride a motorbike and had a clean driving licence, and because he'd never been in trouble with the police, which he hasn't, Bill would be ideal as a special courier for the MoD here in London. Even before war was declared Bill was taking top secret documents from London to-- other parts of the country. Mam and Dad didn't want me to come down at first. Mam was furious. She said London would be the first place the Germans would bomb. Dad was angry because I'd given up a good job. But I'd only been married for a few months and I wanted to be with my husband. I came down to spend Christmas with him and except for going home to fetch my clothes, I've been here ever since.'

'And you're staying with Mr and Mrs Goldman?'

'Not with them, exactly. We have our own cosy little sitting room and kitchenette, bedroom and bathroom. Our rooms are part of the house, but we have our own stairs. I expect they were where the servants lived in the old days. If it wasn't for my sister Bess we wouldn't have such a lovely home. She's a friend of Mr and Mrs Goldman. She met them when she was at college in London. They were very kind to her.'

'I've met your sister several times. She's a very nice young woman.'

'Yes, she's been good to me, has our Bess. So when Bill got the job at the MoD, Mr and Mrs Goldman invited him to lodge with them. They said I could come and stay anytime.' Margaret laughed. 'I'm not sure they meant permanently, but they don't mind me being there. It was Natalie-- Mrs Goldman who suggested Anton spoke to you about me working as an usherette.'

'We do have an opening. One of the girls has been called up. Have you heard anything from the War Office?'

'No. I think they're calling up single women first. At least, I hope they are.'

'I'm sure you're right.' Pamela Lesley smiled and leant forward. 'So why do you want to be an usherette, Margaret?'

'To work in the theatre. I've worked in offices and factories and they are so boring. Sorry!' Margaret took a breath and began again. 'I get on well with people. I'd rather help someone than not help them and…' She sighed, losing the thread once more. 'I can't think of anything I'd rather do in the whole wide world than sit and watch a theatre show every night. Except be in one, of course. That would be a dream come true.' Suddenly seeing a combination of amusement and amazement creep across Miss Lesley's face, Margaret stopped talking and sat up straight. 'If you give me a chance, Miss Lesley, I won't let you down.'

'I'm sure you won't, Margaret. There's just one thing--'

'Ask me anything,' Margaret said without thinking.

'You live a long way away from the West End. Getting to and from the theatre might be a problem. You won't finish work at night until ten or ten-thirty. How do you intend to get home at that time of night?'

'My Bill's a volunteer ambulance driver down the road at St. Thomas's. He'll pick me up after his shift. And if he's going to be late, Mr Goldman said he'd give me a lift home. Getting here isn't a problem. There's a bus that comes all the way to Euston from Hampstead. And there are lots of buses from Euston to Aldwych – some come down the Strand.'

'It seems you've looked into everything, Margaret. I've just one more question...'

Margaret held her breath. What had she said, or not said? She'd made a list the night before and rehearsed what she was going to say in answer to every question on it. Miss Lesley hadn't asked the questions in the right order, but that didn't matter, she was sure she'd told her everything she needed to know. Smiling nervously, Margaret wondered if she'd said too much – gone on a bit. She had a tendency to go on a bit. Bill said she did. 'Yes?' she said, putting as much lightness into her voice as her nerves would allow without sounding superficial.

'You've obviously thought about what you were going to say at your interview. And if what you say is true – and I'm sure it is – you're a perfect candidate. But,' Miss Lesley paused. 'Why are you grubby and dishevelled?'

'Oh my--' Margaret had forgotten about how she

17

looked. 'A building fell on me.' Miss Lesley's mouth dropped open. 'Well, it didn't actually fall on me, but it would have done if a workman hadn't pushed me through the door of a church. I went flying down some steps and,' Margaret looked down at her hands, 'it was very dark down there – and dusty. My stockings got laddered and I didn't have a spare pair. I thought about finding somewhere to tidy myself up, but I didn't want to be late for my interview. I was just going to wash my hands when you came into the foyer. Then I forgot. I'm sorry--'

Miss Lesley laughed and put her hand up. 'I thought there must have been a reason. Come on, I'll show you around. We'll start with the front of house staff room. It has a washbasin.'

CHAPTER TWO

The small staff room was lit by a single bulb in a frosted ceiling pendant. It didn't do much to soften the atmosphere, but it did distract from the ugly brown squiggly wallpaper and toffee-coloured wooden panelling. A portable clothes rail stood behind half a dozen fold-up chairs. Margaret took off her coat and hung it next to a row of maroon tabards. Usherettes' uniforms! She wrinkled her nose. The outdated style was more Lowarth Picture House than West End theatre. On the other side of the room stood a two-ring stove with a kettle, a small table with teapot, cups, saucers, and cutlery on a tray – and next to that, a sink.

'The washroom is opposite,' Miss Lesley said, handing Margaret a towel. 'I'll leave you to it. Shan't be long.'

Entering the tiny room, Margaret caught sight of herself in the mirror. 'What a flippin' mess,' she said aloud. While the basin filled with hot water she scored a tablet of Palmolive soap with a small nail brush and scrubbed the dirt from beneath her fingernails. When her hands were clean she drained the basin of dirty water and refilled it. She washed her face and dabbed it dry with the soft towel. She looked better. After combing her hair, she applied face powder and lipstick.

Miss Lesley poked her head round the door. 'Ready?' Margaret nodded. 'Good. I'll show you around.'

Margaret grabbed her jacket and followed Miss Lesley along the corridor, slowing now and then to look at photographs and posters of famous artists in shows that she'd read about in the *Silver Screen* magazine and *Picturegoer*.

'The company's rehearsing, so we must be quiet,' Miss Lesley whispered, opening the door to the auditorium.

Margaret entered in a dream and stood with her mouth open. The auditorium was huge. Row after row of maroon velvet seats edged with gold disappeared into the shadows under the balcony. Her eyes feasted on the gilded circular balcony and the boxes on either side. Looking up further, beyond the upper circle and the gods, Margaret caught her breath. The ceiling with its huge chandeliers was magnificent. Golden cherubs and seraphs playing harps and flutes lay snug against a cream background. She closed her eyes and inhaled deeply. The smell! 'So that's what greasepaint smells like,' she whispered. The performers were in their rehearsal clothes – slacks, blouses, cardigans – not in makeup, but Margaret felt sure she could smell greasepaint. Standing in the dim half-light of the auditorium she watched the artists on stage. Flooded in bright light they looked magical. She thought her heart would explode with excitement.

'... Margaret?' Miss Lesley tapped her on the shoulder.

'Oh!' Margaret jumped. 'I was--'

'I know, dear.'

'I'm sorry, Miss Lesley. It's just that I can't believe I'm here. I'm in a real theatre, watching real actresses sing and dance. It's amazing!'

'Yes, it is. But we really shouldn't be here, so...'

Margaret followed Miss Lesley to the exit along the side aisle. Before leaving, she looked back at the stage. A beautiful slender dancer stood watching her. Margaret hunched up her shoulders and mouthed,

'Sorry.' The dancer shook her head and smiled, as if to say, 'It's all right.'

'The beautiful dancer at the front smiled at me,' Margaret said, when they were in the corridor.

'That's Nancy Jewel, the soubrette. A soubrette is...'

'A soprano who sings the character solos.'

'That's right!' Miss Lesley laughed. 'The other girls have one, sometimes two songs that they feature in, but Nancy has several solos, in addition to stepping out of ensemble numbers. She's the Prince Albert's leading lady.'

'You have to be very good to sing the lead numbers,' Margaret said.

'And Nancy is. She's an exceptionally talented actress, singer and dancer.'

'I'm going to be an actress one day,' Margaret said. 'I'll be the soubrette too, but--'

'But until then, you're an usherette.'

Margaret nodded. 'Until then I'm-- I am? You mean I've got the job?'

Miss Lesley laughed again. 'You've got the job if you can do the matinee on Saturday. The girl you're replacing would like to visit her family before she joins her regiment.'

'I can start tomorrow if you want.'

'Saturday will be fine.'

'I'm an usherette! Thank you, Miss Lesley. I'm an usherette,' Margaret said again, unable to believe her luck.

Dinner was almost ready. Sausage, egg and chips, Bill's favourite. A tin of Lokreel peaches with Nestle's cream and a small sponge cake for afters. Although she had used the *Health for All Ration-Time Recipes* book, which offered recipes providing the right sort of food under rationing restrictions, Margaret wasn't able to get all the ingredients for the cake and had to improvise. Bill probably wouldn't notice – and if he did he wouldn't mind. She had been saving food coupons for weeks. The plan was to make Bill a special birthday supper. She bit her bottom lip. She'd been so excited after getting the usherette job, she'd blown the lot on the evening meal. Potatoes weren't rationed, and the food coupons had stretched to a couple of eggs and most of the ingredients for the cake. Natalie had given her two sausages. They were kosher – made differently for Jewish people. Margaret didn't ask how. She didn't care. She'd had them before, when she and Bill had been to supper with Natalie and Anton, and they were delicious.

Margaret turned the chips. Bill loved her fat chips. He called them workman's chips. He had promised to come home early, so they could have dinner together. When she was working at the theatre, they'd only be able to have dinner together on Sundays. Not that it would make much difference. Bill was on the ambulances almost every night now he'd passed his first aid higher-something-or-other. Margaret smiled. After Saturday, she wouldn't have to spend the evenings on her own, because she'd be working in a theatre. Margaret felt a flurry of excitement in her tummy. It would be fun working with other young people. She was bound to make friends. The more she thought about it the more excited she became. She couldn't wait for Saturday.

Margaret heard Bill's key turn in the lock while she was tipping the chips onto their plates. 'Wash your hands, Bill; dinner's ready.'

'Will do, Mrs Bossy!'

Margaret took the sausages out of the frying pan and put in two eggs. She splashed hot fat onto them with the flat of a knife. White cooked, yolk runny, just the way Bill liked them. She thought about picking off the tiny bits of sausage that had stuck to the pan and were now clinging to the eggs, but there wasn't time. Besides, with only one frying pan and having to reuse the four measly ounces of cooking fat half a dozen times during the week, they were used to it. She checked the table. Cutlery placed on her best embroidered tablecloth. Salt and pepper in the middle, but no margarine. The last of the marg went into the cake. Margaret shrugged. It didn't matter anyway, because she'd forgotten to get bread.

'Mm… something smells good,' Bill said, entering the room and sitting at the small table.

Margaret placed her husband's meal in front of him and kissed his forehead, before sitting down with her own. 'Enjoy your supper, love. I've spent your birthday coupons on it.'

Bill raised his eyebrows. 'So what are we celebrating if not my birthday?'

'My job. You are looking at the Prince Albert Theatre's new usherette.'

'Well done!' Bill stood up, leaned over and kissed Margaret on the lips. 'I think that calls for a glass of sherry,' he said, his brown eyes sparkling.

Margaret watched her handsome husband open the cupboard in the sideboard. As he reached in for the bottle a lock of thick fair hair fell onto his forehead. Sherry in one hand, he ran his fingers through his hair with the other, pushing the rogue wave back into place before returning to the table.

'To my clever, beautiful wife,' he said, pouring them both a glass. 'I'm proud of you.'

*

'Well I never. If it ain't Miss London,' Margaret heard someone shout. A sudden fluttering in her chest made her catch her breath. It was probably one of the workmen who had been working on the building when the roof of the café collapsed and almost killed her. She wondered if the man who had saved her life was up there, but she daren't look.

"Er Ladyship ain't wearing brick-red today, Chippie,' another called.

'She don't arf scrub up well. Ay, Miss London?' the first shouted. 'Give us a twirl!'

Margaret lifted her head, stuck her nose in the air, and pretended she hadn't heard the commentary. Then, when she reached the Prince Albert Theatre's stage door, she stopped and turned. Putting the fingers of both hands to her mouth, as she'd seen film stars do in the flicks, she blew them a kiss, keeping her arms outstretched for some seconds in an exaggerated pose. She entered the theatre to a chorus of comments and wolf whistles.

'Hello, I'm Margaret, Margaret Burrell. I'm an usherette,' she said proudly.

'Bert Masters, stage doorman.' He put out his hand.

Margaret took the old man's hand and shook it. 'How do you do, Mr Masters?'

'Call me Bert, everyone does. You'll be here to see Miss Lesley then. I'll take you through.'

Margaret followed Bert along a dimly lit corridor, past big black double doors with STAGE written on them in white lettering, down a flight of half a dozen stairs and through a pass door. She recognised where she was immediately.

'Here we are, Miss.' Bert opened the staff room door and stood back to let Margaret enter.

'Thank you.'

'Right you are. Enjoy your first day, Miss,' Bert said, before disappearing through a door with PUBLIC on one side and PRIVATE on the other.

Margaret didn't have long to wait for Miss Lesley, who greeted her warmly and led the way to the auditorium, explaining as they went what Margaret thought was common sense. 'The show starts at seven-thirty. You need to be in the auditorium, in your uniform and with your torch, by seven, which is when the doors open to the public. As the audience enters the auditorium,' she said, opening the stalls door and ushering Margaret through, 'you ask them for their ticket.' Miss Lesley paused and Margaret nodded. 'Each ticket has a letter for the row and a number for the seat. Your section is from J to S, seats eighteen to nine. Is that clear, Margaret?'

Margaret nodded again. 'Seats one to eight are on the other side of the auditorium, aren't they?' she said, walking from row J to S.

'Yes, they are Jenny's responsibility.' Margaret opened her mouth to ask about the other usherettes, but Miss Lesley carried on. 'You point your torch at the floor, at the beginning of the row that corresponds with the letter on the ticket. Then, as soon as they begin to make their way along the row, you go back to the exit and help the next person, or people. When the lights go down and the curtain goes up, you can take your seat. But,' Miss Lesley said, 'stay alert for any latecomers. It can't be helped with the delays in public transport. And if the air raid siren sounds you'll need to be on your feet, ready to show people to the exit. A percentage of the audience will want to stay and have a singsong. For those who don't, show them out and come back as soon as you can. I'll be with you this afternoon and tonight, so don't worry.'

Margaret wasn't worried. She didn't think she needed any help. 'At the interval,' Miss Lesley continued, 'you stand when the orchestra begins to play the last number. Then, as soon as the curtain starts to come down, you open the exit doors. Only after your section of the audience has gone to the bar, toilet, or wherever it is they wish to go, can you leave. And I suggest you do. Have a cup of tea and go to the toilet; the second act is over an hour long. Whatever you do, you must be back at your post five minutes before the second act begins. That way you'll be available if anyone needs you. You then close the door, pull the curtain and find your seat. At the end of the show,' Miss Lesley said, 'you do not leave the auditorium until every member of the audience has left. Your section may be clear, but one of the other usherettes might need help with their section. Just stand by your exit, in case. Well,' she said, smiling, 'any questions?'

Margaret thought for a moment. 'No. I just want to get the first day, and night, over.'

'Good. Go and make yourself a cup of tea. You have an hour before you need to be at your post.'

Margaret left the auditorium and made her way to the staff room. Once inside, she dropped into a chair. All she'd ever dreamed of was about to begin. Hauling herself to her feet, she crossed to the small table, picked up the kettle and gave it a shake. There was water in it. She struck a match, turned on the gas and lit the small ring before putting the kettle on it.

'Hello, I'm Jenny.'

'Ah!' Margaret spun round to see a young woman standing behind her. 'Sorry, I didn't hear you come in. I'm Margaret. How do you do?'

'Better now there's someone my age on the team.'

'I expect most of the young women have been called up,' Margaret said.

Jenny nodded. 'You haven't then?'

'I'm married, so I'm not first dibs.'

'Kids?'

'No. You?'

'Married? I wish! And I love kids,' Jenny said wistfully. 'I'm an aunt. My sister in Whitechapel's got two girls, but it's not the same as having your own, is it? She invites me over all the time, but with work and living in northwest London, I don't get to see them very often. I don't get to do much at all, except travel and work.'

'Don't you have a sweetheart; someone you're walking out with?'

'No. I'm not lucky in love – or anything else, it seems. I had my heart set on being a driver in the Women's Auxiliary Army Corps, but I got turned down at the medical. I went to half a dozen recruitment offices and they all said the same: my eyesight's rotten. I can't remember the long word they used, but it's to do with depth. Plan B is to join the First Aid Nursing Yeomanry. But to be a FANY you need driving experience and a first aid certificate before they'll even look at you. But I won't give up,' Jenny said, taking off her coat.

Margaret felt sorry for her. She didn't have anyone except her sister and nieces. At least she hadn't mentioned any other family. 'Tea?' Margaret asked when the kettle began to whistle.

'Please. I'll get the milk.' Jenny opened the cupboard above Margaret's head. 'There isn't any sugar.'

'That's all right. I don't take it,' Margaret said, pouring the tea. She added milk to both cups and gave one to Jenny.

'Thanks. Met any of the other usherettes?' she asked, as they sat down.

'No, you're the first.'

Jenny laughed. 'You're in for a treat then.'

'Why, what are they like?'

'They're a mixed bunch. A couple of the girls are married with kids. Their husbands are in the forces and their mothers look after the children while they work. They're nice enough, but they go home as soon as the show comes down. There are a couple of older women, Miss Smith and Miss Timmins.' Jenny winked. 'Spinsters, if you know what I mean. They've lived and worked together for so long that they've grown to look like each other. You know, like dogs and their owners. They've been usherettes here for years. Well before Anton and Natalie Goldman's time. They don't mix with anyone and they don't hang around after their shifts. Finished?' she said, taking Margaret's empty cup and putting it on the draining board next to her own. Before she sat down again she handed Margaret a maroon tabard. 'So if you want a pal at the Prince Albert Theatre, you're stuck with me.'

'I can think of worse people to be stuck with,' Margaret said, and they both laughed. Jenny was as dark as Margaret was fair and although they were similar in age, Jenny looked older. She had a bigger bust and hips – and by the way she spoke, she was more worldly-wise.

Over the next few nights Margaret got to know and like Jenny. Bill liked her too. He'd met her when he called to take Margaret home on her first night as an usherette. The two friends had left the theatre giggling. Bill told Margaret later that he was pleased she'd found a friend her own age. He said Jenny looked as if she was fun – and would be good for her.

Jenny had latched onto Margaret as soon as they'd met – and thank goodness she had. Margaret had nothing in common with the two older women, or with the married girls. The older women didn't speak to her and the married ones only talked about babies. Margaret confided in Jenny that she sometimes felt guilty because she didn't want a baby. 'Bill wanted to start a family when he got the job as document carrier with the Ministry of Defence. He said I'd be lonely while he was away in London. He thought a baby would keep me occupied, so I wouldn't miss him so much. But…' Margaret fell silent.

'But what?'

'I had other plans.' What she was about to tell Jenny she hadn't told anyone, not even her older sister Bess who she never kept secrets from. 'If I tell you, will you promise not to tell anyone?'

Jenny nodded. 'Cross my heart and hope to die.'

Margaret took a deep breath. 'I promised Bill that if he let me come to London and get a job in a theatre, I'd go back to the Midlands with him and start a family as soon as the war's over.'

Jenny sighed. 'Poor Bill! Never mind, they say it'll be over by Christmas.'

'They said that last year. But even if it is, I don't want a baby yet.' Jenny looked shocked. 'Now you think I'm horrible, don't you?'

'No. I think you're wrong. If I had a husband

29

like your Bill, I'd have a dozen kids,' Jenny laughed. 'I'd enjoy making every one of them too.'

'Jenny... You are terrible.' Margaret gave her friend a gentle shove towards the door. 'Come on, let's go. It doesn't look like Bill's coming for me tonight. I'll go home on the bus with you.'

It was handy for Margaret that Jenny lived in north west London. They travelled to work together most days and if Bill was stuck somewhere in the ambulance and couldn't pick her up, she travelled home with Jenny. As a Londoner, Jenny had been riding on buses and underground trains all her life. Margaret admired her. She knew all the routes and showed Margaret alternative ways of getting to and from the West End without going on the underground.

'I passed my driving test with flying colours, but I failed the medical,' Margaret heard Jenny say as she opened the stage door. 'I'm only working as an usherette until I find a driving job. So if they ever need an ambulance driver at St. Thomas's you will think of me, won't you, Bill?'

'Er hum! Is that my husband you're trying to lead astray?'

Bill laughed. Sitting astride his Triumph motorbike, he leant sideways and kissed Margaret full on the lips. 'No such luck. Pretty girls have given up on me now I'm an old married man,' he laughed, handing Margaret her motorbike helmet.

Every time Jenny saw Bill during the weeks that followed she pestered him about vacancies at St. Thomas's. She played up to him, jokingly begging him to put her name forward if a driving job, or any job, on the ambulances came up. And her persistence paid off. Squealing with excitement, Jenny threw her arms around Bill's neck.

'Thank you, thank you, thank you!'

'Thank you for what?' Margaret asked, joining Bill and Jenny outside the theatre.

'There's a vacancy at St. Thomas's and Bill's put my name forward. Isn't he wonderful?' Jenny said.

'Yes, he is wonderful. And I'll have him back now, if you don't mind.'

'Sorry,' Jenny said, giggling. 'I got a bit carried away. What happens now?' she asked, her arms firmly by her side.

'Go down to Tommy's tomorrow; they're expecting you at eleven--' Jenny squealed. 'And fill in an application form. Write down your driving experience and don't forget to tell them about your qualifications. Take anything you've got on paper. They'll ask to see proof.'

'I will.' Jenny jumped up and down. 'And then what?'

Bill laughed. 'You wait. They'll let you know if you've been accepted.'

The following week Jenny was offered a job as a trainee ambulance driver. The next week she took the driving course, the following week the advanced course – and passed both with flying colours. The week after that she left the Prince Albert Theatre.

Jenny's replacement was another married girl. She brought sandwiches on matinee days, instead of going out for tea, and left the theatre as soon as the curtain came down at night. Without Jenny to pal up with, Margaret was bored between the matinee and the evening show and often stayed in the theatre by herself. She eventually got to know the other usherettes and one day while they were having their tea break in the cramped staff room she let slip her ambition to be an actress. 'My stage name,' Margaret said, pausing to make sure she had their full attention, 'will be Miss Margot Dudley.'

The spinsters looked at Margaret as if she'd said she was going to be a Spitfire pilot.

'You should have a baby,' one of the married girls said.

'You won't have time for daydreaming then,' her friend said, sarcastically.

'I shall have a baby one day,' Margaret told them. 'When the war ends, Bill and I are going back to the Midlands. And as soon as we've found somewhere nice to live, we're going to start a family. It's just that I've always wanted to--'

Miss Smith and Miss Timmins, dressed in plain brown skirts and white blouses under knitted waistcoats, looked at each other, wrinkled their beaked noses and left.

That night as she was leaving the theatre, Margaret heard one of them say, 'Who does she think she is?' and the other said, 'Miss La Di Dah, that's who.' She couldn't tell who said what because not only did they sound alike, they were shrouded in dark overcoats and wore trilbies over their short grey hair.

They went off cackling like a pair of old witches. It was the first time Margaret had heard the spinsters laugh. And it was the first time she'd felt unhappy in her job.

'Jealous! That's what they are,' she told Bill when he picked her up later. 'In future I shall keep myself to myself like they do.'

Bill smiled, but didn't comment. His wife couldn't keep herself to herself if her life depended on it.

*

The afternoons and evenings ticked by without incident, and Margaret began to put her plan into action. As soon as the lights in the auditorium went out, before the curtain rose and the stage lights came on, Margaret turned towards her seat. Her eyes darted from one exit to the other, taking in the usherettes, to make sure Miss Lesley wasn't with them. Then, quickly and quietly, she made her way to the back of the stalls. Beneath the overhang of the circle, along the walkway that ran parallel with the stage, Margaret was able to watch the show unobserved.

Tap, tap, heel tap – and arms like a windmill. And tap, tap, heel tap – and scoop and tap and scoop and tap. Tap, tap, heel tap... Every night, Margaret practised the dances until she was step-perfect, and she listened to the songs, singing them over and over again until she knew every word.

Better keep an eye on the time, she thought, and she looked at her wristwatch. 'A room with a view, one two! I must be back in my seat, three four! Back in my seat, three four! And...' Margaret needed to keep in time with the rhythm, 'two three four.' She mimed the last verse of the song as she walked back to her seat, and she was standing at her post ready to show the audience to the exit at the interval and at the end of the show.

Wait For Me Dearest was a collection of modern songs and sketches. Margaret knew the words to half the songs already because they were often on the wireless; the rest she worked hard to learn and by her second month as an usherette she knew them by heart. It hadn't been easy learning the dances, because she was constantly looking over her shoulder. Miss Lesley would often turn up at one or other of the usherette stations without warning. Margaret had got away with being absent from her post several times but decided not to push her luck. After tonight, she would practise at home. As the last song of the show came to an end and the stage lights began to dim, Margaret made her way back to her seat. Miss Lesley was sitting in it.

Margaret felt her throat constrict. Her mouth was dry. She swallowed hard. She opened her mouth to speak, but fear had taken her voice. There wasn't anything she could say anyway. She had been caught away from her post and nothing could excuse that. She thought about fainting. She had almost collapsed when she saw Miss Lesley. She could lie. She could say she'd been sick. She felt sick. But Miss Lesley would probably see through her.

Once the audience had left and the auditorium was empty, Miss Lesley led the way to her office. She opened the door, stood back to allow Margaret to enter and followed her in. 'Sit down,' she said, pointing to the chair in front of her desk. Margaret perched nervously on the edge of the seat. Miss Lesley sat down heavily in the chair opposite. Leaning her elbows on the desk, Miss Lesley clasped her hands under her chin. For a long minute there was an awkward silence. 'Well?' she said suddenly, making Margaret jump. 'What do you have to say for yourself?'

'I'm sorry.'

'I'm sure you are, but that is not what I meant.' Miss Lesley looked over the top of her glasses. 'What was so important that you left your station during the show? Were you ill?'

Margaret thought again about lying. She decided against it. 'No, Miss Lesley.'

'What then?'

Margaret lowered her eyes. She hadn't thought about what she'd say if she was caught. She hadn't planned on getting caught.

'What would have happened if a member of the audience had been taken ill?'

Margaret opened her mouth. It was shame this time that had taken her voice.

'Well?'

Tears pricked the back of her eyes. 'I don't know!' she whispered.

'Then I'll tell you. One of the other usherettes would have had to leave her post to help them.' Silence hung heavily in the air of the small office. 'Tonight wasn't the first time you left your post, was it?'

Margaret shot the front of house manager a tearful look, but said nothing.

'What is so important that you'll risk losing your job? What have you been doing?'

'Learning the dances.'

'You've been what?'

There was no going back now. Margaret wiped a tear from her cheek. 'I've been practising the dances from the walkway at the back of the stalls. I know most of them by heart and I thought--'

'You thought what?' Miss Lesley snapped.

Margaret cleared her throat. 'I thought, because the girls in the chorus are always leaving at short notice, there should be someone--' she swallowed hard, 'someone who already works in the theatre that could step in and take over.'

'And that someone would be?'

'Me.'

'You?'

'Yes!' Margaret stuttered on. 'Once I knew the routines well enough to perform them, I was going to ask if you'd have a word with Dick Smiley-- I mean, the director, Mr Smiley – put a good word in for me. I've learned all the songs too. Singing is my strong suit. I could sing before I could walk--'

Miss Lesley put her hand up. 'You're obviously serious about this, Margaret. So if I speak to Mr Smiley on your behalf you must promise not to leave your post again.'

'Thank you, Miss Lesley,' Margaret said, clapping her hands. 'I mean, no, Miss Lesley. I won't leave my post again. I'll practise at home. I'll practise every night.'

'I'm sure you will.' Miss Lesley looked at the clock on the wall. 'You had better go, your husband will be waiting for you.'

Margaret pushed her chair back and stood up. 'Thank you, Miss Lesley.'

'And Margaret?' Miss Lesley said, as Margaret opened the door. 'Be on time tomorrow.'

'I will,' Margaret said, grinning from ear to ear.

It had been three weeks since Miss Lesley promised to have a word with the director about Margaret being an understudy – and she'd heard nothing. She pushed her supper around her plate and sighed loudly.

Bill knew the signs. The novelty of being an usherette was wearing off. Most things did with Margaret – and usually much quicker. 'That was a big sigh. What's the matter?'

'Nothing,' she said, putting down her knife and fork. She waited for Bill to ask her again, but he didn't.

'Well, if you really want to know,' Margaret said, with no intention of telling Bill she had almost lost her job, 'Miss Lesley thought that, because I know the songs and dances in the show, I'd be a good stand-in. She said she was going to suggest me to the director.'

Now it was Bill's turn to put down his cutlery. 'When was this?'

'A few weeks ago,' she shrugged. 'With chorus girls being called up, or leaving to do war work, we thought it would be a good idea to have an understudy on hand.'

Bill put Margaret's plate on top of his own and put them on the draining board in the kitchenette. 'And what did Dick Smiley say?'

'That's just it. He hasn't said anything. He's been auditioning girls all week, but he hasn't called me in.' Bill opened his mouth to speak, but Margaret didn't notice. 'And I know why,' she said. 'He wants to get his hands on the new girls. They're all batting eyelashes and giggles.' Margaret was annoyed and she was jealous, not that she'd ever let him maul her the way the new girls did. 'Miss Lesley must have told him about me by now.'

'The brass neck of the man. And you want to audition for him? I don't think so!' Bill said. 'The mucky bugger isn't going to get his hands on my wife.'

Margaret wished she'd kept her opinions to herself.

Bill said nothing more until they were in bed. 'You keep doing your usherette job, love.'

'I will,' Margaret said, going through the latest routine in her head.

CHAPTER THREE

'Look!' A note on the message board in the front of house staff room caught Margaret's eye. 'CAN YOU SEW? Volunteers wanted to help make costumes for the new show. If you have sewing experience, a few hours to spare and would like to earn some extra money, add your name to the list below. Signed H M Horton, Wardrobe Mistress.'

Annie, Jenny's replacement, squinted at the note and sniffed.

'Can you sew, Annie?' Margaret asked, hoping she couldn't, but making conversation. She still missed Jenny. Although Bill kept her up to date with what she was doing, and how well she was getting on working with him on the ambulances, it wasn't like spending time with her. Margaret missed their chats, missed having someone to confide in.

'Yes, but I don't volunteer for nothing. You get taken advantage of if you do.'

'Good. Not good that you'd get taken advantage, I meant-- Oh never mind.' Margaret took the pencil from the shelf beneath the message board and wrote her name in capitals below that of the wardrobe mistress. 'The less people that volunteer the more chance I've got of getting the job.'

Annie looked bewildered and left the staff room sniffing. She didn't look as if she'd got a cold, Margaret mused, but she sniffed all the time. Margaret wondered if she sniffed while she was showing people to their seats, and she stifled a giggle. All the usherettes were a bit strange. The spinsters – the Sisters Grimm, as she called them – arrived together and left together. They whispered all the time, gave each other knowing looks and rarely contributed to a conversation.

Neither of the married girls had put their names on the list, Margaret was pleased to see. And if the Sisters Grimm didn't, she was bound to get the job. While she was thinking about it the Sisters Grimm arrived, took off their outdoor coats and put on their tabards.

'Hello,' Margaret said, greeting them with a bright smile.

Both women turned and nodded. 'Margaret!'

'Are you volunteering to help in wardrobe?'

They looked at the notice board, and then at each other. 'No.'

'We don't have time,' Sister-Grimm-Timmins said.

'No, we don't have the time,' repeated Sister-Grimm-Smith.

'We'd better get to our posts,' said Sister-Grimm-Timmins, leading the way to the door.

'Yes,' Sister-Grimm-Smith said, hard on the heels of Sister-Grimm-Timmins. 'We'd better get to our posts.'

'Goodbye Margaret,' they said in unison, and they shuffled out.

Margaret stood open-mouthed. You wouldn't believe it if you saw it at the flicks. She put on her tabard and looked in the mirror. Her hair was fine. She'd recently had a perm, so the curls were still a bit on the tight side. She took out the Kirby grip at the front, forced the comb through the deep wave that, without the grip, would fall into her eyes, and replaced it. She straightened her skirt and checked her stockings for wrinkles before following the Sisters Grimm down the corridor into the auditorium.

*

'Morning, Bert.' Margaret's cheeks flushed pink with pride. 'I've been offered the position of wardrobe assistant. I'm here to see Mrs Horton.'

'She's expecting you, Miss. I'll take you up.'

Margaret waited while the stage doorman found a pen and paper. He wrote a note saying, BACK IN TEN MINUTES and pinned it on the door of his small office. 'Right! Follow me.'

Margaret had met the wardrobe mistress several times before with Miss Lesley and Bert, but she had never been to the wardrobe department. She followed the elderly stage doorman up three flights of winding stone stairs. Despite being almost as round as he was tall, Bert was surprisingly quick on his feet. When they arrived on the top floor he was hardly out of puff. Margaret, young and fit, held onto the banister and caught her breath.

Mrs Horton was waiting for them with a pot of tea in one hand and a plate of biscuits in the other. She placed both on a small table that was surrounded by an assortment of chairs. 'Elevenses are early today, Bert.'

'Right you are, Mrs Horton.' Bert lowered his bulk into a large comfortable-looking chair. Margaret waited. She looked around. Dozens of costumes hung on metal clothes racks. In the middle of the room was an oval table. On the far side was a sewing machine and on the nearside a sewing box with a selection of yellow cottons and a canary-yellow blouse. She looked up and gasped. Hanging from a pipe above the ironing board were some of the most beautiful dresses she had ever seen. Red with black frills, navy with emerald green edging, and chocolate-brown with a cream see-through overdress. She brought her focus back to reality. In front of the ironing board a huge basket overflowed with washing. She looked away.

'Take a seat, Margaret. Milk?'

'Yes please, but no sugar. I'm watching my weight.'

Mrs Horton handed Margaret a cup of tea and picked up the biscuits. 'You won't want one of these then?'

Margaret could have kicked herself. She'd spoken before thinking. She had a habit of doing that and nearly always regretted it. 'Well, Peek Frean's are my favourites.' She loved custard creams and the round ones with jam in the middle. 'Perhaps one won't hurt,' she said, taking a custard cream and wishing she had the nerve to take a jam one too.

When they had finished their tea, Bert thanked Mrs Horton and returned to the stage door. Mrs Horton took Margaret to the sewing room and introduced her to the seamstresses who made the costumes for the shows.

'Ladies, this is Margaret.' Margaret opened her mouth to say hello, but Mrs Horton didn't give her time to speak. 'Margaret is going to help us with the costumes for the new show. This is Sylvie,' Mrs Horton said, smiling at a fair-haired girl who looked half-starved sitting behind a big sewing machine at the back of the room. 'Sylvie's a machinist.'

Margaret walked over to Sylvie and shook her hand. Sylvie smiled shyly from under a thick fringe and whispered, "Ello.'

'And this is Violet, our cutter. Violet's been here longer than any of us. She's made costumes for some of the West End's most famous actors and actresses.'

'Welcome to the inner sanctum, Margaret,' Violet said, in a friendly but brisk and authoritative voice.

'This is Ivy. Ivy's a machinist and a cutter.'

Ivy gave Margaret a motherly smile. 'Jack-of-all-trades,' she said, taking Margaret's hand and holding it in both of hers. 'Hello, love.'

'Hello, I'm --'

'And this is where you'll be working.' The wardrobe mistress pointed to a chair and a small kidney-shaped table that was cluttered with boxes of beads, sequins, bits of fur and all sorts of other paraphernalia. Margaret didn't have time to look at it properly before Mrs Horton was speaking again. 'Violet's in charge of the day-to-day running of the sewing room. She'll give you your work and when you've done it, she'll check it.' Margaret nodded and smiled at Violet. 'I also need help with the maintenance of the costumes, but we'll discuss that later. I'll leave you in Violet's capable hands for the time being.' Before Margaret could thank her, Mrs Horton had left the room.

The small table where she would be working was next to an open door. As she passed she peeped in. It was a big room with connecting doors to Mrs Horton's wardrobe and the costume room. It had been painted white from floor to ceiling – and was empty except for a long trestle table in the middle with a low hanging light above it and a dozen mannequins along the back wall.

'That's the white room,' Violet said. 'It's where the costumes are cut out, and then when they're made, the artists have their fittings. Mrs Goldman, the boss's wife, is the designer. She draws the costumes on a big white pad in her studio, dressing room seven, and then she comes and discusses which fabric would be best for which costume with Mrs Horton and me.'

'Then she goes up to Berwick Street and orders it,' Ivy said.

'And that's when the fun starts,' Sylvie added.

'Yes,' Violet said. 'It's fun because the girls and me go to Berwick Street a few days later and collect it. Nine out of ten times the fabric isn't ready, so we go across to Woollies for half an hour.'

'And 'ave a cup of tea and a fancy out of Mrs Orton's petty cash,' Sylvie said, giggling.

'What if the material is ready when you get there?' Margaret asked.

'It never is,' Ivy said, winking.

'And you cut the dresses out in there too, do you?'

'Not before I've made a pattern out of special heavy tissue paper. Only then, if Mrs Goldman approves it, do I begin cutting.'

'Can we try the costumes on?' Margaret asked.

'Not on your life!' Violet looked aghast. 'Only the artists wear the costumes. Mrs Horton takes their measurements, I cut the pattern out and tack it together, and then the artists come in for the first fitting. If it doesn't fit properly at that stage, we can alter it. Once it's been machine stitched it's more difficult, especially to let out.'

'That's what the horsehair dummies and the mannequins are for,' Ivy said. 'They're the models while we're making the costumes. When they're made the artists come in for a final fitting.'

'Sometimes it takes four or five final fittings before the dress is perfect,' Ivy said.

Margaret's first week was spent sewing sequins onto the bodices and hems of evening gowns – gold on gold, red on red, black on black, and so on. Black on black was murder. It was difficult to see the sequins against the shiny fabric, but easy to stick the needle in your finger, which she did constantly. Her next job was to cover tiny buttons in fabric to decorate cuffs, kick-pleats and shoes. She wasn't sure which job was the most awkward. She liked working with silk best, because the needle went through it easily. But when fabric like taffeta was folded over, sometimes twice, it was a devil to get a needle through.

Margaret's job as an usherette was long hours and her second job in wardrobe was hard work. Her back ached from bending over the small work table and her eyes stung from straining to thread needles and sew tiny beads and buttons. She was tired, but she didn't complain. She didn't care how hard she worked, or for how long, because everything she did in the theatre took her nearer to achieving her ambition.

'The first costume fitting,' Mrs Horton announced, 'is Miss Jewel. She'll be here at three this afternoon.'

Nancy Jewel's costume was the most elegant. It was white silk. The skirt was calf length and cut on the cross. Designed to flatter Nancy Jewel's already perfect figure, it fitted snugly and moved with a jazzy swing when she twirled. The bodice of the dress was decorated with tiny seed pearls and the matching coat had a white fur trim. Margaret wriggled her nose. The fur made her sneeze. Because it was white, it had taken her twice as long to decorate. She had to keep stopping to wash her hands so she didn't make the fabric grubby.

'Is the costume ready, Violet?'

'Yes,' Violet said, looking at Ivy and Sylvie, who were both nodding.

'Right! Let's put everything away so we're ready when Miss Jewel gets here.'

Everyone dashed about, folding fabric and putting scissors, pins and reels of cotton into tins, drawers and cupboards. Margaret tidied her work station, making sure each differently coloured sequin, bead and button went into the correct box. By the time she'd finished it was almost three.

'Margaret!' Mrs Horton called.

'Yes,' she said, and then she froze. Nancy Jewel was standing in the doorway. Margaret caught her breath. The Albert's leading lady was as beautiful off stage as she was on. She was slender and elegant, her hair was a rich silky-brown, her skin flawless and her eyes twinkled when she smiled, as she was doing now. 'Oh!' Margaret smiled at her shyly.

'Take Miss Jewel's coat.'

'What? Oh yes. Sorry,' Margaret said, running over to Nancy Jewel, grabbing a coat-hanger on the way, before helping her out of her outdoor coat. As Nancy undressed Margaret hung up her coat, and then returned for her other clothes.

Of all the costumes the white one had caused Margaret the most headaches. Sewing hundreds of tiny seed pearls onto a white dress was slow and painstaking. But the look of amazement on Nancy Jewel's face when she saw it hanging in the white room erased the memory of sore fingers and tired eyes.

'Hang up Miss Jewel's suit, Margaret,' Mrs Horton said, handing her a fashionable dove-grey two-piece. And Sylvie, please ask Mrs Goldman to come in?'

Sylvie scuttled off to get Natalie Goldman who, as the designer, had the last say on the costumes, while Ivy and Violet took Nancy's dress off her dummy and helped her into it.

Mrs Horton circled Nancy, examining first the seams, and then every other part of the costume from the neckline to the hem. Finally she nodded her approval and stepped away to allow Natalie Goldman to take a closer look. Natalie lifted her hands to Nancy's shoulders. She smoothed the fabric and tugged at it gently, as if she was levelling the shoulder pads.

'Are you happy with it, Nancy? Happy with how it feels and looks?' Natalie Goldman asked, running her hands along the fastening at the back.

'Yes, very happy. It feels wonderful and looks amazing.'

'Ladies? Everything to your satisfaction?'

Wardrobe mistress and cutter nodded.

Margaret watched Nancy as she looked at herself in the full-length mirror. She lifted her hands to her lips, palms together, and smiled a wide natural smile. Then she turned gracefully. 'Thank you,' she said, looking at each of them in turn.

'It's a pleasure to make costumes for you, Miss Jewel.' Turning towards the rest of the wardrobe staff, Mrs Horton sighed with relief. Quickly recovering, she said, 'If you'd like to help Miss Jewel out of her costume, Violet? And Margaret, please fetch Miss Jewel's own clothes.'

'Thank you, ladies,' Nancy Jewel said, once she had been helped out of her show costume and into her suit.

'See you tomorrow for Katarina's fitting,' Natalie Goldman called from the doorway. The two women left together. When they were out of earshot, Mrs Horton clapped her hands. 'Well done everyone. Go and get yourselves a cup of tea. Oh, and Miss Jewel brought in a chocolate cake. It's in a tin on the table.'

The girls left the white room chatting and laughing. 'Save me a slice,' Mrs Horton shouted. 'Katarina

Kaplinski's coming in tomorrow. Doubt we'll be celebrating when she's gone.'

'Kat for short and Cat by nature,' Violet said to Margaret as they drank tea and ate cake.

'She's the number two,' Ivy said. 'Lead dancer of the chorus and she thinks she's it!'

'They say she was a Russian ballet dancer before the war. She acts like royalty. She ain't arf jumped up,' Sylvie said. 'She treats everyone as works backstage like her servants.'

'Especially the wardrobe department,' Ivy added.

Margaret couldn't wait to meet the cat of the company. Nor could she wait to get home and tell Bill all about Nancy Jewel who, she decided, was the good fairy of the Prince Albert Theatre, where Katarina Kaplinski was the wicked witch.

'She's foreign, well she would be with a name like Kaplinski.' Margaret jumped into bed beside her husband and wriggled her way into his arms. 'Russian, Sylvie said. I bet she wears expensive clothes. She could be royalty. A Russian princess. She might be a spy.' Still contemplating the various scenarios, Margaret snuggled up to Bill, who had tried to stay awake during the saga of Katarina Kaplinski – royalty, or spy. However, after a long day biking from one government office to another – and an even longer night as a volunteer ambulance driver – he was asleep the instant his head touched the pillow.

Katarina Kaplinski's entrance the following day did not disappoint. She swept into the white room exactly as Margaret imagined she would, and everyone jumped. Everyone, that is, except Mrs Horton. The wardrobe mistress was neither in fear nor in awe of Miss Kaplinski – and didn't acknowledge her high and mighty attitude.

Margaret gasped; she couldn't help herself. Kat was

everything she had hoped she would be. She had an oval face with creamy skin and high cheekbones. Her eyes were blue-grey, their paleness emphasised by black mascara on long lashes, and her eyebrows were sculpted to a dramatic V. She looked like a model. She was tall and sophisticated and elegant, though some of her height had to be credited to the heels on her shoes, which looked as if they were five inches. The classic design of her black tailored costume, with its pencil skirt and buttoned kick-pleat at the back, showed off her long legs to perfection. The cut of her jacket accentuated the smallness of her waist, while drawing attention to the curve of her hips and the fullness of her bust. The finishing touches to the stylish ensemble were a bright red silk scarf round her slender neck, and a black felt trilby that she wore tilted over her left eye. Katarina Kaplinski looked magnificent.

Margaret stood open-mouthed, wondering what an austere young woman who was possibly a spy would wear under her suit. She imagined her in a scarlet blouse with matching underwear, or perhaps steel grey, the year's most fashionable colour. To her surprise, and disappointment, Kat wore white. A white silk blouse, white underskirt trimmed with narrow white lace and beneath that a plain white brassiere and camiknickers. If it hadn't been for her smooth, dark brown hair tied back in a tight ballerina-bun, and ruby-red lips, Katarina Kaplinski would have looked quite ordinary.

While Ivy helped Kat out of her own clothes Violet lifted her new red and black costume from the rail and Sylvie stood by with scissors and pins. Mrs Horton nodded to Margaret, which was her cue to hang up Kat's clothes. By the time she returned Kat was in costume and putting it through its paces. Arms in the air, clicking her fingers in time with her feet, which were pounding the floor boards so quickly they were a blur, Kat danced the Flamenco. Suddenly she gave a small jump, brought her feet together, whipped her arms down by her side and flicked her head forward in a tilt.

Margaret held her breath and when Kat looked up, she clapped wildly.

Mrs Horton shot her a sideways look. But Margaret couldn't help herself. 'Wonderful,' she shouted, 'the dress, the dance--'

'Thank you, Margaret!' Mrs Horton glared at her. Margaret knew it wasn't her place to comment and looked at the floor. Sylvie stifled a giggle. But the others, seeing the seams in the side of Kat's dress, which had weakened from her vigorous dancing, had more important things on their minds.

'I don't understand it. The costume appears to be a little tighter,' Violet said, diplomatically. 'Is it possible that you've put on a pound or two, Miss K--?'

'No, it is not!' Kat spat. 'How dare you accuse me of putting on weight? You obviously made a mistake when you measured me. Or you cut it out wrongly. Where are my measurements?' Kat threw her head back haughtily and stood as tall as she could. Her grey eyes hardened with anger while Mrs Horton slowly and methodically leafed through the pages of the measurements book.

'Miss Kaplinski, your measurements were taken correctly and they were written down correctly,' she said at last. No one, not even Kat, dare suggest Mrs Horton had made a mistake. 'The measurements were then transferred to the pattern, which was cut correctly. Neither myself nor Violet has made a mistake.'

'Never mind, dear, the seams can be let out a touch,' Violet said. 'Leave it to me. Come in the day after tomorrow, same time, and I'll have it ready for you. Good as new, it'll be.'

Kat didn't look pleased, but she nodded.

Margaret brought Kat's clothes while Ivy and Violet helped her out of her costume. As Ivy was fastening the buttons at the back of her own skirt, Kat turned this way and that, looking at herself in the long mirror. Margaret could see Ivy getting more and more frustrated. Finally, when she had fastened the last button, Ivy stepped back and Violet helped Kat on with her jacket.

Before she left Kat turned and smiled – not at the women who had helped her, but at her reflection in the mirror. Kat was a madam, all right!

The following morning Goldie Trick, whose real name was Doreen, was due for a costume fitting. She was late.

Sylvie nudged Margaret. 'She brings us treats,' she whispered, as they waited. 'Chocolates for the sewing room and biscuits for Mrs Horton. Thank you presents, she says, for the work we do. No one knows where she gets 'em from, with everything being rationed, but they say her young man's a gangster, so I expect he gets 'em on the black market. Most of the girls look down their noses at 'im, but they never refuse to eat the chocolates he buys with 'is ill-gotten gains – as Ivy says.' Sylvie giggled.

'It's very kind of her.'

'It is, but she wouldn't eat 'em anyway. She's always on a diet.'

'He's not only a gangster, he's one of Oswald Mosley's lot. A Nazi,' Ivy said. 'And his generosity often coincides with Goldie turning up for work with bruises on her arms, or swollen eyes from crying. It's when that particular penny dropped that the girls began to give him a wide berth. He's a bad lot!'

'You look a bit like her, Margaret,' Sylvie said. 'You've got a tipped-up nose and your hair's the same colour.'

'What, mucky blonde?'

'No, honey blonde. But you're right, Sylvie,' Violet said. 'How tall are you, Margaret, about five feet seven?'

Margaret nodded. 'About that.'

'Here,' Ivy said, taking a tape measure from the table, 'let's see what size you are.' Margaret lifted her arms and Ivy measured her bust, waist and hips. She consulted her notebook and laughed. 'Well I'll be… You're the same as Goldie Trick.'

'Good,' Mrs Horton said, entering the room. 'Miss Trick isn't well and won't be in until later. That bloke of hers has just phoned the stage door. Sylvie, go and fetch Mrs Goldman.'

'But…?'

'Don't argue, Sylvie, do as I ask. We're not putting Miss Trick's costume fitting off; Margaret can stand in for her.' Margaret opened her mouth to say something, but Mrs Horton carried on speaking, as she often did. 'We'll have her in next week, but I'm not holding everyone up for her. Pop along to my washroom, Margaret and give your underarms a good wash.'

'What?'

'And put some talc on afterwards. Can't have you perspiring on the costume. You'll find everything you need in there. Get along. We're already half an hour behind.'

As she ran out of the fitting room, she heard Mrs Horton shout, 'Don't run! You'll sweat more.'

In the washroom Margaret lifted each arm in turn and sniffed. She wasn't perspiring. She didn't much. She took off her blouse and while the basin filled she looked at her reflection in the mirror. She breathed in and lifted her chin. 'Good Lord,' she said aloud. 'I do look like Goldie.' She turned to the right as far as she could and still see herself in the mirror. Her nose did tip up in the same way that Goldie's did. Margaret wanted to scream with excitement, but told herself: 'No, Margaret, you must be professional, and professionals do not screeeeeeeeeeam!' Quickly she washed, dried, and patted talcum powder under her arms.

Walking back to the fitting room, she suddenly needed to go to the toilet. Blow! She'd gone past the Ladies'. Perhaps she should go back. Was there time? No there wasn't. If she went back now she'd keep everyone waiting, so she carried on. It's only nerves, she thought, or wind. Wind? She felt a fluttering in her tummy, or was it a rumble? 'Please God it's not wind.' She stopped again and breathed in. She didn't want her tummy to stick out when she had Goldie's costume on, but then the alternative was worse. 'This is ridiculous,' she said to herself. 'Nerves, that's all it is, nerves!'

At the fitting room door, she was met by Sylvie. 'I'll take your clothes,' she said. After helping Margaret out of her skirt and blouse, Ivy and Violet helped her into Goldie's costume.

Margaret was overwhelmed. One minute she wanted to laugh, the next she thought she'd cry. Having been told it was more than her life was worth to try on the costumes, here she was standing in for

Goldie Trick, wearing her ice blue and silver show gown.

'Lift your arms up, Margaret, so we can check the side-seams.'

Margaret did as she was told, not daring to move any other part of her body, while Mrs Horton and Violet circled her discussing the seams, the beading, the length of the skirt and the trim.

'How does the dress feel, Margaret?' Natalie Goldman asked, having just arrived.

'What?'

'The costume. How does it feel? Does it feel comfortable?' Natalie Goldman said.

'Oh yes. It's comfortable. It's very comfortable,' Margaret cooed.

Mrs Horton looked at Violet and smiled. 'You can put your arms down now, Margaret,' she said, stepping away to view the dress from a distance. 'Turn round so we can see how the skirt falls.'

'Oh my God,' Margaret gasped, catching a glimpse of herself in the mirror, 'I look beautiful.'

'Shush, dear,' Mrs Horton whispered, before turning to Natalie Goldman.

'Thank you, ladies, Goldie's costume is perfect. And thank you, Margaret. You do indeed look beautiful,' she said, smiling. Then to Mrs Horton she said, 'Betsy Evans and George Derby-Bloom tomorrow?'

'Two o'clock and three o'clock, if that's convenient for you?'

'That's fine. I'll see you then,' Natalie said, and she left.

'Betsy Evans,' Ivy told Margaret during their tea break, 'is from Wales. All the men in her family are coal miners and Betsy didn't want to spend her life scrubbing coal dust out of everything, like her mum and aunts.'

'So she left home with her mother's blessing, but not her father's,' Violet added. 'Still George looks after her. Lovely girls and the best of friends, but they're chalk and cheese, Betsy and George are.'

'Why's that?' Margaret asked.

'Well,' Violet said, 'Betsy's an ordinary working class girl and Georgina, or George, is upper-crust, if you know what I mean?'

'She's an ex-debutante,' Ivy said. 'They say her mother, who died when George was a baby, was a showgirl when she met George's father, and after a whirlwind love affair they ran away to Gretna Green and got married. Poor George was brought up by a succession of nannies.'

'George jokes about when her father married again, when she was sixteen. Apparently her step-mother started to introduce her to the sons of her friends. George said she had no interest in men, or in getting married, and told her step-mother so. It was after that she was packed off to finishing school in Switzerland,' Violet said. '"I loved Geneva, but I hated finishing school," she would say. "I learned deportment and dance, how to apply make-up bea-u-tifully, and how to act like a proper lay-dee – perish the thought. But it's here, among my friends at the Prince Albert Theatre, that I learned how to be myself."'

'They came from opposite ends of society – George from money and knowing the right people, Betsy from working in a café during the day to pay for acting and dancing classes at night. But,' Ivy said, 'for both of them the theatre is their world. The Prince Albert Theatre is their home and the people who work here are their family.'

*

Margaret was no longer needed in the sewing room and was moved – or promoted, as she told Bill – to helping Mrs Horton with the maintenance of the costumes. Between them they made sure the costumes were always clean and in good condition. As 'wardrobe assistant' Margaret was responsible for small repairs, sewing up hems and replacing buttons, as well as washing and ironing the gloves and scarves – and making sure each artist had a clean pair of stockings for every show.

'The artists aren't allowed to sit around in their costumes, Margaret. And if you see anyone eating in costume,' Mrs Horton said, 'you must tell me. Be discreet, but tell me at once.' Margaret nodded. 'Not only do most of the costumes crease easily, but stains are impossible to wash out. Costumes with sequins or rhinestones can't be washed in the conventional way; they have to be taken back to Berwick Street and sent away to a specialist cleaner. Before the war it was often cheaper to make another costume. But now material's rationed, fabric's impossible to get, unless you want utility serge.'

Margaret laughed. 'Kat wouldn't wear utility serge unless it came from Harvey Nichols.'

'Kat wouldn't wear utility anything, full stop!' Mrs Horton said.

As soon as she arrived in the morning, Margaret washed the small items and hung them over the hot pipes in the boiler room. While they were drying she joined Mrs Horton and Bert for elevenses. Afterwards, she set about mending and ironing. When the gloves and stockings were dry she sorted them into pairs, folding the stockings and ironing the gloves, ready to take to the dressing rooms after lunch. On matinee days it was at twelve, which gave them time to take the costumes to the dressing rooms before the company arrived.

The artists' names were sewn into their costumes, which Mrs Horton and Margaret took to the dressing rooms and hung on a rail above the shoe rack. Gloves and stockings, and anything else that had been washed or mended, was put on the relevant artist's chair. Jewellery and hats were placed on the dressing table in front of their mirror.

Bert brought up any telegrams, good luck cards and flowers that had been left at the stage door. He was like everyone's granddad. He'd been the stage doorman and first-aider at the Prince Albert Theatre for over forty years. He could have – should have – retired several years before, but the theatre was his life. He was the first to arrive in the morning and the last to leave at night. He spoke to everyone with respect, including Margaret, although she could tell by the way he smiled at Nancy Jewel that she was his favourite. She was Margaret's too.

Until she got to know the artists Margaret decided to keep her opinions to herself. She worked hard and saved her chatter for Bill when she got home.

CHAPTER FOUR

Annie's words came into Margaret's mind. "Don't volunteer for nothing, they'll take advantage of you." Margaret sniffed – as Annie did – at the pile of ironing and mending she'd volunteered to do while she waited for Bill. She sniffed again at the underarms of Kat and George's costumes. 'Phew!' After sponging them with rose water, she took them to the boiler room and hung them up to dry. On her way out she heard a ping, and suddenly it was dark. A bulb had gone. Looking along the corridor, she felt a sudden and icy chill. She rolled her shoulders, but couldn't shake off the feeling. Annie had said the theatre was haunted by the spirit of a young girl. She said there was a cold spot on the landing, where the girl had stood before throwing herself down the stairs. Margaret wondered if she was standing in the spot and shivered. The stairs were steep and winding and made of stone. She looked over the banister and caught her breath.

She ran back to Wardrobe, flew through the door and slammed it shut. Leaning on it, she exhaled slowly. When she was sure no one had followed her, she stopped shaking. She arched her back and pushed herself off the door. 'Bert's downstairs, you silly goose,' she said, 'so get on with your job!'

Banishing all thoughts of Annie's ghost and cold spots from her mind, she started on the repairs. After replacing a button on Betsy's shirt, she took Goldie's costume from its hanger and laid it across Mrs Horton's sewing table. Goldie must have caught her heel in the hem; it had come down in two places. In the sewing drawer she searched the reels of cotton until she found one the same colour as Goldie's dress. Five minutes later the dress looked as good as new.

Margaret ran her hands over the blue and silver beaded bodice. She had sewn the tiny round beads so neatly and close together that they felt level beneath her fingers. It had taken her hours. She grinned as she recalled the expression on Violet's face when she asked her if seamstresses were allowed to try on the costumes "Not on your life!" she'd said, with a scowl that could have curdled the milk, yet just a few weeks later Margaret had been used as a dummy, because she was the same height and size as Goldie. Coveting the costume, she sighed. She would love to try it on now it was finished, but… But what? Who would know? No one!

In one movement she pulled her own dress over her head and threw it across the ironing board. She kicked off her shoes – she didn't want to risk catching her heel in the hem – and stepped into the costume. She didn't do it all the way up; she wasn't able to reach all the small buttons at the back. She twirled and caught her breath. The dress looked as good on her as it did on Goldie.

Her heart began to pound. If she was caught trying on costumes she would get the sack. As quickly as she'd taken off her own dress, but with a great deal more care, she took off Goldie's costume and hung it up.

She put on her own clothes and looked at her wristwatch. Bill was late. The washing basket was full to overflowing. There was nothing she could do about it at this hour, but she could iron while she waited. After plugging in the iron, she sorted through the pile of garments, putting those made of delicate fabrics to one side for Mrs Horton in the morning. As she turned back to the ironing board she caught her reflection in the mirror and jumped. Perhaps being up here alone wasn't such a good idea. Even in the daytime it could be eerie when no one was around. She looked across at the dummies and mannequins in the costume room. The ghostly shadows they cast made her shudder.

Forcing all thoughts of the supernatural from her mind, Margaret picked up the iron and spat on her finger. She was about to test it to see if it was hot enough when she heard knocking coming from the costume room. She froze. She put the iron on its stand and tiptoed over to the entrance. She strained her eyes and looked in. The mannequins, standing in rows, looked like soldiers preparing to march. With the light behind her, Margaret couldn't tell the difference between Kat's mannequin and Nancy's.

She stood still and listened. She couldn't hear anything. Ah! There it was again – knock, knock, knock – and it seemed to be getting louder. Convinced someone was hiding among the dummies she shouted, 'I know you're in there. Come out and show yourself!' She ran back and unplugged the iron. Picking it up with the hot plate facing forwards she wound the flex around her wrist and put the plug in her pocket. Slowly she made her way into the room, weaving in and out of the mannequins. As she ducked under a rack of jackets her hair caught on something. She lifted her free hand and lashed out at the attacking garment. It turned on its hanger but didn't release her hair. Another swipe sent the jacket spinning to the floor with strands of Margaret's hair coiled round a button.

It was unusually cold. She wondered if she was standing in a cold spot like the one on the landing.

Fingers of ice inched their way up her spine and she shuddered. Too frightened to stay any longer, she turned to leave. It was then that she saw the reason for the knocking. A small window at the back of the room had been left open and with every gust of wind the weights in the bottom of the blackout blind banged against a wooden belt rack.

Relieved, Margaret slammed the window shut. 'I'll wait for Bill downstairs,' she told one of the dummies as she passed. She returned the iron, standing it upright because it was still warm, and made her way to the door. She looked back. Everything was safe. Switching off the lights, she ran along the passage and down two flights of stairs. Halfway along the last passage she heard footsteps. They weren't Bert's: his were heavier, and Bill's gait was quicker. She held her breath. The building creaks when it begins to cool down, she thought, but it didn't stumble as these steps had just done. Scared out of her wits, Margaret ducked into dressing room two.

She had been standing in the dark dressing room for what felt like minutes, but could only have been a seconds, when the door flew open and someone staggered in. Without putting on the light the person turned, pushed the door shut, and screamed. Startled, Margaret screamed too.

'Who are you? What do you want?'

Margaret recognised the voice. 'It's me, Miss Kaplinski. Margaret,' she said, switching on the light.

'What the hell are you doing in here?' Katarina Kaplinski shouted. The hostile Russian dancer staggered across the room clutching her stomach and dropped onto the old chaise longue. Her face was as white as a sheet and contorted with pain.

'Are you all right, Miss Kaplinski?'

'Do I look as if I'm bloody all right?'

Margaret recoiled. She'd said the wrong thing to Kat again. She was always doing it. Kat had that effect on her; made her feel stupid. Margaret knew she shouldn't be in the artist's dressing room and wanted to leave, but she could see there was something very wrong with Kat. 'Can I get you anything?'

'Yes, a drink!'

Margaret filled a glass with water and offered it to her.

'What the hell is this?' she said, pushing the glass away. 'I want something stronger!'

'I don't think you should have anything stronger.'

'I don't care what you think.' Kat clutched her abdomen. 'Bloody wardrobe girl telling me what I can and cannot have.' She pulled herself to her feet and staggered across the room to the old stand-alone cupboard, where Margaret knew a bottle of brandy was kept for medicinal purposes. Before she had time to open it, she doubled over again. 'Argh!'

Margaret ran to her. 'All right, all right, I'll get you a brandy, but let me help you back to the chaise first.'

'Leave me alone!' Kat pushed Margaret away, opened the cupboard and took the brandy from it. As she turned she began to sway. She took several deep breaths, which seemed to help her regain her balance, but then she clutched her stomach again. 'You are right, Margaret,' she whispered, 'I will be better lying down. I cannot fall down then, can I?'

Margaret had just settled Kat back to the chaise when there was a knock at the door.

Anton Goldman called from the corridor: 'Margaret, if you want a lift home, I'll be leaving in ten minutes.'

Margaret opened her mouth, but Kat shook her

head. 'Do not answer and he will go away,' she hissed.

'I have to,' Margaret whispered. 'He knows I'm in here.'

'Please do not tell him I am here,' Kat begged, gripping Margaret's arm as if her life depended on it.

'I won't, but if I don't say something he'll come in.' Margaret ran across the room and, putting on a smile, opened the door and stepped into the corridor. 'Thank you, Mr Goldman ... Anton,' she said, in a carefree voice. 'I've got a bit of mending to finish, so I'll wait for Bill.'

'If you're sure?' Margaret nodded. 'Goodnight then.'

'Goodnight.' Margaret watched him turn and leave. 'Oh, Anton? Would you ask Bert to send Bill up when he arrives, please?'

'Yes. Goodnight.'

'Goodnight.' Margaret returned to the dressing room and closed the door. The two women listened as Anton Goldman walked along the corridor, his steps becoming fainter until there was no sound at all. Kat lit a cigarette and lay back on the chaise.

'I'll empty the water, so you can use the glass for your brandy,' Margaret said. 'Shan't be a minute.' When she returned Kat was asleep with her cigarette in her hand. Margaret took it and stubbed it out in an ashtray on the dressing table, before kneeling down and taking Kat's hands. They were as cold as ice. She gently rubbed them; first one and then the other, but she couldn't make them warm. She took off her coat and put it over the sleeping dancer. Her face looked like the Russian doll she kept on her dressing table for luck - round and white. Her hair, usually immaculate, was stuck to her head, lank and greasy. There was a pink spot in the middle of each cheek and dark circles under her eyes that made them look as if they'd been set too deeply in their sockets. Kat looked very poorly.

Margaret paced the floor. She didn't know what to do. She thought about going down to the stage door and telephoning Bill, but she daren't leave Kat. She looked at her watch. Bill would be here soon. Until then, all she could do was watch Kat sleep and hope she didn't stop breathing.

Half an hour later, Bill arrived. 'Kat's ill,' Margaret cried.

'Good God!' Bill said when he saw Kat. 'Do you know what's wrong with her?' Margaret shook her head. 'Kat? It's Bill. Can you hear me, Kat? Can you open your eyes for me? Margaret, pass me that bucket and then go down and ask Bert to telephone for an ambulance.'

Margaret flew down the stairs while Bill, who was used to dealing with sick people, stayed with Kat.

On her return Kat, ghostly white and shivering, began to retch. 'Sit up, Kat,' Bill said, 'or you'll choke.'

Kat did as she was told and began to vomit.

Within fifteen minutes two ambulance men were carrying Kat down the stairs, strapped to a chair. Another five and they were lifting her into the back of an ambulance.

'I'll go with her,' Margaret said.

'She'll be fine once they get her to hospital,' Bill said. 'Come on, you look all-in, let's go home.'

'No, I'm going with her. You go home – you've got an early start in the morning. I'll be all right on my own.'

'No you won't. I'll take you on the bike.'

Margaret opened her eyes with a start.

63

'Hello sleepy head. I think it's time I took you home,' Bill said.

Margaret stood up and stretched. She slowly walked over to the window in the waiting room of the emergency department of St. Thomas's Hospital and pulled back the blackout blind a fraction.

'Careful, Margaret, you'll let the light out.'

'I won't,' Margaret said, yawning. 'It's lighter out there than it is in here.'

Bill stood up, but before he'd taken a step a doctor appeared. 'Are you Miss Kaplinski's friends? Was it you who brought her into the hospital?'

'Yes,' Margaret and Bill said in unison. 'How is she?'

'It's good news. Your friend is still poorly, but you got her here in time. Another couple of hours and we might not have been able to save the baby.'

'Baby?' Margaret gasped. 'Kat is having a baby?'

Margaret climbed onto the pillion seat of Bill's motorbike. She held onto him as he slowly steered the powerful machine out of the hospital gates. Once they were on the road, Bill gave the bike some throttle and Margaret wriggled closer. She laid her head on her husband's back. The leather of his motorbike coat felt cold on her face. She was too tired to care. Besides, she liked the smell, and being cold it might keep her awake.

Before they had travelled a mile, Margaret's eyes began to grow heavy. Thanks to a pothole in the road she didn't fall asleep. If she had, she might have fallen off the back of the bike. She tightened her grip around Bill's waist and felt him lean back. He did that as a sign of affection. He did it in bed, before they went to sleep, and he was doing it now to let her know he was there and she was safe.

Margaret looked around. The streets were empty. It was too late for people to be going home after a night out, and too early for them to be going to work. She looked up at the sky. It was almost dawn but there was still a pale, almost transparent moon. On the south side of the river, black smoke drifted across a ruby sky; a reminder that the East End of London had been blitzed again.

'Brrrrrrrrrrr, it's freezing,' Margaret said when they arrived home. 'I'm so tired I could sleep for a week.'

'Go and put your nightie on while I make us a cup of cocoa,' Bill said.

'Thank you. You are a wonderful husband. But be quick. I hate going to bed on my own,' she said through chattering teeth. Jumping up and down on the spot, Margaret took off her clothes, dropped them on the armchair, and pulled on her nightgown. 'That's better,' she said, putting her arms down the sleeves of her dressing gown and wrapping it tightly around her.

'This'll warm you up.' Bill put a cup of cocoa on Margaret's bedside table. 'And cuddle that,' he said, handing her a hot water bottle.

'I'd rather cuddle you.'

'That can be arranged,' he said, sitting on the bed next to her.

With the bottle in her lap and both hands clasped firmly round the cup, Margaret sipped her hot cocoa. 'Poor Kat. It's almost too much to take in.'

'It is,' Bill agreed. 'Did you know she was expecting?'

'No. I don't think anyone did. They probably wouldn't tell me anyway.'

'Is she engaged, or courting?'

'She doesn't wear an engagement ring, but she's

got a gentleman friend. He's old and posh. Well-to-do, if you know what I mean.'

'How do you know? Have you met him?'

'Good Lord, no! Kat wouldn't introduce him to the likes of me. And I wouldn't dare speak to him unless she did.' Margaret thought for a moment. 'He's a cold fish according to Betsy. I heard the girls talking about him once. They said he was a politician. He must be rich, because he sends Kat flowers almost every night – and they're not from the market.'

'What, with everything rationed?'

'Yes, and he picks her up after the show in a chauffeur-driven car.' Margaret laughed. 'You should see Kat rushing around on the nights she sees him. Don't think he likes to be kept waiting.'

'So if she's got a boyfriend with plenty of money, why are you looking worried?'

'Because I think he's married.'

Bill clicked his tongue. 'Come on,' he said, taking Margaret's empty cup and putting it on the dresser. 'We'll talk about it tomorrow. Let's get some sleep.'

Margaret let her arms drop down by her sides, and her dressing gown slid from her slender body onto the chair to join the rest of her clothes. Then she crawled into bed and pushed the hot water bottle to the bottom by her feet. 'Turn over, Bill, so I can spoon,' she said. And although he was half asleep, Bill turned, and Margaret snuggled up to him.

CHAPTER FIVE

Margaret bumped into George and Betsy coming out of Lyons Corner House. She walked with them along the Strand, turning into Bedford Street, and then Maiden Lane. As they arrived at the Prince Albert Theatre stage door they were met by Natalie and Anton Goldman. Seconds later Bert appeared, followed by Miss Lesley, Mrs Horton, and the rest of the backstage staff.

'Wonder what's going on?' Betsy whispered.

George shrugged. 'No idea.'

Anton Goldman cleared his throat, but before he had time to speak two black cabs pulled up on the opposite side of the road. Nancy got out of one and Kat the other. When both women had joined the gathering, Anton acknowledged them with a smile and continued. 'Last night during the bombing of the East End, part of the water filtration plant at the sewage works was hit, and it's possible that some of the main pipes were damaged. The Water Board has closed the theatre while they investigate. So I'm afraid tonight's show has been cancelled.'

'How long will we be dark?' George asked.

'One night, possibly two--'

'Two?' But we're nowhere near the sewage plant. It's miles away in Lambeth, or Greenwich, or somewhere.'

'It's a precaution in case the pipes across the river are cracked. Tomorrow there's a full inspection and if the pipes haven't been damaged we'll be open at night as usual.'

'Huh!' Kat flicked the air. 'What harm can a little water do?'

67

'It isn't water,' Nancy said, 'it's sewage.'

Kat grimaced and covered her nose. 'You mean--?'

'Yes, it could get very smelly,' Betsy laughed.

'And,' Anton called above the banter, 'if water, or any other liquid, gets into electric wiring it would be very dangerous. So, ladies, tell Bert what you want from your dressing rooms and he'll get it for you. Have a well-deserved night off. Thank you.'

Bert, Mrs Horton and Miss Lesley went into the theatre while the girls said goodnight to Natalie and Anton Goldman.

Margaret watched the lads from stage management leave, discussing which pub they were going to. She wished she could go to a pub, but--

'What about you, Margaret? What are you going to do?' Nancy asked. 'Margaret?'

'Sorry, I was miles away. I'll wait for Bill, I suppose.' It was times like this she wished her friend Jenny still worked at the theatre so she could travel home with her.

'You can't wait out here for four or five hours.' George looked up at the sky. 'Not a cloud in sight; perfect bombing weather. The streets are too dangerous, Margaret.'

'I suppose I could go down to the ambulance station at Tommy's and wait for him.'

'I have a better idea,' Nancy said. 'Come to the club with Betsy, George, and me?'

Margaret had wanted to go to the Prince Albert Club since she first came to London, but Bill wouldn't take her. The girls were always talking about the fun they had there, how good the band was, and how they had danced till all hours. She was desperate to go, wanted to say yes. 'What about Bill?'

Nancy handed Margaret her coat and handbag.

'Bert's staying until eleven, in case the sewage people telephone.' Nancy turned to the stage doorman. 'You'll tell Bill where Margaret is when he gets here, won't you, Bert?'

'Of course, Miss.'

Nancy kissed Bert on the cheek. 'You're a pal.'

'I can't go to a smart club dressed like this,' Margaret said, putting on her coat.

Nancy put her arm around Margaret's shoulder. 'You look lovely, Margaret, you always do. Ladies?' she called. 'Margaret's dressed perfectly all right for the club, isn't she?'

'Fine!' and 'Good Lord, yes,' came the replies.

Margaret turned at the sound of a black cab pulling up. 'Come on, Margaret. Shake a leg,' George shouted, climbing into the back of the cab behind Betsy. 'I'm dying for a drink.'

'It doesn't feel right going without Bill. What will people think, a married woman on her own, without her husband?'

'Who cares what people think?' George shouted.

'No one will think anything, because no one will know. Besides,' Nancy said, 'you won't be on your own, you'll be with us.'

Kat lifted her cigarette in its silver holder to her lips. 'The club will be closed if you do not make up your mind soon, Margaret!'

Margaret closed her eyes, screwed up her face and shouted, 'Yes! I'm coming.'

Betsy laughed and George said, 'Come on then, we mustn't keep the Tsarina waiting.'

Kat shot George a hurt look. 'The *Tsarina* is going home, if Bert will call her a taxi.'

Margaret saw in Nancy's face that she had also noticed Kat's reaction to George's snipe. 'Are you sure you won't come, Kat?' Nancy said. 'We can squeeze up. There's room...'

'Thank you, but no. I will see you tomorrow.' Kat put her hand on Margaret's arm and smiled. 'Have fun.'

'I will.'

'We'll look after her,' Nancy said.

'Come on, Margaret. We're all dying of thirst,' George said, pulling Margaret into the waiting taxi. 'She'll have fun all right. We'll have a couple of drinks at the bar--'

'You couldn't stop at a couple if your life depended on it, George,' Betsy teased, and received a tickling for her cheek.

The Prince Albert Club on Long Acre was owned by Anton Goldman and managed by Nancy's fiancé, Salvatore Russo, who Margaret had never met, but had seen several times when he'd been waiting for Nancy at the stage door. Unlike its neighbour the Club Royal, which the girls said attracted gangsters and black market racketeers, the Prince Albert was where the who's who of London society dined after they'd been to, or appeared in, a West End show.

Margaret felt the butterflies of excitement flying around in her stomach as she waited to enter the club. George rang the bell and within seconds the door opened and the doorman welcomed the party into a dimly lit entrance lobby. Once the street door was closed and the blackout curtains were back in place, the doorman switched on the lights. Margaret looked around in amazement as she took off her coat and gave it to the cloakroom attendant. Smiling her thanks she followed the girls across the maroon and gold entrance lobby to the restaurant, where they were met by the Maître d' who pointed to what looked to Margaret like the only unoccupied table in the place. It was on the edge of the dance floor. Margaret gasped. Entering the restaurant was like stepping into another world, a bright modern world. Men in dinner jackets and women in evening gowns or dresses that were the height of fashion were eating, talking, laughing. Each table had its own table lamp, but all around the room bright wall lights designed to look like half-moons shone upwards. In the ceiling, right in the middle above the dance floor, was a huge mirror-ball. And on the table reserved for the Prince Albert Theatre Company, there were two bottles of champagne in buckets filled with crushed ice and six long-stemmed glasses.

'Sit next to me, Margaret,' Nancy said, as Salvatore pulled out a chair.

'Thank you.' Margaret blushed. Biting her bottom lip she scrunched up her shoulders and smiled at Nancy.

Nancy returned the smile, making her feel very special. Nancy was the kindest, most beautiful, elegant person. She could sing and dance better than anyone, and she had taken a shine to Margaret. Nancy's handsome Italian fiancé, who Margaret had first thought was a bit of a spiv, clearly adored her. She felt the colour rise in her cheeks again when Salvatore sat down on the other side of Nancy, kissed her hand and looked lovingly into her eyes. Margaret looked away.

The Prince Albert Club was what Margaret's dad would have called select. It was select all right. Nancy said lots of film stars went there, and sometimes minor royalty. Looking around the room Margaret spotted high-ranking military men, wealthy-looking business men, and some beautiful young women who were so glamorous, Margaret thought they had to be starlets.

Margaret sipped her champagne. She thought she'd feel out of her depth in a night club surrounded by goodness knows who. Instead, she loved every minute of it. She felt a twinge of guilt, because she was experiencing it without Bill, but then night clubs didn't really interest him. He would rather have a pint of beer in a local pub. Not that they went to a local pub in London. Leaning back and relaxing into her seat, Margaret put her glass to her lips. It was empty.

Salvatore beckoned a young waiter who was standing just a few feet away holding a bottle of champagne. 'See that the ladies get whatever they want.'

The waiter nodded and immediately refilled Margaret's glass. Salvatore bent down and whispered in Nancy's ear. Margaret watched Nancy look up and smile lovingly before he left. He returned a little later in the evening. He rested his hand gently on Nancy's shoulder. 'The diners are asking if someone from the theatre is going to sing tonight.'

'Sorry, but I've had a teeny-weeny bit too much to drink, darling,' George said.

'Me too,' giggled Betsy.

'What about you, Margaret?' Nancy said with a wink. 'You know the songs in the show.'

Margaret choked. 'Me?'

'Why not? You have a lovely voice,' Nancy said. 'We'd like to hear you sing, wouldn't we, ladies?'

'Margaret, Margaret, give us a song!' George and Betsy chanted. 'Come on, Margaret,' Nancy said, 'show them what you're made of.'

At that moment George and Betsy stood up and began to applaud her.

Margaret's mouth fell open. 'What are you doing, George? Sit down, Betsy!'

Nancy leaned forward and whispered in Margaret's ear, 'If you won't sing for them, will you sing for me?'

George and Betsy pulled Margaret to her feet and pushed her forward. 'All right, I will,' she said, looking over her shoulder at Nancy. Everyone was clapping as she walked across the dance floor. She felt so small, and the floor seemed so big.

As she approached the stage the bandleader put out his hand. Margaret took it and, like a real starlet, stepped up with her head held high. 'What's your name?' he whispered.

She opened her mouth to answer, but her mind went into a spin. When she was a child she'd learned monologues and songs and dances, which she performed to her long-suffering family. She'd called herself all manner of names, mostly those of famous actresses that she'd seen in films at Lowarth Picture House. Sometimes she was Myrna Dudley, or Greta Dudley. A favourite was Mae, another Marlene, but mostly she called herself Margot, a shortened version of Margaret. 'Margot Dudley.' The bandleader whispered into her ear again. She replied, '"They Can't Take This…" I mean, "*That…* Away From Me".'

The bandleader instructed the band and Margaret moved nearer to the microphone. Hardly able to contain the excitement she felt, she looked out into the audience, and they began to applaud. She hadn't even started to sing and they were clapping. She was so excited she wanted to clap too. She found Nancy's smiling face in the darkness. She was clapping enthusiastically. Margaret took a breath to calm her nerves and smiled back. Then she turned to the bandleader, her heart beating so loudly in her chest she thought the microphone would pick up the rhythm, and she nodded. The band began to play; she began to sing.

When the song came to an end, the bandleader joined her. 'Miss Margot Dudley, ladies and gentlemen,' he said. And while he and the audience clapped, Margaret took a bow.

'Thank you, Miss Dudley.' The bandleader proffered his arm and Margaret, beaming, took it and allowed him to help her from the small stage. Once on the dance floor the bandleader bowed, and then stepped back onto the stage.

Margaret looked around. The band had begun to play, but people were still applauding her. She tried to smile, but the muscles in her face were paralysed. She peered into the darkness and saw Salvatore walking towards her. She put out a shaking hand. 'Salvatore, thank goodness,' she said, resting her hand on his arm. 'I feel all wobbly. My legs are like jelly.'

Salvatore laughed. 'You were wonderful, Margaret. Listen to the applause. They love you.'

'Do they? Was I? I don't remember,' she said shakily.

'Hold tight, Margaret,' Salvatore said. 'Or should I call you Margot?'

As she turned to answer him someone shouted, 'Lovely song, Margot.' Someone else called, 'Nice to see you, Miss Dudley.' And a third, 'Hope we see you again, Margot.'

'Margot!' she said, smiling up at Salvatore. 'Call me Margot!'

As she arrived at the table the girls stood up, lifted their glasses, and shouted, 'To Margot!'

Margot dropped into her chair and George poured her a glass of wine. 'I don't how I dared do that,' she said, taking a sip.

'You were a hit, Margot,' Salvatore said. 'Would you like to do a spot every Thursday night around this time?'

Margot didn't reply, but stood open-mouthed.

'A couple of numbers for... shall we say, £10?'

Wondering whether the jumble of words in the back of her throat would ever find their way into her mouth, Margot nodded.

'She'd love to,' Betsy and George said together.

'Yes!' Margot gasped finally. 'This could be my big break!' she squealed. 'Oh my God!' She looked at Nancy. 'I've completely forgotten about Bill. What on earth is he going to say?'

'He'll be proud of you,' Nancy said, and everyone agreed. Margot wasn't so sure.

'More importantly,' Betsy said, 'how are you going to get out of the theatre?'

'Oh! I hadn't thought... I-- I can't, can I?'

George nudged Betsy, and then tapped Margot on her arm. 'We'll think of something,' she whispered. 'We'll get Salvatore to arrange for your spot to be in our second act. That'll give you plenty of time to get here, do two songs, and get back to the theatre before the curtain comes down. Easy!'

'Easy?' Margot screwed up her face. 'I don't think it'll be easy, but I'll do it!'

Margot walked the route from the Prince Albert Theatre to the Prince Albert Club a dozen times – and the longest it took was ten minutes. She reasoned that it would take five minutes to get out of the theatre, ten to get to the club, five to change into an evening dress, five hanging about, and ten to do the two songs. Then ten minutes to walk back to the theatre, and five to change back into her usherette uniform. A total of fifty minutes. It was tight, but she was determined to do it.

On the first Thursday night, as the curtain rose for the second act, Margot checked her section of the audience. Every seat was taken. Before the stage lights came up, she side-stepped behind the curtains at the exit and, in one movement, slipped through the door. She nipped to the staffroom and picked up a large bag containing her handbag, gasmask, dress and shoes. Seconds later she was through the pass-door leading from front of house to the backstage area and walking unseen along the passage behind the stage. So far, so good.

The door to the stage door area stood ajar. Margot peered through it. Bert was in his office, reading the *Evening Standard*. Keeping her head down she tiptoed though the door. Suddenly she heard what sounded like a chair scraping on the floor. She froze. She stood up straight and looked into Bert's office again. He had his back to her and was putting something into the top drawer of a chest of six. Like lightning she dashed through the blackout curtain and out of the stage door.

Quickly she walked the length of Maiden Lane, turned into Southampton Street and zigzagged through the narrow streets of Covent Garden to Long Acre and the Prince Albert Club. She looked at her wristwatch. It had taken exactly ten minutes. After giving her coat to the cloakroom girl Margot popped into the ladies' toilet, took off her skirt, blouse, and shoes, and put on a black velvet evening gown that Goldie had worn in one of last season's shows and a pair of black patent leather court shoes. The dress fitted as if it had been made for her – the shoes too.

Checking her hair in the mirror, she was pleased to see it looked the same as it had before she left the theatre. The setting lotion she'd used to secure the finger waves was so strong there wasn't a hair out of place. She wasn't able to put a comb through it and decided to use less next time. After putting on lipstick, Margot smoothed the skirt of the gown over her hips and left the ladies' for the club.

'It's lovely to see you, Margot,' Salvatore said. 'Are you ready to sing for us?'

'Oh yes,' Margot said. 'I can't wait.'

Salvatore took her by the hand and led her though the tables in the crowded restaurant to the stage.

The bandleader put out his hand to help Margot onto the stage and whispered, 'Did you learn the songs?'

'Of course!'

He gave her hand an encouraging squeeze. 'Ladies and gentlemen, I give you Miss Margot Dudley.' When the audience had finished clapping he continued, 'She is going to sing "Cheek To Cheek" from the film *Top Hat*, followed by "I'll See You Again" from the musical *Bitter Sweet*.' The bandleader bowed to Margot and she moved to the microphone. It was bigger than she remembered and when she stood behind it, it covered her face. She moved to the left, and then the right. That was it. Comfortable with her position she looked over her shoulder at the bandleader. He gave her an encouraging wink before nodding to the band.

Margot's stomach was churning. She thought she was going to be sick. Her throat felt dry, but there was nothing she could do about it. She looked into the audience and imagined it was Nancy, George and Betsy clapping – and she smiled. As the band struck the first chords of "Cheek To Cheek" Margot planted her feet firmly six inches apart in an attempt to stop her legs from shaking. It worked. She smiled again, leant into the microphone and on cue began to sing…

At the end of the song the audience applauded long and loud. Margot thought her heart would explode in her chest, she was so happy. She mouthed 'Thank you!' so many times her jaw ached. She daren't look at her wristwatch but she knew if they didn't stop clapping soon she would be late getting back to the theatre. She turned to the bandleader and nodded that she was ready to sing the second number. Again she looked into the audience. This time she wasn't nervous. This time her smile was open and bright, and her eyes were alight with excitement. As the band began to play, Margot reached out to the audience with every fibre of her being as she sang Noel Coward's "I'll See You Again". As she finished singing Salvatore appeared out of the darkness. She turned and bowed to the bandleader, and then to the band, before allowing Salvatore to help her from the stage.

'Thank you. I'm a bit worried about the time,' she whispered. Salvatore smiled as he guided her through the tables. After thanking people for their kind words and assuring them she would be back next week, Margot said goodbye to Salvatore, thanked the cloakroom girl – who was standing at the door holding the bag containing Margot's own clothes – and left.

On the way back to the theatre, Margot relived every second of her performance at the club. She hummed the songs, stopping once and twirling in front of a shop window. She couldn't see her reflection because there wasn't a moon, but she didn't care. Giving the sandbags outside the church a wide berth, she danced along Maiden Lane until she arrived at the stage door. Then, after inhaling and exhaling deeply to calm herself, she slowly turned the doorknob. Once inside she stood behind the blackout curtain and quietly closed the door.

Carefully she pushed the curtain to the side. Bert wasn't in his office. She crossed quickly and quietly to the passage behind the stage. The orchestra was playing the lead-in to the finale. Margot sighed with relief. Everyone was on stage. She ran along the passage and was through the door leading to front of house in seconds. In the staff room she took off her coat and dress. After hanging up the coat she folded the dress, put it in her bag with her shoes and pushed it under the chair. She then put on her skirt, blouse, and tabard. Glancing in the mirror she saw that her hair hadn't moved. Definitely less wave lotion next time, she thought, and she giggled. And there was going to be a next time. "See you at the same time next week?" Salvatore had said when she left.

Seconds later Margot was in the auditorium and, noticed by only one old lady as she wiped off her lipstick, she slipped into her usherette's seat.

She had an overwhelming urge to scream with happiness. She didn't.

CHAPTER SIX

Margot no longer felt anxious leaving the Prince Albert Club. After six weeks, she not only made it back to the theatre before the final curtain, she was often in her seat for the finale. Margot laughed out loud. When she first started doing a spot at the club, she would run back to the theatre in a panic and spend the rest of the night and most of the following day feeling guilty. Now she only felt the thrill of it. She loved the excitement and the danger.

As she entered Southampton Street Margot heard the drone of low flying aircraft followed by the air raid siren. She looked up. The sky on the other side of the river glowed orange and red. The East End was under attack for the ninth night in a row. The rumble and crump of German bombs sounded louder tonight, and nearer. Standing in the shadows, Margot watched as searchlights, their beams crisscrossing in the night sky, illuminated half a dozen heavily-armed Messerschmitts. Directly above her one minute, they went into a dive, off-loading their bombs on the docks. Suddenly the familiar winding sound of the siren in Green Park started up, followed by the ear-shattering cracking sound as streams of bullets were fired into the sky. With an almighty roar the Messerschmitts broke formation, flying off to the left and the right to avoid the anti-aircraft guns. Margot began to run.

'Hey you!' someone shouted. Then she heard the shrill blast of a whistle. 'This way!'

'I've got to get to work,' Margot shouted over her shoulder to an ARP warden who had given chase.

'Not tonight you're not,' he said, catching up with

her. He pointed across the road to the entrance of Aldwych underground station. 'Come on!'

'You don't understand. I'm late,' Margot said.

'And you'll be dead if a bomb drops on you. Now move along!' he ordered.

Margot had no choice but to join the queue of people leaving the Aldwych and Lyceum theatres. She looked at her watch. The safety curtain would have come down at the Albert by now and Anton would soon be addressing the audience, if he hadn't done so already. It was too late for a sing-song; the usherettes would be showing the audience to the exits. An unpleasant taste rose from Margot's stomach and stuck in her throat. She wanted to be sick. Tears of anger and frustration ran down her cheeks. She was in trouble.

The entrance of Aldwych underground station was crammed full. ARP men were trying to control the crowd by blowing their whistles while station employees were shouting for people to make their way down to the platforms. Allowing people to push past her, Margot shuffled on the spot, looking all the time for a way to escape. Once downstairs on the platform she would be stuck there all night. The thought of Bill thinking she was trapped in a raid, dead even, almost outweighed the fear of a ticking off from Miss Lesley. A ticking off? If only. Tears began to fall again. The repercussions of-- 'Hey! Watch what you're doing!' Margot shouted, as a boy of about ten bumped into her.

'Sorry Missus,' he said, his hand on her handbag, pretending to steady himself.

'You're on the pinch, you little devil. I'm going to call the police.'

'I ain't, missus, 'onest I ain't. Please don't call the

Rozzers.'

Holding his false but pleading stare, Margot had an idea. 'All right,' she said, 'but if I don't call them--' Before she had finished speaking the boy, eyes darting this way and that, turned as if to run. Margot grabbed the threadbare collar of his jacket and yanked him back. 'How would you like to earn a shilling?'

The boy shrugged her off and wiped the cuff of his sleeve across his nose. 'Say I would,' he said, squinting at her as if he was sizing her up. 'What would I 'ave to do?'

'Get me out of here.'

'That's easy, follow me. I'll say as you're me mam and your proper poorly, so I'm taking ya to the 'ospital.'

If she hadn't been so desperate to get out of there, Margot would have laughed. By the way they were dressed, no one would have believed they were related, let alone mother and son. However, the scruffy urchin was her only hope and she wasn't about to offend him. 'Good idea, but the ARP warden at the entrance knows me. As soon as he sees me he'll stop me.'

A feral grin crept across the boy's face. 'I've got another idea, but it'll cost you two bob. The ARP bloke knows me too.'

'Go on then,' Margot said, 'but be quick, I'm in a hurry.'

'Not till I've got me money,' the ragamuffin said, holding out his hand.

Margot gave the boy two shillings and, pretending to move along with the rest of the crowd, waited.

'Oi!' she heard the ARP warden shout. 'Stop that child. The little bugger's swiped my whistle.'

As the ARP warden chased after Margot's scruffy

little partner in crime one way, Margot slipped out of the underground station the other – and fled.

As she burst through the stage door, Margot's lungs felt as if they were on fire. She leant forward and, with her hands on her thighs, took several deep breaths.

'Miss Lesley's looking for you, Miss.'

Still breathless, Margot choked back the tears. 'I'm in trouble, aren't I, Bert?'

'I'm afraid so. She asked me to tell you to go to her office when you got back from-- wherever it is you've been.'

'Thanks, I'd better...' Margot forced a smile, left the backstage area and walked along the passage behind the stage. It was deserted. She sighed and whispered, 'Thank God.' She was dreading bumping into someone from stage management. It would be bad enough having to face the other usherettes. Margot stood outside the staff room for some seconds. Finally she plucked up the courage and opened the door. The small room was empty.

Once inside, Margot closed the door and let the tears flow. She took off her coat and hung it up. Then she stepped out of the beautiful gold sequin evening gown that Betsy had 'borrowed' for her from the wardrobe store. She put on her black skirt and white blouse and looked in the mirror. Her hair looked fine, but her makeup had all but been cried off. She took a handkerchief from her handbag, spat on it, and gently rubbed the mascara that had been washed from her eyelashes to her cheeks. She didn't look much better, but she didn't care.

After putting on her usherette's tabard, Margot left the room. Her legs felt like marshmallows, but she held her head up and set off along the corridor at a pace. By the time she arrived at Miss Lesley's office any confidence that she had mustered had gone. Forcing herself not to cry again, Margot lifted her hand and made a fist to knock. However, before her knuckles met the wood the door opened.

'Come in, Margaret.'

Margot followed Miss Lesley into her office and closed the door. Standing in front of the large desk, she clasped her hands so tightly behind her back that her nails dug into her palms.

'I think you know why I have asked you to come and see me?' Margot nodded, but didn't speak. 'I've been told by a reliable source that you've been leaving the theatre during the second act to sing in a nightclub in Soho.'

'Soho? Who told you--?'

'Please don't interrupt, Margaret. Or should I call you Margot?'

Margot opened her mouth again, but shut it quickly when she realised Miss Lesley didn't actually want an answer.

'And,' she went on, 'you return to the theatre, to your job as an usherette, just before the end of the show?' Margot didn't say anything. She didn't know whether she was meant to answer the question, or not. 'Well, is it true?'

'Yes,' Margot whispered. 'But it isn't in Soho and it's only once a week. I--' Margot saw Miss Lesley's eyes spark with anger, so she cut short the explanation.

'The address and the dates are irrelevant, Margaret! You've been leaving your post in the middle of the show!'

Margot felt the tears begin. 'I'm so sorry I've let you down, Miss Lesley. It won't happen again.'

'No, Margaret, it won't! However naïve I think you are for chasing this hobby, or whatever you call it, I'm going to release you from your job as an usherette to pursue it.'

'You're sacking me?' Margot cried.

'No, I'm not sacking you. You are going to leave. Tonight wasn't the first time you were absent from your post, but it was the last. It isn't fair on the other usherettes if they have to do your work as well as their own.'

'Does Mr Goldman know I've been-- I'm leaving--'

'No. As you're a personal friend, I thought it best not to involve him.'

'Thank you.'

'Besides, it isn't as if you're leaving the theatre. You'll still have your job in wardrobe.'

'Will I?'

'Of course. It's only because you're not interested in being an usherette that you've become unreliable. You obviously enjoy working with Mrs Horton, which is why she's always singing your praises. Right, you'd better get off. It's gone eleven. Your husband will be wondering where you are.'

'Thank you, Miss Lesley. I'm sorry I've caused you so much trouble.'

'I know you are. Goodnight.'

'Goodnight.' Margot left the small office and made for the backstage passage. Bill would be at the stage door waiting for her. She wasn't looking forward to telling him she'd been released from her usherette job. Miss Lesley's a lovely person, she thought, pushing open the door that would take her backstage. I don't blame her for getting rid of me. I'd get rid of me, if I was her.

Looking on the bright side, she would be able to

watch the show at night without interruption. She knew most of the routines well enough to perform already, but new ones were being added all the time, sometimes weekly. Working in wardrobe she'd often be backstage when the artists were learning new routines. She would watch from the wings and rehearse at home. Margot brightened. Now she didn't work as an usherette at night, she might be able to do another spot at the Albert Club. And when the time was right, she'd ask George, or Nancy, to introduce her to the theatre's director, Richard Smiley. She could invite him to the club to see her sing and afterwards, over a glass of champagne, suggest herself as an understudy. Tell him that when the chorus girls were called up, or left the show at short notice, she could step in and take their place. She would casually mention that she knew all the songs and dances and-- And she heard Bill's voice. She'd decide what to say nearer the time.

She looked in the mirror at the end of the passage. She looked terrible. She'd cried off her makeup, her face was blotchy and her eyes were red, but there was nothing she could do about it. She cleared her throat, put on a smile, and entered the stage door area. 'Is Bill here, Bert?'

'In here, reading Bert's newspaper.'

Margot peeped through the small hatch. 'It's all right for some,' she joked. 'Are you warm enough sitting in front of Bert's fire?'

'Yes I am.' Bill pushed himself out of Bert's old chair. 'What on earth...? Have you been crying?' he asked, putting his arms round his wife.

'Take me home, Bill.'

'Who's upset you, darling?'

'I've upset me, Bill. I've upset everything.' Margot

buried her head in the sheepskin lining of her husband's motorcycle jacket. Take me home and I'll tell you.'

'Here, drink this.' Bill handed Margot a glass. 'Ginger wine. It'll warm you up.'

Margot sipped the spicy liquid and gazed into the fire.

'Well?' Bill said, after a few minutes. 'It's not like you to cry. What's going on?'

Margot took another sip of her drink. 'I can't tell you, Bill.'

'You're scaring me now, Margaret. Are you ill?'

'No.'

He exhaled noisily. 'Phew! Thank God for that. What then?' he said, his voice lighter. 'Come on, love, we don't keep secrets from one another. Just say it.'

'I've been sacked.'

'You've been what?'

'Sacked?'

'By who?'

'Miss Lesley.'

Bill tilted his head and frowned, the way he did when he knew his wife was hiding something. 'Why would she sack you? She likes you. You like her. And you love the job.'

Margot didn't love the job; she loved the theatre.

'You'd be in that damn theatre day and night if you had your way. So?' Bill put his hand under Margot's chin and lifted her face until her eyes met his. 'What have you done that is so bad you've been sacked?'

'Well,' Margot began. She needed to sweeten the pill. 'Well,' she said again, 'Miss Lesley didn't sack me, exactly. She said she was letting me go to pursue my career.'

'Pursue your career? What the hell does that mean?'

'She knows I want to sing and dance and--' She burst into tears.

Bill waited until Margot calmed down. 'Let me get this straight. Last week you said you liked your boss. You said she was a nice woman. You also said she was pleased with your work and grateful to you for all the hours you put in. Is that right?'

'Yes, but…'

'But what?'

'It was the wardrobe mistress who said that.'

Bill shook his head. 'There's more to this, isn't there? What aren't you telling me, Margaret?' She closed her eyes. Bill was angry. He had every right to be. 'You might as well tell me,' he said, 'or would you rather I ask Miss Lesley?'

'I was late. The air-raid siren started and an ARP warden made me go to Aldwych Underground. And you know how I hate--? Anyway, I was pushed and shoved into the station and almost down the stairs before I got away. Then it took ages to get to the theatre--' Margot burst into tears. 'I'm sorry, Bill.'

'Hold on. It wasn't your fault you were late. We'll explain what happened and everything will be all right. Do you know if she's told Anton?'

'She said she hadn't, but--'

'No more buts! I'm not having you treated like this. Pamela Lesley can't sack you for being late if you were caught in an air raid. Here,' Bill handed Margot his handkerchief. 'Dry your eyes. I'll go and see Anton tomorrow, explain what happened and get you reinstated.' Bill put his arms around Margot and rocked her gently. 'So no more tears, all right?'

'It wasn't the first time.'

'What wasn't the first time? That you'd been late?'

'No. That Miss Lesley had caught me away from my post. It wasn't my first warning either. I'm sorry, Bill. I didn't tell you before because I didn't want you to be angry with me. And the reason Miss Lesley hasn't told Anton is because the Goldmans are our friends. I know they're really our Bess's friends, but Miss Lesley said our friends, and I wasn't about to--'

'Stop, Margaret! Never mind whose friends are who.' Bill frowned, then looked thoughtful. 'When was this air raid? When did the sirens sound?'

'Tonight.'

'Yes, Margaret, tonight! What time? We were called out to an accident at around seven. We drove past the Aldwych. I didn't hear the siren, or see people queuing to get into the station.'

'Just before ten,' Margot whispered, looking at the floor.

'Did you say ten?' Margot nodded, but didn't look up. 'What the hell were you doing walking around the streets at that time of night?'

Tears began to run down her cheeks. 'I'm sorry, Bill, I should have told you. I wanted to, but it never seemed to be the right time. And if I'd told you and you made me stop, I don't know what I'd have done. I love it, Bill. You don't know what it means to me. It's what I've always dreamed of. Please don't stop me doing it, Bill, please,' Margot begged. 'If you do, I'll die. I will, I'll die!' Margot pulled away from her husband, threw herself onto the bed and sobbed.

Bill poured them both another drink. 'Drink this, you'll feel better. Come on,' he coaxed, 'sit up.'

Margot lifted her head from the pillow with a shuddering sob. Her face was red and her eyes swollen. Trembling, she took the glass of ginger wine and spilt a drop. 'Sorry,' she whispered.

'Tell me why you weren't at the theatre at-- whatever the time was. And I want the truth, Margaret!'

Margot told Bill how the theatre had gone dark after the sewerage works had been bombed. How the girls had persuaded her to go with them to the Prince Albert Club, and how Nancy's fiancé, Salvatore, asked if one of them would do a song from the show. 'None of them wanted to sing. They shouted out my name, said I would sing – and I did. I sang a song on the stage, Bill.'

Margot paused to give Bill time to comment, but he just sipped his drink. She couldn't read his expression and she lowered her head. 'Go on,' he said, eventually.

'Well, I walked across the dance floor to the stage. I was so nervous... Anyway, the bandleader helped me onto the stage and there I was, in the spotlight, in front of all those people. He asked me my name and I felt nervous and excited at the same time. I said Margot, because it's kind of short for Margaret. I didn't know whether you'd like it if I sang in a club as Margot Burrell, so I said Dudley.'

'Your maiden name?' Bill shook his head. 'Did you take your wedding ring off, too?'

'Of course not! How could you even think that? Dudley is my stage name, my professional name. All the girls have one and I wanted one too. It has nothing to do with being married or single. I used to call myself Margot Dudley when I was a kid, when the Dudley sisters used to sing in the Christmas concerts at Woodcote village hall.'

Margot could see the hurt and disappointment in Bill's eyes. 'I'm sorry. I love you and I love being your wife, Bill, but this is what I've dreamed of since those days in the village hall. It was a wonderful feeling, singing in front of all those people. I dared to look into the audience once and they'd stopped talking and eating. They were listening to me sing. And when I finished they clapped for ever such a long time. I wish you'd have been there.' Bill lifted his head and raised his eyebrows, but said nothing.

'Salvatore helped me from the stage and walked me back to where the girls were sitting. He asked me if I'd like to do a spot every week. I said no, of course, but George and Betsy said I would. They egged me on, and I suppose I got carried away. And with everybody listening, I had to say yes, didn't I?' Bill didn't reply.

'The girls were laughing at the beginning, when they suggested me to sing – having a bit of a joke, you know? But when I finished singing they clapped me tons.' Bill still didn't comment. 'So there it is. I've been sneaking out of the theatre and going to the Prince Albert Club to sing two songs every Thursday for the last six weeks. And no one would have been any the wiser if the ARP warden had let me go down Maiden Lane.'

'Maybe not, but you'd have worn yourself out doing three jobs, because that's what you would have been doing. All that rushing backwards and forwards... You couldn't have kept it up. And the deceit...' Bill shook his head, finished his drink, and banged the empty glass down on the dresser.

'Are you very angry with me?'

'I'm furious.'

'Don't be, Bill. I won't go to the club again, if you don't want me to. I'll tell Salvatore tomorrow.'

'No you won't Margaret – *Margot* – and I wouldn't ask you to. If I did, you'd end up hating me. Besides, you'll find a way to do what you want, you always do. I'm going to bed.'

Margot sat on the edge of the bed while Bill undressed. Reaching across, she took his pyjamas from under his pillow and handed them to him. He put them on, and then pulled back the bedclothes on his side of the bed and climbed in. Without saying goodnight, he turned over so his back was to her and pulled the eiderdown up to his chin.

Margot watched Bill sleeping, waiting and willing him to turn over and face her. He didn't. She was cold and began to shiver, so she undressed and put on her nightgown. Slipping into bed beside him, Margot brought her knees up behind his. Instead of bending his knees and leaning back to spoon, as he always did, Bill straightened his legs and edged forward.

'Goodnight Bill,' Margot whispered, and she cried herself to sleep.

CHAPTER SEVEN

'Margot?'

Margot stopped and looked around. She could have sworn someone called her name, but there was no one in else in Maiden Lane. At least, there was no one near enough to--

'Margot?'

There it was again. Not much louder than a whisper, but it sounded urgent, desperate. She looked up and down the Lane, but still couldn't see anyone. She looked across to the alley that zigzagged through the side streets of Covent Garden to Leicester Square and-- 'Goldie!' Running across the road, Margot found Goldie Trick on her knees, head against the wall, holding her ribs.

'Help-- please-- Margot,' Goldie begged in breathless whispers. 'Theatre-- better inside.'

Margot wanted to say, you won't be better anywhere until you get away from that bad 'un, Dave. Instead, she said: 'Of course I'll help you. Can you stand?'

Goldie nodded, took a breath in preparation, and fell to the ground. 'Ouch! It hurts when-- I-- breathe.'

'What on earth has he done to you this time?' Margot knelt in front of the bruised and bleeding dancer. 'Breathe really slowly; small shallow breaths, it won't hurt so much.' Margot waited until Goldie nodded that she was ready. 'Take my hands and I'll pull you to your knees. If it hurts we'll stop. But if we do have to stop, try and lean against the wall, that way you won't fall down.'

Trembling, Goldie gripped Margot's hands as she slowly pulled her to her knees. 'Good girl. You're halfway to standing.' Goldie closed her eyes and took several shallow, shuddering breaths. 'You're doing really well,' Margot said. 'Take a rest but don't sit down, will you? I don't think that bugger would dare to show his face around here, but the sooner we get you into the theatre the better.'

Goldie gripped Margot's hands again, tightly. This time, using the wall to steady herself, she struggled to her feet. She wasn't able to stand up straight, but she could walk.

Margot crouched slightly, so she was shorter than Goldie. 'Put your arm round my shoulder and lean on me--' Goldie nodded, and with some effort did as Margot asked. Holding the slender dancer around her waist, Margot was able to take her weight. Slowly, gently, she helped Goldie, one small shuffling step at a time, across Maiden Lane.

As they entered the theatre's stage door, Goldie kept her head down, not only out of shame, but because she was in too much pain to stand up properly. Bert looked out of the small window in his office to greet them, but stepped back quickly when Margot shook her head. Best not embarrass Goldie, she thought.

Because Margot was late, Mrs Horton had hung the artist's costumes in the open wardrobes, placed their show shoes underneath, and laid their gloves on their respective dressing tables. Margot breathed a sigh of relief; she and Goldie wouldn't be disturbed for at least two hours. Feeling useless, Margot sat next to Goldie at the dressing table wishing there was something she could say or do to help her. 'Why don't you have a lie down on the chaise?'

'That's not a bad idea,' Goldie said, pushing herself gently out of her chair. Margot helped her across the room to the chaise longue, lifted her feet up once she was sitting, and put Kat's pillow under her head. 'Will you stay with me, Margot? It's silly, but even here I'm frightened Dave will get me.' Goldie began to cry.

'It's not silly at all. Of course I'll stay; I'll stay as long as you want.' Margot went back to the dressing table, picked up a chair and set it down beside the chaise. After a while Margot suggested she make them both a cup of tea. 'If you're able to drink one,' she said, gently pushing Goldie's hair from her face.

'That would be lovely. Thank you.'

Margot went to the small ante-room. It was not much more than a large alcove with a sink, a side table that had a gas ring on it, a kettle and teapot, and several cups and saucers. After making the tea, she added milk to both cups and a heaped spoonful of sugar to Goldie's. When she returned to the dressing room, Goldie was sitting at her dressing table.

Margot put her tea in front of her. 'I know you don't normally have sugar, but it's supposed to be good for shock, so…'

They drank in silence. When they had finished, Goldie looked in the mirror. 'I can't go on stage looking like this, can I?'

Margot took Goldie's hands. She looked at her swollen face, her misshapen nose, the cut that ran the length of her left cheekbone, the arc of bruising around her left eye, which was almost closed, and her split bottom lip that she daren't clean for fear that if she removed the congealed blood the wound would open and she wouldn't be able to stop it bleeding. Blinking back tears, Margot shook her head. 'No, Goldie, I don't think you can. Besides, you wouldn't be able to dance; you're in too much pain.'

Goldie let go of Margot's hands and pressed gently

on her ribcage. 'Ah!' Tears filled her eyes. 'You're right; I won't be able to dance tonight. There's only one thing for it,' she said, looking at Margot in the mirror. 'You'll have to go on for me.'

'Me?'

'Yes.'

Margot half expected Goldie to start laughing and say she was only kidding. 'You want me to go on stage and pretend to be you in the show tonight?'

'Yes. I know you've learned my songs and dances.' Margot stared at Goldie, embarrassment threatening to engulf her. 'We all know. And we know you could do it too.'

'But how--?'

'You can't keep anything secret in a theatre. Everyone knows you want to be a dancer.'

'Everyone? Even Nancy?'

'Even Kat!' Goldie pulled a face and laughed. 'Ouch! That'll teach me for being horrible.'

Margot didn't comment about Kat knowing. Kat would have taken the Mickey out of her for wanting to be a dancer a month ago, but after the help she and Bill had given her, Kat wasn't spiteful to her any more.

'It's pretty obvious. I mean, why else would you stand in the wings in your spare time and watch us rehearse? So what do you think?'

The thought of going on stage and performing to a thousand or more people overwhelmed Margot. She blew out her cheeks. 'Well… I do know your dances, and your songs,' she admitted, 'and we are the same dress and shoe size. I know we are, because I modelled your costumes when you weren't able to come in for a fitting once before when Dave--'

'Good job you did, now you're going to be me.'

Goldie smiled for the first time since Margot found her in the alley. 'Could be your big break,' she teased. 'Seriously, Margot, if you go on for me tonight I'll be able to give Dave the slip, try to get away from him for good.'

It wasn't the way Margot had planned to make her stage debut, but if it was the only way Goldie was going to escape her fascist boyfriend... 'All right,' she said, the butterflies in her stomach already preparing for take-off, 'I'll do it, if you're sure?'

'I am. This way no one will know it isn't me on stage, and if Dave is waiting for me at the end of the show, he'll be waiting a bloody long time.'

The girls arrived early to run through a new number, but instead gathered in the dressing room. They all agreed that Goldie couldn't go on, and Margot should, so they needed to rehearse some of the numbers that Goldie featured in. They decided not tell the director, Richard Smiley. He'd have brought in one of his many lady-friends, probably a show girl who looked pretty but couldn't dance to save her 'feather boa-ed' life.

Goldie's costume fitted Margot, as she knew it would. Her shoes pinched a bit, but she said she'd manage. Hats and gloves were ignored. The gloves would fit, they were average in size, and the hats could be secured with Kirby grips, if need be. Time was running out, so they went on stage to rehearse.

'What's going on?' a voice called from the wings.

'Mr Goldman.' George ran across to Anton Goldman and said they were trying out an understudy. 'What with bombs going off everywhere, it would be a safety net in case anyone was delayed getting here.'

Anton Goldman agreed and joked, 'As long as it's in your own time.'

'It is,' George assured him.

'I'll leave you to it then.'

Ten minutes later Natalie Goldman arrived. George took her aside and told her what they were really doing. Natalie was amazed that Margot was capable of taking over Goldie's roles. 'Is there anything I can do?'

'Yes,' Nancy said. 'Would you play the piano while we rehearse Margot in?'

After a quick run-through of the numbers where they were all on stage, they concentrated on the numbers that Goldie featured in. When they had done as much rehearsing as time allowed, Nancy and George thanked Natalie for her help. 'If there's anything else I can do, you'll let me know, won't you?' Natalie said to George.

'There is!' George put her hand on Natalie's arm. 'Can you get Goldie out of London? Or at least to somewhere safe, away from that fascist B, before he kills her.'

Natalie nodded. 'Leave it with me. I've already spoken to her. Bert told me Margot had brought her in. He stayed with her in dressing room eight while I came down. They'll be here in a minute.'

'Margot?' Hobbling across the stage, Goldie lifted her arms and hugged her friend. 'Nancy, George-- Ah! Sorry,' she said, distressed and breathing heavily. 'I'm sorry,' she said again, and burst into tears.

'Goldie, you must not cry.' Natalie spoke kindly, but firmly. 'Soon you will walk out of the theatre looking happy, not sad. Margot is going to be you tonight and you are going to be me.'

'Let me help you,' Margot said, holding the collar on Goldie's jacket, pulling it gently until Goldie's arms were free, before helping her into Natalie's outdoor coat. 'Now your shoes,' she said, passing Goldie's jacket to George. Sitting Goldie on the piano stool, Margot took off her shoes and helped her to put on Natalie's. Goldie closed her eyes. She looked exhausted. 'You're doing really well,' Margot said, encouragingly. 'I just need to get rid of your curls.' Margot brushed Goldie's honey blonde hair from her face. 'Kirby grips, anyone?' Betsy took several from her own hair and Margot pinned Goldie's curls into a bun in the nape of her neck. 'Good. With the collar up your hair won't be seen. Let me know when you're ready to stand up.' Goldie nodded and with George's help, Margot pulled her to her feet.

'Now my trilby,' Natalie said. She placed her hat on Goldie's head, tucking her blonde fringe under it. Taking a step backwards, Natalie nodded. 'Will she do, ladies?'

'She will soon,' George said, pulling on the felt hat until it tipped fashionably over one eye. 'That's better,' she said, turning the collar up on her coat, before handing her Natalie's handbag.

Although Natalie Goldman was taller than Goldie, everyone agreed that from a distance no one would know the woman going home with Anton Goldman wasn't his wife.

Backstage, with tears in her eyes, Goldie said, 'You're the best-- I'll miss you all.'

Margot kissed her goodbye, followed by each of her friends. 'You mustn't cry, sweetheart,' Nancy said, wiping the tears from Goldie's cheeks. Everyone except Margot and Nancy returned to their dressing rooms after saying goodbye. More for Goldie's sake than their own, Margot thought. They knew that if they stayed, there was a chance Goldie would break down, lose her nerve. 'We'll all miss you too, but you must pull yourself together. Stop crying,' Nancy said. 'Come on, it's time to go.'

Goldie nodded and let Nancy lead her to the stage door.

'Good luck tonight, Margot, and thank you,' Goldie said before leaving.

Nodding, unable to speak, Margot blew a kiss and forced herself to smile.

'Look after yourself, and let us know where you are once you're settled,' Bert said, putting out the light before opening the stage door. Margot and Nancy watched from the small window at the side of the door as Anton and Goldie followed Bert across Maiden Lane to the Goldmans' car. Anton unlocked the passenger door and Bert held it open for Goldie, as he always did for Natalie. Margot held her breath, praying Goldie wouldn't look back. She didn't. She sat down sideways on the passenger seat and lifted her feet into the car, as Natalie did. Then she smiled up at Bert and he closed the door. Nancy put her arm round Margot's shoulders and exhaled with relief. Once she was safely in the car, Anton went round to the driver's door, unlocked it and slipped in behind the steering wheel.

After two sharp raps on the car's roof, Margot heard Bert shout, 'Goodnight, Mrs Goldman – Mr Goldman.' And as the stage doorman walked back to the theatre, Anton Goldman drove down Maiden Lane.

The mood in the dressing rooms was subdued. 'I've taken Mrs Horton into our confidence,' Nancy told the girls. 'She'd have known something was up as soon as she saw Margot in Goldie's first costume, but

I've asked her not to tell the dressers. I told her to tell them that George was so late for rehearsal that,' Nancy shook her head, pretending to be exasperated, 'by the time we'd finished it wasn't worth getting changed, so we've stayed in our opening costumes.'

'What about my costume changes?' Margot asked.

'Mrs Horton will look after you this week, instead of me. She'll be with you every time you come off stage and make sure you go on stage on cue. It's important that she helps you until you're used to your costume changes and your entrances and exits. We might have to tell one of the other dressers something. We'll say Mrs Horton and I have had words and I'd rather she didn't dress me.' Nancy smiled reassuringly. 'Don't worry, I'll think of something. You just concentrate on your first night. I know you have a lot to remember and I'm sure you'll feel terrified at times, but we'll all be there for you, won't we, girls?'

Everyone agreed. And while they dressed for the opening number, they reminded Margot of Goldie's cues. At the five minute call everyone hugged and kissed her, and as they waited in the wings, they gave her the thumbs-up, wishing her good luck and assuring her again that they would be there to help her in any way they could.

Margot waited nervously for her call – Goldie's call. She took several deep breaths, which made her feel dizzy. She cleared her throat a dozen times, rotated her shoulders and sipped water from a small glass that Mrs Horton had put at the side of the flats. Suddenly she was aware that the orchestra were playing the opening chords of the first sketch. It was time. She looked across the stage to the wings opposite and in the dim light she saw Betsy waving.

Margot waved back before running onto the stage. The lights came up on a 1920s speak-easy and Margot and Betsy, dressed as flappers, shimmering from head to foot in golden tassels, danced the Charleston with a couple of gangsters. When Betsy circled her hands to the right, Margot mirror-imaged her, circling her hands to the left. At the end of the dance, before Goldie made her exit, she always struck a pose, held it for two beats, and then blew a kiss at the middle of the first row of the balcony before taking an exaggerated bow. Margot copied the routine exactly; she struck the pose, looked up at the balcony and blew a kiss. But instead of taking a bow she stumbled. The recipient of the kiss was Nazi Dave.

At the interval the girls took it in turns to look through a small hole in the curtains.

'I can't see anyone in the middle of the balcony,' George said, crouching down so her eyes were level with the small hole.

'Here, let me look. I know where Margot blew her kiss,' Betsy said, taking George's place. 'There's no one there now, Margot. He's probably satisfied himself that he didn't hurt Goldie too badly and gone home.'

'Or he's waiting outside for her,' Margot said.

'Well, we won't know until the show's over, so it's pointless worrying. Come on, it's time to get changed for the second act.'

'Hats, masks, feathers, fans, parasols, we've got all manner of paraphernalia so your face won't be seen too clearly. If it was Nazi Dave out there earlier,' Mrs Horton warned, 'we mustn't let him see you're not Goldie.'

'But Goldie doesn't wear all this stuff. Won't he suspect something?'

'No. He's been around the theatre long enough to know she couldn't go on stage looking like she did. He'll expect her to wear something to hide the bruises.'

'He might not have realised how badly he hurt her,' Margot added. 'When I first found her it was only the cut on her lip that was really noticeable. She couldn't stand, of course, but he wouldn't have known that. The bruising and the swelling on her face came out later, in the dressing room, so he might not suspect anything.'

Margot copied Goldie's songs and dances perfectly. She remembered every smile, tilt of the head and wink, unique to her friend's performance. No one would know it was me in the show tonight, she thought, as she took Goldie's curtain call, sandwiched between George and Betsy.

In the dressing room afterwards, while the girls hugged and kissed her, Nancy opened a bottle of champagne. 'I've been saving this for a special occasion,' she said, keeping her voice to a whisper. 'And I can't think of anything, or anyone, more special than you, Margot. What you did today, helping Goldie, was wonderful and we're all very grateful. But what you did tonight, on the stage, was amazing. You gave a star performance and we're all very proud of you.'

Everyone raised their glasses and mimed their congratulations. Mrs Horton popped in and joined the silent applause, but refused a glass of champagne. 'Well done,' she whispered to Margot. 'I'll be back for the costumes in ten minutes,' she said in her normal voice. And then, quieter, 'Don't want any changes to the routine.'

'Mrs Horton's right. We still have to be very careful,' George warned. 'We must act as if tonight is an ordinary night.'

'I agree,' Nancy said. 'Margot, you'll still have to go to the club and do your spot, or it'll look suspicious. Finish your champers darling, and when you've changed, meet me at the stage door as normal. I'll give you a lift to the club.'

For the next few nights, Goldie Trick performed on stage at the Prince Albert Theatre as usual, George and Betsy did, or didn't, go to the Prince Albert Club, and the only person that knew what was going on, outside the theatre, was Bill. Margot had hurt him by not telling him she was singing at the club, and wasn't going to upset him again. Besides, she was so excited, she thought she'd explode if she didn't tell someone.

'Tell me you're joking, Margot,' Bill said, shaking his head. 'You said Goldie's bloke was a gangster. Think of the repercussions.'

'There won't be any repercussions.'

'He's dangerous!' Bill shouted. 'If he could do that to someone he's supposed to care about, because he thought she might leave him, what the hell do you think he'll do to you when he finds out he's been watching you on stage every night, not Goldie, because you've helped her to leave him?'

'He won't hurt me like he did Goldie, Bill. He's not a gangster, he's a fascist; the police will be watching him. They watch all the--'

'He's what? The police-- What are you going to get mixed up in next, Margot?'

Unable to stem the flow of tears, Margot ran to her worried husband and threw her arms around his neck. Looking up into his eyes, she said, 'Don't shout at me, Bill, please. Finding Goldie beaten up, and knowing I could help her-- I'm sorry, but I had to. And,' she hesitated, wondering whether Bill would understand what she was about to tell him, 'when I was on stage it was wonderful, of course it was, but it felt right too.' She lowered her arms, put them round his waist and laid her head on his chest. 'I wish you'd been there,' she cried, 'I wish you'd seen me dancing and singing like a professional.'

'Shush... don't cry. I know how much you wanted this. Not Goldie getting hurt, of course, and I'm pleased for you, really I am, but--' Bending down until his eyes were level with hers, he said, 'You don't seem to understand danger, Margot, you don't see it. There's a war on and when everybody's running to safety, to a shelter or the underground, you're running around the streets to a theatre, or a night club.'

'I'm sorry, Bill.'

'If anything happened to you, Margot,' he said, wiping away his tears with the back of his hand, 'I don't know what I'd do.'

For the first time Margot realised how reckless she had been during the last few months. She had so desperately wanted to be a singer and dancer that she'd allowed her needs and her wants to override everything else, even her safety. She looked into Bill's tired, sad eyes. 'Do you want me to stop working in the theatre and the club? If you do...'

Bill shook his head. 'Then you'd hate me.'

'No I wouldn't!'

Smiling, he pushed a curl of hair from Margot's face and kissed her on the nose. 'Yes, you would, which is why I would never ask you to.'

Margot opened her mouth, but before she could protest, Bill put his finger to her lips. 'If you promise not to walk to the club on your own – either go with one of the girls or get a cab – and if you wait for me to pick you up at the end of the show, I'll feel happier.'

Margot nodded and whispered, 'I promise.'

'Now, tell me all about it. What was it like to sing and dance in front of all those people?'

Bert beckoned Margot over to the small window at the side of the stage door, put out the light and pulled back the blackout curtain. 'I don't want you to go out there yet. Someone's watching the stage door,' he said, stepping to the side to let Margot take his place. 'Been standing in the shadows at the entrance of that alley for the past half hour.'

Margot's eyes soon adjusted to the charcoal darkness that London had become at night without street lights, and she saw a movement. There it was again: the shadow of a man in a trilby hat. She strained her eyes. He was tall, with square shoulders. He struck a match, but must have shielded the flame, cupped it in the palms of his hands to stop the wind from blowing it out, because it disappeared for a second before reappearing and then falling to the ground. In the darkness she saw the end of a cigarette brighten and dim several times. She watched, transfixed, the nerve ends on top of her stomach tightening like the skin of a drum. Suddenly the cigarette flew across the alley and almost immediately the man walked out of the shadows to where it had landed. He crushed the burning stub, twisting and turning his foot until there couldn't have been anything left. Then he reached into his pocket and took out a pack of cigarettes and a box of matches. He took a cigarette from the box, returned it to his pocket and struck a match. And as the match flared, Margot saw his face. 'It's him. It's Goldie's ex-boyfriend, the Nazi.'

Margot and Bert watched as Dave, dressed in his usual black leather overcoat and a black trilby, left the alley. He stopped walking after a few yards and turned up the collar of his coat. Then, with his hands pushed deep into his pockets, he swaggered along Maiden Lane as if he owned it. Margot kept watching. She wanted to be sure he wasn't going to hide in a doorway, pounce on one of the girls as they passed and force her to tell him where Goldie was. Suddenly he stopped. Margot flinched as she watched him turn and walk back towards the theatre. He slowly looked up at the dressing room windows and down again, his gaze settling on the small window where Margot was standing. Her heart leapt in her chest. She knew Dave couldn't see her, but she felt vulnerable. Then she saw his expression. It had changed from his usual cocky smirk to an angry glare. And she went cold. Slowly, so she didn't cast a shadow or jerk the curtain, she stepped away from the window. 'He gives me the creeps,' she said, and she shuddered.

'Lord knows how long he's going to keep this up,' Bert said.

'What? You mean this isn't the first time?'

'No. I've seen him several times, standing in the shadows, watching the stage door. He's hoping to see Goldie, I expect.'

'I feel as if he's watching me.' Margot shrugged the idea from her mind. 'He can't know it's me on stage in place of Goldie, can he?'

'No. Even so, I don't want you leaving on your own tonight, Miss. Wait in the office with me until your husband gets here. By then the Nazi bugger will have gone home, or wherever it is he goes. The sewer, I shouldn't wonder, with all the other Nazi rats.'

Margot followed the old man into his office and perched on the arm of his chair.

George and Betsy were next to come down. 'Bye, Bert,' George called, heading for the stage door. 'See you tomorrow.'

'Night-night, lovely,' Betsy said, sticking her head through the small window of Bert's office and blowing him a kiss. 'Margot? Why are you still here? Not going to the club tonight?'

George turned at the sound of Margot's name and followed Betsy into Bert's office. 'What's going on?'

Margot confided that she and Bert had seen Goldie's Nazi boyfriend. 'He's gone now, but he was standing in the alley staring at the stage door.'

George's brow furrowed. 'I'm surprised he's still hanging around. I thought he'd got the message after coming in here and threatening Bert.'

'He did what?'

Bert waved his hand dismissively. 'It was something and nothing.'

'Come on, Bert. We said we'd look after each other, and that means you too.'

'He came in earlier in the week, just after the show came down. He asked if Goldie was here. I didn't say she was; I said if she hadn't left already, she'd be down when she'd changed. He went, but he'd know if he was watching the stage door that she didn't come down.' George looked perplexed. 'And,' Bert said, 'he came in the next night, asked for Miss Goldie again, and I told him the same thing. I busied myself with some drawer tidying, so as I didn't have to talk to him. I don't think he was fooled by my domestic chores, because when I turned to see what he was doing, he made a fist of his right hand and punched the palm of his left hand.'

'How dare he threaten you? The damn bully!'

'He dare all right. The last time was after you'd all gone. He didn't say a word, he just stood over there.' Bert pointed to the window at the side of the stage door. 'I asked him to leave. I told him that I had to hand the keys over to Arthur, the night watchman, and I couldn't do that until I'd checked the dressing rooms, made sure everyone had left. He laughed. "Tell you what," he said, "I'll check them for you." "No you won't!" I said. "Get out, or I'll call the police."'

'What did he do?'

'He came right up to me and laughed in my face. He made that fist again and said, "Tell her I'll be waiting – and when she least expects it!" Then he left, slamming the door behind him. I was shaking when he'd gone, I don't mind telling you.'

'Was that the last you saw of him until tonight?' Margot asked.

'No, I saw him sitting in his car on Butte Street. I expect he was there because Miss Goldie used to walk that way home – if he didn't fetch her.'

'Thank God he doesn't know it's me up there on stage,' Margot said. The sound of a motorbike engine attracted her attention. 'That's Bill. I'd better go.' Saying goodnight to George and Betsy, Margot followed them out. 'Lock the door after us, Bert, and put the bolt on.'

'Will do.'

As Bill pulled up outside the stage door, Margot waved goodnight. Returning the wave Bert went into the theatre and, Margot hoped, locked and bolted the door.

CHAPTER EIGHT

Margot thanked the bandleader and band and looked into the audience. She bowed again, and then put her hands to her mouth and blew a kiss. The audience were always generous with their applause, but tonight it seemed they were never going to stop. She took a final bow and was about to step down from the stage when she saw a man in a black leather coat standing at the bar. He wasn't clapping. The room was smoky and the spotlight was on her, but she knew that hard face and those cold menacing eyes. She forced herself to smile but he didn't return the gesture; he just stared at her, his black eyes boring into hers, penetrating and threatening. She looked across the room to the table where Nancy and Salvatore were sitting and gave one short nod – the signal that Dave Sutherland, Goldie's fascist boyfriend, was in the club. She glanced back at the bar. He was leaving. Salvatore jumped up, summoned two of his men, and followed him out.

The audience were still clapping as Margot stepped shakily from the stage. She walked through the tables, stopping occasionally to say hello or thank someone for a kind comment. At Nancy and Salvatore's table she smiled broadly and took a final bow before sitting down.

'Gone. Disappeared into the night,' Salvatore said when he returned. 'Was it him?'

Margot shuddered. 'Yes! Who else would just stand there and glare at me like that?'

Salvatore beckoned a waiter and motioned to their empty glasses.

'Have a drink, darling,' Nancy said. 'If Bill isn't here in half an hour, Salvatore and I will take you home.'

Margot drank her champagne, followed by a second glass. Safe among friends, she began to feel better. Bill arrived twenty minutes later, by which time she had decided not to tell him that she'd seen Nazi Dave in the club. She didn't want him to worry. Nor did she want him to stop her working there.

'There's a bouquet for Miss Dudley,' Bert said to Nancy when she arrived for the evening show. 'It was on that table when I came down from having tea with Mrs Horton. I don't know how it got there. I could have sworn I locked the stage door.' Bert picked the flowers up. 'They're wilting a bit.'

'They're wilting more than a bit, Bert. They look half dead. Not to worry, I'll take them to the dressing room and put them in water. They'll revive in no time. Poor Margot, her first week is almost over and she hasn't been able to celebrate. Do you think we could throw a small party in the dressing room after Saturday night's show? We can celebrate Goldie arriving at her sister's in Ireland too,' she whispered.

George arrived before Bert had time to answer. 'Who died?'

'What do you mean, who died?'

'The arum lilies. They're funeral flowers. What they use to decorate the church, and put on coffins.' George wrinkled her nose. 'Who are they for?'

'They're for Margot.' Nancy frowned. 'Why would someone send Margot funeral flowers?'

'Why would they send her flowers at all?' George asked.

Nancy rounded on George. 'Because she's doing a very good job--'

'That isn't what I meant.'

'What then?'

'Why would anyone outside the four of us, Mrs Horton and Margot's husband send Margot a bouquet? No one knows she's in the show. As far as the audience is concerned it's still Goldie they're watching on stage.'

'That's right.' Nancy turned to Bert. 'Which florist's boy brought the bouquet?'

'No idea. I didn't see him. But it couldn't have been one of the usual lads. They'd have waited for me to sign the delivery docket. Mind you, they don't always wait these days. The younger lads don't anyway. And there are more younger ones than ever now so many of the regular lads have been called up. There's been quite a turnover recently – a different face every few days, so--'

'It isn't your fault, Bert,' George said, cutting the old man off – which for once he didn't seem to mind. 'What does the card say?'

'I don't know. It's in a sealed envelope.'

'Open it and have a look. It might be from Nazi Dave.'

'What might be from Nazi Dave?' Margot said from behind George.

'Margot! I didn't hear you come in.'

'What's up? Why are you all looking at me as if I've grown another head?' Margot lifted her hand and pretended to check. 'No, still only one,' she laughed.

George and Bert looked at each, but said nothing. Nancy showed Margot the bouquet. 'This came for you earlier.'

'Funeral lilies?' Margot shivered. She put her gas mask and handbag on the floor, took the lilies and laid them on the table next to Bert's door, and then opened the envelope and took out the card. 'R.I.P.'

At that moment, Betsy came bounding in as she always did, full of energy, and opened her mouth to greet everyone. She smiled at Margot, who was facing in her direction, but after registering the look of terror on her face, said nothing. Instead she tapped George on the arm and when she turned, raised her eyebrows as if to ask what was going on. George stepped to one side to allow Betsy to join the group and Margot handed her the small card. Betsy gasped.

Kat arrived a minute later. Margot showed her the flowers and Betsy gave her the card. Kat's eyes flashed with anger. 'Right!' she said. 'We must find a way to protect Margot from this snake! Let us go to the dressing room, where we will not be disturbed, and discuss it!'

Nancy took the card from Kat and put it back in the small envelope. 'Bert, would it be possible to seal this envelope up again? Make it look as if it hasn't been opened?'

Bert nodded. 'I've got special thin glue that I use for pasting up the newspaper reviews. Leave it to me.'

'Good. And when you've done that, would you put the bouquet on the table exactly as it was when you found it? That way, if the Nazi comes in later he won't know Margot's seen it. He might even be stupid enough to think it isn't her on stage.' Bert disappeared into his office with the small envelope. 'I'll let you know the plan when we've got one,' Nancy said. Bert, already thinning the paper glue, nodded and Nancy left.

A couple of minutes later, Nancy put her head round the door of dressing room two. 'Shan't be long getting dressed. Start without me. I'm sure I'll agree with whatever you decide.' She looked at Margot. 'You're not alone in this. We're all in it together.'

Assured by Nancy, Margot nodded, and the girls shouted, 'Too right!' and 'Absolutely.' George entered as Nancy left. 'All for one and one for all!'

'Who do you think we are,' Betsy said, poking George playfully in the stomach as she squeezed past her, 'the three musketeers?'

'There were four musketeers. Everyone forgets d'Artagnan.' George plucked a silver-handled walking cane from the props box just inside the door, pointed it at Betsy, and began to advance.

'Stop it, George!' Betsy squealed, giggling.

'There is only half an hour until the half,' Kat said, glaring at George. 'I shall change into my opening costume while we discuss what we are going to do. I suggest you do the same.'

'Yes, sorry, I, we…' Trying not laugh as Betsy stood, open-mouthed at Kat's reprimand, George clapped her hands. 'I shall also change into my opening costume. I suggest you do the same!' she told Betsy, in the worst Russian accent.

Kat ignored George. 'There must be someone with Margot at all times,' she said. 'She must not be left on her own. Not even in the theatre. Agreed?'

'Agreed!'

'With Bert on the stage door I'll be safe in the dressing room.' Margot looked at Kat, then at George and Betsy. 'Won't I?'

George shook her head. 'I don't believe for a minute that Bert went upstairs this afternoon and forgot to lock the stage door.'

'You think Dave came into the theatre and put those flowers on the table without Bert seeing him?' Margot felt pricking at the back of her eyes. It was possible, because she'd done it herself when she was sneaking in and out to sing at the club. She blinked quickly to stop the tears.

'Can't rule anything out, which is why one of us will be with you at all times, even in here. Chin up,' George said, putting her arm around Margot's shoulder and giving her a squeeze. 'We'll look after you.'

'We should give Pamela Lesley a description of him. Ask her to circulate it to the box office staff and the usherettes.'

'Do you think we should tell her why?' Margot asked.

'It isn't necessary,' George said. 'Besides, the fewer people who know the better. That he's a fascist will be reason enough for Pamela Lesley to keep a look-out.'

'I've got the gist of the plan, and I agree,' Nancy said, entering. 'We'll take it in turns to be with Margot before, during, and after the show. Tonight's my turn. We'll stay in here until Bill arrives.' As she left the dressing room she said, 'Enjoy the show, Margot, and don't worry. We'll look after you, won't we, girls?' Everyone shouted in agreement.

Nazi Dave hadn't been seen in the theatre or the club for weeks – nor had he been backstage. Bert kept the stage door locked during the show and anyone wanting access had to knock. Even then, before he answered the door, he looked through the small window. And every time he let someone in he took the opportunity to check the street – giving special attention to the alley opposite. To all intents and purposes Nazi Dave had disappeared.

Margot was no longer chaperoned in the theatre and as time passed the rule that she was never to go out alone was relaxed. The girls still went for tea together between the matinee and the evening show,

Bill picked her up at night, and Salvatore still sent a car for her and Nancy on the nights she performed at the club, but Margot travelled to the theatre by bus, on her own. She loved the freedom, although since the day of the arum lily bouquet, she looked over her shoulder more often. And she didn't always feel as relaxed or confident walking among the crowds in Covent Garden. But at last she was able to enjoy performing on stage. She could look into the audience without fear of seeing Dave's threatening, sneering face. The icing on the cake came when Anton Goldman announced the new programme would be on sale from Saturday.

'Now Goldie is safe, it's time you performed under your own name, Margot.' He opened his briefcase and took out a proof copy. 'The printers sent me this to check; make sure there aren't any mistakes. There aren't. So,' he said, handing the copy to Margot, 'this is for you.'

Margot squealed with joy. Everyone cheered and clapped as Margot threw her arms around Anton's neck. 'Thank you so much.' Releasing him, she opened the programme and turned to the cast list. 'My name's in a real theatre programme... Who would have thought it?'

'Pamela Lesley,' Anton said. 'It was Pamela who arranged for the programmes to be printed.' Everyone laughed and clapped again. 'And,' he shouted above the chatter and laughter, 'she sent her congratulations. Have a good show tonight, everyone.' No one responded; they were all too busy congratulating Margot.

On Saturday morning Margot went into the theatre early and bought six copies. One for her mam and dad, one for each of her sisters, and most importantly one for Bill. She was keeping the first copy off the press for herself. It was a special copy and Margot liked nothing better than feeling special. 'The first of many,' she said aloud, placing the programmes in her shopping bag. Later she wrote a personal message in each programme, signed and dated them.

As soon as they arrived home that night Margot told Bill to sit down and close his eyes. 'I've got a surprise for you!'

Bill quickly took off his coat and hung it up before dropping onto a chair at the dining table. 'I hope it's something to eat, I'm starving.'

'What I've got for you is much more important than food.' Bill opened his mouth to protest and Margot kissed him passionately on the lips. Bill grinned. 'No, it isn't that!' she said, slapping him playfully on the shoulder. 'Come on, do as you're told or I might change my mind, then you won't get anything.' Bill chuckled, put his hands up in submission and closed his eyes. 'And keep them shut,' she whispered in his ear. Watching him to make sure he didn't peek, Margot took his theatre programme from her shopping bag and placed it on the table. 'Don't look yet!' she warned. Then she moved round the table so she was standing opposite him. 'You can open them now!'

Bill looked up at Margot, who was staring at the table directly in front of him. He followed her gaze. 'A theatre programme?'

'Not just any theatre programme. Open it,' she said excitedly, 'and read the list of artists.'

Bill scanned the names until he came to Margot's. He looked at her, his eyes moist with emotion. 'I'm very proud of you.'

'Read the message,' she ordered. 'It's especially for you.'

Bill cleared his throat. '"To my wonderful husband Bill. Thank you for understanding me and putting up with me. This is my dream come true, which would never have happened without your love and encouragement. I love you, Margot. xxx" Thanks, love,' Bill said. 'I love you too, with all my heart. Now it's official,' he said, looking again at Margot's name. 'I'll be able to go to the theatre and watch my beautiful wife on the stage.'

'And I'll blow you a kiss.' Margot danced across the room to the larder. 'Spam sandwich all right?' She didn't wait for Bill to reply. 'I forgot to go to the shops.'

Margot had forgotten about Nazi Dave too, until she saw him, or thought she saw him, at Oxford Circus. Her stomach lurched as she approached the station. She had no intention of travelling on an underground train, but she was late for a hairdresser's appointment in Bond Street and decided to take a short cut through the station. On her way across the ticket hall she bumped into a man, or rather he bumped into her. She turned instinctively to apologise, but he'd gone. She didn't take any notice at the time but as she was going up the steps at the Oxford Street North exit the same man bumped into her again. 'Hey!' she said, turning to confront him. But again he had disappeared, melted into the crowd.

Bending down outside the station, Margot adjusted the strap on her shoe. She looked under the brim of her hat and saw the man pushing his way past people entering the station. There was something familiar about him, but Margot couldn't put her finger on it.

She backed into a doorway and watched him as he looked up and down Oxford Street. After a few seconds he turned to join the sea of people going into the station and she saw his face. It was Nazi Dave. Her heart began to pound and she could hardly breathe, but she forced herself to follow him.

She kept him in sight as they went down the steps and into the ticket hall, but lost him in a crowd of people heading for the moving stairs and the trains. 'Damn! Gone again!' Margot looked at the clock above the ticket office. She had missed her hair appointment, so she made her way through the crowd to the Regent Street exit. There he was, at the top of the steps that she was about to mount. She pushed her way out of the station and looked around. She couldn't see him. She climbed onto the bottom rung of the railings and scanned a crowd of people crossing Regent Street – and there he was. Keeping him in sight, she ran across the road. A lorry screeched to a halt. She put her hand up to say sorry and stepped back onto the pavement. When she looked again, he had gone.

She had almost given up when she saw him looking in a shop window. 'Got ya!' She wasn't going to lose him again so, as soon as the traffic eased, she zigzagged her way south determined to catch up with him.

'Blast!' For a second Margot couldn't see him – but there he was, just a few yards ahead. She watched as he took off his trilby and ran the fingers of his right hand through his hair. She froze, shocked. She was sure this was the man who'd been following her – the man she thought was Nazi Dave – but this man's hair was light brown; Dave's was almost black. He stopped suddenly and looked over his shoulder. Fearing he would see her, Margot ducked into a bus shelter. She lifted her hand so her arm partially covered her face, and pretended to check the timetable. She watched him take a packet of cigarettes and a box of matches from his pocket. He put a cigarette between his lips and struck a match. After lighting it, he inhaled deeply, blew out the flame and flicked the match into the street. Margot was confused. She felt sure the man who had bumped into her in the station was Nazi Dave. If it was, who was she following along Regent Street?

She needed to speak to the man, but he was on the move again. He began to walk quickly. Margot walked faster. 'Excuse me!' she shouted. 'I want to talk to you.' The man ignored her and carried on walking, but Margot stayed with him. She grabbed hold of his sleeve. 'Who are you and why have you been following me?'

The man didn't turn round. He pulled away from her and began to walk away at speed.

Margot ran after him and caught hold of his arm, and he spun round. Her heart was pounding. She looked up at the man's face and her heart sank. 'You're not... I'm sorry,' she said. 'I thought you were someone else.'

The man said nothing. At first he looked angry. Then he bent down until his face was so close to hers she could smell cigarettes on his breath and said, 'Go away! Now!'

Shaking, Margot stumbled into a nearby café, ordered a cup of tea and sat down. She hadn't seen Dave, or anyone resembling him for weeks, until today. The last time was at the Prince Albert Club. She shuddered at the memory.

When her tea came she wrapped her hands around

the cup and drank absentmindedly. Refreshed, she paid at the counter and left. Buttoning up her coat in the café's doorway, Margot examined the face of every male that passed. She sighed with relief. She couldn't see either man. At the end of Regent Street, in Leicester Square and again in Covent Garden, Margot stopped and looked back. She'd taken a roundabout route to get to the theatre, but it was worth it, because she knew she hadn't been followed.

After the first air raid the safety curtain came down and when the girls had changed into their own clothes, they came back on stage, stood in front of the curtain, and began to sing "Roll Out The Barrel". In no time the audience were singing and cheering. "There'll Always Be An England" followed, and then "We'll Meet Again." When the second raid began, wave after wave of German planes roared overhead, drowning out the sing-along. As soon as the all clear sounded the audience were shown to the exits and the company went home.

Grateful for the lift, Margot sat in the passenger seat of Anton Goldman's car while he navigated his way around a huge bomb crater at the top of the Strand, which, with capped lights, took ages.

'Your sister Bess telephoned earlier. She sent her love.' Margot turned to hear more clearly what Anton was saying. 'She rang to let us know the children are safe after the bombing of Coventry. We were a little concerned, with Foxden being so near to two RAF aerodromes, but she assured me the cellar walls are five feet thick and will protect the Foxden residents if the bombers return. Have you heard from Bill?'

'Yes, he telephoned the stage door. His mum and dad are all right, thank goodness. They live quite a long way away from the centre of Coventry and apart from having their windows blown out, there's not a lot of damage done. It's the city centre that's been blitzed to smithereens. The cathedral has been gutted. It's a shell, Bill said.'

Anton clicked his tongue. 'I suppose they were after the aircraft factory.'

A cold shiver took Margot by surprise and tears welled up in her eyes. 'Oh my God. I used to work there, before I came to London. I've got friends who still do. I hope…'

Anton glanced at her briefly. 'I'm sorry, Margot, I didn't think. But I'm sure your friends would have finished work for the day and been at home, or in shelters, when the bombs fell.' The night shift wouldn't have been, Margot thought. They drove in silence for some time, and then Anton said, 'What are you and Bill doing for Christmas this year?'

'I'm not sure. We're staying in London,' she said, wiping tears from her eyes. 'We thought about going up to the Midlands, but it isn't possible. Travel's bad now, but Bill says it's going to get worse. The MoD has asked anyone who doesn't have to travel not to. They want to keep the roads clear for the emergency services and the trains for moving troops.'

'We'll miss the children, with them being at Foxden. We don't celebrate Christmas,' Anton said, 'but we take the holiday. It's an excuse for a rest!' he laughed. 'Why don't you and Bill come to us for your lunch on Christmas Day?'

'Thank you, Anton, I'll ask him.'

'And I'll ask Natalie.'

They both laughed.

*

'Listen to that, sweetheart,' Bill said, opening the window. Margot pulled on her cardigan and joined her husband. Hampstead was a long way from the City of London, further still from the East End, but they could usually hear the distant rumble and crump of falling bombs. 'Silence. I'd forgotten what it sounded like. And tonight,' Bill said, 'no bombs and no ambulance work.' Margot whooped. 'The married chaps have been given Christmas Eve and Christmas Day off. So,' he said, closing the window, 'did wardrobe give you any chocolates this year?'

'Yes. And they're mine,' Margot shouted, jumping on Bill's back in an attempt to stop him from reaching her present. Bill fell sideways, rolled over, and pulled Margot on top of him. Laughing almost hysterically, Margot pulled at his shirt. Bill grabbed her and kissed her. Then, lying on his back, he gently pushed her until she was sitting up, straddling him. He took off her cardigan and blouse. Margot undid his belt and the buttons on his trousers. He pulled her down again and, holding her with one hand, slipped the other inside her slacks. As he caressed her, Margot arched her back and moaned with desire. Unable to wait any longer, Bill picked her up and carried her to the bedroom – all thoughts of the chocolate forgotten.

CHAPTER NINE

Betsy screamed. 'Damn, I've dropped my lipstick. Who switched the bloody light off?'

'No one,' George said. 'There must be a power cut.'

'Stay where you are, girls, I'll get a candle.' Margot felt her way to the old chaise longue. To the left of it was a small cupboard. She opened the door and, feeling around, found the medicinal brandy. She then found a box of matches and half a dozen candles. 'Got them,' she said, lighting one. By its pale light she returned to the dressing table and lit candles for George and Betsy. There was a knock on the door.

'Company on stage please, ladies,' Bert said, entering the room with a torch in one hand and several candles in the other. 'Mr Goldman is making an announcement.'

'What's happened, Bert?'

'Power cut. The electrician's checking now. He says it isn't the fuse box and there's nothing wrong with the wiring. External, he reckons, caused by heavy bombing across the river.'

'Bloody Luftwaffe,' Betsy said. Crawling around on the floor she found her lipstick. 'It's been every bloomin' night for the last six months.'

'Follow me, ladies, and bring your candles. I don't want you falling down the stairs. But please blow them out before you go on stage. There's so much wood and paint – and it's as dry as tinder. We don't want the place going up in flames, do we?'

Anton Goldman and Pamela Lesley were on stage by the time the artists arrived. Without lights it felt cold. Margot nudged Betsy, and shivered. Betsy exhaled loudly, forcing the air to reverberate between her lips indicating that she was cold too.

'Ah! What's that?' Betsy hissed. 'Something as cold as ice just touched me on the shoulder. Was it you, Margot?'

'No. Stay where you are,' Margot said, straining to see in the dark and stretching out her hand in the direction of Betsy's voice. 'I've lost you.'

'Ah! There it is again. George?' Betsy hissed. 'If you're playing silly beggars...'

'Ooooooaaaaaaaaaaaaah! Betsy Evans, I'm coming to get you.' George flicked on a torch and held it under her chin. Her face, illuminated grotesquely, made Betsy squeal.

'Found you,' Margot said, following the light of George's torch. 'Let's hold onto each other.'

'Good idea.' Betsy grabbed George's hand with the torch.

'Spoil sport,' George laughed.

'What's that grinding noise in the wings?' Margot said. 'It sounds as if someone's dragging an iron bedstead across wooden floorboards.'

'Portable overheads,' George said. 'About time too.'

From both sides of the stage stagehands appeared holding large round battery operated lights. They walked so slowly and carefully they might have been carrying coffins. Margot felt the hairs on her arms stand up. At the front of the stage the lads lifted the lights onto their shoulders – leaving the artists in the dark again – and pointed them above the heads of the audience. The usherettes did the same with their torches.

'Oh my God! I didn't realise the curtain was up. How embarrassing,' George said. 'I hope they didn't hear us.'

'Hear you, you mean. It was you being daft, not me and Margot,' Betsy said.

'Ladies and gentlemen,' Anton Goldman shouted, but the audience didn't hear him. Half a dozen ladies in the middle of the stalls got up and began to push their way past people who had remained seated. From the wings Bert handed Anton a loudhailer. 'Ladies and gentlemen!' he boomed. A hush spread through the auditorium and at last he had their attention. 'There has been a power cut. It is not internal, therefore we are unable to do anything about it.' There was a rumble of muted comments. 'Would you please remain seated and the usherettes will guide you, one row at a time, to the exits. Once you have left the auditorium members of the front of house staff will show you out of the theatre. The fire doors and the main entrance will be open, so please use the nearest exit. Goodnight. Have a safe journey home.'

As the audience began to leave the curtain came down and Anton turned to the artists. 'As almost half the house has been sold for tomorrow night's show, we're hoping the electrical problem will be resolved and we can open as usual. The matinee has very few bookings, so Miss Lesley and I think it would be prudent not to open in the afternoon, but to be here at six o'clock prepared to do the evening show. If everyone is happy with that, I'll say goodnight and see you all tomorrow.'

The artists made their way from the stage into the wings, and then to their respective dressing rooms with the help of Mrs Horton and the wardrobe assistants, who shone torches on the floor and stairs for the artists to follow. Back in the dressing rooms, candles were lit again and the wardrobe department went down to help the usherettes and front of house staff to clear the theatre.

George passed Margot a coat hanger and she hung up her costume. The cliché that theatre people were like family was true, she thought, remembering how they helped one another and how the girls had looked after her when Dave the Nazi was around. She swallowed and forced back a tear. There was a knock on the door and as she was nearest she opened it.

'Come in, Bert.'

'To what do we owe the pleasure?' George said. 'Thought you'd be front of house.'

'Not until I've seen you ladies off the premises safely,' he beamed. 'Make sure you've got all your belongings and your candles are out – we don't want the place going up in smoke.'

'How are we going to see to get downstairs without candles, darling?' George asked.

'Like magic, Miss George,' he said, producing a torch. After switching it on he pushed it between the belt of his trousers and the arch of his back. 'This way, if you please?'

Holding onto each other, the human convoy descended the stairs one tentative step at a time until Bert's small candle-lit office came into view. 'Just a couple of steps and we're down. There! Hang on a minute,' he said, taking the torch from his belt. 'Hold on for just a second longer.' Turning, he pointed the torch at the stairs and backed down the last few steps. 'Right! Follow me,' he said, crossing to the stage door.

The girls trailed out one after the other, discussing whether the club would have electricity. 'We could call round and have a look,' George said.

Betsy turned her nose up, but changed her mind. 'All right, but I'm only staying for one drink. Are you

127

listening to me, George?'

'Darling, I cling on your every word. Ta-ta everyone. See you tomorrow.' Linking her arm through Betsy's, George dragged her playfully along the Lane.

'Hang on for me, you two,' Nancy shouted. 'I'm seeing Salvatore later anyway, so there's no point in going all the way home. Are you coming, Margot?'

'No thanks, I'll hang on for Bill. I don't expect they'll have electricity at the ambulance station with it being so close. He'll probably be here soon.'

'If you're sure?' Nancy said, and blew Margot and Bert a kiss before running off to join Betsy and George.

'Is there anything I can do to help here, Bert?'

'No, Miss. Now the backstage is clear, I'm going to lock up and go through to the front of house, see if I can help Miss Lesley.'

'Goodnight, then. See you tomorrow.'

'I don't like leaving you out here on your own, Miss.'

'I'll be all right. If Bill isn't here in the next ten minutes, I'll come and find you. Or I'll go and find him,' Margot said cheerfully.

'Make sure you do. Goodnight.' Returning to the theatre he closed the stage door.

'Damn!' It had started to drizzle and Margot had left her umbrella in the dressing room. She turned, but before she had time to knock she heard the bolt clunk into place.

She sheltered in the doorway for ten minutes, and then another ten, before walking round to the front of the theatre. The double doors were already locked and sandbags had been stacked in front of them. Arthur Armitage, the night watchman, must have secured them and returned to the theatre by the fire exit. She expected the audience to have been evacuated by now, but she thought Bert and Miss Lesley might still be inside. Balancing on top of the sandbags she began to knock. No one came.

She looked up. The sky above the docks was a palette of oranges and reds. Every night for almost six months the Luftwaffe had bombed the East End. Margot thanked God she worked and lived on the north-side of the Thames – though the bombs were getting closer every night.

Several ambulances sped past as Margot walked down the Strand. She waved down the only black cab she'd seen in twenty minutes. 'The ambulance station at St. Thomas's, please.' The cabbie nodded and pulled out into the traffic. By the time she arrived, Bill and his crew had been called out to Fleet Street.

'Will you give him a message when he gets back? Tell him I've gone home.' The controller cupped his ear. Margot shouted above the scream of sirens and the ringing of the ambulances' bells as they raced through the gates. 'Tell him not to go to the theatre. We haven't got any power, so I'm going home.'

'There aren't any buses going your way from here, Mrs Burrell. I've just been told nothing's going north over Waterloo or Westminster Bridge. Gerry's been targeting buildings along the river. Fleet Street's been hit--' The controller's two-way radio began to buzz and crackle.

'I'll walk until I see one.'

'It's too dangerous to walk. Get yourself down the underground. It's the only place you'll be safe in London tonight.'

'I suffer from claustrophobia,' Margot shouted, which was a slight exaggeration. But the thought of spending the night with hundreds of strangers huddled together like sardines, not knowing when or if they'd get out, sent an icy ripple up her spine. If one of the underground stations close to the river took a direct hit the whole network would flood. She shuddered. 'I hate the thought of being trapped in an underground station.'

The ambulance controller looked at her as if she'd brought something unpleasant in on her shoe, and shrugged. 'It's up to you. But it is the *sensible* thing to do!'

'You're right, but there'll be city buses going to Euston and North London from Kingsway – I'll pick one up there. Will you tell Bill, please?'

The controller nodded. 'Be careful,' he shouted after her, but before she had time to reply she heard a shrill whistle followed immediately by an earth-rocking explosion. It was too close for comfort, so when the controller's two-way radio console began to buzz like a hive of demented bumble bees, she made a bolt for Westminster Bridge. 'Taxi!' she called, running into the road.

The taxi swerved to a halt. 'What the 'ell?' the cabbie shouted out of the window. 'Not waiting for Gerry then?'

'What?'

'Running into the road like that, you could've got yourself killed.'

'Sorry, but there's so little transport about. Can you take me to the Aldwych?'

'Sorry love, I'm not going that way. I can drop you off at Trafalgar Square.'

'That'll be fine.' She jumped into the cab and it sped off. It wasn't fine, but it was better than nothing.

'How much?' she said, getting out of the cab on

the south side of the square.

'Have it on me, love. I've done for the night. I'm on my way home.'

'Thank you,' she shouted above the high pitched wail of the air raid siren as he drove away. She squinted and looked through the drizzle. Trafalgar Square's landmark in the blackout was Admiral Nelson – if there was enough moonlight to see his silhouette – and if you didn't walk into a lion first. Margaret crossed at St. Martin in the Fields and ran up to Charing Cross station. From there she walked up the Strand to the Aldwych.

The taxi rank outside the Waldorf Hotel was overflowing with people, as was the bus stop further along. It seemed pointless to queue at either. She looked around, half expecting an ARP Warden to march her across the road to Aldwych underground station. But not tonight. The entrance hall was packed. Two brawling men tumbled out of the station, stopping only when the air raid siren began to wail again. As enemy aircraft roared overhead, Green Park's searchlights chased them across the sky, followed by the ack-ack of anti-aircraft guns. Men and women who couldn't get into the underground station turned and ran in every direction. Thankful there wasn't room for her, Margot walked on. Bill knew her fear of the underground and wouldn't expect her to be down there anyway.

Before turning into Kingsway, Margot was stopped in her tracks by a thunderous explosion. The docks were being blitzed again. She looked ahead. It wasn't only the docks; Fleet Street had been hit too. Flames, whipped by the wind, rose hundreds of feet in the air above the roofs of a dozen buildings. Pinkish-white smoke ballooned upward in a great cloud. Margot stared into the sky, transfixed by the tiny bright specks of flashing light as anti-aircraft shells burst, lighting up the barrage balloons, turning them from silver to pink. She put her hands to her ears to muffle the sound of the shells.

She jumped back onto the pavement as several fire engines, bells clanging the warning that they weren't going to stop, flew past. When the road was safe to cross she ran to the beginning of Fleet Street. She watched as the first engine pulled up in front of the first burning building, the second in front of the next, and so on. As they pumped water onto the flames the buildings hissed and thick smoke billowed into the sky, falling back to earth as black rain. Margot wondered whether she should offer to help, but Bill always said however well-intentioned the public were they often got in the way of the professionals. She decided against it, lifted her scarf over her mouth and nose and walked back to Kingsway. With the gut-churning crump and rumble of exploding bombs ringing in her ears, she suddenly felt frightened. Bill had been sent to Fleet Street earlier in the evening. She prayed he wasn't still there. She shook the thought from her mind and carried on walking. There wasn't a bus in sight. She would probably have to walk all the way to Euston to catch one now.

The drizzle of half an hour ago had turned into rain and the smoke from Fleet Street's burning buildings was making it difficult to see. She stepped into a shop doorway to tie her scarf around her head and stumbled over something bulky. She began to withdraw her foot from what she thought was a bundle of rags when it kicked out. She caught her breath. A man, mumbling to himself in what smelt to Margot like a pub cellar, was slumped against the door. She daren't move. Suddenly the man belched loudly, jolting himself out of his drunken stupor. His eyes shot open and, seeing Margot, he began to curse. Margot made a bolt for it, knotting her scarf as she ran.

At Russell Square there was a barrier across the road. Margot strained her eyes and could just make out a gaping hole on the other side. Unable to follow the bus route, she followed a faint line on the road that pointed to a sign that read DETOUR.

The rain was sheeting down. The new moon gave little light and without streetlights one house looked much like another. There was always a window or a door that allowed a chink of light to escape, but not tonight – tonight Margot felt as if she was walking through a ghost town. She looked about. Not a soul in sight. She told herself not to panic, that there was bound to be fewer people in the streets now than there had been an hour ago, or however long ago it was since she left the Strand. But she hadn't reckoned on the streets being completely deserted. She turned into a tree-lined avenue of three-storey terraced houses with tall shuttered windows. 'Bloody blackout,' she said under her breath.

Everything about it looked familiar. She stopped for a moment to think. Had she been here before this evening? Without streetlights one city avenue looked much the same as another. Each terraced house was built to the same design. Each had window boxes instead of a garden, and a small paved area between the gate and the steep steps leading up to the front door. What made each house different from its neighbour was the door, windows and curtains, which couldn't be seen in the blackout.

Margot needed to know where she was, so she

opened the nearest gate and ran up the steps. At the door she lifted a brass knocker. It was heavy and shaped like the head of an animal. She put her hand into what felt like a mouth and rapped several times. There was no reply. She put her ear to the door, but there was no sound. She was about to knock again when she heard footsteps. They were coming from the direction that she had come – and they were getting nearer. Margot turned, ran down the steps and was through the gate in seconds. She walked as quickly and as quietly as she was able to the end of the road, and then she flew round the corner to goodness knows where and stopped. Leaning against a wall she held her breath and listened. All she could hear was her own pulse beating.

She waited for several minutes and when she was sure she wasn't being followed, she walked on. She hadn't gone more than a few yards when she heard footsteps again – and they sounded closer. Margot stopped, and the footsteps stopped. After a minute's silence she began to walk again – and she heard the footsteps again. Convinced now that someone was following her, Margot ran for her life, the clip-clip of her heels sounding louder as she pounded the uneven pavement.

At the end of the avenue she saw a derelict builder's yard and her heart sank. She had seen the yard already this evening. She had gone round in a circle. She was lost. In a frenzy to escape whoever was following her, Margot ran through the open gate. Her left shoe came off in the mud, but she daren't stop. Praying there were no unexploded bombs in her path, she hobbled across a stretch of wasteland littered with broken furniture and motorcar tyres, a stove, and other discarded objects. She looked over her shoulder to see if she was being followed, tripped and fell. On her hands and knees she crawled to a rusting oil drum and pulled herself up.

Sitting on the drum, covered in mud, exhausted from running in what had turned into torrential rain, Margot burst into tears. She looked up at the sky. The rain was sheeting down. She cuffed a hot tear from her cold cheek and smeared mud across her face. She didn't care. She was soaked, cold and frightened, and she knew she couldn't stay there; it was too open, too exposed. Shivering, she hauled herself to her feet and set off across the expanse of mud and puddles.

'Ouch! Damn! That hurt!' Margot stubbed the toes of her shoeless foot on something sticking out of the rubble. It happened so suddenly that the momentum carried her forward and she slammed her foot down hard on the ground. She wanted to scream. She stopped for a second. But the footsteps behind her didn't. In agony every time she put her foot to the ground, Margot hobbled on.

'Hello? Who's there?' she heard someone shout. She ran into a derelict building and hid behind the door. It was a man that was following her, she could tell by his voice, and he was near. Should she stay where she was and hope whoever was out there would give up and go away, or should she run into the building? She didn't want to go further in; it was pitch black in there and she could hear water pouring onto what sounded like a corrugated iron roof. If the water pipes had been damaged, the gas ones might have been too. She heard the man call out again, and this time she recognised her name. 'Margot? Are you there?'

Leaning forward, Margot looked between the rusty hinges of the door and the frame. The man was sitting on the oil drum. He sat sideways on to her and half hidden by shadow, but then he turned and looked in her direction. He was holding her shoe. 'Margot?' He sounded like Bill, but... 'Please God,' she whispered, 'please let it be Bill.' Margot held her breath, not daring to reply. She watched the man stand up and walk away. At the entrance of the yard he stopped, turned and bellowed, 'Margot? Margot?'

'Bill! I'm here!' Margot ran from the building. Managing to avoid a dozen dangerous objects she fell into her husband's arms. 'I was so frightened,' she said, trembling.

'All right, all right, you're safe now.' Bill wrapped his arms around his young wife and rocked her. 'Shush... I've got you.'

'Oh Bill,' Margot said, collapsing in tears, 'I thought you were the Nazis.'

'You silly goose,' he said, lovingly. 'What would Nazis want with you? He handed Margot her shoe. 'Come on. The bike's round the corner. Let's get you home.'

Margot kicked off her other shoe, picked both up by their heels, and threw them into a pile of rubbish. Trembling from the cold, she looked up at Bill, her eyes sparkling with fear. 'I was being followed, Bill. We need to get out of here now!'

'That imagination of yours will get you into real trouble one day.' Bill bent down. 'Put your arms around my neck and hold on tight.' He picked Margot up as if she was a doll and she leant her head on his shoulder. His coat was wet and cold. She didn't care, she was wetter and colder. Bill held her tightly. 'Nazis indeed!' he said, kissing her on her forehead. 'It's a good job you've got me to look after you.' Bill carried Margot out of the gate and along the avenue to his motorbike. 'It's a bit wet,' he said, and they both laughed.

Bill put Margot down and after mounting the bike he put out his arm for her to hold, and she climbed onto the pillion seat. 'Next stop Hampstead,' he said, kicking the stand from beneath the bike.

Margot looked back into the darkness, relieved that it was her husband's footsteps that she'd heard and not someone out to do her harm. As she turned to face the way they were going, she saw a movement out of the corner of her eye. In the shadows, coming from where she had been hiding, she saw a match flare. A second later there was a red glow. It brightened as if air was being sucked through a cigarette.

Margot tightened her arms around Bill's waist and in a hoarse voice cried, 'Get us out of here!' As they drove away, Margot laid her head on Bill's back. She felt safe for the first time since she'd left the theatre, five hours earlier.

CHAPTER TEN

Kat's dances had been modified several times over the last few months. She no longer did high kicks. Nor did she perform pirouettes, or stand on her points when she was the black swan in the tableau of *Swan Lake*. And her costumes had been let out as much as they could be. Some even had the same, or contrasting, fabric sewn in at the sides.

'There's nothing more we can do, Miss Kaplinski,' Mrs Horton said. 'The seams won't hold for much longer. They'll split one of these nights and then what shall we do?'

Kat looked at the strained stitching on her costume and nodded. She knew, as wardrobe did, that it was time she hung up her dancing shoes.

'If it wasn't that fabric was so hard to get,' Violet said, 'we might be able to make new costumes, but--'

'It isn't hard to get,' Mrs Horton said, 'it's impossible. And even if it wasn't, I'm afraid we wouldn't be able to conceal Miss Kaplinski's condition for much longer.'

Kat laughed. 'My condition will no longer need to be concealed, Mrs Horton. Thank you for all the work you have done to keep my secret, but this week will be my last as a dancer – at least for a while. My doctor says that although I no longer do strenuous work on stage I must rest more. I will tell Mr Goldman and the director tomorrow. I think they will understand.' Standing sideways on to the mirror, with one hand on top of her tummy and the other beneath it, Kat proudly exaggerated her baby-bump and everyone laughed.

On Kat's last night the show was a great success,

although the company, backstage staff, and orchestra were aware that some scenes were a little subdued. The tradition when one of the Prince Albert's leading ladies leaves was for Anton Goldman to join the cast on stage for the last curtain.

'Ladies and gentlemen,' he began. 'It is with sadness that tonight we say goodbye to one of the Prince Albert Theatre's leading lights.' Anton turned, smiled at Kat, and offered his hand. Kat, smiling graciously, joined him. Slowly Anton led her to the front of the stage, bowed, and then stepped back, leaving her on the apron to enjoy the applause. A couple of minutes later a pageboy appeared from the wings holding a bouquet. The audience stood up and cheered. And as the company gathered round Kat, kissing her and wishing her well, the curtain was slowly lowered.

Artists came and went regularly at the Prince Albert, especially the girls in the back row who didn't sing or dance, but filled in as handmaidens and servants, or held poses in friezes. It was an occupational hazard of war that women as well as men were called up to fight for their country. The Phoney War, as the politicians called it, had come to an end with the blitzing of the East End. Since then the turnover of women employees had doubled. To the audience, Kat leaving was just another artist moving on. To the company at the Prince Albert Theatre, her leaving was not only sad, it presented a huge problem. When Goldie left, Margot was able to take over her role. But there was no one waiting in the wings to take over from the feisty Russian.

Getting anywhere on time in London had become almost impossible. With more air raid warnings since the Luftwaffe had stepped up their assault on the East

End, two understudies had been employed to go on at short notice when artists were delayed. They were both professional dancers and had agreed to understudy if they were given the chance to take over when a member of the company left. Richard Smiley had promised to audition them for Kat's roles. He hadn't even considered Margot.

Kat hadn't been able to stand on her points for months, nor had she been able to spin or perform pirouettes, which Margot could do if the routine wasn't too complicated. She smiled, remembering when she took dance classes on Saturday mornings in Woodcote's village hall. She didn't have the shoes needed to learn some of the dances, so the dance teacher brought in her older daughter's ballet and tap shoes for her to borrow. She said she was too good a little dancer to miss out. Margot's eyes filled with tears. It was so easy then, not only because the dance teacher recognised she had talent, but because she liked her for being confident. Not so now. Richard Smiley didn't seem to notice her talent and resented her confidence. Margot dried her eyes. She knew she could do Kat's dances – she was as good an actress and her voice was better than Kat's. But it didn't matter how good she was if Smiley wouldn't consider her.

Before she left on Saturday night, Margot went to see Nancy. She knocked gently on the door of dressing room one and heard Nancy say, 'Come in.'

'Oh, I'm sorry,' Margot said, opening the door and seeing the choreographer, Lena Di Angelo, sitting on the chaise. 'I didn't know you had anyone with you.' She smiled at Lena. 'I'll come back.'

'We're only chatting. What can I do for you, Margot?'

Margot looked from Nancy to Lena and, as they were the two people who could help her the most, launched straight in. 'I'd like to take over from Kat.'

Nancy smiled. Lena looked surprised. 'Have you spoken to Richard?'

'No. He kind of doesn't see me. He hasn't forgiven me for stepping in without telling him when Goldie left.' Margot looked at the floor. 'I thought – hoped – you might put a good word in for me with him. Then he might consider me.'

Lena looked at Nancy. 'I think we can do better than that. Kat's dances were modified during her pregnancy, so there aren't many ballet moves to learn. Richard will expect some, but he doesn't expect Kat's replacement to be a ballet dancer.' Margot exhaled with relief. 'I'm guessing you have ballet shoes?'

Margot scrunched up her shoulders and nodded. 'I borrowed a pair from the wardrobe store.'

Lena smiled. 'How's your balance?'

'Good.'

'Fluidity and grace, like in the Adagio?'

Margot thought for a moment and nodded. 'Yes. Good.'

'And how are you on the small quick steps of Couru?'

'I've been practising since I knew Kat would be leaving, and I'm confident I'm good enough. I can stand on demi points, and I've learned the fast steps of the Deboulé.'

'I'm impressed,' Lena said.

'Don't be. My Deboulé leaves a lot to be desired. I'm fine doing half turns, stepping onto one leg and completing the turn by stepping onto the other, but I find it hard to step high and keep my legs together. And I can only travel in a straight line.'

Lena laughed. 'We'll soon put that right. What are you doing tomorrow?'

'Nothing. With Bill and me both working long hours we just eat and sleep on Sunday.'

'Good. See you here at ten o'clock. I won't be able to turn you into a prima ballerina, but I'll have you dancing a damn sight better than the girls Richard has lined up to audition on Monday.'

Margot put her hand to her mouth. 'I can't tell you what this means to me, Lena,' she said. 'See you at ten.' She looked at Nancy and bit her bottom lip.

'Get a good night's sleep, Margot. You're going to need it,' Nancy said, smiling at Lena.

Margot left the dressing room and danced down the corridor. 'Night, night, Bert,' she sang, as she crossed to the stage door. Through it in a flash she waved to Bill, who had just turned into the Lane.

'I'm working tomorrow.'

'What?' Bill looked disappointed as he passed her helmet.

Margot kissed him before putting it on. 'I'll explain later.'

On the way home Margot put her arms around Bill's waist and held him tightly. As they approached Hampstead she inhaled the cool clean air of the Heath and smiled. Tomorrow couldn't come soon enough.

When she arrived at the theatre on Sunday morning, Lena was already on stage dressed in ballet shoes and dance leggings. She watched as the choreographer performed pliés on a portable bar. 'I don't think I could ever be as graceful as that,' Margot exclaimed.

'You don't have to be,' Lena said. 'Richard won't expect you to do pliés, only demi-pliés. But you will have to perform them more gracefully than the other dancers auditioning if you want the job. Right!' she said, turning away from the bar. 'Warm up exercises. Start with bending and stretching. Shan't be long,' she said, and she ran out, laughing.

Margot had warmed up at home, in a fashion, but began now in earnest. When Lena returned she was sweating and breathing heavily.

'Keep going or you'll get a chill.' Ten minutes later she shouted, 'Slow it down... Right down, and... Stop! Grab your towel and come over here, I have something to show you,' she said, waving a brown folder in the air.

Margot rubbed the perspiration from her face and arms and put the towel round her neck. 'Oh my God,' she said, reading the name on the front. 'Is that what I think it is?'

'Yes. It's a list of what Richard wants to see tomorrow, so have a drink of water,' she said, handing Margot a glass, 'and let's get down to it. You obviously know your positions – first to fifth?' Margot nodded. 'Show me.' Margot returned to the bar and did as directed. 'Good!' Lena shouted. 'Now show me your demi-pliés.' When Margot had finished Lena said, 'Lovely.'

Margot rolled her shoulders and stretched her arms. 'Show me what you can do with your arms. Reach out into a broad sweep. Further,' Lena shouted. 'Further still.' Margot thought the muscles in the tops of her arms would burst into flames they felt so hot and strained. 'That's lovely. Now bring them into your body... Sweeping, brushing the air. Head down and-- lift it! That's lovely. Straight back. Head high. Tummy in. Watch your eye line and sweep out again. Bend your knees and follow your hand. Look at it, look at it. Keep looking. Look along your arm all the way to your fingertips. And… bring your hand back, slowly. Slowly… that's it. Perfect.'

'You've worked hard,' Lena said when they stopped for a break. 'You're better than the understudies, which I expected you to be.' Margot smiled and tucked a stray strand of hair behind her ear. 'Which doesn't mean you can stop work,' Lena said.

'Not even to eat?' Nancy appeared from the wings. 'Thought you might like something sweet, give you some energy,' she said, handing Margot and Lena a jam doughnut each.

Delighted to see Nancy, Margot took the doughnut. 'Should I?'

'Of course,' Lena said, taking a bite out of hers and letting the jam drip down her chin. 'And tea!' she said, spotting three cups. 'I'm dying for a cuppa.'

Nancy held out the tray. 'Yours is nearest to you, Margot. I put a couple of sugars in it. I know you don't take sugar, but you have the rest of the afternoon to dance it off.'

'We won't ask where you got the sugar,' Lena said.

'That's good, because then I won't have to lie,' Nancy said, and they all laughed.

The afternoon went quickly. The routines weren't as difficult as they had been earlier, which was good because halfway through Margot's calf muscles hurt so much she wondered if she would be able to walk in the morning, never mind dance.

That night, after a hot meal and a long soak in a Radox bath – both courtesy of Bill – Margot fell into bed and slept like a baby. When she woke the following morning she ached all over and had blisters the size of sixpences on her heels and toes. Only slightly concerned about the pain, she took a couple of aspirin. They didn't help, but Margot knew that if she got the chance to audition for Kat's roles, Dr Theatre would kick in and she'd perform through the pain.

Natalie was sitting at the piano on stage when Margot slipped backstage to watch the auditions. The director, Richard Smiley, and choreographer – now friend – Lena Di Angelo were in the stalls. The first and second dancers to perform were no competition to Margot or the understudies and were told to stop before they'd completed the director's list. The third and fourth were the understudies – both familiar with Kat's roles. Margot watched from the wings. The dark one was as tall as Kat, but to Margot's delight she was nowhere near as good a dancer. The second, a pretty fair girl, had a sweet voice and could dance beautifully, but she lacked Kat's physical presence and vocal range. But, Margot thought, she'd be perfect to take over from me.

'We'll let you know,' she heard Richard Smiley say to the second understudy. And as she left the stage he shouted, 'Next?'

Margot strained her ears, hoping to hear his reply to Lena's suggestion that she could play Kat's roles. 'Margot's in this morning, Richard. I said I was sure you'd audition her. I mean, there's no reason why you won't, is there?'

'No. No reason.' Margot wrinkled her nose. He didn't sound very enthusiastic. She heard a seat go up with a slam. 'Will someone get Margot Dudley?'

'I'm here.' Running onto the stage, Margot put her hand up to shade the glare from the stage lights, and looked into the auditorium.

'Waiting in the wings again, Margot?' She ignored the sarcasm. 'Do you know the routines?'

Margot couldn't see Lena's face and wasn't sure whether she should admit to having seen them.

'I have a spare set,' Natalie said, handing Margot a list of the dance moves and a song sheet.

'You know Kat's work, so when you're ready.' He sounded irritated, impatient. Margot didn't delay. She looked at Natalie and took a breath. Natalie winked and began to play. She wasn't going to let Richard Smiley intimidate her, nor was she going to have Lena think she'd wasted her time the day before. When she finished singing the first song, Smiley shouted directions to the moves she'd learned and rehearsed the day before.

'Thank you,' he shouted, after putting Margot though several routines that weren't on the list, and were much more difficult. 'We'll let you know.'

Margot was in the dressing room, putting on her coat, when Lena burst in. 'I've got something to tell you,' she whispered. 'You've got the job.'

Margot threw her arms around Lena. 'What did he say?' she giggled, unable to contain her excitement.

'He said you were the best of the dancers. "An exceptional talent," he said.' Lena laughed. 'Then he said, "Tell her she's got the job, but keep her waiting a couple of hours. She's too cocky by half, that one."' Lena laughed again. 'He doesn't believe you just happened to be backstage when the auditions were taking place. He said, "The little madam used the situation to her own advantage, prepared for it, the way she did when she took over from Goldie Trick."'

'Can't imagine what made him think that,' Margot said, linking arms with Lena. 'Let's go to Lyons Corner House for tea – my treat. You can tell me if I've got the job over jam doughnuts.'

'There's a message for you, Miss Dudley,' Bert said,

when Margot poked her head through the window in his door to say good morning. 'Would you go up to wardrobe before you go into rehearsal?'

'Will do,' she said, making for the stairs. 'See you later.'

Mrs Horton and the blonde understudy Tilly Bronte, who Margot had thought from the beginning was perfect to take over her roles, were looking at her costumes. Although Tilly was the same height and dress size as Margot, she was a little smaller on the bust and hips, so Margot's costumes needed a nip and a tuck. Kat's costumes, on the other hand, needed major surgery. Kat was a couple of inches taller than Margot and over the last four months had become quite a size.

'If we removed all the panels we put in to make Miss Kaplinski's dresses bigger, I'm sure they'd fit Margot,' Violet mused.

'Couple of years ago we'd have made her new ones,' Ivy said. 'Now, even if we could afford to buy new material, there isn't any.'

'It's the government saw to that with their controls on importing and manufacturing cloth.' Violet shook her head and clicked her tongue. 'There hasn't been any material to be had for love nor money since those restrictions were brought in.'

Violet and Ivy cut and cobbled Kat's costumes. 'That looks fine,' Violet said during Margot's first costume fitting. 'All right for you, Ivy?'

Ivy nodded. 'Margot?'

'No! It isn't all right, Ivy. I'm the number two dancer now. I shouldn't have to wear costumes that look *all right*!' She pulled at the neckline. 'This is miles too big.' Then she turned and looked over her shoulder at the back of the dress in the long mirror.

'The bodice bags and the waistline is too low. If it was lifted and taken in....' She saw Violet look at Ivy and roll her eyes. 'I'm sorry if it means more work for you, Violet, but Kat wouldn't go on stage in something that didn't fit and nor will I!' Margot allowed Ivy to help her out of the costume and took her own clothes from Sylvie who, although she daren't comment, gave her a quick nod.

The following afternoon, Margot went for a second fitting and to her delight the costume she had tried on the day before fitted. By the end of the week all Kat's costumes had been altered properly and fitted well. Mrs Horton looked tired; Violet, Ivy and Sylvie looked exhausted. Margot knew from her time working as a seamstress that to remodel Kat's costumes to this standard they had worked very hard and for long hours.

'We are happy with your costumes, Margot. How do you feel now?' Natalie asked.

Margot nodded and smiled. 'Thank you,' she said, 'They look wonderful and they fit perfectly. Thank you ladies, they look as if they've been made for me.'

'They have,' Ivy whispered.

'Each costume has been taken apart and remade to your measurements, which is what we should have done in the first place,' Mrs Horton said, standing back and admiring the dress from a distance.

'Can't have the number two looking anything but perfect,' Violet winked.

Margot looked from Ivy to Violet, her eyes wide and sparkling with tears.

'What is it, dear?'

She wiped her tears and laughed. 'I've been so busy learning Kat's songs and dances that I haven't had time to think about it, but I really am the number two, the second lead in the show, aren't I?'

Her old friends from wardrobe laughed and congratulated her as they helped her out of the costume and into her own clothes. 'And we're all very proud of you,' Violet said.

On Margot's first night as second lead the show opened with Nancy, dressed in white, alone on stage. Margot heard a gasp ripple through the audience as first the stalls, and then the circle, followed by the upper circle and the gods, watched her being lowered from the fly-deck on a swing dressed as the black swan.

Once on the stage, Margot performed the Deboulé. Stepping from one leg to the other high on her toes, she danced effortlessly in a circle around the white swan. The dance of the swans ended to rapturous applause.

The extra work she'd done with Lena before and after rehearsals paid off. She turned slowly and gracefully, her steps quick and smooth; she looked beautiful.

In the second act Margot allowed herself to relax as she performed routines and sketches – tragic or comic – with perfect timing. At the curtain call, she was the penultimate artist to enter the stage. Standing alone in the spotlight she took her bow. As the audience stood, she thought she would burst with happiness. She looked into the wings. Nancy was applauding too. As she arrived at Margot's side to take her curtain, Nancy turned to Margot's young replacement and applauded her, which encouraged the audience to clap louder. She then took her own bow before taking Margot by the hand. Together they bowed several times to an audience that were on their feet and clapping wildly. Eventually Nancy nodded to Margot and after one last bow they left the stage, followed by the company. The audience were still clapping.

After the show Kat, who sat with Bill, Natalie and Anton in the Goldmans' box, was the first to arrive backstage and, apart from Bill, was the first to congratulate Margot. 'You were wonderful, darling.' Kat threw her arms around Margot. 'I leave my black swan in good hands. Congratulations, my friend.'

Everyone who came into the dressing room congratulated Margot, but it was the praise that Kat had given her that touched her heart and brought tears to her eyes.

Tilly Bronte, who had taken over from Margot, received congratulations too. And, she told Margot later, the most important were the compliments that Margot and Nancy had given her.

Before they all went to the first night party at the Albert Club, Kat took her leave. She was tired. She didn't feel up to going to a party, but she promised to call in the following day between the matinee and evening performance.

After waving Kat off in one taxi, the company piled into several others that were waiting at the stage door. Margot travelled with Nancy and Bill in the car Salvatore had sent for them.

The following day, when Kat arrived at the theatre, everyone was on stage except Nancy and Margot, who were waiting for her at the stage door. 'So many people wanted to say goodbye to you, Kat, that we thought we'd get everybody together on the stage,' Nancy said.

'There isn't enough room to swing a cat in the

dressing room,' Margot added. 'And we didn't want to leave wardrobe and stage management out.'

Nancy and Margot led the way, chatting excitedly, because the Goldmans had arranged a surprise tea party. And that wasn't all. They had bought Kat a Bluebird pram.

Kat's eyes filled with tears when she saw the beautiful pram with its navy hood and cover and its chrome handle and wheels. 'It is beautiful,' she said.

The pram stood centre stage, surrounded by tables laid with sandwiches and cakes, tea and cold drinks.

'No alcohol, I'm afraid,' Anton said. 'We have a show tonight.'

Several of the girls protested jokingly, as they tucked into egg sandwiches and slices of cheese on Jacobs biscuits.

'Will you be all right?' Margot asked Kat when they were alone.

'Yes, I think I will. I have spoken to my parents. I have been trying to get in touch with them for a long time.' Kat put her hand on her stomach. 'The baby's father tried for me but… It was difficult, even for him I think. My embassy was sick of me pestering and arranged a telephone call. I can't go home now, but when the war is over the baby and I will go back to Ukraine. If things work out we will stay, if they do not we will come home to England. I have lived here for so long I feel as English as I do Russian.'

'I'm pleased you got in touch with your parents.'

'Yes, I am too. My mother is excited about the baby.'

'And your father?'

'Papa is not excited. He is ashamed of me, as I expected him to be. He is very old-fashioned. When I became a dancer he almost disowned me, so now…?'

Kat laughed. 'Don't worry about us, Margot. My mother will have talked him round by the time I get home.'

Margot hugged Kat for a long minute. 'It may be a year, longer, until the war ends. You'll come and see us, won't you? And when the baby's born, I'd love to see--'

'And you shall. You shall be godmother. After all, if it hadn't been for you...'

Before Margot had time to say anything, the girls surrounded them. 'Come on, Kat, we want to give you your leaving presents.' The girls gently pulled Kat to the centre of the room to a table laden with gifts, and sat her down. Tears filled her eyes as she was given beautiful baby clothes and soft toys.

'How did you find such lovely things with everything being rationed?'

'We weren't going to tell you in front of Mr Goldman,' Mrs Horton said, 'but there's plenty of soft fabric around if you know where to look, and plenty of friends who are willing to give up their time to knit and sew baby clothes.'

By the time Kat had kissed and thanked everyone for the gifts she was in tears again.

Ten minutes later Bert arrived to say Miss Kaplinski's cab was outside.

Once Kat was seated in the taxi, her friends packed the presents around her. There were so many, she could barely move. The pram, Anton said, would be delivered the following day.

Everyone waved and shouted goodbye and the taxi sped off with Kat waving out of the back window. The cab disappeared into the traffic and was out of sight in seconds, but Margot knew that Kat, her talent and her friendship would have a lasting influence on her life.

CHAPTER ELEVEN

'It's time we got a place of our own,' Margot said, the second Bill sat down to supper. 'I'm working longer hours, and so are you. If we lived in the West End we'd be nearer to work, and there'd be no risk of me getting lost in the blackout.' Margot stopped and shuddered, hoping that reminding Bill of that terrible night would persuade him. It didn't. 'Hampstead is so far away from everything. Besides,' she went on, 'it isn't fair on you having to wait around for me at night, especially now I'm doing the late spot at the club. Not when you've been driving to and from goodness knows where all day for the MoD and been on the ambulances half the night.'

'I suppose we do live quite a way from where we work,' Bill conceded. 'And as much as I don't want to leave these rooms, because they're where we began our married life, I suppose it would make sense.'

'So we're moving?'

'We'll see.'

'We'll see? What do you mean, we'll see? I want to move, Bill. I want us to have a home of our own with our own front door. I want to paint it and buy pretty ornaments and things. I want to be able to nip home and have my tea after the matinee. I want to invite friends for drinks and...'

'Wow! Slow down, Margot. This is the first I've heard of moving and you're already throwing parties.'

Flushed with anger, Margot put down her knife and fork with a clatter and glared into the mid-distance. She hated it when Bill cut her off, especially when she was saying something important.

Placing his cutlery gently on the table, Bill took

hold of Margot's hands. He waited until she looked at him. Then, when he was sure he had her attention, he said, 'Anything as important as moving house is something we need to discuss.'

'We were discussing it!'

'No Margot, we weren't. You were telling me what you wanted, assuming I'd agree like I always do. But it isn't just about moving house. It's leaving our home. It's a big step. So, whatever we decide, we'll decide together when we've discussed it properly. It won't be because you've had another crazy idea.'

'Crazy? It isn't a crazy idea! What's crazy about wanting to live with your husband in your own home?' Margot knew if she pushed Bill too far he would dig his heels in. He could be stubborn sometimes. She softened her tone. 'At least say you'll think about it.'

'I'll think about it! Now, could we please eat our meal while it's hot?'

Margot also hated it when Bill patronised her. He was right of course, anything as important as moving home shouldn't be rushed. But that didn't stop her asking him every night until he gave in.

'Have you given any more thought to us getting our own place, love?'

'Yes I have, but--' Margot leapt out of her chair. 'If you let me eat my supper in peace,' Bill said, 'I will go and see Anton and Natalie. It's only fair that we tell them that we're thinking about moving.'

'Thinking?'

'All right! That we might – will – be moving. We'll start looking in the morning. There's a notice board at work that advertises apartments--'

Margot squealed with excitement. 'And there are newspapers.'

'And there are newspapers,' Bill repeated. 'There's a local one, the *Covent Garden News*. And there are a couple of letting agencies in Neal Street. I'll call in tomorrow.'

'And with me working so near, I can pop in every day.'

'There are bound to be vacancies. People are moving out of the West End because of the nightly bombing of the East End, which is getting closer.' Bill looked into Margot's eyes and shook his head. 'Who in their right mind would want to live in the West End of London?'

'Me!' Margot said, jumping up and throwing her arms around Bill. 'I want to live there!'

'I meant other than you, Margot.'

Margot moved her face close to her husband's until their noses were touching. She gave him several Eskimo kisses before kissing him full on the lips.

That night, after they had made love Margot lay in Bill's arms, content and sleepy. 'A place of our own,' she whispered. 'Thank you, lovely husband. I'm so happy... You make me so....'

The following night Margot arrived home with newspapers, leaflets, For Sale and For Rent cards that she'd taken from shop windows, promising to return them the following morning, and half a dozen sheets of paper with the address and description of a dozen or more apartments in and around Covent Garden. After supper, she spread them out on the bed while Bill made their bedtime drink.

'Are you sure you have enough information there, Margot?' Bill said, handing her a cup of cocoa.

Margot laughed. 'For now, but I can show you more if you want. I've whittled them down to a couple of dozen, so pay attention,' she said, wagging her finger. 'These are the possible-stroke-probable apartments. I have a batch of maybe-could-be and another of not-on-your-life in my shopping bag. I wonder if they have carpets and curtains? Probably will,' she chattered on. 'We might like them of course, but if we don't we can change them. Our own little love nest,' she said, pursing her lips and blowing Bill a kiss. 'And a bed,' she said suddenly. 'I don't want to sleep in a bed that anyone else has slept in. Will we be able to buy a new bed? I've never thought about it before. Are beds rationed?'

'Someone slept in this bed before we did, and you've been happy sleeping in it.'

'Yes, but this bed is different, we know who slept in it before us, or at least we know it would have been someone clean. In a rented apartment in Covent Garden there's no telling who has slept in the bed.' Margot lifted her hand and flicked the possibilities away. 'No, we'll have a new bed and that's that!'

Bill made no further comment. He slipped out of the room, leaving Margot ticking off the good and the bad points of what looked to him like every available flat in the West End. He settled down on the settee and read the newspaper.

Eliminating those that didn't come up to her standard, Margot was left with two properties that she wanted to see. She went into the sitting room to show Bill. He was asleep, so she cleared the unwanted literature from the bed, put the two she wanted to view into her handbag, and pulled down the bedclothes.

'Come on, sleepy head,' she said, returning to the sitting room and shaking Bill by the shoulder. 'Time to go to bed.'

Bill pushed himself up and, squinting through

sleepy eyes, shuffled into the bedroom and fell onto the bed. 'G'night love.'

Margot took off his slippers, pulled the bedclothes up, and tucked him in. Then she switched off the light and slid into bed beside her already snoring husband.

Margot flew into Bill's arms. 'I've found it. I've found our new home and it's perfect,' she said, showing Bill a photograph of a spacious sitting room, one double bedroom and one single. 'I love it, Bill. I want it. The kitchen is so modern. It's got a big sink, hot water on tap, and a mangle in one of the cupboards. Oh, and there's a bathroom and toilet and guess what? Go on,' she said after waiting only a second. 'Guess what it's got that I've always wanted.'

'I don't know,' Bill said. The happiness radiating from his wife overwhelmed him. It always did. 'I give in.'

'A front door! We've got what we've always wanted,' Margot said, as if it was the only apartment in London with a front door. 'Please say you'll come and see it tomorrow,' she said, jumping up and down on the spot.

'Tomorrow?'

'Yes... Pleeeeeeease.'

The flat was all Margot said it was, and more. It did indeed have its own front door. Made of solid wood with a brass door knocker and handle, it opened onto a cobbled side street. Number 3 Oxford Mews was between the offices of a film company and a theatrical agency. At the end of the Mews there was a wrought iron fire escape belonging to a late night gambling club. The letting agent had told Margot that the club's clients kept a low profile and never bothered the residents of the Mews. There was a door beneath the fire escape, which was the entrance to the club's kitchen, and a door next to that with a small window above. There had been a red light in the window the first time Margot visited the Mews. Today, she was relieved to see, there was no light and the curtains were drawn.

'It will be quiet at night,' Margot said, opening the front door leading to the apartment she so desperately wanted. 'The offices close at half past five and whoever lives at the end of the Mews is far enough away that we won't hear them, or anyone else, come to that.'

Bill nodded. 'Good location,' he said, giving Margot's shoulder a squeeze.

Margot led Bill up the stairs to a small landing. The door was on the left. She put the key in the lock and turned to Bill. Her eyes sparkled with excitement. 'Well, this is it! I hope you like it,' she said, and she threw open the door.

The square entrance hall was bright with clean straight lines and four doors. The door directly ahead of them led to the sitting room and kitchen. Margot opened it. 'Look Bill, isn't it lovely? Nice big settee and armchair, and the dining table and chairs look perfect here, next to the kitchen.' Margot sighed. 'It's smart, isn't it?'

'It looks like a doctor's waiting room,' Bill said.

Margot pretended she hadn't heard him. 'The kitchen's through here. You'll love it, I know you will. It's so modern. I'll be able to bake you a cake and things, like a proper wife.'

Bill laughed, 'That'll make a pleasant change.' Margot punched him playfully on the arm.

She ran her hand along the edge of the worktops.

'Cream and cherry are the latest colours. Oh, Bill, look at this cabinet. It isn't only for keeping food in.' She pulled the handle in the middle. 'Look, it turns into a work surface.'

'Where's the bedroom?'

'This way, sir.' Margot led Bill back to the hall. 'After you,' she said, opening the door and following him into the double bedroom. The room had three matching mirrors: one on the dressing table, one on the wall opposite, and a huge oval one on a wooden stand. Margot looked at herself in all three, turning to the left, and then the right, before jumping onto the bed. 'Come and try it, Bill,' she said, patting the mattress. 'It's ever so comfortable.'

Bill laughed and lay down beside her.

'Close your eyes and relax for a minute.'

Bill closed his eyes and Margot rolled over and kissed him. 'You do like the apartment, don't you?' she purred, walking her fingers up his chest to his chin.

'Yes,' he sighed, 'I like it.'

Margot squealed and jumped up. 'I knew it, I knew it, I knew it! I knew you'd love it!'

'I love you, Margot,' Bill said, 'and if you want to live here, I want to live here. I don't care where I live as long as I'm with you.'

'But you do like it, don't you, Bill? Please say you do.'

'I like it. I love it.'

Margot squealed again. 'Then what are we waiting for? Let's go and tell the letting agent, and give him the deposit.'

The agent was delighted and asked when they wanted to move in.

'Next Sunday,' Margot said, grabbing hold of Bill's

hand.

The man raised his eyebrows at Bill. 'Next Sunday it is then,' he said. 'If you'd like to pay the deposit, you can sign the tenancy agreement.'

Margot skipped out of the letting agency, chatting and laughing. Nothing could be done that day. Being a Saturday, there was a matinee and an evening show to get through. But she spent the following day packing the things that she and Bill could manage without until they moved into their new home.

The week flew by, but Margot managed to pack a little each day, before and after work. The day before they moved, Bill couldn't find any clean socks – Margot had packed them.

Two of Bill's mates from St. Thomas's and Margot's friend Jenny, who worked with him now on the ambulances, arrived at ten o'clock and loaded up a van that Bill had borrowed from work. The rooms, which had been home to Margot and Bill for so long, looked sad without Margot's bright furnishings.

With his arm around Margot's shoulder, Bill said, 'We've been happy here, haven't we?'

'Yes we have; very happy. But we'll be happy in Covent Garden too – and without so much travelling we'll be able to spend more time together.'

'There's that,' Bill said, giving her a gentle squeeze. 'Right!' he said, kissing her on the cheek. 'I'd better go down and tell the lads they can get off. Next stop Covent Garden.'

'I'll have a quick look round, check we haven't forgotten anything. I'll be down in a sec.'

'Okay, don't be long.'

Margot walked through each of the rooms that had been home to her and Bill since soon after they were married. She stopped for a moment in the living room with its tiny kitchenette, where she had often burnt their dinner, before checking the bedroom. She sighed. Even when she'd kept secrets from him and he found out, Bill always forgave her, and they always made up. There had been some tears, but there had been much more laughter. As she left, Margot looked back and smiled before closing the door.

Having invited their friends Anton and Natalie to lunch the following Sunday, Margot and Bill said goodbye and travelled to number 3 Oxford Mews on Bill's motorbike.

'Well, Mrs Burrell,' Bill said, after locking their helmets in the panniers. 'Isn't this where I carry you over the threshold?'

'I think it is, Mr Burrell.' Margot put her arms around her husband's neck and lifted one leg.

'Give me the key and I'll open the door,' Bill said.

'You've got the key!' Margot put her leg down. 'I gave it to you before we left. Oh Bill! What have you done with it?'

'Only joking,' he said, producing the key from a pocket inside his jacket.

'Thank goodness. I thought we'd have to go all the way back to Hampstead.' Margot watched Bill put the key in the lock and, squeezing his arm, jumped with joy when he turned it and she heard the click that said it was unlocked. Together, laughing like a pair of teenagers, they pushed the door open.

Margot clapped her hands before putting her arms around Bill's neck again. Bill smiled and lifted her up. He carried her over the threshold, kicked the door shut behind them, and mounted the stairs. Outside the apartment, Bill set Margot down and took another key from his pocket. 'I think you should open this door, Mrs Burrell.'

Margot took the brass key, put it in the lock and turned it. When she heard the lock click a broad smile spread across her face. She pushed open the door. 'I don't think I'm strong enough to carry you over this threshold though.'

'Then I'll have to carry you again,' Bill said, picking her up. 'There's a new piece of furniture in the flat.'

'Oh? What is it?'

'I'll show you.'

Margot squealed with delight when Bill took her into the bedroom and laid her on the new bed. An hour later there was a knock at the door. Giggling, Margot pulled on her skirt and blouse and slipped her feet into her shoes. 'Coming!' she shouted out of the window, before running downstairs to welcome the friends who had brought their belongings.

'What are you doing here?' Margot said, throwing her arms around Natalie. 'I didn't think we'd be seeing you until next week.'

'Thought we'd surprise you,' she said, beckoning Anton. 'Anyone for champagne?' Natalie shouted, waving a bottle in the air.

Margot laughed. 'Lovely idea, but we haven't got any glasses.'

'We have,' Anton shouted, from the boot of his car.

'Then yes please!'

'What are you doing standing on the doorstep? Come in,' Bill said, arriving at Margot's side. 'Take everyone up, sweetheart,' he said, standing to one side to let them pass. 'I'll hang on for Anton.'

After a toast of champagne, the men brought in Margot and Bill's belongings.

'If you tell the lads where you want the boxes, it will be less work for you and Bill later,' Natalie said.

'Good idea.'

Anton brought the first box. 'Bedding,' Margot said, pointing to the bedroom. 'That box too, it's dressing table stuff. Cutlery in the kitchen – and that's bathroom. Suitcases in the bedroom – I'll unpack them later – and coats in the hall. Everything else can go in the single bedroom. It's the door on the left as you come in. I'll sort it out later.'

When the pots, pans and crockery had been stacked on the work surfaces in the kitchen, Natalie said, 'There's one more box. Anton, would you fetch it?'

'Of course.' When he returned it was with a hamper, which he placed on the dining table.

Margot opened it and caught her breath. 'There's enough food here to feed half the theatre.'

Everyone laughed. And as if on cue there was a knock at the door. 'I think you'd better answer that, darling, as you're the hostess!'

Margot scrunched up her shoulders and put her hands up to her cheeks. 'Bill Burrell, I love you!' she said before running down the stairs and opening the door to see Nancy, George, Betsy, Mrs Horton and Miss Lesley, who said at the same time, 'Surprise!'

Margot flung her arms round each of her friends and kissed them before taking them up to the apartment. As they entered the sitting room there was more hugging and kissing. When they had finished greeting each other, Anton filled everyone's glasses with champagne, Natalie found plates and Margot unpacked the hamper.

CHAPTER TWELVE

Margot caught a break in the traffic at Lancaster Place and ran across the road. She sidestepped around the water tank outside the Savoy Hotel and looked at her wristwatch. Half an hour until she was due to meet Nancy. She enjoyed being with her fellow dancers, loved the camaraderie, the chatter and laughter, but tea with her beautiful mentor on Thursday afternoons was special, something she looked forward to all week. She'd better get a move on; she didn't want to be late.

There was still so much she needed for the new apartment, but every week there was less in the shops. Earlier in the day Margot had called in to the Imperial Ironmongery off Leicester Square, but there wasn't a saucepan, frying pan, or pie dish to be seen. "They are using metal to repair aeroplanes," the snooty shop assistant said – as if Margot didn't know. "You'll just have to make do."

With next to nothing in the windows of the shops going south on the Strand, Margot crossed over at Charing Cross station. There was less produce and even fewer goods in the windows on the north side. She looked at her reflection in the empty window of Dutton's Hardware, and sighed. A sign saying No Kitchen Appliances or Utensils looked back at her. Oh well, she would have to do what everyone else was doing. She straightened her hat. She would make do.

As she passed Simpsons Confectionery a Thornton's poster caught her eye, reminding her of the chocolates left at the stage door by American servicemen. She felt a warm blush on her cheeks. She had quite a few American admirers. They were harmless enough. Most of them were very young. Some, like so many British servicemen, didn't look old enough to go to war. She passed a newspaper stand. "AT LAST THE YANKS ARE HERE" and "IKE WILL SHOW HITLER". Almost every week for the last two and a half years the newspapers had reported on the US situation. One week the Americans were on their way to help Britain, the next the war in Europe was nothing to do with them. But since the Japanese attack on the US naval base at Pearl Harbour in December 1941 the country was slowly becoming flooded with American servicemen. Margot stifled a giggle. They didn't leave flowers like the English stage door Johnnies, they left silk stockings, chocolate and sweets, which they called candy. The girls preferred stockings to flowers. The American boys – GIs, they were called – could be a bit loud and sometimes made cheeky comments during the show, but they were harmless, and they were very generous.

Margot was miles away when she felt someone touch her arm.

'Excuse me, Miss Dudley, can I have your autograph, please?'

Margot turned to see a young woman standing at her side. 'Yes, of course. What's your name?'

'Doreen. Doreen Adams.' The girl dove into her shopping basket and brought out a programme.

'Oh, you've seen the show. Did you enjoy it?'

'Yes,' the young woman gushed. 'You're my favourite. Well, you and Miss Jewel. She's very beautiful, isn't she?' the girl said with a sigh that was almost a swoon.

'Yes, she is. She's very nice too.' Margot took a pen from her handbag. 'To Doreen, best wishes, Margot Dudley. There you are,' she said, returning the programme.

'Thank you ever so much.' The young woman made no attempt to leave.

'Was there something else?'

'Well.' She cleared her throat. 'I was wondering if you'd take the programme and ask Miss Jewel to sign it for me. I'd go to the theatre and ask her myself, but I've got to meet my mother at Lyons Corner House. She doesn't like it if I keep her waiting.'

'Of course I will. I'll ask her as soon as she comes in. I'll leave it for you to collect at the stage door. Will that be all right?'

'Oh yes.' The excited young woman handed over her programme, said goodbye, and skipped off.

Margot turned, dropped the programme into her bag, and walked in the opposite direction. Who would have thought it? Me, Margot Dudley, signing autographs. It wasn't the first time, of course. Every night there were at least a dozen people at the stage door with their programmes. And each time she wrote her name was as exciting as the first time. "Dreamer", they used to call me at school. "Margaret is a bright girl if only she concentrated." "Margaret could do better." The head mistress wrote that, or something similar, on her school report every year. Well, Miss 'Pinky' Pinkerton, I think you would agree that I have now done better!

Margot looked at her wristwatch – it was almost six. If she didn't get a move on she'd be late for tea with Nancy. Tonight was a big night. Nancy was performing a new song at the end of the show – a love song that had been written specially for her – and it was beautiful. Most shows ended with an uplifting number which was meant to distract the audience from the death and destruction going on all around

167

them. That wouldn't be the case tonight. Tonight there wouldn't be a dry eye in the house.

Nancy had taken Margot under her wing, helped her and given her confidence when she took over from Kat – as she had when she took over from Goldie. Margot smiled, remembering how Nancy and Lena had helped her to learn Kat's routines and dances so that when Richard Smiley auditioned her she was good enough to get the job and take over Kat's roles. Now, with no sign of the war ending, there were fewer classical dances and more comedy acts and sketches, which were more fun.

Margot couldn't remember a time when she'd been happier. She loved the hustle and bustle of London. She loved the apartment, she loved Bill, and she loved her job. Life was perfect. Or as perfect as it could be considering the country was at war and the city she lived in was bombed every night. Grateful that she lived in the West End, not the East End, she turned into Bedford Street and quickened her step.

As she approached Maiden Lane, Margot heard the explosion. She began to run, but an ear-shattering second explosion stopped her in her tracks. It was close. She looked around. Nothing. She looked up at the roof of the bookshop opposite the theatre. The impact of the bomb had cracked the ornate pillars of the Juliet balcony on the third floor. As if in slow motion they began to sway. It was as if they couldn't make up their mind whether or not to fall. Suddenly flames filled the window between the pillars. Red hot and smoking, they licked at the window frame until, distorted and grotesquely misshapen, it gave way. Frozen with fear, Margot watched as the window blew out, showering Maiden Lane with shards of shattered glass. She brought her focus back to the Lane. There was a taxi parked outside the theatre. Bert came running out. Margot screamed and waved hysterically. 'Bert! Go back inside!' She looked up at the bookshop's roof again. The pillars had started to buckle. 'Bert!' she screamed. 'Bert!' Get back! The roof! It's going to come down!'

Bert couldn't have heard her because he kept running. Seconds later the pillars crashed to the ground. Huge lumps of masonry landed on top of the taxi, the impact crushing it until the windows bowed and burst out. Several large lumps of brick and mortar fell on the bonnet. One bounced, flew through the air and hit Bert on the side of his head. The old doorman's body jerked and for a second he stood perfectly still. Then he closed his eyes and slid to the ground.

'No!' Margot screamed. 'No!'

In her haste to get to him, Margot stumbled and fell. 'Damn!' Her right leg became entangled in steel wire sticking out of a block of plaster. She ripped it from her ankle, tearing the flesh and exposing the bone. Slates were falling, hitting the ground, splintering, and cutting her already bleeding legs. She didn't care. 'Bert!' she screamed, and she dropped to her knees to help the old man. 'Bert?' He wasn't moving. A large lump of plaster lay on his chest. Margot knew not to move it; it could cause internal bleeding. Blood flowed from his right temple. She couldn't bear it. Where was everybody? She got to her feet. 'Help! Someone help!'

She could hear hammering coming from the stage door. She didn't want to leave Bert, but she needed to get him help. She ran to the door and pushed. It was stuck. She pushed again and again until finally it gave way and Mrs Horton, followed by Miss Lesley, came running out.

'It's Bert,' Margot said to Miss Lesley. 'I think he's dead.'

'What about Nancy?' Mrs Horton asked.

'Nancy?' Margot turned towards the taxi. 'No, no, no. No!' she screamed. 'Please God, no!' Her beloved friend was in the passenger seat. She had been there all the time. Margot ran to her. Most of the glass in the window had gone. Nancy was leaning on what was left. Her arm hung from her shoulder at a strange angle. Margot knelt until her face was level with Nancy's and pulled on the door, cutting her hands on what remained of the window, but the door wouldn't open. 'Oh Nancy.' Margot stroked her hair. It was sticky, reddish-brown and matted with blood. Her face was white, translucent like alabaster, and her eyes were staring and sightless. There was a trickle of blood at the corner of her mouth and another on the lobe of her ear.

Margot opened her mouth to scream, but no sound came. The pain in her throat was excruciating and threatened to choke her. She looked into the unseeing eyes of her friend and fell to her knees. Somewhere deep inside her the pain rose and strangled screams burst from her. 'Get her out! Get her out! Get her out! She's stuck. Nancy's stuck inside. Won't somebody help her?'

Bill, suddenly at Margot's side, tried to pull her from the taxi.

'Bill? Why-- how--?'

'I was on my way to Tommy's when I heard the explosion.'

'You'll help Nancy, won't you, Bill? You'll help her?'

'Of course I will, love, but you must let go of the

door. Come on, sweetheart, the ambulance and fire brigade are here now. If we move away they'll be able to get Nancy out of the taxi.'

Margot shook her head vigorously and gripped the door even harder. The man standing beside Bill was holding a pair of cutters. 'You be careful!' she said. 'Don't hurt her!'

The fireman turned to Bill. 'Get her out of here, will you, mate?'

'Come on, sweetheart. There's nothing you can do here.'

'I'm not leaving. I'm staying with Nancy. She'll need me when—'

Bill put his arms round her and held her tightly from behind, so she was unable to move. 'Nancy's gone, love,' he whispered. 'There's nothing you can do for her. Come away now and let the fireman do his job.' Margot shook her head and tried to break free. Bill tightened his grip. 'She's gone, Margot!' he said, firmly. 'She's gone!'

'No!' Margot cried. 'Please, Bill,' she begged, 'say it isn't true.'

Bill prized her hands from the door of the taxi and Margot spun round. She beat her fists against his chest and Bill held her until she wore herself out, emotionally and physically. With her head resting on his shoulder and her body limp and moulded to his body, Bill looked down at her tear-stained face.

A minute later he was carrying Margot to the ambulance. 'Emergency,' he said. 'My wife has lost consciousness.'

The headlines read FANS KEEP ALL NIGHT VIGIL OUTSIDE HOSPITAL.

'Can she hear me?' Bill asked.

'We can't be sure in cases like your wife's.'

Bill? I can hear you, Margot wanted to say, but only tears came. Bill sounded concerned, worried. She could feel his hand on her arm. Another man was speaking, but she didn't recognise his voice. She didn't know who he was, and she didn't care. They were talking about her as if she wasn't in the room.

The other man said, 'It's shock. We've given her a thorough medical and apart from the cuts on her hands and legs – and of course her ankle – there's nothing physically wrong.'

Her mouth was dry. She was thirsty. She tried to lick her lips.

'Doctor? My wife moved,' Bill said, stroking Margot's hair. 'She tried to open her mouth.'

'Bill?'

'I'm here, love.'

Margot felt wet cotton wool on her lips. She tried to suck the moisture from it. 'Bill,' she said again, opening her eyes, and then closing them against the light.

She heard a rustle of fabric and what sounded like curtains being drawn. 'It's a lovely day,' a cheery female with a Southern Irish accent said, 'but the sun's shining directly into your eyes, and we don't want that now, do we?' When Margot opened her eyes again, the blinds were closed.

'Where am I?'

'You're in hospital, sweetheart.'

'Hospital?'

'Yes. But there's nothing to worry about,' Bill said, dabbing gently at her tears.

Margot tried to sit up. 'Here, let me.' The Irish nurse helped Margot to lean forward and slipped a pillow behind her back.

'Thank you.' Margot closed her eyes. The small amount of effort had tired her.

Bill pulled up a chair and sat beside the bed. He thanked the nurse as she left.

Margot opened her eyes at the sound of Bill's voice, smiled, and closed them again. When she woke, Bill was still there, his hand on her arm.

Margot tried to move, but couldn't. 'My legs feel numb. They're stiff. And my right ankle hurts. What's the matter with my legs, Bill?'

'They're bandaged. There's nothing to worry about. You got tangled up in some rusty wire and they were cut pretty badly.'

What little colour there was in Margot's face drained away.

'They're on the mend,' Bill said.

'Doctor says when he's finished with you,' the nurse said, returning with fresh water, 'you won't even have scars.'

'Scars?' Margot looked at the raised quilt over her legs. 'What's the matter with my ankle?'

'Badly sprained,' the nurse said. 'But it will be as good as new in no time. Right! Let me know if you want anything.' She plumped up Margot's pillows. 'I'm only outside, at the nurse's station.'

Margot watched the nurse leave the room. Then she turned to Bill. Tears filled her eyes. 'Nancy's dead, isn't she?'

Bill nodded. 'I'm so sorry, Margot. There was nothing anyone could do...'

'How's Salvatore? Have you seen him?'

'Yes. He's been in to see you every day since--'

Exhausted, Margot closed her eyes. She was asleep in seconds.

*

She had no idea how long she'd been asleep. The sun was no longer on the window, so an hour, maybe two, had passed. Bill was speaking quietly to someone. She opened her eyes to see Salvatore standing in the doorway. He was shaking Bill's hand. Was he leaving? She didn't want him to leave. 'Salvatore? Don't go.' Margot pushed herself up to a more comfortable position and motioned to the chair at the side of the bed.

'Dear Margot, I am sorry we woke you.' Salvatore came to her and sat in the chair. Bill stood behind him.

'You didn't.' Margot choked back her tears. She wouldn't cry in front of Nancy's fiancé. His loss was far greater than hers. She would be brave for him, and for Nancy.

'How have you been?' she asked, and then said immediately, 'Sorry, that was a stupid question, forgive me.'

Salvatore shook his head. 'Not stupid, Margot. You could never be stupid.' He didn't speak for a minute. Then he said, 'The light in my world has gone out. It is as if the last five years were make-believe. As if I was living in a beautiful and loving dream that turned into a dark and lonely nightmare.' Tears spilt onto his cheeks.

Margot laid her bandaged hand on Salvatore's arm and at the same time Bill squeezed his shoulder. Salvatore half turned to acknowledge the gesture. 'I am like a machine. I get up as soon as it is light, and I walk the streets until it is time to go to work. When I finish at one, two o'clock in the morning, I go back to my apartment. The apartment where my beautiful Nancy and I were going to live when we married.' Salvatore buried his head in his hands and wept.

Margot didn't know what to say. It was Bill who broke the silence. Looking at Margot, he said, 'Never having lost anyone I love, I can only imagine how you must be feeling. If there is anything I can do, my friend, anything at all...'

Margot looked at Bill, fighting to hold back the tears.

Salvatore nodded. 'Thank you, Bill. Everyone says once the funeral is over, there is closure. I don't want closure. I want my beautiful Nancy.'

Margot spoke softly. 'When is Nancy's funeral?'

Salvatore took a short sharp breath and put his hands up to his face. He turned to Bill.

'What? Salvatore? Bill? What aren't you telling me?'

'The doctors said you weren't well enough to go to Nancy's funeral,' Bill said, 'and I agreed.'

Margot shot him a fierce look. 'Are you telling me I've missed Nancy's funeral?'

'Margot, the doctors were right. Bill was right. You were too ill to attend,' Salvatore said.

'When was it?' Margot asked, looking straight ahead.

'Yesterday.'

'I see. I'd like you both to leave now.'

Salvatore stood up and moved away. Bill took his place. He bent down and kissed her. 'Get some rest, sweetheart. I'll be back in the morning.'

'Good. You can bring my black suit and black court shoes with you.'

'Court shoes? What for? You can't wear heels. You can't walk in slippers, so how--'

'High heels, low heels, I don't care. There's a pair of flat shoes somewhere. Bring them if you like.' Margot looked squarely into Bill's eyes. 'I am going to Nancy's grave tomorrow. I won't stay long. I'll come straight back. But I am going, and that is that!'

Salvatore's smile told Margot that he understood her need to see her friend's grave. 'Goodbye, Margot. I will see you soon.'

A little later, Bill was despatched with a list, promising to call on her hairdresser on the way home and arrange for her to go to the hospital and wash and set Margot's hair.

No sooner had Bill gone than Betsy and George arrived, followed by the doctor and nurse.

'Did you see Bill on your way out?'

'Yes. He's worried that you're not up to--' George looked at the doctor. 'So are we, aren't we, Bets?'

'Nothing to worry about, ladies,' the doctor said, cutting in on the conversation. 'A couple of weeks and Miss Dudley will be on her feet and dancing the light fantastic.'

'Did you hear that, Margot?' George asked. 'A couple of weeks.'

'I'm going to Nancy's grave tomorrow and that's all there is to it.'

The doctor spun round. 'I'm afraid you are not going anywhere tomorrow!'

'Yes I am. I am going to the grave of my friend – with or without your permission.'

The doctor picked up Margot's notes and flicked through them. 'It seems the patients are running the hospitals these days.' He handed the notes to the nurse and looked down at Margot. 'If anything goes wrong with your ankle and you're not able to dance again, don't come crying to me.' He shot a look at the nurse, who nodded in agreement, and he left the room.

'Doctor's right, you know,' the nurse said. 'You could undo all the work he's done. You could end up crippled for the rest of your life, if you're not careful.'

'Then I'll be careful.'

'You'll have to go in a wheelchair.'

Margot wrinkled her nose and frowned.

With her hands on her hips, the nurse stood her ground. 'If you want to leave the hospital, Miss Dudley, we can't legally stop you. But doctor won't let you out of this room unless you're in a wheelchair. It's up to you!'

'All right! We can't have the inmates making decisions for themselves, can we?'

The nurse didn't reply. 'And you're to come back immediately you've--'

'I will.' Margot rolled her eyes.

'And no!' the nurse laughed. 'We can't have the inmates making decisions, especially when they're contrary to what doctor says.'

CHAPTER THIRTEEN

'"Margot Dudley Crippled! A friend close to the actress said…" What friend?' Bill shrugged and shook his head.

'"Will Margot Dudley Ever Walk Again?" Where do they get this rubbish? Walk again? I intend to dance again – and soon.' Margot threw the newspaper onto the chair at the side of the bed and pushed herself up into a sitting position. 'I swear I'll go mad if I have to spend another night in this damn bed. Where the hell's the doctor?' She swung her legs over the side of the narrow cot, stood up too quickly and stumbled.

Bill leapt forward, arms outstretched. 'Are you sure you're ready to leave, Margot?'

'Yes!' Allowing Bill to steady her, she looked into his eyes and put her arms around his neck. 'I'm very sure. I want to cuddle up to my husband and fall asleep in his arms. And when I wake up in the morning, I want to be in my own bed and…' She laid her head on Bill's shoulder and walked her fingers from his belt to his chest. 'I've missed you. It's been weeks…' she purred.

Spotting the nurse in the corridor, Margot pursed her lips as if to kiss him, but Bill turned his head and cleared his throat.

'Don't worry, Mr Dudley, your wife doesn't shock me,' the nurse said, entering the room.

Margot giggled. Bill was always being called Mr Dudley. He didn't mind and she had long since given up correcting people.

The doctor arrived at last. 'Up and dressed already?'

'Yes!' Margot sat on the bed. 'No offence, doctor, but the sooner I get out of here the better.'

'What if I don't think you're ready to leave?'

Margot took the walking stick from the back of the chair and brandished it in the air. 'If you won't let me out of here, Doctor Frankenstein, I shall whack you with my stick.'

The doctor took a step backwards and put his hands up. 'I surrender,' he laughed. The nurse passed him Margot's notes. Reading them, his smile faded to a frown.

'What now?'

'You're still not sleeping.'

'Of course I am. Well, I'm sleeping better than I was, aren't I, nurse?'

The nurse, looking sideways at the notes the doctor was holding, pressed her lips together and said nothing. 'And the bad dreams?'

'Haven't had one for weeks.' The doctor looked from Margot to the nurse who, Margot thought, was about to shop her. 'All right! I do occasionally have a bad dream, but they're getting less, honestly.'

After what seemed like an age the doctor inhaled, then blew out his cheeks. 'You win! But,' he said, handing the notes back to the nurse, 'there is a condition.' Margot clicked her tongue and looked at the ceiling. 'You can go home if you promise to come back if the dreams persist?'

'Cross my heart and hope to die,' Margot said.

'I'll see that she does,' Bill said. He turned to Margot. 'Got everything, love?'

'Yes.' She looked at the clock on the wall above her bed. 'It's almost six. If we don't go now, there'll be a dozen newspaper reporters outside.' Bill helped her to the wheelchair and settled her into it. 'Thank you for all you've done for me,' she said, offering her hand to the doctor, and taking in the nurse.

Smiling, he leaned forward and took Margot's hand in his. 'It has been a pleasure, Miss Dudley.' Then, standing up straight, he turned and said, 'We'll miss her, won't we, nurse?'

'That we will, doctor. It will be very dull around here without her.'

Tears pricked the back of Margot's eyes and she swallowed hard. The slightest show of kindness made her emotional. 'And don't forget,' the doctor said, 'plenty of rest. Your legs are beginning to heal. Your ankle will take longer, but in time, if you take care--'

In time? Margot wondered if in time she would be able to accept Nancy's death. And if in time the horror of that terrible day would stop playing out in her dreams. She wondered if the guilt that twisted and wrung the nerves in her stomach would ever lessen. She knew she couldn't have saved Nancy, but knowing didn't help-- Margot realised the doctor was still speaking. 'Sorry?'

'Try to get away for a week or two. Get out of London. Go to the country; fill your lungs with fresh air – it'll help you sleep.' Margot nodded. 'And when you return come and see me.'

'Thank you, I will.'

Bill shook the doctor's hand before picking up the suitcases and following the nurse as she pushed Margot out of the room and along the corridor.

Before leaving the hospital Margot put on dark glasses and a headscarf.

Bill opened a fire door leading to a side street at the back of the building and the nurse whisked Margot through it. The rubble-strewn road was empty except for Anton Goldman's black Rover. Anton jumped out and opened the back passenger door – and while Bill lifted Margot into the car, Anton put her bags in the boot.

As they turned onto Westminster Bridge, Margot saw several newspaper reporters standing outside the small café opposite. They had their hands clasped around tea and coffee cups, laughing and joking, but they were all facing the hospital's main entrance. Ready to drop everything and run across the road, Margot thought. Eyes fixed on the front of the hospital, they didn't notice the Rover cruise past.

Whitehall and Trafalgar Square were relatively traffic free and they made good time. On the Strand, however, a lorry offloading panes of glass outside the Prince Albert Theatre had caused a bottleneck in the traffic. As they waited for a break in the oncoming traffic, Margot heard Anton sigh. Bill looked out of the window on his side of the car and focused on the shops. He tried to engage Margot in conversation, but she wasn't listening.

As tears streamed down her face, Margot looked out of the nearside window. Except that the windows of the theatre had been boarded up there was no evidence of the bomb that killed--

Margot looked ahead and closed her eyes. Bill squeezed her hand, but said nothing.

Bill and Margot sat on the settee like bookends, Bill reading his newspapers and Margot her magazines. 'My leave ends on Sunday. It's back to the grind next week but…'

'Mmmm? But what?'

'But I don't want to leave you on your own. The cuts on your legs are almost healed, but your ankle is still--'

'A mess?' Margot leant forwards and pulled up the right leg of her slacks. 'I'm not sure I'd capture the heart of Rhett Butler showing him this ankle, but at least you can't see the bone now,' she laughed. 'So go back to work and don't worry,' she said, throwing a cushion at him. 'My ankle's healing.'

'But you're not sleeping.'

'I've done nothing but sleep!'

'No you haven't, Margot. I've woken up several times recently and you haven't been in bed.'

'So what?' Margot dropped her magazine on the occasional table with a sigh. 'It isn't going to make any difference to me sleeping at night if you're working in the day, is it? Or even if you do a few shifts on the ambulances?' Bill opened his mouth to protest. 'I'll be fine! I promise I won't slide down any banister unless you're at the bottom to catch me.'

'It isn't a laughing matter, Margot!'

'I know… Oh, come on, Bill.' Margot shuffled sideways until she was sitting right next to him. She smoothed the worry lines on his forehead with her thumb. 'Anyway, Monday's three days away.' She slowly pushed herself up and stood in front of him. 'Look! My ankle is almost better. It doesn't hurt half as much when I put my weight on it. I don't need the stick, but you keep telling me I've got to use it.'

'Yes, you have!'

'And I will! Bossy old…' she muttered.

'I heard that,' Bill said, picking up his newspaper.

'I know,' Margot said, sitting down and picking up her magazine. Giggling, she flicked through the pages until she found the article she'd been reading. A few minutes later, she laid it on her lap. 'You know, I wouldn't mind some time on my own without you fussing over me. So you can go back to work if you want to.'

'Are you trying to get rid of me?'

'Yes! Back to work with you, husband.'

Bill laughed. 'I'm not going back until I have to.'

'Good. We'll have what the toffs call a long weekend. You, me, and the box of chocolates GI Joe sent to the hospital. Where are they? You haven't eaten them, have you?' Seeing her husband wasn't sharing the joke, Margot said, 'Now what's the matter?'

'It isn't going to be just you and me.' Margot opened her mouth to protest. 'Let me finish,' Bill said, putting his forefinger to her lips. 'I'd like you to go home.'

'I am home.'

'To Foxden.'

Margot let her head fall backwards to rest on the settee. 'I don't want to go to Foxden. I want to stay here with you.'

'Just hear me out. I think it would do you good to get away from the bombs and the memories. The doctor said you need rest and fresh air and you'll get plenty of both at Foxden.'

'And our mam saying, "I told you so!"'

Bill helped Margot out of the cab at Euston, paid the driver and took the cases. With the aid of the walking stick, Margot made her way into the station and Bill followed. A newspaper vendor selling the *Daily Mail* was shouting, 'Margot Dudley has left hospital! Miss Dudley whisked away to secret hideaway.' Bill stopped to buy a paper.

'Miss Dudley? It is Margot Dudley, isn't it?' a young woman called, before walking in front of Margot and blocking her path.

Margot looked round for Bill.

'Miss Dudley, look this way, please?' There was a sudden flash, which made Margot jump. 'Would you like to say something to your fans?' a man shouted.

'Over here, Miss,' shouted a second man. 'How did you feel when you saw your friends dead in the street? Do you feel any remorse, or guilt, because you survived when Miss Jewel was killed?'

'Your friend told us that if she hadn't delayed you on the Strand, you would have been outside the theatre when the roof collapsed and you would have been killed too.'

'Do you have anything to say to the friend who saved your life?' the woman added.

'What friend? Who said that?' Margot's head was spinning. Another flash bulb went off, temporarily blinding her. 'Stop it!' she shouted. The newspaper reporters were circling her like vultures – shooting questions at her. She felt dizzy, nauseous, and her ankle was throbbing. 'Please!' she gasped, leaning heavily on her walking stick. 'Where's Bill? I can't breathe. Please, would you find my husband? Bill!'

'What the hell's going on?' Bill shouted. 'Get out of here,' he said, pushing one reporter and catching another on the chin. With a look of utter surprise the man staggered backwards and overbalanced, ending up on the floor. 'Can't you see my wife isn't well?' A woman reporter stepped over the man on the floor. She took a notebook from her pocket. 'For the record, Miss Dudley is going to spend some time on the coast with friends,' Bill lied. 'She would appreciate some privacy to grieve for her friends while she recovers from her injuries.'

The reporters stood back and let Margot and Bill pass. Someone shouted, 'Get well soon, Margot.'

Another called out, 'We look forward to your return, Miss Dudley.' And a third, 'We didn't mean to...'

Margot nodded that she understood they meant well. Bill put his arm round her shoulders protectively and they moved slowly through the crowd. 'Come on, darling. Let's get you to the train.'

Margot pulled up the collar on her coat and looked down, hoping no one would recognise her among the queues of people on the platform, but they did. First one and then another called, "Margot?" and "Hope you're feeling better soon." "Get well, Margot." Someone ran in front of her with a camera. Shortly afterwards there was a flash. Margot put her hand up to shield her eyes.

'Stop that!' Bill shouted. The man ran away, but another took his place.

'Miss Dudley?' he called. 'I'm from the *West London Gazette*. Could you say something to our readers, please?' There was another flash and Margot put her hand up again.

Bill let go of Margot's arm and stepped between her and the reporter, snatching the camera from him. 'If you want this damn thing back, you'll find it in lost property.'

The photographer began to protest, but the crowd of onlookers clapped and cheered.

Margot turned to Bill, touched by the crowd's obvious love for her, and said, 'It's all right, Bill, let him take a picture.'

Bill returned the camera to the reporter and while Margot smiled at the sympathetic faces in the crowd, he took his photograph. 'Thank you, Miss Dudley.'

Bill took her by the arm again and, walking as fast as she was able, Margot smiled and thanked people as they moved to make way for her and Bill to cross the platform. Her ankle was not only throbbing, it had swollen to twice its original size. But with Bill on one side of her and the platform attendant now on the other, she mounted the steps of the train. 'Can you manage?' Bill asked. Margot stood to one side and let him pass. Then she shook the hand of the platform attendant and waved goodbye to the crowd, who were shouting get well wishes.

Margot hobbled into the first class compartment and fell onto the seat, while Bill shut the door and pulled down the blind.

'Damn parasites!' he fumed, lifting Margot's cases onto the overhead rack. 'We could have missed the train because of those damn reporters.'

'You can't blame them,' Margot said. 'They were only doing their job. A few weeks ago I'd have been grateful for the attention, courted it even. I'd have stood and posed for ten minutes if they'd asked me.'

'That may be true, but today they could see you weren't well.'

As the train pulled out of the station Margot glanced out of the window. A piece of white material – paper or fabric, she couldn't tell – had been swept up by the wind and was stuck among the branches of an ash tree. It flapped as if it was waving goodbye. Below, in a small park that had been turned into allotments, children dressed in thick coats and wearing woollen scarves and matching mittens played happily among runner bean canes and rows of cabbages while their fathers tended the earth. Margot turned away and looked at Bill. He was sitting opposite, asleep. His head lolled to the left, in anticipation of a pillow.

Watching him sleep brought it home to Margot just how hard the last few months had been on Bill. There seemed to be more and more trips to Bletchley and Hastings. The blitzing of the East End had been relentless, which meant he and his ambulance crew worked later, sometimes into the early hours of the morning. And however hard she tried she wasn't able to get over the deaths of Nancy and Bert, which she knew worried Bill. He also worried about the physical pain she was in, her mental state, and the fact that she wasn't sleeping at night. Poor Bill.

Margot rose and hobbled over to sit beside him. She put her arm through his and snuggled up. The next time his head lolled to the left he didn't jerk it back, but left it to rest on her shoulder. He smiled contentedly and Margot, while her husband slept, looked out of the window again. She watched as the train sped past woods and fields, towns and villages. Eventually her eyes grew heavy and she closed them, drifting into a shallow, fitful sleep.

Balancing on a tightrope, she poked her head through a knife-thin gap in the stage curtains and looked into the auditorium. She strained to see who was in the audience, but the fog was too thick. She stepped back, but the curtains were made of cobwebs and stuck to her, tightening around her neck. In a frenzy she clawed at them, tore them from her. Free at last, she watched them rise high in the air, but suddenly they swooped down even thicker. Margot ducked. She batted them away with a beautiful silver hand-mirror. The cobwebs wound themselves around the looking glass until she could no longer see her reflection. She held the mirror with bleeding hands. The cobwebs held it too. She mustn't lose or break the mirror; it belonged to her sister Bess. Granny gave it her when she passed the eleven plus. Bending down until she was level with the cobweb, she looked into its glazed and staring eyes. Then, mustering all her strength, she gave the mirror a final tug. 'No!' she screamed. It slipped through her bloody fingers and flew through the air. In slow motion she watched the mirror fall from the Juliet balcony. It landed in the alley opposite the theatre and shattered into a thousand pieces.

'Goldie? What are you doing here?' Margot said. 'He's still following you. You've got to get away from him.' The fog was getting thicker, choking her. 'There's Nancy. Nancy?' She began to run, but the nearer she got to Nancy the further away she seemed to be. 'Stop!' she shouted. 'Can't you hear the footsteps?' Margot stopped and the footsteps stopped. She looked over her shoulder. The fog was curling, beckoning her, and getting thicker. At least if she couldn't see Nazi Dave he couldn't see her. Happier now, she turned for home. Home? Where is home? She was lost again.

'Go back the way you came, Margot.'

She looked round. 'Who said that? Shush,' she whispered.

'Can't you hear the footsteps? Well, can't you? Run, Margot! Run! "Run rabbit, run rabbit, run, run, run." You must get away from the footsteps.'

'I can't, I'm frightened of the shadows and cobwebs.' Crouching, Margot looked up into a shimmering light. 'Nancy, you're safe,' she said with relief.

'Why didn't you help me, Margot? Why didn't you help me?'

'I didn't know you were in the taxi. It had gone six. I thought you were in the theatre.'

'I thought you were my friend.' Nancy's image began to fade.

'I am your friend, Nancy. Please don't go,' Margot

cried, but Nancy had turned into Bert.

'Run for your life Margot, the Nazi bugger is after you,' he shouted.

As she turned to run she saw Dave Sutherland. Eyes the colour of pitch, his fat mouth slobbering beneath his stupid moustache. She began to scream. She couldn't get away, the fog was thicker now. It wrapped itself around her like a filthy blanket and held her in its disgusting grip. 'Bill, I can't breathe,' she gasped. 'Help me, I've lost my shoe. Bill!' she screamed. 'Where are you?'

'I'm here, Margot. Sweetheart, it's all right, you're safe,' Bill said, 'you're safe.'

Clinging onto him, Margot opened her eyes. She looked around the compartment as if she was seeing it for the first time. 'Safe,' she whispered.

'Yes, my love, you're safe. It was only a dream. A bad dream, but you're safe now.' Bill held Margot tight and rocked her until she stopped crying.

CHAPTER FOURTEEN

In torrential rain, with the wind cutting across the platform, Margot's older sister Bess helped her from the train while her father helped his son-in-law with the suitcases.

'Welcome home, lad,' Thomas Dudley said, shaking Bill's hand. 'You look all in!'

'I'm all right, it's Margot who isn't well,' he said, looking at her through the sheeting rain. 'She looks so small in Bess's arms.'

'There's never been more than an ha'porth of meat on her. Don't worry son, she'll soon have some flesh on her bones, her mother'll see to that.' When Bill and Thomas Dudley caught up with the sisters, Margot turned to her father and broke down in tears.

'There, there, Margaret love.' Her father dropped the suitcase he'd been carrying and wrapped his arms around his sobbing daughter. 'You'll be home soon; home and safe. Come on, let's get you out of this rain.' Margot didn't argue. She let her father take her by the arm and steer her to the tunnel leading from the platform to the road. Protected between her father and her sister, she left the station, followed by her adoring husband.

'Your mother's looking forward to seeing you.'

'She'd have come,' Bess said, 'but there wasn't room in the car. She's made stew and dumplings.'

'Don't ask where she got the meat,' Thomas said, winking at Bill. 'There's enough to feed an army, so I hope you're hungry.'

'I haven't got much of an appetite, but I'm sure I'll manage something.'

Holding Bill's hand in the back of the car, Margot

gazed out of the window at the familiar landmarks: the churches, houses, and farms. The countryside was not so familiar. As far as the eye could see, land which only a few years ago had been pastures where sheep and cattle grazed had been ploughed. Inhabited now by scarecrows and haystacks, the lush green meadows that Margot remembered were furrows of brown soil.

Having driven though several small villages between Rugby and Lowarth, the River Swift and The Fox Inn public house came into view. 'Next stop Foxden,' Bess said, turning right onto the Woodcote Road. 'You won't recognise the estate, Margaret. I'll show you round as soon as your ankle's up to it. You'll love the land girls. They work really hard, but they have fun too. Mrs Hartley's looking forward to seeing you. Oh look, Margaret!' Bess shouted. 'Look out of Bill's window and you'll see the land girls working.'

Margot leaned across Bill. 'Good Lord. The meadow's gone. It's--'

'Hay. It's the last to be harvested. You should see the rest of the estate. It's all arable land.'

'Even the meadow where Mam used to send us to pick mushrooms?'

'Yes, it's potatoes now.' Bess laughed. 'If you're still here in November you can go up there and do some potato picking.'

'I don't think so,' Margot whispered into Bill's ear, before nibbling it.

'Shush,' he said, doing his best not to laugh.

She hadn't eaten properly for weeks but she didn't want to upset her mother, or cause an argument, so Margot made an effort. She ate a small bowl of stew and a slice of bread – and felt better for it. When they'd finished eating, Bess cleared the table with her mother and took the dishes into the kitchen.

'I'll take the cases up, Dad,' Bill said. 'Which room are we in?'

'The girls' room. Claire's been seconded to some sort of special RAF task force because of her languages. She'll not be home on leave while Margaret's here or she'd have let us know. And Ena's gone into Tom's room.' The creases on Thomas Dudley's forehead deepened. He looked worried. 'Tell you the truth we don't know where Claire is, and the last letter we had from Tom, he said he was going overseas.'

When Bill left the room, Margot put her feet up on the old settee in front of the fire, leant her head on the arm and stared into the flames. Her eyes filled with tears.

'Hey now,' her father said, 'what's all this?'

'I can't stop crying, Dad. I keep seeing Bert, the stage doorman, lying in the road. And then I look up and I see Nancy in the black cab. She looked as if she was awake, because her eyes--' Margot wiped away her tears. 'I keep wondering if she knew what was happening, if she felt anything. Bill said she wouldn't have, that she was killed outright, but how can he know?'

Thomas Dudley lifted his daughter's legs, sat down beside her, and put them on his lap. 'From what Bill told me, your friend--' Margot's father stopped speaking and cleared his throat. Then he nodded as if he had found the right words. 'The first piece of masonry that fell on the cab would have killed your friend. And because she couldn't have seen it falling, she wouldn't have known anything about it, Margaret.'

Margot looked up and searched her father's face.

Looking into his eyes, she held his gaze. His face was kind and honest. 'Thank you, Dad.' She knew her father wasn't just saying it to ease her pain. He was telling her the truth. Tears rolled down her cheeks. 'I'm tired now, Dad, but one day I'll tell you all about Nancy. You'd have loved her. Everybody loved Nancy,' she said, closing her eyes.

Thomas Dudley took a handkerchief from his pocket and dried Margot's face. 'Why don't you go up and have a lie down?' he whispered.

'What about Mam? What will she think if I'm not here when she and Bess come through?'

'She won't mind. I'll tell her you're tired. Do you want me to help you up the stairs?' Margot shook her head. 'You go up then,' he said, lifting her legs from his lap. 'I'll be here when you've had a rest. I've taken a couple of days off. We can go for some gentle walks. Strengthen your legs and put some apples back in those beautiful cheeks.' He helped her to her feet.

Margot limped across the room. At the door she turned, and with great almond-shaped tears in her eyes she said, 'Thank you, Dad.' Her father smiled, but Margot could see in his eyes that he was worried; that he was hurting because he couldn't take away her pain. Only time could do that. 'Thank you, Dad,' she said again, and left.

'I'm bored, Bess,' Margot said.

'Come up to the Hall, then. I'll give you so much work you'll never be bored again.' Margot didn't reply. 'What about it?'

'I don't know…. I'll see how I feel. Perhaps I'll come up later.'

'Right. I'm off.'

'Do you really have to go?' Margot whined. 'The

harvest's in. What else is there to do?' Bess, open mouthed, put her hands on her hips. Sensing her sister was losing patience, Margot said, 'Sorry. Stupid question.'

Bess came back into the room and sat next to Margot on the settee. 'It's been weeks now, Margot. Lying here day in day out, wallowing in self-pity, isn't going to bring your friend back and it won't make you feel any better about her dying either, believe me.' Bess waited for Margot to say something, but she didn't speak. 'I'm sorry, Margot, but somebody has to say it. There isn't anything Dad, me, Mam, or anyone else can say to make you feel better about losing your friends. But helping those who are worse off than you might help you to feel better about yourself.'

'You're right.' Margot lifted her head from the cushion and sat up.

Bess put her arm round her sister's shoulder and drew her near. 'You were very lucky, you know. If you'd have been five minutes earlier...' Bess shuddered. 'It doesn't bear thinking about. So, Miss Margot Dudley, remember how lucky you are and get on with your life. You only have one, get out there and live it!' Bess glanced at the window. 'Talking about getting out there, I'd better go, or it'll be too dark to do any work. Will you be all right?'

'Yes, you go.' Margot got up and followed Bess out of the room and along the hall to the front door, where she watched her put on her wellingtons.

'You know where I am if you change your mind,' Bess said, opening the door and stepping out.

A gust of cold air blew in and Margot shivered. 'Thanks, but I think I'll stay in the warm,' she said, and she closed the door.

In the living room, Margot knelt on the armchair

under the window and stared into the rain. It was only three o'clock in the afternoon, but the sky was bulging with charcoal-grey storm clouds. It was so dark it could have been six, or even seven in the evening. Margot turned her back on the window. It was gloomy outside. It matched her mood. She threw herself onto the settee and read again the letter she'd received from George that morning.

'Still here, Margaret?'

Margot jumped. She quickly put the letter back in her pocket. 'My name is Margot now, Dad.'

'You'll always be Margaret to me. Margaret, after young Princess Margaret Rose, same as Bess after Princess Elizabeth.'

'Hang on! I'm not allowed to be called anything other than Margaret according to you, but Bess has always been called Bess, even though she was christened Elizabeth. That isn't fair.' Margot thought for a moment. 'You old fibber,' she said to her father. 'Bess and I weren't named after Princess Elizabeth and Princess Margaret, they were born after us.'

'Well I'll be blowed.' Margot's father scratched his head. 'The King must have named his daughters after you and your sister, then.' Thomas Dudley laughed. 'All right, I give in. Have it your own way, *Margot*, you usually do.'

'Thanks Dad. You may not be royalty, but you'll always be a prince to me – plus you're the best dad in the world.'

'So long as I keep letting you have your own way.' Margot's father kissed her on the top of her head. 'But don't expect your mother to call you Margot.' He walked across to the kitchen and put his head round the door. 'Where is she?'

'No idea!'

'Right, I'm off to the Hall to help Mr Porter clear out the old foaling stables. We're going to turn them into a winter feed store for the livestock. It's too wet to cart any more bales across the Acres to the store barn – besides, it's almost full.'

'Aren't you supposed to be at the foundry today?'

'I asked for a couple of extra days. With all this rain, Bess needs help up at Foxden. Why don't you come up with me? See Mrs Hartley. The land girls have their tea about now. Come and say hello.'

Margot thought for a second. 'All right! If you can't beat 'em, join 'em.'

Her father shook his head. 'You've lost me.'

'It's between me and our Bess. Don't ask!'

At the front door, Margot put on a small pillbox hat the colour of autumn leaves. She looked in the hall mirror and tilted her head this way and that until she was satisfied with the angle. Reaching up, she took her cream-coloured coat with red fox fur collar and matching trim from the coat hook. After giving it a shake, she swung it round as if it were a matador's cape. 'Perfect,' she said, as the coat fell onto her shoulders. After sliding her arms down the sleeves, she reached for the door handle. 'Are you coming, Dad, or what? If we don't go now it'll be too dark to do anything,' she winked.

Thomas Dudley stood open-mouthed. 'You can't go up to the Hall in those shoes, Margot. You won't get as far as the gate before those high heels--'

'Kitten heels,' she said. 'Aren't they lovely? They came from Paris.'

'Never mind what they're called, or where they came from. They'll get stuck in the mud and break off, and then they won't be any kind of heel. And what about your ankle? It's only just got better. One twist and you'll be back where you were three weeks ago. Where's your common sense, child?'

'Left it in London, I shouldn't wonder,' Margot's mother said, striding through the gate. 'Wait a minute and you can have my wellingtons. And when you see Bess, ask her to lend you some. She's got half a dozen pairs up at the Hall. She's bound to have some your size.'

Newspaper carpeted the front hall floor. Standing on it, Margot's mother kicked off her wellingtons. 'I'll leave this paper down, so as you don't get mud on my clean lino when you come home. And don't forget to bring my wellies back,' she said, sliding her feet into her old slippers before disappearing down the hall to the living room.

'Thanks, Mam.' Margot took off her shoes and put on her mother's wellingtons. They were cold and caked in mud – and so were the centre pages of the *Lowarth Advertiser*.

Trudging along behind her father in footwear that was too big for her, holding her shoes by their heels in one hand and her handbag in the other, Margot wondered which was worse for her ankle – wellingtons that were two sizes too big, or shoes with heels. Not much in it, she decided.

'You're quiet,' her father said, when she caught up with him.

'I was thinking.'

'About the letter you were reading earlier?'

Margot laughed. 'No flies on you, Dad. Yes, it was from my friend George Derby-Bloom. She and my friend Betsy Evans are going to try to get into ENSA.' Margot paused to pluck up the courage to tell her father that they wanted her to go with them. They walked on for a few minutes without speaking. Then

Margot laughed. 'George wants me to join them. Betsy said we should call ourselves the Albert Sisters, after the theatre. We'd be touring air force and army bases, singing songs mostly, to cheer the lads up. We'd probably do the odd comedy sketch...' She realised she was rambling and stopped talking. 'Dad?' She put out her hand and caught her father's arm. He stopped walking. 'Tell me what you think?'

'It doesn't matter what I think, Margot. What matters is whether you are ready to go back.'

'I think I am. I hope I am.'

'Thinking and hoping doesn't make it so, love.'

Margot looked up at her father. 'Is that right?'

They both laughed. 'Well in your case, it probably does. You're a headstrong girl, Margot Dudley. All you girls are.'

They walked on for a few minutes, and then her father said. 'Is it what you want, Margot? To go back to the theatre?'

'Yes it is. I'm just not sure I can do it any more. I suppose if I spend some time with the girls, working with ENSA, I'll find out.'

'What does Bill think?'

Margot didn't answer until she felt her father's step begin to slow. 'He doesn't know. I'm due to ring him tomorrow. I'll tell him then. I don't suppose he'll like it. He'll think it's too soon, like you do.' Her father gave her a sidewise glance and tilted his head, as if to say he didn't know whether or not it was too soon. 'But I'm better. I'm eating well, sleeping through the night, and I haven't had a nightmare for weeks. My only worry is whether I can still do it.'

'Why don't you ask your friends to come up here? You could put on a show for the lads at the Hall, as a practice for ENSA, and then you'll know.'

'That's a brilliant idea, Dad. You clever old stick,' Margot said, tugging on her father's arm. When he turned she kissed him. 'I'll telephone George in the morning and invite them up. And if all goes well, I'll go back to London with them.'

'You'd better telephone your husband first and tell him your plans,' her father said, shaking his head.

Bill felt so strongly that it was too soon for Margot to go back to work that despite his crippling workload he asked for leave. His boss, aware that Margot had been hospitalised after being injured in a bombing raid, granted him twenty-fours. He left for Foxden immediately.

When she heard Bill's motorbike, Margot ran out to meet him. 'Hello, you've made good time,' she said, throwing her arms around him.

Leading him to the door, Margot shouted, 'Bill's here! Mam and Dad are dying to see you. Mam's put some food up, so I hope you're hungry. Dad'll be back soon. You can stay till he gets home? He'd be sorry if he missed you.' Margot took Bill's jacket and hung it up. 'I've got lots to tell you,' she said, 'but come into the living room and have something to eat first.'

'Margot, stop! We need to discuss this ENSA thing,' Bill said, closing the front door. 'Stop trying to bamboozle me with lots of chatter.'

Margot bit her bottom lip. 'Sorry, it's just that this is important to me.'

'It always is!' he said.

Margot's mother opened the living room door. 'Come in, lad, it's draughty out there. You must be starving,' she said. 'Margaret, get Bill's plate from the larder.' Margot did as she was told, relieved that, for

199

the time being at least, the discussion about ENSA had been postponed.

'You're not strong enough, Margot. Look at you. You need to put some weight on before you even think about going back to the stage. And sleep? Are you sleeping?'

'Yes. And I haven't had a nightmare for months.'

'You haven't been here for months, Margot.'

'Weeks then!' She clicked her tongue. 'I'm better, Bill, physically and mentally, really I am. I've enjoyed it up here, but I want to come home. I want to be with you,' she pouted.

'You won't be with me if you're touring aerodromes and army camps with ENSA.'

Margot plonked herself down on the settee and, with a face like thunder, glared into the fire.

Bill sat next to her. 'So,' he said with a sigh, 'what's the plan?'

'We're going to see Basil Dean. See if we can support some of the acts,' she said without emotion. 'We don't want to steal anyone's thunder; we just want to keep our hand in until the theatre reopens. Please say you understand, Bill?' she pleaded.

Bill shook his head. 'You'll do what you want, Margot, you always do. I'm going for a walk to clear my head.'

'What did Bill say?' Margot's mother asked from the doorway, seconds after he'd left.

'You know what he said.' Margot glared at her mother who stood red faced. 'Sorry, that wasn't fair. He doesn't want me to join ENSA, he thinks it's too soon.'

CHAPTER FIFTEEN

Margot watched as Bess pulled a Fair Isle jersey over her head. Then, looking in the mirror above the fireplace in the sitting room, she brushed her hair. Holding her thick auburn curls in the nape of her neck with one hand, and a ribbon in the other, she chopped and changed hands until she had tied the ribbon securely. Then she folded a headscarf corner to corner, and after floating the floral triangle over her head, tied it under her chin.

'How do you do it, Bess?'

'Do what?'

'Hold it all together?' Looking at her sister's reflection in the mirror, Margot saw a combination of strength and sadness in her eyes. She didn't reply. Instead she busied herself by tucking stray curls under her scarf. 'You work on the estate, organise the land girls, keep the farmers happy – and if you're lucky you get an hour to yourself to exercise your horse. And what about the servicemen up at the Hall, and James...'

'The servicemen are not my responsibility. As for James, I promised him I would look after his estate, and that is what I'm doing. I also made a commitment to the Ministry of Agriculture to turn Foxden Estate into arable land, and that is what I've done. And I shall keep doing it until this damn war is over.' Bess turned and walked across the room to the hall door. 'I keep busy, Margot,' she said pointedly. 'And talking of keeping busy--'

'Which I wasn't,' Margot said.

Bess wiped a tear from her cheek and at the same time laughed at her sister. 'Why don't you come up to the Hall with me? Meet the boys in the hospital wing? They know my sister, the famous Margot Dudley, is here and they keep asking me when you're coming up.' Wrinkling her nose, Margot bit her bottom lip. 'I know you don't like hospitals,' Bess said, 'but the lads aren't ill. They're at Foxden to convalesce. Most of them don't even need medical treatment. They're recovering from pneumonia or shell shock. A couple have lost limbs, and our old friend Frank Donnelly has lost an eye, but there's nothing unpleasant to see. And they're all in good spirits.'

'Right.' Margot said. 'I'm coming up!'

'Atta girl! I'll wait for you.'

'No. I need to do my hair and put on some decent clothes if I'm going to meet my public,' she said, laughing. 'I can't have the friends of my clever sister seeing me like this, can I?'

Margot popped in to see Foxden's housekeeper and cook, Mrs Hartley, and swapped her wellingtons for shoes. While she was there she checked her appearance in the mirror hanging in Mrs Hartley's washroom. Dark rings under her eyes made her look tired. She felt a hundred years old. Fishing in her handbag she found her make-up. After patting rouge on her cheeks and applying red lipstick she looked and felt much better.

It was raining when she left the kitchen, so she kept her head down and walked quickly. She hadn't worn shoes with heels for what seemed like an age. Every time she put her foot to the ground a sharp pain stabbed at her ankle, so she slowed down and walked more carefully. After mounting the steps to Foxden Hall's main entrance, she leant against a pillar to steady her nerves. Could she do this; could she put on a smile and be Margot Dudley?

'Hello?'

'Ah!' She spun round. 'I didn't see you there.'

'Sorry.' A young soldier stepped from behind the pillar. He threw down his cigarette and put his hands up. 'I'm Sid,' he said. 'Bess told me to come and find you.'

'Margot! How do you do?'

Sid opened the door and stood back to let Margot enter. She followed him across the marble hall. Except for the floor to ceiling blackout curtains, it looked pretty much the same as it had the last time she was there, before the war. Sid opened the door to the ballroom and ushered her in. As soon as they caught sight of her, the boys began to whistle and cheer. She was amazed to see so many soldiers, sailors and airmen. Some were in beds along the walls, others were in armchairs in the bay windows – and they were all clapping and smiling. She took a few steps into the room and they cheered again. She laughed, put her hands up as if in a prayer and mouthed, 'Thank you.' One of the boys approached her on crutches. 'I play the piano, Miss Dudley. Would you sing for us?'

Margot turned too quickly and went over on her already painful ankle. The boy's request had taken her by surprise. Her stomach lurched. She was out of practice. She didn't know whether she could do it. She looked around the room and found Bess. 'I want to meet you all first.'

'Over here, Miss Dudley,' several of the lads shouted at the same time. 'No, over here.' Margot waved to the lads on the left side of the room as she walked over to Bess on the right. 'We'll start at the beginning,' Bess said, steering Margot to the first bed inside the door, where she received more applause.

Margot shook the hands of the soldiers and answered their questions; questions that she had been asked a hundred times before.... 'What is it like being famous? How can you live in a place like London? Aren't you scared you'll be bombed in your bed? Do you drink champagne every night? What does your husband think about you singing and dancing in a West End show? Is he jealous because you're a pin up?'

Margot burst out laughing. 'Me? A pin up? I've never been a pin up. Betty Grable's a--' She stopped mid-sentence as two lads unrolled a poster of her in a skimpy two-piece swimming costume. 'Good Lord, I am a pin up!' she laughed. 'Did you ever think the scrawny little sister that you gave your pocket money to so she could have dance lessons at Woodcote village hall would one day be a pin up, Bess?'

Laughing, Bess said, 'If I'd have thought about it at the time, I probably would. There wasn't anything you couldn't do when you put your mind to it, Margot.'

Margot was gracious and honest, and answered all the servicemen's questions. She stood at the side of every bed and talked to every patient. She then went over to the bay window and sat and chatted to the lads who were further along in their recovery.

'Sid will play for you, Margot, if you'll sing for the boys.'

Margot stuttered, 'I, I don't know Bess. I haven't-- since Nancy--'

'All the more reason to sing now, I'd have thought, while you're among friends.' Bess paused and then said, 'You're a professional, Margot, so what about it?' She walked away and then turned back to her sister. 'I'm sorry, Margot, that was unfair. You must do what's best for you. If you don't want to sing the boys will be disappointed, but they'll understand. I think it would do you good. But what do I know? Perhaps you've lost it.'

'Lost it? Of course I haven't lost it!'

'I didn't mean lost it, exactly. But you do hear about people who have gone through a traumatic experience losing their voice.'

'I'm not people, Bess! I'm Margot Dudley. I may not be anyone important to you, but I am to my fans. And if I can please these boys, these poor boys, I will!'

Bess put her arms round her sister. 'I love you, Margot Dudley. You may be a West End star, but you'll always be my contrary little sister.'

'And you'll always be my clever big sister who knows me far too well. I can't get away with anything around you, our Bess!'

'No you can't! Besides, I want to hear you sing as much as they do. You'd like to hear Margot sing, wouldn't you lads?'

Everyone cheered and Margot put her hands up, which made them cheer even louder. Eventually, when they were quiet, Margot said, in a loud and uplifting voice, 'Right boys, what do you want to hear?'

So many song titles were called out at the same time that Bess stepped in. 'Since none of you can agree, Margot will decide on the song, and Sid will play it.' That seemed to satisfy them. After a couple of able-bodied servicemen pushed the piano into the middle of the room so everyone could see Margot, she sang "The Boogie Woogie Blues".

Sid could hardly keep up with her. As soon as she finished one song the boys called for another. Halfway through the evening a young soldier sang

"Kiss Me Goodnight Sergeant Major" to give Margot a break. After a cup of tea Margot gargled with port and went back to the ballroom. She began the second part of the evening with "The Lambeth Walk" from the West End musical *Me and My Girl*, which the lads sang with her, followed by "I'll See You Again" from Noel Coward's *Bitter Sweet*. Physically tired, but with adrenalin pumping through her veins as it had the first time she sang at the Prince Albert Club, Margot took her final bow. It was ten o'clock. She promised to return the following evening.

The next morning she telephoned Natalie Goldman from Woodcote post office. Natalie was well and eager for news of her three children, whom Bess had taken to Foxden as evacuees. Margot wanted news of the Prince Albert Theatre and asked how her friends in the company and backstage were faring. They were all well and wanted to get back to work. Anton was at the theatre, overseeing the building work that everyone thought would be completed before Christmas. However, after the recent bombing of the Aldwych and Fleet Street, London's builders were stretched to the limit. Demolishing unsafe buildings and making safe public buildings took priority over repairing theatres. Recent delays meant the refurbishment of the Prince Albert Theatre would not be completed in time for the advertised Christmas Show. It was more likely to be early 1943 before the Prince Albert's doors opened again.

Margot asked the exchange to connect her to another London telephone number, and a few minutes later she was speaking to her friends and fellow dancers, George and Betsy.

*

That evening, Margot told the servicemen that she would soon be returning to London. 'After my friends were killed and I'd spent what felt like an age in hospital, I didn't want to go back to the theatre. The truth was I didn't know whether I could still do it. Losing my friend Nancy, the leading lady at the Prince Albert and my mentor, was too much to bear. But,' she said, looking at each of the servicemen in turn, 'you have inspired me with your bravery and strength of character. I was going to give up everything I had worked for, but not any more. You are all determined to get on with your lives. Well, thanks to you, I am going back to London to get on with mine.'

Cheers and humorous complaints drowned Margot's words. 'And,' she said when the racket had died down, 'along with two of my friends from the theatre, I am going to join ENSA. And,' Margot put her arms around Bess and stopped talking until the lads stopped whooping and whistling, 'it is thanks to my sister Bess that I am able to sing again. So,' Margot put her finger to her lips and the room quietened. '"Thanks for the memory…"' As she sang the servicemen joined in.

When they'd finished someone shouted, 'If ENSA stands for every night's something awful, will you come back to us, Margot?'

'No!' she said, laughing, 'Not if you're going to be rude. We, the Albert Sisters, will be touring aerodromes, army bases, and factories, starting on Friday at the Foundry in Lowarth. And on Saturday night there is going to be a special concert here at Foxden Hall. Thank you!' She left the hospital wing to the sound of cheers and calls for more, followed by a rendition of "For She's A Jolly Good Fellow".

*

Forgetting her ankle, Margot ran across the platform as Betsy leapt from the train. Hugging each other, the two friends squealed with delight. George waved briefly from the train's open door before calling the porter to help her haul two large suitcases from the corridor onto the platform.

'Costumes!' George shouted, abandoning the cases when they were safely off the train, and joining Betsy and Margot.

When they had finished greeting each other, Margot remembered Bess was with her. 'Sorry,' she said. 'This is my sister Bess. Bess, meet George Derby-Bloom and Betsy Evans, my best friends from the theatre.'

'How do you do, Bess?' George said.

'Lovely to meet you,' Betsy added.

Before Bess could reply, George said, 'And this is Artie.'

Putting the two black cases he was carrying on the ground, he shook Bess's hand. 'Artie Armitage, at your disposal.'

Margot's mouth fell open at the sight of the Prince Albert Theatre's night watchman. 'Arthur – I mean Artie. How nice to see you. I didn't recognise you out of uniform.' Artie held the lapels of his coat and waddled like Charlie Chaplin. They all laughed. Margot looked at George, her eyes wide and questioning.

'Our pianist,' George said.

Margot shook Artie's hand and looked at the case at his feet. 'Small piano.'

'Don't be absurd, darling, that's Artie's accordion. The other is his banjo.'

'Of course. Silly me!'

'Before the war Artie was a piano tuner and teacher. So, being too old for the services – sorry darling,' George said, 'when the children were evacuated and the upper classes stopped spending money having their pianos tuned, Artie came to work at the Prince Albert. Working as a night watchman gave him time to practise his music during the day.'

'You weren't the only one watching the shows from the wings, Miss,' he said to Margot. 'I was there too, on the other side of the stage.'

'And we're jolly pleased you were, darling.' George turned her attention to Margot. 'So my dear, Artie plays accordion and banjo, and he tickles the ivories superbly. He knows every number from the show and all the popular songs. Isn't he wonderful?'

Margot nodded. 'Yes, except we don't have a piano. There's a grand at the Hall, but Lady Foxden would never agree to it leaving the estate. We can use it for the show we do for the lads in the hospital wing, but our first public performance is in a factory in Lowarth – and we need to rehearse.'

'The village hall at Woodcote has a piano,' Bess said.

Margot threw her arms around her sister and kissed her. 'Bess, you're a genius! Why didn't I think of that?'

George, Betsy and Artie looked from Margot to Bess. 'Woodcote is just down the road from Foxden. I'm sure you'll be able to use the piano. I might even know someone who will transport it to Lowarth for you. Especially if it's professionally tuned after you've done with it,' she said, winking at Artie. 'Apart from Home Guard meetings, the hall's rarely used. I'll check with my father, see if it's free for a couple of days. If it is you've got a rehearsal room.' Bess looked at her wristwatch. 'We'd better make a move.'

George picked up the larger of the two cases as Bess picked up the other.

'How are we going to fit everything into your car?' Betsy asked.

'I thought we'd put my sister on the roof,' Bess said.

Margot rolled her eyes. 'Very funny! Mr Porter, who works with Bess on the estate, is here with the farm truck.'

'I didn't know how much luggage you'd have, so I thought it best to bring back-up.'

'My sister thinks of everything.'

'Not quite everything. I didn't think about sleeping arrangements for Artie.'

'You didn't know about Artie. *I* didn't know about Artie.'

'That's true!'

On the way to Foxden, George told Margot how her father had written to Basil Dean, the director of ENSA, at the Drury Lane theatre. 'He's seeing people on Tuesday,' she said.

'Tuesday? Next Tuesday?' Margot said.

'Yes, but if you think it's too soon. If your ankle's still--'

'No! No, my ankle's fine.' Margot's voice cracked and she cleared her throat. Her eyes felt moist and there was a stinging sensation at the back of them, but there were no tears.

'This is it, ladies,' Bess said, pulling into the cobbled quadrangle at Foxden Hall behind Mr Porter and Artie. 'I expect you're hungry,' she said, jumping out of the car. Mr Porter took the cases from the back of the truck and carried them into Mrs Hartley's kitchen. Bess and the London visitors followed.

'Come in, come in,' Foxden's cook and housekeeper said, ambling across the large kitchen. 'Kettle's on, so if you want to take your cases upstairs, Margot will show you where your rooms are. Oh, and the Goldman children have been in and out of here all day. They're so excited about seeing you. 'Course they're too polite to say, but I think they're hoping you've got presents for them.'

'We have!' Betsy said. 'Where are they?'

'Doing sums and such like in the old nursery with their nanny and nurse. Margot will show you where to go, won't you my duck?' Margot nodded and took one of Betsy's bags. 'I'll have tea on the table by the time you come down.'

Foxden's guests picked up their belongings and followed Margot, while Bess and Mr Porter headed for the door. 'I'm going to the stables to check on the horses,' Bess said. 'Won't be long.' Mr Porter, nearest to the door, opened it and was almost knocked over as the land girls piled in.

By the time they returned to the kitchen the land girls and the Londoners were seated round the big wooden table drinking tea and eating muffins.

'I see introductions aren't needed,' Bess said to Margot, who was watching Mrs Hartley test the dumplings in the stew.

'Can't get a word in edgeways,' Margot said.

'First time for everything,' Bess laughed.

'Go on you two, scoot!' Mrs Hartley said, pouring two cups of tea. 'Go and join your friends while I refresh the pot. You sit yourself down, Mr Porter, and I'll bring your tea over.'

'Right-ho,' he said, lowering himself into one of two rocking chairs at the side of the fire.

Tea was loud and lots of fun. Kitty Woodcock, a cockney sparrow from the East End of London, kept them laughing with stories about her mum and the pub she worked in. Margot asked her if she'd heard from her mother lately and Kitty said she had. Looking relieved, George, who had been talking to a land girl named Sylvia, smiled across the table at Margot. Like Margot, she knew how dangerous it was for anyone living in the East End. One or another borough was blitzed every night.

After tea, while a couple of the land girls helped Mrs Hartley with the pots, the others took their London friends upstairs and helped them hang up the costumes. The weight of the clothes would pull any creases out overnight, they decided, but the ironing board had been put up in Mrs Hartley's scullery in case it was needed.

During supper, sitting around Mrs Hartley's kitchen table, they discussed the songs they could sing. One of the land girls tuned the wireless into the BBC Home Service, saying it would give them inspiration, while another found a sheet of paper and a pencil to make a list. The type of songs being sung in munitions and engineering factories were uplifting songs; songs that the BBC called "songs to work by". "Roll Out The Barrel" was a good one. And "We're Going To Hang Out The Washing On The Siegfried Line" was another. Both were put on the list.

'I heard a new song by Glen Miller and his Orchestra, with Ray Eberle and the Modernaires, on the wireless the other day. Aren't they just swoony?' Betsy said, and she launched into "Don't Sit Under the Apple Tree with Anyone Else But Me". Everyone joined in and it was added to the list.

'A song we must sing at the Foundry is "Sing As We Go",' Margot said.

'Yes!' Betsy said. 'But who's going to sing the opening lines?' Betsy launched into her Gracie Fields impression.

'Not you, darling, that's for sure. Our Gracie is from Lancashire, not Llanglovey.'

Everyone laughed again and Betsy made a show of pretending to be disappointed.

'What about you, George?' Margot said.

'Me?' George guffawed. 'With my accent, darling, the northern charm of Gracie Fields' opening lines would be annihilated. No,' George looked at Margot. 'Leicestershire is a damn sight nearer to Lancashire than Surrey. Besides, you're a better actress than me.'

After supper, Artie went out for a smoke with Mr Porter while the girls, still laughing and singing, trooped upstairs to sort out costumes for the Foundry and Rover engineering factory, and the night at Foxden. Natalie had loaned them some amazing outfits from the theatre's costume store. Most of them they had worn before, so alterations weren't needed, and the shoes fitted perfectly.

After a fashion parade to decide which costumes would be worn at which concerts, the newly formed 'Albert Sisters' went downstairs to Mrs Hartley's kitchen and practised songs with Artie on accordion and the land girls joining in as the orchestra. More laughing was done than rehearsing, which was just what Margot needed.

The village hall was freezing and the air musty with damp. Margot shivered. A fire had been laid in the small fireplace, in preparation for the next Home Guard meeting. Grinning, Artie took a box of Swan Vesta from his pocket and struck a match. Margot raised her eyebrows and looked the other way as he lit a rolled up newspaper under a handful of sticks and a couple of logs. 'Got to have heat to dry the keys,' Artie said, on his hands and knees, blowing the damp paper until it caught. Once the fire had taken hold the girls helped him to move the piano nearer. According to him, the Joanna needed air and heat. The Albert Sisters sat around the fire, coats buttoned up to their chins, while they went over the lyrics of the songs they were going to sing. By late morning the songs and routines, and the order in which they were going to be performed, had been decided. And the piano, whilst it wasn't yet in tune, sounded better.

'I think you ladies should take a break,' Artie said, gently pressing the piano keys. 'Go across to the pub and have a sandwich or something, and I'll fetch you when I've tuned the old girl.' The three women took no persuading and left for the Crown.

Sitting in front of the pub's roaring fire, George with a tankard of beer and Margot and Betsy with glasses of sherry, they began to thaw out. George put her feet up and rested them on the corner of the inglenook. 'This is the life. I could get used to this,' she said, relaxing back in a big old armchair.

'Too quiet for me,' Betsy said. 'Reminds me of the village I was brought up in in Wales. Give me London every time.'

George closed her eyes. 'I feel like Lord what's-his-name sitting in this chair.' She tapped the padded arm. 'It's like a throne.' Lifting her tankard she took a long drink. 'I'm surprised he asked a woman to run the estate,' she said thoughtfully. 'Must be a forward thinker.'

'Lord Foxden's always thought a lot of our Bess, but it wasn't him who asked her, it was his son, James. Bess was a teacher in London and when the children at her school were evacuated James asked her to come back to Foxden and turn the estate into arable land.'

'Crikey,' Betsy said. 'That's a hell of a lot of work.'

'And responsibility,' George added.

'Talking of responsibility,' Margot said, 'shouldn't we be getting back to Artie?'

In a slightly warmer rehearsal hall with an almost perfectly tuned piano, the Alberts rehearsed the song they were going to open with at the factory the following day, which they decided would also be the best song to do for Basil Dean and ENSA next Tuesday. Once satisfied that "Don't Sit Under The Apple Tree" was the right song to perform they added the other songs. Each song and dance routine needed to be perfect, because after the initial song for ENSA, they didn't know which of their repertoire Basil Dean would ask them to perform next. There was no guarantee he'd ask them to perform another number, but if he did they wanted to be prepared.

By mid-afternoon the Albert Sisters had an audience. As people walked past the village hall and heard the music they stopped and came in – and with only a few hours to perfect their act they welcomed the feedback. After a final run-through, the audience of local ladies and customers from the Crown pub, who had wandered across the road at closing time, cheered and clapped for more.

The following day at twelve o'clock, the Albert Sisters performed their show in the canteen of the Lowarth Foundry where Margot's father worked and later, during an extended tea-break, at the Rover where Ena, Margot's younger sister worked. Both workforces sang along with the popular songs and some of the women danced. For the Albert Sisters it was a taste of what performing with ENSA would be like, if they got through the audition.

That evening Margot took George, Betsy and Artie up to the Hall to meet the men in the hospital wing. She took them round the room and introduced them, as Bess had introduced her earlier in the week. Exhausted after performing two shows that day, they made their excuses and left after an hour, promising to return the following night to entertain them. And true to their word, at eight o'clock the next night, dressed in WAAC, WAAF and WREN uniforms, Betsy, George and Margot marched into the hospital wing at Foxden Hall and stood to attention. Artie had arrived earlier and was seated at Foxden's grand piano. 'From the top!' he shouted in his best Sergeant Major's voice, whereupon the girls saluted before bursting into song with "Run Rabbit Run". During the evening they performed their entire repertoire to cheers and applause. Thanks to the men and women in the factories at Lowarth and the servicemen at Foxden Hall, the Albert Sisters were ready for ENSA.

The following morning, after a tearful farewell with her parents, Margot joined Bess and the land girls at Foxden Hall for breakfast. Artie, having brought the cases down some time before, had finished his breakfast and was on his second cup of tea. George arrived ten minutes later. She'd been to say goodbye to the Goldman children, who had given her letters and drawings that she'd promised to deliver to their parents in London. As Mrs Hartley heaped scrambled eggs onto Betsy's plate the land girls went off to work and Artie and Mr Porter took the cases out to the truck.

By the time Margot and the girls were ready to leave the drive was lined with servicemen. Some had walked down with the aid of sticks or crutches, some were sitting on top of the semi-circle of stone steps outside the Hall's main entrance in wheelchairs, and those who weren't mobile had their beds pushed in front of the ballroom's French windows.

Mr Porter waved to Margot, indicating that he and Artie were ready to leave. Having said goodbye to Mrs Hartley and the Goldman children – who had come out to wave them off – George and Betsy walked down the steps to the car, shaking hands and saying goodbye to the servicemen.

'Come on,' Bess said, linking her arm through Margot's, 'or you'll miss your train.'

As they began their descent a cheer went up and Margot waved. She shook hands with some of the lads wishing them good luck and to get well, and promising them that she would come back as soon as she was able. To those in the distance she waved and blew kisses.

'You've made a big difference to the lives of these lads,' Bess said.

'Not half as big a difference as they've made to mine.' Margot stopped for a moment to take in the scene. She looked back and waved to Mrs Hartley and the Goldman children – and she blew kisses to the servicemen looking out of the ballroom's windows.

As she lowered herself onto the passenger seat of the car, tears that had threatened all morning filled her eyes. She took a deep breath and smiled bravely. Following the farm truck along the drive, Bess reached over and squeezed Margot's hand. Margot wiped her tears and nodded that she was all right.

CHAPTER SIXTEEN

Stretching all the way down Catherine Street to Aldwych one way and back up to Drury Lane the other, the queue to the stage door of The Theatre Royal Drury Lane appeared endless. For what seemed like an age Margot, George, Betsy and Artie inched their way from one paving slab to the next behind jugglers, comics, belly dancers and other singers and dancers. After three hours they entered the theatre through the stage door. After another hour they were invited to sit on wooden benches in a backstage corridor.

Betsy wriggled, transferring her weight from side to side on the bench. 'My bum's sore. I never dreamt there'd be this many people trying to get an audition.'

'Me neither,' George agreed. 'But it shouldn't be long now, Bets.'

It was twenty-five minutes past six when a smartly dressed woman appeared from a door marked Private. 'Mr Dean will see one more act today.' She looked around. 'Miss Derby-Bloom?'

'I'm Derby-Bloom.' George jumped up, beckoning the others.

'That's it for today,' the woman said, turning to the disgruntled queue. 'Interviews will resume tomorrow at nine o'clock. The doors will open at eight.' Without waiting for a reply the woman turned, opened the door to Basil Dean's office and stood to the side.

Margot followed George into Dean's office with Betsy behind her and Artie bringing up the rear. Basil Dean, sucking on a pipe, sat behind a large desk. As he lifted his head to acknowledge them the telephone began to ring.

'I'll take it, Mr Dean,' his secretary said, leaving the office.

Basil Dean nodded, took off his glasses and rubbed his eyes. He looked tired. He was older than Margot thought he'd be. Or perhaps it was that he had a receding hairline. He wore a dark blue pinstripe suit and waistcoat over a white shirt and blue tie. He pulled at the collar of his shirt and loosened the tie. 'Good afternoon,' he said, picking up something Margot thought could be their letter of introduction. 'What can I do for you?' he asked, directing the question at Artie.

It was George who replied. 'We are part of the Prince Albert Theatre company. I'm sure you know the theatre was damaged some months ago and is being repaired. Anton Goldman had hoped to be up and running before Christmas. Unfortunately the work has been delayed, which has put the opening back until March or April of next year. So we would like to offer ENSA our services until the Prince Albert re-opens.'

'We can provide our own costumes and props,' Betsy said.

'And we have Anton Goldman's support,' Margot added.

Basil Dean picked up the letter again. 'Yes, Anton has been in touch. So has your father, Miss Derby-Bloom. He has made a substantial contribution to-- Most unusual, but I'm in no position to turn down such a generous offer. I wish we had more sponsors like him,' he said. 'Be in costume and ready to show me what you can do at three o'clock tomorrow.'

As if on cue, the door opened and Dean's secretary appeared. 'Thank you,' George said. But by then Basil Dean had his head down and was busy writing.

The theatre was buzzing with artists, both professional and amateur. Illusionists, jugglers, singers, dancers, comedians – it seemed everyone who had ever trod the boards was there. And the worst of it was, after each act had performed they went into the audience and watched the other acts.

When the Albert Sisters were called, Artie entered the stage first in top hat and tails. Walking over to the piano, he took a bow. He flicked the tails on his evening jacket and flexed his fingers several times. Everyone laughed when, instead of sitting down to play, he stood to attention. Then he shouted as loud as any sergeant-major: 'Please give a big welcome to the Prince Albert Theatre's conscripts, Misses WAAFY, WAACY and WREN.'

Margot marched in first dressed in a short WAAF costume and high heels, followed by Betsy and George in army and navy costumes.

'Halt!' Artie called, when they were level with him. Artie was the smallest of the Alberts so, leaning backwards as if it was an effort to look up at them, as well as accentuate the difference in their height, he shouted, 'About turn!' and the girls turned and faced the audience. 'At ease!'

As Artie played the opening bars to "Boogie Woogie Bugle Boy of Company B" the girls began to swing their hips. The song went well. Just before the end, Margot stepped forward and sang, 'In the army now!' George barked 'In the navy now!' and Betsy followed with 'RAF!'

When they had performed their three songs Artie stood up and shouted, 'Atteeeeeeeeention!' and the girls stood to attention. 'About turn!' They turned so their backs were to the audience. 'And... Left, right. Left, right.' Marching off, the girls looked over their right shoulders, saluted, and held the pose until they were in the wings. A second later Artie took his bow and marched off behind them.

Back stage the three women danced round Artie. Betsy shushed them. 'Listen! They're clapping.' She looked round the flats separating the stage area from the wings. Then, turning back, she said, 'Basil Dean's nodding and writing something in his note book.' She looked again. 'Now he's saying something to the bloke sitting next to him. Oh my God,' she said, 'it's Tommy Trinder! And he's smiling. They're both smiling.'

'I think the big man like us,' Artie said, mimicking Basil Dean. The girls huddled round him, hugging and kissing him – and purposely leaving red lipstick kisses on his cheeks.

'Where have you been, Margot?'

'The telephone box,' she said, going to the oven and taking out a small joint of brisket. Holding the roasting tray with an oven cloth, Margot carefully placed it in front of Bill before passing him the carving knife and fork. 'I phoned George to see if she'd heard anything. She hadn't, so I telephoned Basil Dean's office.'

Bill carved the joint, putting a couple of slices onto Margot's plate before putting the same onto his own. 'And?'

Margot shook her head. 'Dean wasn't there. I left my name and address again. It's been two weeks since we auditioned. Anyway, I'm going down to see George tomorrow.'

'All the way to her father's house in Essex?' Bill asked, concerned.

'Yes. Betsy's already there, she's lodging with them

and George is going to get in touch with Artie. We're meeting to discuss what we're going to do if ENSA don't want us.' Margot strained the vegetables. 'Apparently there's an independent theatre group starting up. George's dad is looking into it for us. Oh, and there's Stars in Uniforms. Not sure we fit the bill, but if all else fails...'

'Promise you'll leave before it gets dark, Margot? The train will be coming through the East End. The stations are always being targeted. And the raids are starting earlier.'

'Of course I will! But I have to go, Bill.' She spooned a couple of roast potatoes onto her plate and the rest onto Bill's before putting the oven dish on the draining board. After adding vegetables and gravy to both plates, Margot sat down to eat her Sunday lunch.

The following morning Margot caught the 11.45 train from Liverpool Street to Ongar, promising to catch the 3.20 back so Bill could meet her and take her home when he'd finished at the MoD. That way they could have an early supper together before he went to Tommy's.

For once – probably because it was to do with show business – Margot was as good as her word and arrived back as promised. She ran across the platform and out through the exit. Bill, sitting astride his motorbike, had seen her and was waving. Out of breath, she fell into his arms. 'We've got to think of something else to keep us together until the theatre re-opens.'

'You don't have to, Margot, I--'

'I know,' she said, stopping him from speaking further by kissing him. 'I know you'll look after me.' She kissed him again. 'And I'm going to let you. I'm going to stop trying to prove myself – and stop being so selfish. My poor Bill,' she said, looking into her husband's soft brown eyes. 'I didn't consider what you were going through when I was in hospital. All I could think about was Nancy and how *I* was going to miss her – and of course whether or not the hospital would be bombed. And when I got back from Foxden, all I could think about was how *I* wanted to join ENSA – and how George, Betsy and I could stay together. I've been so selfish! Am so selfish! I don't mean to be,' she cried. 'I do love you, Bill. Can you ever forgive me?'

Bill laughed. 'I know you do. And there's nothing to forgive, you silly goose.'

Margot smiled thinly through her tears. 'Thank you. Not many men would put up with me, I know that.'

Bill held Margot by the shoulders and looked into her eyes before putting his hand under her chin and lifting her face to his. 'You're not selfish. Maybe a little self-orientated perhaps, but that's who you are. You're driven and ambitious, but you're not selfish.' Taking a handkerchief from the inside pocket of his jacket, he wiped the tears from her eyes. Then he kissed her. 'Better?'

Margot nodded and said again that she was sorry. Bill put his arms around her and pulled her close. 'You don't have anything to be sorry for,' he whispered.

'Thank you for saying that, but I do,' Margot said, taking Bill's handkerchief, blowing her nose and then giving it back to him. 'But I'm going to make it up to you. I'm going to be a good wife. I shall cook all your favourite meals – well, those that I can get the ingredients for. Your slippers will be by the fire and your dinner will be on the table every night as soon as you get home. Oh,' she said, as an afterthought, 'I shall keep the house spotless. I'll wash and iron--'

'No you won't!'

'Yes I will!' Margot said, indignantly. 'I want to and I'm going to. I know I haven't always had the time, but--'

'Stop!' Bill shouted, laughing. 'Stop talking for one minute you silly, beautiful, wonderful girl, and listen to what I'm trying to tell you.'

Margot began to say she was sorry again, but thought better of it.

'I've been trying to tell you about this!' Putting his hand into his jacket pocket again, he brought out an envelope. 'It came for you this morning,' he said, handing it to her. 'It's from ENSA. I opened it before I saw it was addressed to you.'

Margot's mouth fell open. 'Why did they write to me?'

Bill laughed. 'It couldn't be because you've been pestering them?'

'I only dropped a letter in, and telephoned a few times… Oh Bill! You realise what this means, don't you?'

'It means the Albert Sisters are officially members of ENSA.'

'Yes, but rehearsals start on Wednesday – 9 am,' she said, in a subdued whisper.

'What's the matter? It is what you want, isn't it?'

'Give me your hankie,' she said, as tears rolled down her cheeks. After wiping her face Margot looked up at her husband. 'What about you? What about all the promises I just made you? About being a proper wife, being there when you get home at night, cooking your dinner?'

'And you will, when you come back. It'll only be

for a few months – six at most. When the theatre re-opens you might not have to go out with ENSA again. Then everything will be back to normal. If you can call being bombed nightly normal,' he said, trying to make light of the situation.

Margot looked at the letter in her hand, and then at Bill. 'I don't know what to say. I don't deserve you.'

Bill shook his head and laughed. 'Then say yes! I've asked for tomorrow off. Passionate leave,' he said, passing Margot her helmet. 'I thought a lie-in, breakfast in bed, and…'

Climbing onto the pillion seat, Margot put her arms around her husband and held him tight. 'I love you, Mr Burrell.'

'I love you too, Mrs Burrell,' Bill shouted over his shoulder as he drove the motorbike away from the curb and into the traffic.

Dear Bill,

I've never been so cold in my life. We're billeted at the local lord's place – Compton Marsh Hall. It's nothing like Foxden Hall. It's more like a derelict, but big, estate worker's cottage without heating. It's unbelievably cold and the old skinflint who owns the pile – and it really is an old pile – won't let us build a fire. Last night we slept in our clothes, but still couldn't get warm. Betsy's recovering from a cold, which has left her with a husky voice. Last night she sang George's melodies and George sang hers. It was so funny. It didn't work, but the lads didn't notice. George is fit and as uncomplaining as ever, but I'm worried about Artie. He's had a chesty cough. The poor chap had a serious bronchial illness when he was a child, which is the real reason he isn't in the forces.

Please God our billet next week is warmer, or he'll

be ill again.

My ankle nips now and again, but I'm taking care of it. I'm putting it up whenever I'm not on stage. I'm eating properly and sleeping well, so stop worrying about me. I don't have much more to report, so I'll get on with ironing the costumes.

Look after yourself, my darling. I miss you too.

Your loving wife, Margot. xxx

PS We're going to Leominster tomorrow. So my next letter will be from somewhere in Herefordshire. X

Margot flexed her ankle. She couldn't feel any pain. The pills she'd been given the week before by a medic at Blackmore Park in Worcester seemed to be working. Sighing with relief, she put the top on the small brown bottle. It was half empty. She wasn't sure how she'd cope when they'd gone. But she didn't have time to worry about that now. Her priority was to get to the tent which had been erected at the end of a rutted track a hundred yards away in the middle of a waterlogged field.

'Ready when you are,' Margot called, knocking on Betsy's bedroom door.

'Coming! And I have a voice.' Betsy trilled to prove it. 'Not bad, eh? I've been gargling with the old man's port. He might be stingy with his coal, but he's generous with his booze. The lonely old love is more than happy to share a tipple with anyone who'll listen,' she said, following Margot downstairs.

'I have the shoes and Artie has the frocks,' George said when Margot and Betsy arrived. 'Put your wellingtons on and let's get going.'

'Look sharp, ladies or we'll be late,' Artie said, opening the back door of Compton Marsh Hall. 'Thank God it's our last night here,' he said, trudging out into the muddy lane. 'I don't think my chest could take any more of this damp old place.'

'Tomorrow night,' George said, 'if our billet is anything like this one, my father will foot the bill for a hotel.'

'That's lovely,' Betsy said. 'When did he tell you that?'

'He didn't. It's a surprise,' George said, and they all laughed.

'Doing our bit is one thing, but this is ridiculous,' Betsy said, mud squelching almost to the tops of her wellingtons.

They were met at the main gate by the entertainments officer. 'Tonight you're starting with Tommy Trinder,' he told Artie. 'His warm-up man's gone down with the flu – all right?'

'Yes!' Artie said eagerly. He winked at the girls. It was better than all right, it was a great opportunity. The more people he worked with and the more experience he could get the better the chance of him finding work in a theatre when the ENSA tour ended.

Artie was fantastic and Tommy Trinder took to him straight away. The Alberts also went down a storm. 'All the way from the Prince Albert Theatre in London's West End... Please give a great big welcome to the Albert Sisters,' Artie shouted into the microphone. As the girls entered the stage in their short uniforms, the boys whistled and threw their caps in the air.

At the end of the concert, Tommy invited them back to his hotel.

'Does your hotel have a fire?' Betsy asked.

'Yes? Doesn't yours?'

'Come on!' Betsy shouted, and The Alberts piled into the back of Tommy Trinder's car.

CHAPTER SEVENTEEN

The train from Durham was a troop train, which Margot had been given special permission to travel on because of her ankle. Packed in like sardines, the servicemen – Royal Engineers in full kit – were on their way to Kitchener Barracks in Chatham for their final three months' training. They looked very young.

In pain because the pills she'd been taking were wearing off, and tearful because she'd had to leave George, Betsy and Artie to finish the tour without her, Margot limped across the platform at Kings Cross. 'Oxford Mews, please,' she said, falling onto the back seat of the cab.

'It's Miss Dudley, isn't it?' the cabbie asked, looking at Margot through the reversing mirror.

Usually excited that she had been recognised, she forced a smile. 'Yes. I'm surprised you recognised me looking like this.'

'The papers have been full of the ENSA shows, the flicks too. You was on last night, Miss, singing "We're In The Army" with two other ladies.'

Margot hadn't thought about the cine cameras actually putting the footage on at the pictures. Suddenly feeling happier, she began to wonder if she might one day have a career in films.

'We're here Miss. Miss Dudley?'

'Sorry, I was miles away. How much is it?'

'Three and six, please.'

Margot gave the cabbie five shillings and thanked him, before taking her gas mask and carpet bag from the seat next to her. Stepping carefully from the taxi, she bent down and looked under the plant pot at the side of the door. The spare key was still there. If Bill was at home she'd surprise him. If he wasn't he'd be more surprised to see a meal on the table when he came in. That's if there was any food in the larder, she mused.

Unlocking the door, Margot mounted the stairs. Careful not to put weight on her right foot so she didn't stress her ankle, she took the stairs one a time, bringing her right foot up to meet her left. Music from the wireless and the smell of cooking met her as she opened the door at the top of the stairs. Bill was in. Just the thought of seeing her kind and caring husband brought tears to her eyes. Relieved to be home, Margot dropped her bag and gas mask on the floor of the small hall.

'Hello?' Bill called from the sitting room. 'Who's there? What on earth?' he said, opening the door and seeing Margot leaning against the wall. 'Margot, why didn't you let me know you were coming home?'

'It was a last minute thing. My ankle's been playing up. It started to swell, and then it became too painful to dance.'

'My poor darling. Let's get you inside.' With Bill's help she limped into the sitting room and slumped onto the settee. Kneeling in front of her, Bill began to take off her shoes. 'My God Margot, how long has your ankle been like this?' She didn't tell him; she daren't tell him. Holding her right calf with one hand, he eased her foot out of her shoe with the other. 'There!' he said, giving it one last gentle tug. 'It's off. I'm sorry if I hurt you.'

Margot smiled at his concern. 'You didn't.' Resting her head against the back of the settee, she closed her eyes. 'Something smells good,' she mumbled, before drifting off to sleep. Aware that her leg was being lifted up and placed onto something soft, Margot smiled. She was home. And with Bill looking after her, her ankle would be better in no time.

The sound of a woman whispering penetrated Margot's conscious and nudged her awake. An uncomfortable feeling swept over her and she opened her eyes. Jenny – her friend and Bill's colleague – was standing in the doorway of her bedroom, wearing Margot's towelling bathrobe and smiling up at Bill.

'Bill?' Margot stood up without thinking, put her foot to the floor, screamed with pain and fell.

'Margot!' Bill ran across the room. 'What on earth are you doing?' He helped her back onto the settee.

'You need to keep your foot up, Margot,' Jenny said, following Bill and bending down as if she was going to lift Margot's leg.

Margot's eyes glistened with anger. 'Get away from me!'

Startled, Jenny jumped back. 'I – I was only trying to help.'

Help yourself to my husband, Margot thought. 'I don't need your help. What are you doing here? Why were you in my bedroom with my husband, wearing my bathrobe?'

Jenny didn't answer. Instead she looked at Bill. 'I'm sorry, Bill,' she whimpered. 'I didn't mean to…'

'Jenny's lodgings were bombed last night, so she stayed here.'

'In our bedroom?'

'Well, yes. It was late and the spare bed wasn't made up, so I gave Jenny our bed and I slept in here on the settee. I'd just changed the sheets and was about to make up Jenny's bed when you arrived.'

Jenny appeared tearful and her voice was shaky. 'After my shift I went home and the house where I had rooms was gone. It had taken a direct hit. An

ARP Warden said it was too dangerous for me to look for my belongings and he moved me on. The only clothes I had were what I was wearing. I didn't know what to do,' she said, and she broke down in tears.

'So she came back to the station and I said she could stay here until she finds somewhere else to live.'

'I don't know what I'd have done if Bill hadn't been there,' she said, with a catch in her throat. She smiled up at him.

'I see.' Margot didn't see at all. Jenny had a sister who lived a damn sight nearer to St. Thomas's than she and Bill. 'Was your sister's house bombed too?'

'What? I – I don't know. I was in shock. I just ran to the bus stop and caught the late bus to Westminster Bridge. I thought I'd go and see her before my shift tonight. Perhaps I should go now,' she said to Bill in a little-girl-lost voice. 'Give you and Margot time to discuss things.'

Margot hauled herself to her feet. 'I'm going to *my* bedroom.' Bill tried to take her arm. 'I can manage.'

'Don't you want something to eat, love? Jenny's made a stew.'

Margot flashed an angry look at her husband, and another at Jenny. 'Would you bring me a glass of water please, Bill?'

'I'm sure there'll be enough for you as well,' Jenny said sweetly, taking Margot's arm.

'No thank you, I've lost my appetite.' Snatching her arm away, Margot limped into the bedroom, collecting her bag on the way, and closed the door behind her.

She lay on the bed and stared at the ceiling. She needed to relax, to calm down. If she hadn't left the sitting room when she did she might have hit the lying little-- She hadn't been in the bedroom long when the door opened.

'I've got your water,' Bill whispered.

'Put it on the bedside table, will you,' Margot said, sitting up. 'Would you pass my bag, please?' Rummaging in it, she found the small bottle of pills.

'What are they for?' Bill asked, taking the bottle from her and turning it over in his hand. 'There's no label.'

'They're to help me sleep.'

'Sleeping pills?'

'No! They take away the pain in my ankle so I can sleep. I'll go to my own doctor now I'm back, but tonight a couple of these will do. So please,' she sighed, holding out her hand, 'give me the bottle and go and entertain your house guest.' Margot unscrewed the top, shook two pills into her hand and then threw them into the back of her mouth, before washing them down with half a glass of water. 'I'm tired,' she said. Lying down, she turned her back on Bill.

Bill left the room, closing the door quietly and Margot buried her head in the pillow and sobbed. She felt guilty, angry and confused, and she wished she hadn't come home.

As the bus approached The Cut, Waterloo, posters of Sybil Thorndike and Ann Casson caught her eye. Standing ten feet tall alongside Bernard Miles and Frank Petley, they advertised a tour of The Old Vic's production of *Medea*. The theatre had been damaged in an air raid in May of that year, but it was soon to reopen.

The bus turned at Elephant and Castle and trundled up through Borough. Once over Tower Bridge Margot could see the devastation the Luftwaffe had wrought on the East End. Row after row of blitzed and burned out buildings. Shops that once served a close-knit community, proud to be born within the sound of Bow Bells, had been gutted. Businesses stood empty and homes derelict. A single wall of a wet fish shop stood erect among buildings that had been reduced to rubble. On its facia, covered in brick and plaster dust, a sign said "Whitechapel Fish". Beneath it, "Closed until further notice".

She couldn't remember exactly where Jenny said she lived. She wasn't interested and consequently hadn't listened. She wished now that she had. When they worked together as usherettes, Jenny had lived near Margot in Hampstead. She moved to Whitechapel when Margot and Bill moved to Oxford Mews. She said she wanted to be near her sister, whose husband had been called up. Margot wasn't sure now if that was the reason. Jenny had made a joke about King Henry VIII, but that wasn't what the avenue was called. Margot consulted the A to Z and found Tudor and Wolsey Avenue.

'Tudor Avenue!' the bus conductor shouted.

Margot took her handbag, gas mask and stick from the seat next to her and, with the help of the conductor, left the bus.

Tudor Avenue wasn't tree-lined, like the avenues in North West London, but from the little that was still standing, she could see it had once been a pleasant place to live. Houses at the beginning of the avenue were inhabited – curtains twitched as she passed and washing hung on stretched clothes lines. Further down the avenue houses that were still in one piece had some of their windows boarded up. Further down still, solitary walls stood amid rubble and beyond that was wasteland.

Margot walked the length of the avenue. The houses that were unsafe through bomb damage looked as if they'd been like it for some time. She walked along Wolsey Avenue and, like Tudor, the houses that were severely damaged had been damaged months before, not days.

'Excuse me?' Margot called to a couple of boys playing football on the wasteland. 'Do you live around here?'

The boys stopped kicking their ball. One picked it up and the other came towards her.

'We ain't doin' nothin' wrong Missus. It's me bruvver Alf's ball.'

'I know you're not,' Margot said, smiling. 'I just want to ask you something. If you live around here you might be able to help me. If you don't--'

'We do. Go on Missus, what do you want to know?'

'A friend of mine used to live here, but she lost her home this week in an air raid. Do you know which houses were bombed?'

'That's easy. None of 'em. We ain't bin bombed this week. It were too foggy at the weekend.' The boy put his dirty finger to his mouth and frowned thoughtfully. 'Gerry was Stepney way last night, Dulwich the night before, Bethnal Green one night this week and the docks the other. We don't know the exact places 'cause we ain't bin to 'em, but we know near enough where the bombs was fallin', which direction like.'

'And you're sure?'

'Wot?'

'That this area hasn't been bombed for a week?'

'Ye-ah!' The boy looked shocked that Margot could doubt him. 'Me and our Alf 'ave got all the places and times of the bombin's written down in a book wot a Yank give us. The aeroplanes too. Do you want 'im to fetch it, so as you can see for yaself?'

'There's no need, I believe you. Thank you for your help. Here are two sixpences,' she said, placing two small silver coins into the boy's grubby hand. 'One for you and one for Alf.'

'Thank you, Missus.' The boy held out his hand to show Alf the bounty. 'Reckon Gerry ain't gunna waste bombs on somewhere what's already bin flattened.' With that the boy ran off to join his brother, who was still holding the football.

Leaving the bus at Lancaster Place, Margot crossed the Strand and walked down to the theatre. The windows in the doors and the glass in the poster cabinets were smeared with a fine film of grease. Dust had settled in the corners like snowdrifts and the sills were thick with what looked to Margot like ash. With so much traffic going up and down the Strand there was bound to be dirt. And if there was no one to clean them... Apart from being laced in a film of London grime, the theatre looked much the same as it always had. In the glass cases on either side of the door there were posters saying Opening Soon. Margot wondered when that would be.

Leaning heavily on her stick, she made her way to Maiden Lane and the stage door. It was open. She looked inside. There was a gaping hole where Bert's office used to be. She took a step forward, but stopped at the sound of voices. Two men were joking and laughing, as if nothing had happened. Her hands were shaking and her heart hammered in her chest. She turned away, steadied herself on the doorframe, and focused on the road. A shuddering breath escaped her throat. She was looking at the place where Bert and Nancy were killed. There was nothing to see.

In a daze she walked to the spot. The road looked the same as it had before. She walked on to the pavement on the far side and sat down. There was no trace of that day left. Nothing to show for her tragic loss. The only evidence that anything had happened on that terrible, terrible day was a couple of ill-fitting kerbstones. Grief took hold of her as it had then, and she began to tremble.

'Are you all right, Miss?' a young man asked.

'What?' Margot looked up from the pavement.

'Let me help you,' he said, kneeling down beside her and taking her hands in his. 'It's dangerous to sit so close to the road,' he continued, helping Margot to her feet.

'Thank you.' The young man picked up her stick. She took it and smiled. 'You must think I'm a fool,' she said. 'I have no idea why I... One minute I was crossing the road from the theatre,' Margot looked across at the Albert's stage door, 'and the next...' Tears filled her eyes.

'Can I walk with you to wherever it is you're going, Miss Dudley?' the young man asked, holding Margot's elbow to support her.

Margot looked at him. 'Do I know you?'

'No. But I know you. Mostly from the newspapers, but I brought my mum to see you in a show last year, on her birthday. Well,' he said, a shy blush spreading across his cheeks, 'I'd better go.'

'What's your name?'

'Harry. Harry Ward.'

'Thank you for helping me, Harry. When the theatre re-opens come to the stage door and ask for me, or tell--' Margot swallowed hard, 'tell the stage doorman when you and your mum would like to see a show, say you're my guests, and I'll leave complimentary tickets for you at the box office.'

'Thank you, Miss Dudley,' Harry Ward said, beaming. 'Mum'll love that.'

Margot watched her young helper walk away, and after one last longing look at the Prince Albert Theatre's stage door, she set off in the same direction.

As she approached the Church of St. Saviour she heard organ music and a choir singing. She limped down the steps that she had fallen down in 1940, when she first came to the theatre, and saw the door was open. Quietly she slipped into a pew at the back of the church and listened to the Gloria.

Except for a new door, which had elaborate brass hinges, the outside of the building was unremarkable to look at. Tall and narrow, it looked as if it had been crammed in between the other buildings on the lane as an afterthought. Except for the large crucifix, the vestibule was dark and plain. But the interior was magnificent. The walls were covered in colourful tapestries and gilt-framed paintings. The wooden pews were relatively simple, but the pulpit was elaborately carved. Beyond the choir stalls the ornate altar was decorated with silver candlesticks and vases of flowers. In the middle beneath the east window was an ornate silver cross. Margot closed her eyes and was calmed by the fragrant scents of lavender furniture polish and incense.

She sat in the beautiful church listening to the choir rehearse for some time and wondering what she should do about Jenny. She had been furious with her the night she arrived home from ENSA and saw how she looked at Bill. And now, after finding out that the house she said she lived in hadn't been bombed, she wanted to go home and throw her out, challenge her in front of Bill and show him what a conniving liar

Jenny was, as well as a potential husband stealer. Margot went over and over what she should do and decided that, since Jenny was studying to be a First Aid Nursing Yeomanry driver – and was bound to pass their first aid exam because according to Bill she was brilliant – she'd be leaving Tommy's in the not too distant future.

The real reason Margot decided not to tell Bill about Jenny while he was working with her was in case she 'accidentally on purpose' let slip to him that Margot didn't want children until she'd achieved her ambition. She wished she'd never confided in Jenny, but she had, so-- No. She wouldn't confront her. There was a much better way to control the lying little bitch.

Margot kicked off her shoes. She shouldn't have gone out, at least not in high heels. 'Is that you, Bill?' she called, hearing the door open. Throwing her shoes in the bottom of the wardrobe, she slipped her feet into her slippers.

'It's me – Jenny. Bill's locking the bike. How are you feeling today? Better?'

'Much. You?'

'Me?' Jenny's cheeks flushed. 'Why do you ask?'

'Well, with you losing your home in the blitz. I wondered if you were still upset about it. It must have been terrible for you. If you want to talk about it,' Margot said, 'I'm always here. They say talking helps. So let me help you, Jenny. Tell me how you felt when you arrived home this week and found the house you lived in had been bombed? It was this week, wasn't it?' Jenny didn't answer. 'Or was it last week, or last month?'

'I don't know what you mean,' Jenny said, wringing

her hands nervously.

'Oh, didn't I say? I went to Tudor Avenue today.' Jenny shot her a frightened look. 'There haven't been any bombs dropped on Tudor or Wolsey for almost a week. So where were you living before you gave Bill the sob-story about losing your home?'

'With my sister,' she whispered.

Margot hobbled into the kitchen. Jenny followed. 'Are you going to tell Bill?'

'No.' Jenny sighed with relief. 'You are, if you don't go and see your sister tomorrow and ask her to take you back.' Margot turned and faced her. 'Any reason why she wouldn't?' Jenny shook her head. 'Good. Then you can come back here before you go down to the ambulance station and give Bill and me the good news.'

'If I do, will you promise not to tell Bill?'

'I won't tell him if you stay away from him. Bill's my husband, Jenny. I know he's your friend, and your partner on the ambulances, but he's married to me.' Jenny began to cry. Margot thought about putting her arms around her, but there was something about her tears that didn't ring true. 'Even when we were usherettes you flirted with him when you thought I wasn't around. You pretended it was so he'd put a good word in for you at the ambulance station, but I knew it was more than that.' Margot paused. 'You're in love with him, aren't you?'

'In love? Of course I'm not,' Jenny protested. 'Bill and I are friends. He's my best friend.'

'Stop lying! I've seen the way you look at him!'

Jenny broke down. 'Please don't tell him. I'm begging you, Margot. If you tell him he won't work with me, and I won't get the first aid experience I need for the nursing yeomanry exam. I'll never be overfriendly again, I promise. Please Margot, I'm sorry.'

'Sorry I've caught you out in a pack of lies,' Margot said, throwing down the tea towel and walking away. 'And stop crying! It's too late for tears.' Margot's patience was wearing thin. 'All right! I won't tell him. But you must promise me that this-- this obsession you have with Bill stops now!'

Jenny nodded. 'Thank you, Margot. Can you ever forgive me? Please say you can.'

The bombed out houses in the East End, the gaping hole where Bert's office used to be, the curb stone on Maiden Lane, the boy who helped her and the choir at St. Saviour's singing the Gloria flashed through her mind. 'I forgive you,' she said, 'but if you ever--'

'I won't. I know now that Bill's kindness and friendship was just that. Can we still be friends?' Jenny asked.

'I can hear Bill. Go and wash your face. Splash cold water on your eyes so he doesn't know you've been crying. Supper's in ten minutes.'

Christmas 1941 was the first Margot and Bill spent in their new apartment. Bill brought home a Christmas tree and Margot made lots of decorations out of shiny paper and offcuts of fabric. And thanks to Natalie and Anton Goldman, they had a chicken for their Christmas dinner.

Margot put on the wireless, tuned it to hear the King's Speech and sat down next to Bill. She put her feet on his and picked up her glass. 'Mmmm, this sherry has gone to my head,' she cooed. Bill leaned forward, kissed her and laughed. 'What a perfect day,' she said, snuggling up to him. She hadn't told Bill about Jenny's lies at the time and now, after two months, it was too late. Jenny was right, they did have to work together – and their jobs were extremely important. Anyway, Margot trusted Bill completely. She knew he hadn't done anything to encourage Jenny. She looked up at her husband's kind face. He did like Jenny, but not in *that* way. He respected her for the work she did, which was very different.

Bill topped up her glass and Margot relaxed with her head on the back of the settee. If Jenny hadn't gone back to live with her sister when she did, she thought, I'd have told Bill about her lies and dragged her out of my home by her hair. Margot drained her glass.

CHAPTER EIGHTEEN

Margot had kept the promises she made to Bill when she thought ENSA didn't want her – to be a proper wife, keep the house spotless and cook dinner every night – and she'd enjoyed doing it. But now her ankle had healed and the nightmares were a thing of the past, she had become restless. Being a housewife wasn't enough. She was bored.

Margot flopped onto the settee and picked up a magazine. She flicked through it, found nothing interesting, and dropped it onto the occasional table. She pulled her legs up to her chin and hugged her knees. What next? She looked at the clock on the mantle. Almost time to start supper. When Bill left for the MoD in the mornings Margot counted the hours until he came back. She loved that the two of them were able to sit down and have supper together. But then he went out to Tommy's and she was on her own again until ten or eleven o'clock at night – worrying that he would be caught in a raid, injured or killed.

She pushed herself off the settee, went over to the sideboard and picked up the letter from George and Betsy. Reading it again, she took a pen and a writing pad from the drawer and wrote a reply.

Bill had reservations about Margot going out on tour again – he didn't think she was fit enough – but Margot bamboozled him as always. 'The timing is perfect,' she said, as they sat down to supper. 'I spoke to Natalie today and she said there's such a shortage of timber and other building materials that the reopening of the theatre has had to be postponed until the end of April. Oh Bill,' she went on, 'you don't really mind, do you? I mean, it's only for a few weeks and George and Betsy are desperate for me to join them.' Margot whipped Bill's plate away the second he put down his knife and fork. 'I'm going to pack,' she said, putting the dishes in the kitchen sink with a clatter. 'I'll wash up later.' Bill opened his mouth to speak, but Margot didn't give him a chance. Dashing from the kitchen to the bedroom she stopped to plant a kiss on his cheek. 'Thank you, love. I knew you'd understand.'

Waterloo Bridge was closed. Margot heard the taxi driver curse as he pulled into the traffic. Cutting in front of the car behind, he put his foot down and drove down the Strand and along Whitehall. When Big Ben and the Houses of Parliament came into view he swung the taxi onto Westminster Bridge. A few minutes later they were at Waterloo Station.

'We've got less than ten minutes, Margot,' Bill said. He paid for the taxi and followed Margot onto the concourse. 'I'll get your ticket,' he shouted. 'You make your way to the train.'

On the platform outside a second class carriage she watched a crowd of young American airmen talking to a group of girls. Someone shouted, 'OK men! Let's go!' Immediately the young men and women fell into each other's arms, hugging and kissing, until the man barked again. 'I said now! Next stop Southampton!' The Americans dragged themselves away, leaving the girls on the platform consoling each other and crying. She looked up to where the orders had come from and caught the eye of a tall, fair haired airman standing in the doorway. He smiled and saluted. Margot smiled back and felt her cheeks redden.

Looking away, she wondered if they would be at

the ENSA concerts.

'Margot,' Bill called, interrupting her thoughts. He opened the door of a first class carriage, which was next to the one the Americans had filed into, and leapt in with her suitcase. He checked the ticket and then the number on the door. 'This is it,' he said, sliding back the door of the compartment. Margot watched as he stood her case against the seat, end-on to the window. 'No need to put it up,' he said, indicating the overhead rack. 'Doesn't look as if you'll be sharing the compartment.'

Suddenly a whistle blew. 'Better leave!' Bill said, squeezing past her. At the door he kissed her passionately. 'I'd got used to having you at home.'

Margot reached up and kissed him, Eskimo style. 'I'll be back before you know it,' she said, and she kissed him properly.

Bill stroked her hair and looked into her eyes. 'Take care of yourself.'

'I will. I promise.' The train clunked and hissed as steam was released, and Bill jumped off. He slammed the door and jogged along with the train as it slowly chugged south.

'Don't overwork your ankle,' he shouted. 'Put it up as often as you can.'

'I will,' Margot shouted back. She waved until Bill had disappeared in a cloud of steam. After pushing up the window she returned to the compartment, closed the door, and made herself comfortable in the seat next to the window.

While the train sped past the smoke-stained terraced houses and cobbled back yards of South London, Margot read a magazine. Once in Surrey she looked out of the window. Bright sunlight flickered through budding trees, settling on daffodils and tulips in full bloom. The sun reflected on the train's window and she put her hand up to shade her eyes. In the distance a lake shimmered as the wind created ripples on its surface that looked like dancers under spotlights. Margot closed her eyes.

Somewhere far away, or maybe she was dreaming, she heard wood sliding against wood followed by a click, and a light breeze brushed her ankles. She opened her eyes.

'Excuse me, Miss?' The young officer who was in charge of the American airmen was standing in the doorway of her compartment. 'I'm sorry to wake you, but the carriage,' he said, pointing along the corridor, 'that I reserved for my men and me has one too few seats. Would it be OK if I sat in here?'

'Of course.' She could hardly say no, sitting on her own in an empty carriage. 'Oh, but it's first class.' The airman looked disappointed. 'I won't tell if you don't,' she joked.

'Thank you.' The young airman took a newspaper from his kit bag, and then swung it up onto the overhead rack. Sitting down with the paper on his lap, he took a pack of cigarettes from his pocket. 'Would you like a smoke?'

'I don't, thank you,' Margot said, and began to laugh.

'What?' Shaking his head, he started to laugh with her. 'Come on, give?'

Still laughing, she pointed to the no smoking sign on the door. 'I won't tell if you don't.'

'I can wait.' Returning the cigarettes to his pocket, the airman picked up his newspaper and Margot picked up her magazine. They sat in silence reading for some time, but as Margot had read most of the articles earlier she became bored and looked out of the window again. She watched the towns and villages of Surrey go by in the distance. With the sun warm on her face she closed her eyes, but opened them almost immediately when the train rattled into a tunnel. Startled by the sudden contrast of brightness to darkness, she jumped. Dark outside, the train's window became a mirror and she could see the airman's face reflected in it. He was looking at her.

'Excuse me, Miss,' he said, closing his newspaper and dropping it onto the seat next to him. 'You look kinda familiar. Have we met?'

'I don't think so. I'm sure I'd remember if we had.' Margot felt her cheeks flush and she began to chatter to hide her embarrassment. 'I'm in show business. Perhaps you've seen my photograph outside the Prince Albert Club in Covent Garden. I'm with ENSA at the moment. I worked at the Prince Albert Theatre on the Strand, until--' Margot felt a lump in her throat and busied herself putting the magazine in her bag.

'Well, how about that! I'm in the movies back home. Have you made any movies, Miss...?'

'Dudley, Margot Dudley,' she said, regaining her composure.

'First Lieutenant Boyd Murphy. Pleased to meet you,' he said, standing up.

Margot shook the lieutenant's outstretched hand and watched him sit down. Damn, why hadn't she said something? By not speaking she'd ended the conversation and she was desperate to know about the movies and movie stars. How could she take the conversation back without appearing to be a gushing fan? 'To answer your earlier question,' she said at last, 'I was filmed when I was with ENSA last year. I haven't actually made any movies, but I should like to.'

'Well, if ever you're in California--'

'I'll be sure to look you up,' Margot laughed. 'Do you live in Hollywood?'

'No. My dad does, and I stay with him all the time. Mom and my sisters and me live in Santa Monica. It's only eighteen kilometres away. That's about eleven of your English miles, or a half-hour drive.'

'I read that James Stewart joined up.'

'He sure did.'

'Is he in England as well?'

'No. I don't know whether it's to do with his age – he's over thirty – or because he'd been training guys to fly for about a year, but he's still in the US and he's still an instructor.'

The train whistled and juddered as it began to slow down. 'Soon be in Southampton,' the lieutenant said, jumping up and taking down his kit bag. 'Is Southampton your destination, Miss Dudley?'

'No. I'm going to Stony Cross air force base in the New Forest to do a concert for ENSA.'

'Well I'll be! That's my base. Since we're both going to Stony Cross, could I offer you a lift? The base bus is picking us up. If you don't mind sitting among a bunch of rowdy Yanks, I'd be happy to give you a ride.'

'If my friends aren't at the station, I'll take you up on it, Lieutenant.'

'Call me Murphy,' he said, his blue eyes sparkling.

'Margot,' she said, holding his gaze.

As the train pulled into Southampton station Margot picked up her handbag and gas mask in one hand and her suitcase in the other.

'Let me,' Murphy said, covering her hand with his. Margot's heart began to flutter with girlish excitement and she felt the heat of a blush on her cheeks. She slid her hand from under his and let him take the handle. With his air force bag over his shoulder he picked up the suitcase.

As she stepped from the train, George and Betsy were waiting. Throwing their arms around each other they hugged and kissed and all spoke at once. 'Come on, let's get out of here,' George said, taking Margot's case.

Margot turned and looked along the platform. The US air force boys were filing off the train. Murphy was with them. He had turned at the same time as Margot. When she waved, he saluted.

RAF Stony Cross was the first date of the Albert Sisters' final tour. They opened with Artie's piano gag, followed by his impersonation of George Formby. Then Artie called in the troops. The airmen, RAF and USAAF, whistled and cheered as Margot, George and Betsy strutted on stage. Instead of standing to attention by the piano, they marched to the front of the stage and swiped caps from the heads of the three nearest Americans. Then, marching back to the piano, they turned and stood to attention, saluting American-style. With their GI caps sitting at an angle on their perfectly coiffed hair they sang The Andrews Sisters' song, "Boogie Woogie Bugle Boy of Company B" followed by "I Can Dream, Can't I?" As they marched off stage for their quick change, RAF boys and GIs cheered and threw their caps in the air. When they returned, Margot and Betsy in long evening dresses and George impersonating Noel Coward in white dinner jacket and black bow tie, they sang "A Room With A View" followed by "Putting On The Ritz". The audience went wild.

Each night after the show, Tommy Trinder, who had asked for the Albert Sisters to support him after working with them the previous autumn, invited them to his makeshift dressing room. The great man was charming and instructed his dresser to keep their glasses filled. He then disappeared to sign autographs. They didn't think it would be polite to refuse the star of the concert's generosity and, trying to hide the fact that they were in awe of the biggest star of British films, they allowed his dresser to fill their glasses.

On the last night at Stony Cross, Tommy returned from signing autographs with a brown paper sack. 'Thank you presents for the Albert Sisters,' he said, giving each of the girls a gift. 'And a bottle of Hooch for you,' he said, handing Artie a bottle of bourbon. 'You lucky people!' he shouted, and everyone laughed. 'Oh, and there's one for me,' he said, looking deep into the paper sack, and everyone laughed again.

Margot opened her gift and caught her breath. Lying on a cushion of cream satin was a pair of silver wings. Apart from being smaller, they were identical to those that Murphy wore. Betsy ripped the paper from her present to reveal a pair of fully-fashioned silk stockings. She squealed with delight, while George wrapped a beautiful long white silk scarf round her neck.

'Am I allowed to wear these?' Margot asked. 'Isn't it against the law to wear military badges if you're not in the services?'

'Might be if they were the real thing, but these aren't,' George said. 'These are smaller – and they're silver.'

Artie poured himself and Tommy a glass of bourbon. 'Who have I got to thank for this, Tommy?'

'No idea. A young GI gave me the bag when I was

signing autographs. Said he'd enjoyed the show and would never forget us.'

Margot looked at George and Betsy. They knew it was First Lieutenant Boyd Murphy who had sent the gifts, but they said nothing. Margot had been friends with Murphy, nothing more, but it didn't stop her from feeling guilty as she pinned the silver wings onto her jacket.

It had been sad saying goodbye to Tommy, but the Sisters were happy to be back in London and were looking forward to the grand reopening of the Prince Albert Theatre. While the finishing touches were being made to the theatre, Margot, George and Betsy spent their days at Margot's apartment running lines and learning songs. Artie, having had a taste of show business, had no intention of going back to his old job as a night watchman and turned up after a couple of days with his accordion.

One Wednesday morning at the beginning of March Margot was woken by a furious hammering on the outside door. 'All right, I'm coming,' she shouted, dragging on her dressing gown and running down the stairs. It was George. 'Hello. I didn't think we were working today. Where's Betsy?'

'She's been called up,' George said, beads of perspiration on her forehead and out of breath from running. 'She received a letter this morning telling her to go for a medical.'

'Damn! Just when things were going so well! Come in, love,' Margot said, leading the way to the apartment. 'Sit down while I get dressed.' A few minutes later, wearing slacks and a button-through cardigan, Margot joined George on the settee.

'What if she's sent overseas, to the front line?'

George burst into tears. 'I couldn't bear it, Margot. I don't know what I'd do if she was.... I couldn't live without her.'

Margot put her arms around her friend. 'I didn't realise you felt that way about Betsy. Does she know?'

'No! And she must never find out. She'd be mortified if she knew I ... had feelings for her.' George pulled away and, looking terrified, said, 'You won't tell her, will you? Promise you won't, Margot.'

'Of course not. Not if you don't want me to. But I think you should.'

'No! Never! I would lose her. Swear you'll never say anything.'

'I swear.' Margot smiled at her friend. 'I'll make a cup of tea and we'll decide what we're going to do.'

'If there is anything we can do.' George put her head in her hands.

'We'll think of something. Come on,' Margot said, 'chin up. She hasn't been accepted yet. It's silly worrying till we know. Besides, she's a member of ENSA. That's it! Betsy's still in ENSA. She's already working for the war effort – so are we. Surely they won't ask her to leave the work she's already doing.' Margot made tea and took it into the sitting room. George was at last dry-eyed. 'Drink this.' Margot handed George a cup. 'Did she say where she was going?'

'Seven Dials.'

Margot smiled. 'It won't take us long to get there from here. And when we find her we'll take her to the club for a drink.'

'Drown our sorrows?'

'No,' Margot said, 'celebrate that the conscription office has made a mistake.'

The queue along Monmouth Street was a mile

long. It reminded Margot of the day they auditioned for ENSA except everyone waiting to go into the Drury Lane theatre looked hopeful. Some of these women looked scared to death. Betsy was nowhere to be seen.

'Are you sure she said twelve?'

'Positive.' George looked at her watch. 'She's either already in there, or she's late.'

'We'll hang on until a few more come out and if she isn't among them, we'll go back to the beginning and start again.'

As four women came out of the recruitment office, four went in. 'This is hopeless!' George turned and marched back the way they'd come.

Margot ran and caught her up. 'Stop!' she shouted, pulling on George's arm. 'Look! She's over there.'

'Where?'

Margot pointed to a low wall on the opposite side of the street, surrounding the paved garden of an official-looking building. Betsy was sitting on the wall, frowning.

'Betsy!' they called in unison. Running over to her friend, George flung her arms around her. 'Bets, I'm sorry.'

'Me too,' Margot said.

'Anyone would think I'd been accepted.'

'What?' George looked worried, while Margot jumped with joy. 'You mean they've turned you down? Why? Are you ill?'

'Yes. No! Not ill, but I had scarlet fever as a child. They said I wasn't fit for duty. So it's back to Every Night Something Aaaaaabsolutely wonderful.'

Relieved, the three friends danced along Monmouth Street arm in arm, singing "Sailors Three" from Tommy Trinder's film.

CHAPTER NINETEEN

Margot inhaled deeply before opening the stage door. Taking a tentative step, she looked around at what should have been a familiar place. It didn't look or feel familiar. Cards and telegrams were piled up on the post table in the usual way, but the table was round, not square. Margot didn't like it. Nor did she like the regulation green coloured paint on the door to Bert's office, or the frosted glass in the window. 'Bert's office,' she said. 'That's Bert's office,' she told a man who had suddenly appeared at the window. 'Bert's window and Bert's office,' she said, nodding frantically, willing the man to nod that he agreed, but he didn't. Instead he stepped back and picked up the telephone. He said a couple of words that Margot couldn't hear and replaced the receiver. He's got a kind face, she thought. Bert had a kind face, but he's gone. 'I'm sorry. For a moment I--' She spotted the rehearsal schedule on the wall. It was in a different place, but that didn't matter. She read the artists' names over and over, looking for Nancy's name. She shook her head. 'I thought I could cope,' she said to the man in Bert's office, 'but it's too hard.'

'Margot?' How lovely to see you. Welcome back.' Pamela Lesley was standing in the doorway leading to the backstage area. 'You're early, dear. Let's go through to the front of house and have a cup of tea. Stan will let us know when the rest of the company arrives.'

Margot looked at the new stage doorman, 'I'm sorry, Stan,' she said. 'What must you think of me? Please accept my apologies.'

'Nothing to apologise for, Miss Dudley.'

Margot acknowledged Stan's kindness with a smile. Then she took a deep steadying breath and turned to Miss Lesley. 'Thank you, Miss Lesley, I should love a cup of tea.' Still feeling overwrought, Margot allowed the front of house manager to lead her along the corridor behind the stage, through the pass door and into the small staff room that she had known when she was an usherette.

Once inside, Miss Lesley took the kettle from the stove, filled it with water from the tap in the washroom and replaced it. Then she turned on the gas, struck a match and held it against the ring of hissing jets until they ignited with a loud pop. Margot jumped.

'I have some sugar in my office,' Miss Lesley said, conspiratorially. 'I'll be back in a jiffy.'

Margot hadn't been in the front of house staff room for a long time; probably since she was an usherette. She looked around. There was no bomb damage. The staff room was far enough away from the stage door. She ran her fingers along the shelf. She could see by the shine that it had been recently painted – and about time.

The kettle began to whistle, softly at first and then louder, until it became shrill and piercing. Margot turned off the gas and the whistle lessened until there was no sound at all. She spooned two scoops of tea into the pot and added the boiling water.

A second later Miss Lesley returned. 'Thank you, dear,' she said, taking the caddy spoon out of Margot's hand. Margot sat down and watched Miss Lesley pour the tea. She added two spoons of sugar to Margot's and handed her the cup. 'That will do you good.'

Margot smiled at the kind woman who had given her a job when she first came to London. Because of

Miss Lesley's tolerance she had climbed the career ladder to where she was now. And where was she now, she wondered.

They drank their tea in silence and when they'd finished Miss Lesley said, 'Feeling better?'

'Yes, thank you. It was seeing Stan in Bert's place, and then not seeing Nancy's name on the call-sheet.' Margot broke down. 'She's gone, Miss Lesley. Nancy's gone, hasn't she?' Pamela Lesley held Margot in her arms. 'She was so beautiful, and so kind. If only I hadn't stopped to autograph that girl's programme, I might have been on Maiden Lane earlier. And Nancy might have got out of the taxi before--'

'There was nothing you could have done,' Miss Lesley said. 'Besides, if you had arrived sooner, you would have been there when the building collapsed and you would have been killed too. It was lucky that you--'

'My good luck, but Nancy and Bert's bad luck. How unfair is that?'

'I know.' Then, gently pushing Margot away and holding her at arm's length, Pamela Lesley looked into her tearful eyes. 'It was unfair, Margot, terribly unfair. Thousands of people have been killed in this war – mothers and fathers, sisters and brothers, husbands and wives – and their deaths were unfair too. But we can't change what has happened. All we can do is remember our loved ones and get on with our lives.'

Margot looked surprised, but said nothing.

'It might sound harsh, but we owe it to them to carry on,' Pamela Lesley said. 'And we must!'

A knock on the staff room door startled Margot, and she flinched.

'It's all right. It'll only be Stan,' Pamela Lesley said, and she called, 'Come in.'

The stage doorman poked his head round the door. 'Rehearsal is about to start. Shall I tell them five minutes?'

'Yes, thank you, Stan.' When the doorman left, Pamela Lesley said, 'Ready, Margot?'

Margot nodded and dried her eyes. 'Thank you, Miss Lesley. I am.'

As she entered the auditorium Margot was aware that the chatter and laughter, which was as much a part of getting ready to rehearse as the warm up, came to a sudden hush. George and Betsy ran over to her, and Natalie and Anton Goldman, who were sitting in the stalls, left their seats and joined her on stage. Anton turned to the artists and nodded to them to carry on, while Natalie put her arms around Margot and assured her that if she needed to take a break, she only had to say.

Margot looked into the auditorium. The lights were off, but she could see Pamela Lesley sitting in the usherette seat that used to be hers. Grateful to her for her kindness, Margot blew her a kiss. Then she turned and hugged Betsy and George – who weren't scheduled to rehearse until later – and welcomed the chorus members, old and new. Then, after shaking hands with the director, Richard Smiley, and hugging choreographer Lena Di Angelo, Margot kissed and congratulated her friend Artie Armitage, the Albert Theatre's new pianist.

'Everyone had time to look at their song sheets?' Smiley asked. And without waiting for a reply, he shouted. 'From the top!'

As Artie played the opening bars of the first song, Margot's heart was breaking with the injustice of it all, but her head told her to sing, to do what she had worked so long and so hard for – and she did.

She sang and she sang and she sang.

Margot sat on the apron of the stage on the afternoon of opening night and looked around. On either side of the stage there were new canvases, flats and curtains. Above, new lights shone down from the flies and below, surrounding the orchestra pit, was a new mahogany partition. The smell of recently waxed wood filled her nostrils. It reminded her of the ballroom at Foxden Hall before her sister Bess turned it into a hospital wing. Bess would be in London now. She had come down for her old housemates' wedding and stayed on. Claire wasn't able to get leave from the WAAF, but Ena was coming. Margot couldn't wait to see them. She looked over to where they would be sitting with Natalie and Anton Goldman. The box didn't look as if it had been refurbished. Most of the seats in the auditorium hadn't either. Only the first three rows had been replaced; the rest had been cleaned. They'd have been covered in brick and plaster dust after the--.

'Time to get you into your opening costume, Margot,' Thelma, her new dresser called from the wings.

'I'm coming.' Margot jumped up and followed Thelma to the dressing room.

'What do you think of your name on the door?' Thelma asked, helping Margot out of her jacket. 'Stan did it while you were on stage.'

Margot went back to the door, opened it and smiled. 'That was kind of him, but it's a bit big. A bit showy, don't you think?'

'No I don't! The big star was my suggestion. I thought you'd like it.' Thelma looked disappointed.

'I do. Thank you.' Margot secretly enjoyed being in

the number one dressing room. It was the only one with a gold star but, more importantly, it had been Nancy's dressing room. 'When I was at school,' she said, laughing, 'whoever came top of the class at the end of each term was awarded a gold star. I was always near the top, often second or third, but I never came top, so I never got the gold star.'

'Stand still.'

'Sorry.' She laughed again. 'I wonder what my teacher would say if she could see me now with a gold star that big on my door?'

Dressing room one was nearest the stage and was the female lead's dressing room. Number two was the male lead's room, except there wasn't a male lead, so George and Betsy were in it. Artie was in dressing room three with a couple of musicians. And the rest of the orchestra were in room four – the biggest dressing room. Five and six, on the first floor, housed jugglers, magicians and other guest acts. Wardrobe and the white room were where they'd always been and Natalie Goldman's studio was still in dressing room seven. Eight and nine, which were only used when there was a large cast, were home to the chorus – boys in eight and girls in nine.

It was a fairly big cast, although there were no glamorously dressed back-drop girls standing at the back of the stage holding elegant poses in picturesque tableaux. Until last summer there had been quite a turnover of young women. They didn't do much and they didn't say anything. But dressed as Indian maidens, Greek goddesses, or Spanish flamenco dancers, they looked stunning.

'Your five minute call, Miss Dudley.'

Margot looked at Thelma. 'Did he say the five? I don't remember him calling the half.'

'You had your eyes closed. I thought you were asleep and didn't want to disturb you.'

Getting up, Margot looked in the mirror. She bit her bottom lip. 'This is it then?'

Thelma nodded. 'This is it. Get out there and show them what you're made of,' she said, hugging Margot. 'Break a leg.'

'Don't say that. My ankle has only just healed.' They both laughed.

'You'll be fine; better than fine. I'll see you for your first costume change.'

George and Betsy, Artie, the entire orchestra, dancers, musicians, everyone backstage and front of house, had wished Margot good luck one way or another. And she was ready. When the stage manager said, 'This is your cue, Miss Dudley,' she walked out onto the stage as if she'd never been off it.

The show was a massive success. It was a series of sketches and songs that were familiar to many people in the audience. They sang along with "Run Rabbit Run" and "Don't Sit Under The Apple Tree" and all the other songs. Artie Armitage had them rolling in the aisles, jugglers on stilts had them gasping, and at the finale Margot, George and Betsy, dressed in their ENSA uniforms, sang their interpretation of The Andrews Sisters' hit "Bei Mir Bist du Schoen" to rapturous applause and a standing ovation.

Margot's dressing room was buzzing with members of the company as well as friends. Natalie and Anton arrived with Bill and Bess but not Ena, who had been refused time off work at the last minute.

The first night party at the Prince Albert Club was a little subdued, but everyone was exhausted anyway. The bandleader asked Margot to sing, which she agreed to do only if George and Betsy sang with her. The three friends ran across to the stage. They sang, "Putting On The Ritz", which went down a storm. Margot and Betsy left George on stage to do her new party piece "Burlington Bertie" and she brought the house down.

When they had finished and were back in their seats a waiter gave Margot a card and pointed at the bar. It was from Bernard Rudman, the manager of The Talk of London, asking her if she would consider working for him. Margot looked over her shoulder. Bernard Rudman was easy to spot. He wore a black tuxedo with a satin grosgrain shawl collar and an overcoat with an astrakhan collar draped over his shoulders. Margot smiled and nodded. Performing at The Talk of London would be good. She dropped the card into her handbag. Topping the bill was what she wanted.

CHAPTER TWENTY

'I have the newspapers, Miss Margot.'

Margot laid her hand on the new stage doorman's arm. 'Thank you, Stan.'

Margot meant more than thank you for the newspapers, and saw in Stan's kind eyes that he knew. 'Congratulations, Miss,' he nodded, handing her half a dozen dailies.

'Anyone in yet?'

Miss Betsy and Miss George. Both weighed down with papers,' he laughed.

'Thank you, I'll join them.' With her own bundle of newspapers tucked under her arm, Margot ran to George and Betsy's dressing room.

'You've hit the headlines,' Betsy said, throwing her arms around Margot as soon as she stepped through the door.

'Damn right too,' George said.

'You were spectacular last night. Considering-- I mean, how upset you were before the show.'

George handed Betsy *The Stage* and the *Evening Standard*. 'Find the reviews in these while I look through *The Times* and the *Guardian*. Then lay them open on the table. What have you got, Margot?'

'*Telegraph* and *Mirror*.' Dropping the rest of the papers on the floor, she laid the *Mirror* on the table and began to read the *Telegraph*.

'Right, let's see what the critics have to say! Come on, you two,' George said, 'don't be shy.'

'Oh my God!'

'What is it?' Seeing tears in Margot's eyes, George went to her and looked over her shoulder. 'Let me see what it says.'

"'No one could take the place of the wonderful Nancy Jewel…'" Margot burst into tears. 'I wasn't trying to take her place. I wish she was here more than anyone.'

'We know,' George said. 'Hang on; what you read was out of context.' She took the paper out of Margot's hands. '"No one could take the place of the wonderful Nancy Jewel, the toast of London and star of The Prince Albert Theatre in London's West End, except the equally talented Margot Dudley. It must have been hard for the relatively unknown actress, Nancy Jewel's protégée, to take over her mentor's role, but she did and she did it brilliantly. We toast you, Miss Dudley. Theatreland is agog!"'

'I'm sorry. When I read the opening sentence it made me feel as if I was stepping up on Nancy's coat tails. Made me feel--'

'Oh I think you've earned your stripes, Margot. I think the theatre critics and reviewers know it too.'

'"Margot Dudley stole the show. Not the first time and it won't be the last, I hope."'

'It says in *The Stage*, "Regional actress Margot Dudley, who arrived in London a couple of years ago and began her life at the Prince Albert Theatre as an usherette, stole the show."'

'"A star performance!" the *Guardian* says. "The Prince Albert Theatre at its very best," from the *Evening Standard*, and *The Times*, "Margot Dudley gave the performance of her life." Do I need to go on, Margot?' Margot shook her head and put her arms around George. 'I think Nancy would be proud of what you did last night-- what we all did.'

At that moment Richard Smiley came into the room. 'Does anyone around here have time to rehearse, or should we just go up tonight in the slip-shod fashion we went up in last night?'

The three girls turned and glared at him. Unable to keep up the pretence, he broke into a broad smile and ran across the room. Lifting Margot off her feet he swung her round, before dropping her and putting his arms round George and Betsy. 'Stars! You're all bloody stars!'

'Does that include me, Mr Smiley?' Artie said, entering the dressing room.

'You're all included,' the director said. 'But we have to keep up the standard. Today we enjoy our fame. Tomorrow we start re-working the opening number. I want it tighter, sharper and more energetic.' Richard Smiley left to good-humoured protests and sounds of mock rebellion.

'Shush everyone,' Betsy shouted. 'Shush, listen!' she shouted again.

'What is it, Bets?' Margot said.

'That Dave. Goldie's ex-bloke. That's him, isn't it?' she said, taking the *Daily Mirror* from the table and passing it to Margot.

'Looks like him. Oh my God!' Margot began to read. '"Three men taken into custody for their own protection were later arrested. At Speaker's Corner in Hyde Park, three men were heckling an elderly Jewish man speaking about the plight of Jews in Germany. Several people in the crowd recognised the hecklers from an earlier confrontation in the East End and set about them, accusing them of having been members of the disbanded British Union of Fascists."'

'So was Nazi Dave one of them arrested?' Betsy asked.

'It doesn't give names,' Margot said.

'Let's see if there's anything in *The Times*.' George flicked through the paper. 'There's a short report here.

"Ex-BUF members David Sutherland, Harold Alsop and Richard McCauley, taken into custody for their own protection after being attacked in Hyde Park, were later charged with membership of an illegal organisation, failing to answer the call up and resisting a constable in the execution of his duty. All three men have been kept in custody pending a court hearing."'

'Woo-hoo!' Betsy hooted. 'He's in the clink.'

'Well! That's one to celebrate.'

'And we should. Let's go to the club after the show. Margot, you won't have to look over your shoulder ever again,' Betsy said.

'Depends on how long they give him.'

'It won't matter, Bets. He'll be interned until the war ends, like Mosley,' George said.

Margot felt conspicuous sitting in the court, but she was determined to see Dave Sutherland put away. With a guard, he was first up from the cells. The other men followed. He wore a brown shirt buttoned up to the neck. His hair was greased down and he'd grown a stupid moustache like Adolf Hitler. When he entered the dock he stood to attention and looked straight ahead.

'What does he look like?' George shook her head. 'God knows what Goldie saw in him.'

'Or why she stayed with him for so long,' Betsy said.

'Fear,' Margot whispered. 'She was scared to leave him. Frightened for her life in the end. She told me he was really nice to her in the beginning. It was after she found his BUF membership that he began to show his true colours.'

'The bastard!' George said. 'I hope they throw away the key.'

There were the normal questions about name and address. And then the Clerk of the Court read out the first charge, failing to answer the call up. All three admitted their guilt. What else could they say?

The judge asked them if his information was correct – that they continued to support the aims and principles of the British Union of Fascists, even though it had now been disbanded. Dave Sutherland brought his heels together and shouted, 'Guilty as charged and proud of it!' His two mates nodded.

The judge slammed his gavel down on its block. 'Eighteen months on the first charge. If the war is not over by the time you have served your sentence you will be interned under Section 18B until it is. Take them down.'

The judge stood up and the court followed. Margot, George and Betsy, holding hands, gripped each other tightly as Dave Sutherland and his cronies were escorted down to the cells.

For a moment the three women stood as if frozen, speechless. It was George who broke the silence. 'Thank God the pathetic bully got what he deserved.'

Margot nodded. 'He'll be in jail until the war ends at least. That's a much longer sentence than he'd have got for beating Goldie up.'

'And they won't be given an easy time by the other inmates,' George said, 'or the prison warders. No one likes traitors and cowards.'

George put her arms round Margot and Betsy. 'Let's go. We've got a show to do.'

CHAPTER TWENTY-ONE

'It's been a year since the theatre re-opened and we're still getting fantastic reviews,' Margot said, drinking tea and eating toast while reading the reviews in the newspapers. 'They're still walking out of Sherwood's *There Shall Be No Night* at the Aldwych. Don't know how it keeps going. It says here that it's too tragic, too close to what's going on in real life. Well it would be, wouldn't it?' she said, more to herself than to Bill. 'Bob Hope's still in London. There's a lovely photo of him with a crowd of GIs. Look, Bill...' Margot pushed the newspaper under her husband's nose. 'I'd love to see him while he's here. Not much chance of that though. Vera Lynn's been in town too; in Trafalgar Square, entertaining the Navy. Good Lord, the BBC's complaining about *Strike A New Note* at The Prince of Wales. They're saying that, because Zoe Gail sings "I'm Gonna Get Lit Up When The Lights Go Up In London" she's encouraging people to get drunk.'

'Well, getting lit up is modern slang for getting drunk,' Bill said.

'It might be,' Margot said, laughing, 'but no one's going to get "lit up" on a ration of one bottle of gin every eight weeks, are they? I like Zoe Gail, she's fun. So,' Margot said when she'd finished reading, 'the Prince Albert Theatre is still at the top of the West End theatre listings.' She folded the last newspaper and added it to the pile at the side of her chair. 'You're quiet,' she said, looking up at Bill. 'What's the matter?'

'I was thinking. Well, wondering really.'

'What about?'

'Whether or not you're going to do The Talk of

267

London?'

'I'd forgotten about it. Bernard Rudman hasn't been in touch for ages.'

'What if he gets in touch?'

Margot knew Bill wouldn't like what she was about to say and wished he hadn't asked. 'I'd probably do it.'

'I knew it!'

'How could I turn it down?'

Bill wasn't listening. 'Seven shows a week, two late spots at the Albert Club and a late night at The Talk. You'll be ill again.' He got up from the table, picked up his wallet and went into the hall.

'Where are you going? You haven't finished your breakfast.'

'To work.'

That night when she got home from the club, Margot took off her coat and tiptoed into the flat hoping Bill was in bed, but not asleep. She needed to speak to him, persuade him that a spot on Saturday night at The Talk of London wasn't going to be too much for her. Also, they hadn't made love for goodness knows how long. She opened the bedroom, but Bill wasn't there. A surge of panic rose from her stomach. She felt nauseous and swallowed hard. What if he'd been injured in a raid? Had she pushed him too far this morning and he'd left her? Margot's heart began to thump against her ribs. If he talked to Jenny, she'd do her best to persuade him to leave. She ran into the sitting room. 'Bill!' she shouted, feeling relief and anger at the same time when she saw him asleep on the settee. 'What are you doing in here? Why aren't you in bed?'

'Must have fallen asleep,' he said, yawning and rubbing his eyes. He squinted at the clock on the mantle shelf. 'Good God, it's one o'clock. I've got to be up at six.'

'You should have gone to bed.'

'I did go to bed, but I couldn't sleep for worrying about you. Where the hell have you been until now?'

'Working! It's Friday night. I do a late night spot at the Albert Club on Fridays, remember?' As Margot dropped onto the settee Bill pushed himself up. 'You're obviously not interested in what I've got to tell you,' she said, as he made his way to the bedroom.

'What's so important it can't wait until morning?' Bill said, turning in the doorway and yawning again.

Margot felt like saying nothing, but that would cause another argument. 'Bernard Rudman was at the club with Salvatore tonight.'

'Is that what you're keeping me from my bed to tell me?'

'No!'

Sudden realisation crept across Bill's face. He hit the doorframe with the flat of his hand and shook his head. Margot jumped, but said nothing. 'He's asked you to do a spot and you've said yes, haven't you? Well, am I right?'

'Yes! You're right! Are you happy now you've spoilt it for me?' Margot screamed.

'I'm tired. Don't wake me when you come to bed,' Bill said, closing the bedroom door.

The following morning when Margot got up, she was pleased to see Bill had already left for the MoD – she didn't feel up to another argument. Bill said it was because of her health that he didn't want her to take on any more work, but it was because when the war ended – and those in the know were saying it would be sooner rather than later – he wanted her to leave London with him and go back to the Midlands to start a family. She had managed to change the subject every time he brought it up, but she wouldn't be able to do it for much longer.

'Ladies and gentlemen, I give you Miss Margot Dudley.'

Margot stood up to overwhelming applause. After kissing Bill on the cheek, she made her way across the room, elegantly weaving through tables of diners, smiling and greeting them.

The bandleader offered her his hand, which Margot graciously accepted. After a brief exchange she turned to the audience. 'Thank you,' she said into the microphone, smiling, and she waited for the applause to die down. When it did, she nodded to the bandleader. The band began to play and Margot began to sing "A Nightingale Sang In Berkley Square".

At midnight, after singing for almost an hour, Margot ended the set with "Smoke Gets In Your Eyes" followed by "I'll Be Seeing You", to a standing ovation. She bowed to the band, thanked the bandleader and blew kisses to the audience. Then she made her way back to the table where Bill and her friends were sitting, smiling and thanking people on the way.

'Bravo!' George shouted as Margot approached the table. 'You were wonderful, darling.'

'Thank you, George. Pour me a drink, will you?'

Bill pulled out her chair. 'Sit down, Margot, you look exhausted.'

'I am a bit. Cheers!' she said, taking a glass of wine from George and drinking half of it in one go. 'I needed that. It's hot under all those lights. Bright too; given me a headache,' she said, more to herself than to her friends.

After congratulating her, Natalie and Anton got up

and made their way to the dance floor.

'Do you want to dance, Margot?' Bill asked.

'Not at the moment, darling, if you don't mind,' Margot said, leaning back in her chair and smiling lovingly at her husband. 'Give me ten minutes to shake off this damn headache and I'll dance you off your feet.'

'I'll dance with you, Bill,' Jenny said, jumping up.

'See you later, ladies,' Bill called over his shoulder, as Jenny led him to the dance floor.

George poured another drink. 'Do you trust her, Margot?'

'Who?'

'Jenny.'

'Why do you ask?'

'It's probably nothing, but she's been making eyes at Bill all night. Agreeing with everything he said and laughing at his jokes, which frankly weren't all that funny.'

'Making eyes at him and agreeing with him is one thing, but laughing at his jokes? That's grounds for divorce,' Margot said, putting her arm around George. 'What do you think, Bets?'

'I think she's got a crush on him, that's all. But there's no harm in keeping an eye on her. Bill's a good looking fella and they do spend a lot time together on the ambulances.'

Margot scanned the dance floor until she found them. Bill stood head and shoulders above Jenny. With a straight back he held her at arm's length. She waved the idea away. 'Loyal to the core, my Bill.'

'He might be,' George said, 'but is she?'

'No, she isn't!' Margot's eyes flashed with anger.

'But I thought she was your friend,' Betsy said.

'She was. Bill thinks she still is, so don't say

271

anything. She tried to pinch him off me while we were touring with ENSA.' Margot's pulse quickened and she felt her cheeks flush. Not at the memory of Jenny, but at the memory of her own near indiscretion with Lieutenant Boyd Murphy on the second ENSA tour. If she hadn't felt so guilty she might easily have--

'What happened, Margot?' George asked. 'Margot?'

'Sorry, I was miles away... She said she'd been bombed out and had nowhere to live, so Bill took her in.'

'And had she?'

'No. It was a pack of lies. Anyway, I threatened to tell Bill and she promised not to try it on with him again.'

'Do you believe her?' Betsy asked.

'Oh yes! She knows if I told Bill it would put the kibosh on her working on the ambulances.' Margot laughed. 'She won't try anything again. If she does, I'll get her sacked.'

'Shush, they're coming back,' George said.

'I think this is my dance,' Margot said to Bill when he and Jenny returned to the table. 'Sir?' She slipped her arm through his.

Bill stood up very straight. 'It would be my pleasure, Madam.'

While they danced, Margot asked Bill if he'd noticed Jenny making eyes at him.

Bill laughed and said he hadn't. 'I only notice when you make eyes at me.' He held her tight, her body moulded to his.

The last dance was a waltz. Margot laid her head on Bill's chest and they danced closely and slowly, making up their own steps.

'Right!' Margot said when they were back at the table. 'This place is about to close, but I haven't had nearly enough fun. Let's go back to our apartment and carry on the party.'

'We must go home,' Natalie said. 'It's been lovely, but it takes a while to get back to Hampstead.' She took Margot's hand. 'Look after yourself, my dear, and get a good night's sleep,' she said, kissing her goodbye.

Anton said goodnight to Bill, and Natalie said goodnight to George and Betsy, kissing each of them in turn.

'You were wonderful tonight,' Anton said, turning to Margot. 'You won't give up your theatre job now you're a famous cabaret star, will you?'

'How could you ask such a thing?' Margot looked suitably shocked and kissed Anton goodbye. 'I'll be on stage at the Prince Albert Theatre on Monday morning, ten o'clock sharp, to work on my new songs.'

'Bets and I are off too.' George said, kissing Bill and then Margot. And while Betsy was saying goodnight, George said, 'We'll take Jenny with us.' Jenny opened her mouth to protest, but George ignored her. 'Bets and I are getting a cab,' she said, looking sternly at Jenny. 'It's no trouble to swing by the East End, make sure you get home safely.'

Jenny looked at Bill but, seeing Margot with her arms around him, she said, 'If you're sure?'

Walking the short distance home, Margot said, 'She's got one hell of a crush on you, Bill.'

'Who? George?' he said, laughing.

'No! You know who! And, cheeky, there's nothing wrong with George,' Margot said, defending her friend.

'I know that, you silly goose. George is a good sort. I just don't think I'm her kind of-- beau.'

'You're definitely someone's kind of beau.'

'If you mean Jenny,' Bill said, as they turned into Oxford Mews, 'you're wrong. Jenny is just a nice kid who's a bit lost.'

'Is that what she is, a bit lost? We'll see.'

'Yes,' Bill said, opening the street door to the apartment. 'And she does a good job on the ambulances, so don't be so horrible, Margot!'

'Me? Horrible? That girl is infatuated with you. And if you can't see it, Bill Burrell, you're dafter than I thought you were.' In the living room, Margot went straight to the drinks cupboard and took out a bottle of brandy.

'Thank you!' Bill took the brandy from her. 'I think it's time you went to bed.' After returning the bottle to the cupboard, he helped Margot out of her coat and hung it up. 'Come on, I'm tired.'

She gritted her teeth. She was so close to telling Bill about Jenny and her lies. Another drink and she would have done. Serve the little bitch right. Bill too, for always taking her side. In a huff, Margot stomped into the bedroom.

'"The assassination attempt on Adolf Hitler may have failed, but thanks to the Americans – and the other allied forces involved in the Normandy landings – the major cities of Europe are being liberated,"' Bill said, reading the newspaper to Margot when she entered the sitting room. 'They've listed the cities – Cherbourg, Florence, Paris, and on October 14th, Athens. Hitler won't last long now.'

'Good morning to you too, Bill. Yes, I am well, thank you for asking. No, I didn't sleep through the night, because I was in agony with my ankle.' Seeing the concerned look on her husband's face, Margot put up her hand. 'But this morning it feels much better,' she said, plonking herself down on the chair opposite him at the breakfast table. Leaning on her elbows, Margot put her chin on her hands and looked up at Bill through tired eyes. She sighed loudly.

'Sorry, sweetheart. For once the papers have some good news in them. Tea?' He felt the pot. 'It's still hot.'

Margot nodded. 'Toast?'

'Have this,' he said, buttering the last slice in the rack and handing it to her. 'I'll put another couple of slices under the grill.'

Returning almost immediately with the kettle, Bill topped up the tea pot. After taking the kettle back to the kitchen, he returned with two slices of toast. While he buttered them, Margot poured a second cup of tea.

'It'll be over soon,' Bill said, picking up the newspaper again. 'It says here, "June 6th 1944 will go down in history as the beginning of Adolf Hitler's demise. Thanks to the amphibious invasion in Nazi-occupied France earlier this year, when allied troops landed on the beaches of Normandy and invaded the heavily guarded coastline, important headway was made towards overtaking Hitler's armies." I told you, didn't I?'

'It hasn't stopped him from bombarding us with flying bombs. Those damn Doodle Bugs have done more damage and killed more people--'

'Not for much longer. Listen to this. "Allied paratroopers and glider units were dropped behind German lines along the coast, from Caen through Sainte Mere-Eglise beach--"'

'I hope Claire isn't there,' Margot said, suddenly all ears.

'What makes you think she might be?'

'Because...' Margot wished she'd paid more attention to what Bess had told her about Claire's work in France.

'I tell you, Margot, it's going to be over soon. I can't say anything, but Whitehall's buzzing with optimism.' Bill folded the newspaper and got up. Standing behind Margot, he bent down and kissed the top of her head. 'And then, my love, we are going home.'

Margot sighed. Going home to the Midlands wasn't what she wanted. She loved her life as a West End star. She loved the work, the fame, being recognised in the street. She still felt a tingle in the pit of her stomach when she was asked for her autograph. 'Why are you in such a rush to go back to the Midlands? I thought you were happy here?'

'I am happy, if you don't count dodging V1s and V2s every day on the roads, watching people die because you can't get them to a hospital fast enough because the roads have been blown up, or trying to stop an old lady from going into what's left of her home after it's been blitzed. London was never going to be forever, Margot,' he said, bending down and looking into her eyes. 'We were only ever going to be here until the war ended. We said we'd go home once it was over and start a family. Or have you forgotten?'

'No, I haven't forgotten. How could I, you're always reminding me.'

'What? I can't remember the last time we talked about going home, or starting a family.'

'That's because *we* don't talk about it. *You* do.'

'That's not fair, Margot.'

'I'm sorry. Of course I haven't forgotten,' Margot said, putting her arms around Bill's neck. 'It's just that things are going well for us at the moment. We have a nice home, good friends--'

'We'll have a nicer home and make new friends. We can live wherever you want: Lowarth, Rugby, Coventry-- You choose,' Bill said, resting his chin on her head and rocking her gently.

'What about my job?'

'There'll be other jobs. I'm sure your old employers--'

'You're not listening, Bill. What about my job in the theatre, at the club and The Talk of London? How many theatres and clubs are there in Lowarth and Rugby? As for going back to working in a factory or an office, how the hell can I do that?'

'But you said--'

'That was five years ago, before the war. Before I'd worked in the theatre. It's different now.'

'No, Margot,' Bill shouted. 'It isn't different! Nothing has changed except you are going back on your word. As usual it doesn't matter what *I* want, it's all about you and what *you* want.' He stormed out of the room.

'The war isn't over yet!' Margot shouted after him. Seething, she took the breakfast dishes into the kitchen. When she returned she heard the front door slam.

Out of breath and drenched to the skin from running in the rain, Margot knocked on the door of the Ambulance Controller's office. She didn't wait to be invited in. 'Did Bill come in to work this evening?'

'Yes. They've just come back. I don't know where they are, but you could try the cafeteria.'

'I didn't think Bill was on tonight.'

'He wasn't, but he was here when a couple of FANYs called in sick, so he went out on a shout.'

'Who with?' Margot asked, even though she knew what the controller would say.

'Jenny was driving. Bill was her first-aider.'

'Thank you.' Margot forced herself to smile, and left. She hadn't taken more than a couple of steps across the ambulance park towards the hospital's main entrance when a strip of light, hardly more than a flash, cut through the darkness from a side door, attracting her attention. She peered through what was now driving rain. She hoped it was Bill. It was Jenny.

'Looking for Bill?'

'Yes!' Margot said, misjudging the depth of the curb and stumbling. To save herself from falling headlong into a puddle, she put her right foot down heavily and twisted her already painful ankle.

'Ooops!' Jenny said, laughing. 'Bit early isn't it, Margot, even for you?'

Treating the insinuation that she was drunk with the contempt it deserved, Margot carried on walking, her ankle throbbing.

'You'll lose him, you know,' Jenny shouted after her, 'but then you don't deserve him anyway.'

Ignoring the pain in her ankle, Margot spun on her heels. 'What do you mean, I'll lose him and I don't deserve him? You know nothing about me, and even less about my relationship with my husband.' She moved towards Jenny, who stepped backwards. 'Yes! *My* husband!' Margot spat. 'Not yours!'

'Not for long,' Jenny said, regaining her confidence. 'Look at you. You're a drunk, Margot Dudley. You're an argumentative, conceited, self-centred drunk! And when Bill sees you for what you are, he'll come back to me.'

Margot's eyes blazed with anger. 'Come back to you? How the hell can Bill come back to you, when he has never been with you? You're deluding yourself again, Jenny.'

'After my flat was bombed, Bill and me--'

'What?' Margot laughed out loud. She couldn't believe what she was hearing. 'Your flat wasn't bombed, Jenny – except in the twisted fantasy world you live in – because you didn't have a flat. I went to your imaginary flat, remember?' Jenny looked at Margot, her lips a tight line, her eyes black with hate. 'You promised me if I didn't tell Bill you'd made it up, you'd leave him alone.'

Without taking her eyes off Margot, Jenny put her hands over her ears. Then, jerking her head from side to side, she started to sing. 'La-la-la-la! La-la-la-la…'

'You begged me not say anything to Bill,' Margot shouted above Jenny's insane chanting, 'and I didn't. I didn't tell him, and I didn't tell your controller, because you'd have been sacked if I had – and this is how you repay me!'

'Bill would be with me now, if you hadn't come back from ENSA before I had time to--' Jenny looked wide-eyed, like a rabbit caught in the headlights of a car.

'Time to what?' Jenny didn't answer. 'Before you had time to what?' Margot shouted.

'Make him love me! And he would have done too, if you hadn't come back and ruined everything. He wanted me as much as I wanted him. He loved me, I know he did. We'd have been happy if it hadn't been for you,' she screamed, and she lunged at Margot, knocking her to the ground. Standing over Margot, Jenny laughed hysterically. 'Not so high and mighty now, are you?'

Margot lifted her arms up to protect her face as Jenny kicked out. The toe of her shoe caught Margot in the ribs. As she turned to avoid a second blow, Margot saw a dim shaft of light coming from the door that Jenny had come out of. She saw a man pull on the collar on his coat before stepping out. It was Bill. 'Bill!' she shouted.

'Margot?' Seeing his wife on the ground, Bill began to run. 'What the hell's going on?' Bill took hold of Jenny by the shoulders and dragged her off Margot.

Jenny stumbled but quickly recovered. 'She attacked me, Bill. I was defending myself. She's drunk,' Jenny cried, trying to put her arms round Bill's neck.

'Let go of me, Jenny!' Bill bellowed.

Jenny let go and stepped back. She shook her head in disbelief. 'What are you doing, Bill? I love you, and you love me, you know you do.'

'I don't love you, Jenny. I have never loved you. I have never loved anyone but my wife,' Bill said, helping Margot to her feet.

Margot put her foot to the ground and cried out. 'Good God, what have you done to her?' he barked.

I'm sorry, Bill. I didn't mean to... Please don't tell the controller. I couldn't bear it if I lost my job. Please, Bill. It's all I've got.'

'Then you'd better get on with it, hadn't you!' Bill shouted, putting his arm around Margot. 'Come on, love, let's go home.'

'You're just in time for a cup of tea,' Margot said, hopping across the sitting room to greet Bill. 'Would you get it, love? It's in the kitchen. I daren't risk carrying it in case I drop it.' Margot turned on her good foot and dropped onto the nearest chair. 'Damn ankle.'

Bill went to the kitchen and brought back the tea

tray. 'I'll pour,' he said, sitting next to her.

'You're quiet,' Margot said, as Bill handed her a cup. 'What did the controller say?'

'He wouldn't accept my resignation.'

Margot sighed loudly. 'As angry as I am with Jenny I don't want her to lose her job, but if the controller won't let you leave you'll have to tell him you won't work with her. And if he wants to know why, tell him. Serves her right,' Margot said, taking a sip of her tea. 'If he sacks her it's her own fault.'

Bill leant his elbows on the table and put his head in his hands.

'What is it?' Margot asked. 'What's the matter?'

'The controller didn't accept my resignation,' Bill said, looking at Margot with tears in his eyes, 'because there's no need for me to leave.'

'Why? Has Jenny left?' She rubbed a tear from Bill's cheek with her thumb. 'What is it, love?'

'Jenny's dead.'

Margot looked into Bill's eyes, her own filling with tears. 'When? How?'

'Last night. She went out in my place.'

Margot's feelings were in turmoil. She thanked God Bill hadn't gone out with the ambulance the night before, or he might have been killed, but she was sad and sorry that Jenny had. She felt guilty too, because she'd argued with her, told her she was deluded. It was a cruel thing to say and would have hurt her more because it was true. The truth didn't matter now. Not the argument, not Jenny attacking her, or trying to steal Bill. None of it mattered any more. 'I'm sorry,' she whispered.

Bill gently pushed a wisp of hair out of Margot's eyes. 'I know.' The frown lines on his forehead deepened. 'Because I left early to-- Jenny took my ambulance out to the East End. The controller said Poplar had been given a thrashing and he put a call out asking every available crew to attend. When they got there a row of houses had been blitzed to rubble. Most of the residents had been in the shelter; the rest – minor cuts and bruises – were attended to on site. The firemen thought they'd got everyone out and began to pack up, but Jenny said she could hear someone shouting for help and went to investigate.' Bill paused and took a drink of his tea.

'Is it cold, love? Shall I'll make you another?'

He shook his head and cleared his throat. 'She found a man trapped beneath an iron girder. She managed to move the girder enough for the man to crawl to safety. It was then, the man said, that they saw the bomb. Jenny said she daren't put the girder down in case the weight set the bomb off, and she told him to fetch help.' Bill put his head in his hands again and wept.

Margot wanted desperately to say something that would help him. 'She was brave--'

'She was stupid,' Bill roared. 'Careless! She knew better than to put her own life in danger. She knew the procedure. We'd gone over it a hundred times. You never go into a dangerous situation alone; you wait for the fire brigade. They're equipped, trained. They'd have got the man out... Silly, silly girl! Why did she do it?' he cried. Bill took a handkerchief from his trousers pocket and wiped his face. 'The man she saved said her fellow ambulance workers were making their way over to her when the bomb exploded.' Bill broke down and sobbed. 'She didn't stand a chance.'

CHAPTER TWENTY-TWO

Margot turned over. She reached out in the dark, waved her hand about anxiously until she found the lamp on the bedside table and switched it on. She squinted at the clock. It was half past two – an hour later than the last time she looked. Her stomach felt hollow and ached. She was hungry. She hadn't eaten since…? She couldn't remember. Tea and toast! That's what she needed. Swinging her legs over the side of the bed, she wriggled her feet into her slippers, stood up and yawned.

By the lamp's pale glow, she staggered into the small hall and through the sitting room to the kitchen. She struck a match and lit a ring on the stove for the kettle, and then the grill for the toast. After filling the kettle and putting it on the gas, she took the lid off the bread bin. What was left of the loaf was covered in mould. She turned off the grill. Tea would have to do. Putting a couple of spoons of tea in the pot, she took a cup and saucer from the cupboard and a spoon from the drawer and placed them on the work surface before taking the milk from the stone slab in the small pantry. Sniffing it, half expecting it to be off, she smiled. The milk did smell a little rich, but it hadn't turned.

While she waited for the kettle to boil, she pulled back the blackout curtain and peered out of the window. The sky, as clear as glass, was dotted with stars. The moon was full with an eerie mustard yellow halo around it. She looked down and shivered. The Mews was full of shadows – some denser than others. Her heart began to hammer against her ribs. Every nerve in her body was jumping. Her chest was tight with fear and she began to panic. She held her breath and waited for the feeling to subside. It didn't. She inhaled deeply and exhaled slowly – that didn't help either.

Saved by the kettle whistling, Margot turned and let the curtain fall back into place. In the kitchen she made a pot of tea and riffled through the cupboards for something to eat. Nothing! Pouring tea into her cup, she remembered the Christmas present that Mrs Horton had given her. She went into the sitting room, knelt by the small fir tree and dragged the prettily wrapped gift from under it. Like an excited child she ripped off the paper and prised off the lid to find a tin of assorted Peak Frean's biscuits. She picked out her favourites - custard creams and the round ones with jam in the middle – and ate them hungrily while she drank her tea. Then she ran to the bathroom and was violently sick.

'OK! Take ten, everyone,' Richard Smiley called from the stalls. 'Not you, Margot,' he said, beckoning her with his forefinger.

Walking to the edge of the stage, Margot looked into the auditorium. As her eyes adjusted to the darkness she saw the director walking towards her. He mounted the steps at the side of the orchestra pit and stood on the apron with his hands on his hips. 'What the hell is going on with you, Margot? Are you ill?'

'No. I'm just a bit tired. I'm not sleeping well. You know how it is; stuff goes round in your head...' Smiley didn't look convinced. 'I'll be as right as rain after a good night's sleep,' she promised.

'Then go home and get some. You're no good to me as you are.'

She began to protest, but Smiley turned his back

on her and flicked his hand as if he was brushing away a fly.

Exhausted, Margot took off her coat, kicked off her shoes and went into the bathroom. She opened the door of the cabinet and took out a small brown bottle. Trembling, she unscrewed the cap, tipped a couple of pills into her hand, tilted her head back and threw them into her mouth. There wasn't a glass for water and the bitter tang as the pills began to dissolve made her heave, so she turned on the tap and put her head under it. Balking, she gulped water until she had swallowed the tablets. Wiping the back of her hand across her face, she stumbled into the bedroom – and, fully dressed, dropped onto the bed. She was asleep in seconds.

The following morning, Margot forced herself to get up. She washed and dressed, and went to see her doctor. Sitting in the waiting room she thought about the first time she'd seen him. He said there was nothing wrong with her, that all she needed was a good night's sleep. He prescribed pills for the pain in her ankle, which she took three times a day, and sleeping tablets that she took half an hour before she went to bed. They worked for a while, but then she started waking up after seven or eight hours feeling shattered, as if she hadn't slept at all. She couldn't face getting up. When she did eventually drag herself out of bed, it was often with a blinding headache. She felt sluggish, irritable, had no energy. She was repeatedly late for rehearsals and would argue with the choreographer and the director. But the worst was not being able to remember her songs and routines. She made excuses, blamed other people, but she knew it wasn't them. Even Lena, the choreographer, who had become a friend, accused her of not listening. But she had listened. She'd heard every word. She just couldn't remember.

The receptionist was suddenly standing in front of her. 'The doctor will see you now, Miss Dudley.'

'Thank you.' Margot followed her along a short corridor to the consulting room. Sitting down in front of his desk, Margot told the doctor that the effects of the sleeping tablets he'd prescribed for her lasted too long. She overslept most mornings. And when she did eventually wake up, she felt as tired as she had done before going to bed. It wasn't until mid-morning that she was able to function properly. 'Should I stop taking the sleeping tablets? They make me feel…' She searched for the right words. 'Lifeless,' she said at last, 'and irritable. I'm having bad dreams and headaches, and I can't concentrate.'

'Well,' he said, leaning across his desk and looking sympathetically at her. 'It isn't advisable to just stop taking tablets that your body has become used to. I'll lower the dosage and give you something to help you feel livelier in the mornings. Fifteen minutes after taking one of these,' he said, writing the prescription, 'you'll feel as bright as a button.'

Margot took the prescription and read it. It meant nothing to her. 'I wish I didn't have to take more tablets. Can't I go back to taking just one, for the pain in my ankle?'

'Yes, in time, but you have to reduce the dosage of the other tablets first. Coming off medication too quickly can be harmful. There are side effects--'

'Side effects?'

'Yes, but that's nothing for you to worry about. You're a very special patient, Margot, and I'm going to look after you personally. In time I shall have you as fit as a fiddle,' he said, walking her to the door. I'm sure you will, Margot thought. As long as I keep paying, you'll keep looking after me. 'Book Miss Dudley in for the next six weeks at around this time,' he said to the receptionist.

'Six weeks?'

'If I'm going to wean you off the sleeping tablets, as you've asked me to do, I need to monitor you every week. First we'll see how you get on with the new tablets. Then, if everything's satisfactory, we'll lower the dosage of the old ones.' Smiling, the doctor shook Margot's hand and returned to his office.

The receptionist wrote Margot's name in the appointment book, then handed her a card with the times and dates of her appointments written on it. 'We'll send the bill,' she said. Then she got up and went into the waiting room, presumably for the next patient, and Margot left.

The following week Margot cancelled her appointment. She was no longer going to line the private doctor's pockets. He'd had enough money out of her and as far as she could see, done very little for it. She would take herself off the sleeping pills and pick-me-ups when she was ready. Besides, she was too busy to take the time off. She was rehearsing in the day, performing at night and after doing cabaret at the Albert or The Talk of London she was going to parties, or jitterbugging into the early hours at Rainbow Corner, the American canteen in Piccadilly. One small pill put her to sleep at night, another woke her up in the morning, and one took away the pain in her ankle. She had never felt better.

'Margot? What on earth's the matter?' Natalie Goldman said, seeing Margot on the floor in the corner of her dressing room. With her eyes shut, clutching her knees and rocking back and forth, Margot began to shake her head and cry. 'Would you take Margot's other arm, Miss Lesley and we'll help her to her feet?' Natalie said. She nodded her thanks to Stan, who had alerted Miss Lesley to how ill Margot looked when she arrived at the theatre, and he left the dressing room, closing the door quietly.

'Leave me alone,' Margot hissed, resisting help from the two women. 'He mustn't know I'm here, or he'll-- Shush! If he finds me he'll kill me.'

'Who'll kill you, dear?' Pamela Lesley asked.

Margot's eyes narrowed, darting round the room like a frightened child. Breathing in short, sharp gasps she said, 'Listen! Can't you hear him? He knows I'm here. Please God, save me.' Her eyes flashed from Pamela Lesley to Natalie Goldman. 'Natalie?' Margot said, as if she was seeing her for the first time. 'You won't let him hurt me, will you? Say you won't. Say it!' she begged.

'I won't let him hurt you. I wouldn't let anyone hurt you, Margot. Nor will Miss Lesley, will you, Pamela?'

'No, Margot dear. You're safe with us.'

Reassured, Margot allowed the two women to help her to her feet. 'I'm so tired,' she said as they steered her across the room to the chaise longue.

'Why don't you have a lie down?' Natalie put a pillow under Margot's head. A second later she closed her eyes. Natalie Goldman motioned to Miss Lesley to move away. 'I don't want her to hear... Thank you for coming to me, Pamela. And thank you for helping me now. I couldn't have managed her on my own.'

'I'm very fond of Margot,' Pamela Lesley said, 'very fond indeed.' For some time the two women stood without speaking and watched Margot sleep. It was Pamela Lesley who broke the silence. 'What I'm about to tell you is for your ears only, Natalie.'

'Of course. Go on.'

'As you know, there is always chit-chat and gossip in the theatre – and most of it is harmless. However,' Pamela Lesley said, 'I overheard the usherettes talking about Margot last night. They were saying she drinks in the dressing room.'

'There is always a bottle of champagne, brandy, or some sort of alcohol in the cupboard--'

'She brings it in and hides the empty bottles, one of the casuals said.' Natalie's eyes widened. 'But don't worry. The girl gave me her word she wouldn't tell anyone. I promised her a job as soon as there's an opening to make sure. But that's by the by,' she said, turning to look at Margot. 'What people do, or don't do, is their business, but Margot has worked so hard to get where she is, it would be a terrible shame if she threw it all away.'

Natalie sighed. 'It would. I wonder if Bill knows?'

'No! And he mustn't,' Margot shouted, reaching out to Natalie. 'I'll stop. I won't drink any more, I promise. I'll do anything, but please don't tell Bill,' she begged.

'I won't tell him, if you let me help you.'

Margot looked at Natalie for a long minute, and then nodded. 'All right,' she said, leaning heavily on Natalie and Pamela as they helped her to stand up

'Are you sure you don't want us to tell your husband, Margot?' Pamela Lesley asked.

'No!' Margot shot the front of house manager a frightened look. 'No. Please don't tell him. He's visiting his parents in Coventry. He'll come back, and it's not fair. Besides, there's no point. I told you. I won't drink again, I promise. I just need a good night's sleep.'

'Which you won't get on the floor of your dressing room. Come on, let's get you out of here before someone comes in. Pamela, would you mind having a look round?'

'Leave it to me,' Pamela said. 'I'll make sure nothing's been left behind.'

'Margot, how long will Bill be away? When will he be back?'

'I can't remember... I think another week.'

'Right! You're not going home to an empty apartment. You can stay with Anton and me.'

'But I don't have any clean clothes.'

'That's the least of your worries, dear,' Pamela said, helping Margot on with her coat.

'We'll call at the apartment on the way and pack a bag.'

Margot nodded and let Natalie and Miss Lesley take her by the arms. 'What about the show?'

'You've got an understudy. She'll be only too happy to go on for you.'

'But--'

'No buts, Margot. You know you can't work in this state.'

Margot took a shuddering breath as great almond-shaped tears spilled onto her cheeks.

'Come on now, you'll soon feel better,' Natalie said, putting her arms around Margot and walking her to the dressing room door. 'The Prince Albert Theatre can't do without you, you know that.'

Margot smiled through her tears, but she said nothing.

The week Margot spent with Natalie and Anton passed quickly. She went to bed at a reasonable time and slept until she woke up naturally, getting up when she felt like it – sometimes it was mid-morning before she bathed and dressed. Natalie took the week off and together the two friends went for long walks over Hampstead Heath. Most days they called at a small coffee shop on their way home, drank Camp coffee by the fire to warm up, or went shopping for food – such as it was.

On Saturday morning Margot was mixing powdered egg when Natalie arrived downstairs.

'Mm, can I smell coffee?'

'Yes. Just made it,' Margot said. 'I hope it's all right. It's been a while since I made real coffee. Where did you get it from?'

'Germany. The last time I visited my parents I persuaded a local shopkeeper to sell me a couple of packets. He had cupboards full of the best coffee beans, packaged and priced, but the SS had been to his shop and ordered him not to sell it to anyone, except them. Not that they would pay him for it. The SS take what they want. If they had even suspected the shopkeeper had sold me some, a Jew, he would have been--' Natalie shuddered. 'It doesn't bear thinking about.'

'When was the last time you saw your mother and father?' Margot asked, placing a plate of scrambled egg on toast in front of Natalie, before sitting down with her own.

'Eighteen months ago longer. After the Luftwaffe intensified the bombardment of vessels sailing across the Channel it became impossible to travel to Germany. I don't know where my parents are now. They were planning to go to Switzerland, to stay with relatives of George--'

'Our George?' Margot said. 'George

Derby-Bloom?'

'Yes.' For some minutes they ate in silence. 'George and I have been helping Jewish students to escape the Nazis,' Natalie said, when they had finished eating.

'How did George get involved?'

'When she was at finishing school in Switzerland she got to know people in a Jewish organisation that helped students cross the German border. To cut a long story short, George persuaded her father to finance getting the students out of Germany, and asked Anton if he would hide them when they got to England.'

'Is that what dressing rooms eight and nine are for? To hide Jewish students?'

'Yes, but after the children and their nanny and nurse had been evacuated to Foxden with your sister Bess, the students were able to stay here. There were only two or three at a time. A couple of house guests every now and then went unnoticed. It was the same at the theatre. With young women being called up on a regular basis no one noticed that there were more walk-ons one week and fewer the next.'

'What happens to the students? Where do they go?'

'First to Ireland and from there to America. There is a wonderful network of people in New York who find homes for them.'

'Is that what happened to Goldie?'

'No. Goldie is living with her aunt in Ireland.'

Margot smiled at the thought of her friend being safe, and began clearing the table.

'It goes without saying that this conversation stays between us, Margot. We must never speak of it outside this house. Walls really do have ears,' Natalie said. 'The network of people, and the escape route out of Germany across the Swiss border, was the reason Goldie's fascist boyfriend befriended her. He might have killed her if you hadn't stepped in. That's why, when he realised it was you who had taken her place on stage, he followed you.'

'Good God. I'm glad I didn't know I was in that sort of danger.'

'You weren't really. While Goldie's boyfriend was following you, we had people following him. You were never in mortal danger. Anton made sure of that.'

Margot laughed. 'A couple of things make sense now. Once when I was lost in the blackout I was followed. And in Oxford Circus underground I bumped into David Sutherland, or rather he bumped into me. I followed him, but lost him on Regent Street. When I saw him again and caught up with him, it wasn't him, if you know what I mean. The other man told me to go away. Was he one of Anton's people?'

'Yes. We wondered whether we should tell you at the time, but decided it would be best if you stayed on your guard. Eventually David Sutherland and his fascist blackshirts must have been satisfied that you didn't know anything, because he stopped following you. However,' Natalie said, her tone serious, 'if they find out you know now, you will be in danger again. Sutherland may be in prison, but there are many others.'

'I won't tell anyone, don't worry. I won't even let George know you've told me.' Margot finished her coffee. 'If there's ever anything I can do, you will let me know, won't you?'

Natalie put her hand on Margot's and nodded. 'Of course.' After pouring them both a second cup of coffee Natalie said, 'You're looking much better today. Did you sleep well?'

'Yes I did. And I'm feeling better too, so I'm going home.'

'Are you sure? You're welcome to stay as long as you like. Bill can stay too. It will be like old times,' Natalie said, smiling at the memory.

'I don't want Bill to stay here. And I don't want him to know I've been staying here.'

'But surely you'll tell him that you've been unwell, Margot?'

'No, he'll only worry. Besides, I'm better, so there's no need.'

At that moment Anton walked in and Natalie went over to the stove. 'What do you want for breakfast, darling?'

'Nothing, thank you, there's no time.' He looked at his watch. 'Got a breakfast meeting with the Association of West End Theatre Managers. I'll see you later,' he said, taking a drink of Natalie's coffee, before kissing her goodbye. 'Ready, Margot?' he called, leaving the kitchen.

'Yes, my bag's in the cloakroom. Thank you for looking after me, Natalie,' she said, hugging her friend. 'I appreciate all you've done for me this week, but I need to be at home when Bill gets back.' At the front door, Margot hugged Natalie and thanked her again. 'You won't tell Bill I was-- that I'd been drinking and I've been staying here with you and Anton, will you?'

Natalie shook her head. 'It isn't my job to tell him, Margot, it's yours.'

'And I will tell him, I promise, but not just yet. With our workloads we hardly see each other as it is. I don't want what little time we have together spoiled because Bill's worrying. Thank you, thank you, and thank you!' she said, kissing her friend, before running down the path and jumping into Anton's car.

CHAPTER TWENTY-THREE

The wireless crackled and spat for a few seconds before sparking into life with the voice of Winston Churchill. "Hostilities will end officially at one minute after midnight tonight, Tuesday, May 8th, but in the interests of saving lives the cease fire began yesterday." Margot cried with joy. Unable to see through her tears, she brought her attention back to the broadcast. "... celebrating today and tomorrow as Victory in Europe days."

Switching off the wireless, she grabbed her handbag and house keys, and ran downstairs. She flung open the street door and ran into the Mews to the sound of bells. The bells of St Paul's Cathedral were ringing for the first time since September 1939. Laughing and crying at the same time, she hugged and kissed everyone who lived or worked in the Mews as they came out of their homes and offices to share the good news.

She pushed her way through the crowds and made her way to Covent Garden. There was a party in almost every street and Margot was offered glasses of beer or cups of tea at every turn. Eventually she arrived at the Strand. Standing in the doorway of the theatre to protect her ankle from being trampled on, she listened to the horns of the river tugs as they sailed up the Thames. Suddenly they were drowned out by the drone of aeroplanes. Everyone looked up at the sky as five Spitfires roared overhead. The crowd went crazy, cheering and waving.

Margot searched the sea of faces hoping to see her friends. It was impossible to distinguish one face from another as thousands of people poured out of the underground stations. Someone pushed a Union Jack into her hand and pulled her into the crowd. She had no choice but to join the throng and go with the flow. Waving the flag high in the air, she was carried along the Strand, singing and dancing – and praying she wouldn't damage her ankle.

As Trafalgar Square came into view, Margot gasped. She could hardly believe her eyes. Tens of thousands of people were cheering and waving. Youths were climbing on the lions, draping them in red, white and blue bunting. Others were splashing about in the fountain. The fountain! Margot laughed out loud. When she first came to London in 1939 the fountain had been turned off to conserve water. She had walked through Trafalgar Square hundreds of times and never seen water coming from it. Now, for the first time in six years, people were jumping in it, cheering and laughing, scooping water up in their hands and throwing it over each other as if it were a symbol of freedom. In a way it was.

Suddenly a great snake of people dancing the conga passed and a soldier pulled Margot in. She danced along until she reached the steps of the National Gallery, where she ducked out.

'Margot?' she heard someone call. 'Margot?'

She looked around.

'Up here. On the steps.'

Looking up, Margot saw three American air force officers. One of them was First Lieutenant Boyd Murphy. 'Come up!' he shouted.

Margot wanted to but knew she shouldn't. Not after...

Suddenly the American film maker was at her side. 'Hi. Remember me?'

'Of course,' she said. 'What are you doing here?'

'We got orders to go to Hendon in north London.' He pointed to two other USAAF guys on the steps. 'We got stuck in traffic,' he shouted above a sudden burst of hoots and cheers. 'The roads around Buckingham Palace and the Mall are at a standstill, so we abandoned the jeep and came here to have some fun. We were heading for Rainbow Corner, but got key-holed by some wireless guys. You know the thing. "How do British girls compare to the gals back home?"'

'Who did you say they were?'

'BBC wireless guys. Come and say hi.'

Before she had time to answer Murphy's two pals were at her side. 'What are you doing?' she said as they knelt down beside her. 'Put me down!' she screamed. The two guys slowly stood up, arms outstretched around each other's shoulders, with Margot sitting in the middle, as if she was on a swing. With nothing to hold onto to keep her balance she began to scream.

'They won't drop you, Margot,' Murphy shouted, as the two airmen marched through the crowds shouting, 'Make way for Margot Dudley.' At the top of the steps, outside the main doors of the National Gallery, they put her down to calls from the crowd for her to sing.

'Will you sing for us, Miss Dudley?' Margot recognised the BBC announcer from his photograph in the *Radio Times*. He was the "Dig for Victory" man, Cecil Henry Middleton.

'I'd love to when I stop shaking.' Middleton handed her his microphone and she asked if there were any musicians in the crowd that would play for her.

A couple of men put up their hands and were

helped up the steps by cheering onlookers. An elderly chap dressed in a navy blue doorman's uniform appeared suddenly with what looked to Margot like a dustbin lid. Taking two spoons from his pocket, he winked at her before rapping them – first on his arm and then the tin lid. Margot laughed, and winked back. In no time, mouth organs and harmonicas were being played, spoons were beating out the rhythm and Margot was singing "Red White and Blue". The revellers nearest joined in and by the second verse, everyone was singing. She sang "Oh! Johnny, Oh! Johnny, Oh!" to one of the young Americans who had carried her up the Gallery's steps. Then, instead of singing the last line of the song, Margot turned to the crowd and waved the microphone, encouraging them to sing, "Oh, Johnny! Oh, Johnny! Oh!" Looking into the throng, Margot spotted George and Betsy. 'They are my friends,' she called to the GIs. 'Can you help them to get up here?'

'George? Betsy? Over here,' she shouted through the microphone. Her friends waved and, chaperoned by the two Americans, pushed their way through the crowds and up the steps.

'Want a couple of sisters to sing with?' George asked when she and Betsy reached her.

'You bet!' Margot said. And after huddling together for a couple of seconds to decide which numbers to sing, the *reformed* Albert Sisters lined up as they had done when they toured with ENSA and sang "Don't Sit Under The Apple Tree" followed by "Rule Britannia".

As if on cue, Big Ben began to chime and everyone in Trafalgar Square cheered.

'Bets and I are off, Margot,' George shouted, articulating the words.

Margot looked at her watch. Motioning for her friends to wait for her, she shouted, 'I'll come with you.' She waved and mouthed 'Thank you!' to Cecil Middleton, the BBC technicians and the musicians, and then kissed Murphy's pals goodbye.

Murphy smiled and Margot found herself looking into his eyes. She stretched up to kiss him on the cheek, but he turned his head and she kissed him full on the lips. Shocked, she leaned back but he leaned forward and held her tightly. Margot's heart was thumping in her chest and she felt excitement stirring in the pit of her stomach. She pulled away. 'I'm sorry, I must go.'

'Do you have to leave? We're going to Rainbow Corner for an hour. Won't you come and jitterbug with me?' he shouted above the cheering and singing.

For a split second Margot wanted to say yes. She wanted to dance and have fun. But she didn't trust herself to leave after an hour. She shook her head. What the hell was she thinking? Today of all days she should be at home when Bill came in from work. 'I'm sorry, I can't. I'm at The Talk of London later. I have to get ready.'

He put his hand on his heart, pretending to be hurt. 'Just one more number then?' he said, taking in George and Betsy, who both nodded. They stood shoulder to shoulder on top of the steps and, holding their hands high in the air, made Winston Churchill's trademark V for Victory sign. Cecil Middleton handed them the microphone and they sang "There'll Always Be an England". When the song ended the crowd went mad. For fear they would be mobbed, a couple of BBC wireless technicians huddled the three women – waving and blowing kisses – into the National Gallery where the doorman, Margot's spoon playing

300

drummer, showed them out of a side door. Ending up in Charing Cross Road, Margot accompanied George and Betsy to the Prince Albert Theatre.

'Do you miss being in the show, Margot?' Betsy asked.

'Yes. I miss you and George too.'

'Well, don't worry, darling,' George said, 'I'm only keeping your dressing room warm until you're ready to come back.'

'From what I hear, you're doing a fantastic job.'

George laughed. 'I wish! See you later at The Talk.'

'Have a good show,' Margot said, kissing George and then Betsy.

She watched her friends enter the theatre and, as the streets were still swarming with people and there would be no chance of getting a cab, walked the short distance home.

Margot took off her coat and shoes and looked in the hall mirror. Her hair was dry, her eyes dull, and her complexion sallow. She leaned forward and pulled at her eyelids. The whites of her eyes were bloodshot. Her tongue felt furry. She studied it in the mirror. It was coated in a white film. She was out of sorts.

Singing in Trafalgar Square on VE Day had been an honour. It was the day Germany's planned domination of Europe officially ended. The day Britain and her allies defeated Germany and brought peace to Europe after six years of bloodshed. And with a bit of luck the name Margot Dudley would go down in history after singing on such an historic day. But that wasn't important. Being in Trafalgar Square on the day the war ended with George and Betsy – and with people from all over London, as well as soldiers, sailors and airmen, from Britain, America and all the Empire countries – that was important.

Margot ran a bath, dropping in a rose-scented bath cube. Bill wasn't back from the MoD. He would have celebrated in Whitehall while she was a stone's throw away in Trafalgar Square. Margot wondered if he'd heard her on the wireless. She hoped he had. There was still three hours before the taxi was due to pick her up to take her to The Talk of London for another Victory celebration. Plenty of time for a long soak.

'You'll turn into a mermaid if you stay in there much longer.'

'Bill?' Margot looked up to see her handsome husband standing beside the bath. 'I didn't hear you come in. How long have you been home?'

'Half an hour. Come on,' he said, holding up a large towel. As Margot stood up, Bill folded the towel around her and lifted her out of the bath. After kissing her, he rubbed her dry playfully, as if she was a child, before helping her into a bathrobe and leading her by the hand into the sitting room.

Margot stood open mouthed as she looked at the spread on the table. 'What on earth--?' She caught her breath. 'Are these real eggs?' She touched one and squealed. 'Oh my God, they are real! Where did all this food come from?'

'The MoD. I wasn't the only one called in before dawn. Everyone was. And because we knew we wouldn't get out until after Churchill's speech, we each took something to eat. I took the tin of salmon you were saving for a special occasion.'

Margot laughed. 'I can't think of a more special occasion than the end of the war. But eggs?' she said again. 'I haven't seen an egg since Foxden.'

One of the ladies lives on a farm in Surrey. She keeps chickens, so she brought a dozen in – boiled, of course. There was a lot of food left over, so she gave a couple of us blokes bags to bring home. I think she feels sorry for me because you're always working.'

The excitement drained from Margot's face and she gave Bill a hurt look. 'She doesn't, does she? Please say that's not true. I couldn't bear it if anyone thought I didn't look after you.'

'I'm joking, you silly goose. Come on, sit down and tuck in. I don't expect you've had time to eat with all the singing you did in Trafalgar Square.'

'You heard me?' Margot jumped up and threw her arms around Bill's neck.

'I wish I had. One of the chaps told me.' Margot put on a frown and pushed out her bottom lip in a pout. 'I'm on the lowest branch of the MoD tree. I wasn't privy to a wireless, except to hear Churchill's speech.' Bill walked round the table and pulled out Margot's chair. 'I'll hear you sing tonight at The Talk of London. They won't!' As she sat down Bill kissed her. 'Now eat!'

Entering through the double doors of The Talk of London always took Margot's breath away. The floor of the foyer was marble, the ceiling a mirror and the walls were adorned with framed posters by Frederick Charles Herrick, prints from the Paris Exhibition in 1925, and portraits and illustrations of beautiful women in elegant evening gowns by Erté and Georges Barbier. A reminder that there was glamour before utility clothing – and hopefully would be again, now the war was over.

The Talk of London was the biggest night club and restaurant in London and VE night was the biggest occasion. It was no surprise to Margot that every table in the fashionable club had been reserved. She walked slowly round the room and marvelled, as she always did, at the gilt framed signed photographs of Ivor Novello, Joyce Grenfell and Noel Coward. A smile crept across her face, making her eyes sparkle, as she passed her own photograph, which was next to Tommy Trinder. She liked that; she liked Tommy. Vera Lynn and Gracie Fields were separated by George Formby.

She looked up. A net above the dance floor held dozens of red, white and blue balloons. This was going to be a night to remember.

Bill sat at the bar with their friend Salvatore and the Talk's owner, Bernard Rudman. Salvatore had popped in to ask Margot if she would do an hour at the Prince Albert Club the following night. Margot said she'd love to, and after kissing him goodbye she dashed off to change into her evening dress.

The dress she had bought for this, the most important night of the last six years, was stunning. And so it should be. She had spent her and Bill's entire clothes ration, plus dozens of clothes coupons that she'd bought on the black market for 2/6d each. She slipped the dress over her head and knew immediately that it was worth every coupon and every penny she had spent. The royal blue skirt, soft and flowing, was made of parachute silk and fell from her hips gracefully when she moved. The bodice, strapless and in the design of the Union Jack flag, was covered in red, white and blue sequins.

Looking at her reflection in the mirror as she applied her lipstick, Margot could see how tired she looked. Gently she dabbed face powder under her eyes and rubbed a little more rouge into her cheeks – she looked better.

Seeing Lieutenant Murphy at Trafalgar Square had

reminded Margot of the silver wings he'd given her when she was touring with ENSA. She took them from her handbag and put them on. They were lovely and set the dress off perfectly.

Waiting in the wings, Margot listened to the applause as the band played the first few chords of her signature tune. When she felt the audience had clapped enough, she entered the room smiling. Thanking them and blowing kisses, she made her way to the stage and the microphone. "'They Can't Take That Away From Me,'" she said, 'for my husband, Bill.' Margot looked over to the bar and blew him a kiss.

Her second song was a Talk of London favourite, "That Old Black Magic". Coincidentally an elderly gentleman walked across the dance floor as Margot began to sing "It Had to be You". She sang the first line of the song to him and everyone laughed, including the man.

Taking a short break to mingle with the audience, as she always did, she spotted Lieutenant Boyd Murphy walking towards her. 'You're wearing the wings?'

'What?' She put her hand up and touched the brooch he had given her. She could feel her heart beating. 'What are you doing here?'

'When we got to Hendon we were given our papers to go home,' Murphy said. 'I leave tomorrow. I won't be coming into London again, but I wanted to give you this.' He handed Margot his card. 'My address in the States. On the flip side is the movie studio. You're made for the movies, Margot.'

'I don't know what to say.' She looked down at the small card.

'Say you'll come! Or at least say you'll think about

it,' he said, taking her hand. 'This blue bird is done flying over the white cliffs of Dover, it's the Atlantic tomorrow.'

'I'm sorry. I have to go.'

'Promise you'll think about it,' he said, his eyes penetrating hers.

With butterflies of excitement flying around in the pit of her stomach, she nodded. 'I'll think about it.' The band began to play the opening chords of "Every Time We Say Goodbye". 'I must go.' Letting go of his hand, Margot returned to the stage. She looked into the audience, to where her American film maker had been standing. He had gone.

Margot brought the first day of VE celebrations to an end with "I'll Be Seeing You" and left the stage to rapturous applause. After talking to people, accepting their compliments and thanking them, she joined Bill at the bar.

'You were wonderful, sweetheart.'

'Thank you,' she said, kissing him on the cheek.

'Drink?'

'Please. Make it a large one,' she whispered to the bartender. 'It's been quite a day.'

'What did the GI want?' Bill asked as soon as they were home.

Margot looked at him quizzically before remembering the card that she'd tucked down the front of her dress. 'Ah,' she said, producing it. 'He's in films.' She handed Bill the card. 'He said if I ever go to America I should get in touch with him, and he'll get me work in the movies.'

Bill rolled his eyes. 'And what did you say?'

'I didn't say anything.'

'You were a long time not saying anything.'

'He'd been given his papers and was going back to America. He'd come from Hendon specially. I could hardly ignore him.'

'Still, it's academic, as my boss would say.'

'What is?'

'You going to America. It's academic, because we're going home now the war's over. I'll be demobbed from the MoD soon, and then we'll go home.'

'I've signed a contract to do the summer at the Albert.'

'What the hell have you done that for?'

'My contract at The Talk takes me up to August, so when Salvatore asked me, I thought I might as well. How was I to know the war was going to end?'

'Because I've been telling you for a year it was gearing up to end,' Bill shouted. 'You just didn't bloody listen!' He stormed off. 'Do what you like Margot, but I'm going home as we *both* agreed we'd do.' Margot heard the bedroom door slam.

CHAPTER TWENTY-FOUR

Margot took her bow, threw back her head and opened her arms to the audience. They weren't clapping. They always clapped when she finished singing, often before. She bowed again. Still no applause. She looked around the audience and settled on the table nearest the stage. The couple looked familiar. Of course they do, she thought. They come to see me every time I appear at The Talk of London. 'Hello,' she said, smiling. The man looked away and busied himself with his cigarette case. He took out a cigarette and immediately the waiter nearest to him struck a match. Margot smiled at his wife. She smiled back, but looked sad. How could that be? She dropped her head. She looked as if she was going to cry. 'Don't cry,' Margot whispered.

The band began to play and Margot stepped back behind the microphone and into her light. She turned to the bandleader and frowned. The band was playing a tune she didn't recognise. Why were they doing that? She bit her bottom lip and shook her head, trying desperately to remember the words. Perhaps the tune didn't have any. Ah, that was it. There were no words. She gave the bandmaster a hard stare. He should have told her she wasn't singing the next number. She'd report him to Bernard ... Bernard... Exasperated that she couldn't remember his name, she looked up. Swaying from side to side, her eyes darting from left to right, she began searching the ceiling for something. She wasn't sure what. Bringing her focus back to the room she squealed with delight and threw her arms open wide as Salvatore appeared out of the shadows and walked towards her. 'My dear beautiful friend Nancy's fiancé, Salvatore,' she told the audience, and began to applaud him. 'What are you doing here?'

'I've come to see you, Margot.' Salvatore put out his hand to help her from the stage.

'I haven't finished my set yet. Will you tell the band to play something I know, please?'

'Yes, but it is time for your break. Let us go to your dressing room. We can talk, and they will play your song when you come back.'

'Will they play "They Can't Take That Away From Me"?'

'Of course.' Salvatore stood to the side of the stage while Margot took a bow. At first there was only a ripple of applause among an audience that wore worried expressions. But when Salvatore put his hands together they took his cue and applauded Margot as they always had.

'It's not a coincidence that you're here, is it?' she said, when she and Salvatore were in the dressing room.

'No,' he replied kindly. 'Bernard telephoned me. He's worried about you, Margot. We both are.'

There was a knock at the door, which Margot ignored. Salvatore answered it while she squinted in the mirror and put on more lipstick.

'Margot?' Salvatore held her by the shoulders and turned her round gently. 'This is my good friend, Doctor Thurlingham,' he said, pointing at the man who had just entered the room.

'I saw you earlier with your wife. You were sitting at the table nearest the stage.' Seeing the look of concern on the doctor's face, she put up her hand. 'So what is it?' The doctor didn't answer. 'Don't be shy. Are you here to tell me to take a week off? Two?' She began to pick at the fabric on the sleeve of her dress. 'He loves me, he loves me not. He loves me – hooray! He loves me,' she said, lifting her left hand and showing them her wedding ring. 'What? I'm fine. I'm just tired. Bill's up in the Midlands and I never sleep when he's away.' Suddenly she looked at the doctor as if she'd remembered what she was saying. 'Don't say longer than two weeks. Well?'

'Salvatore and I have been concerned about you for some time, Margot. You don't look well and it isn't just that you are tired. In my opinion you are heading for a breakdown if you don't have a complete rest away from--'

'I knew it! Longer.'

'You're not listening to me, Margot.'

'I am! I'll rest – tomorrow! I don't know why Salvatore asked you to come backstage. He's ruined your evening, and mine.' Margot glared at Salvatore. 'You can go now,' she said. 'Shoo!' She looked into the mirror and stuck out her tongue. 'Look. Pink. I don't need a doctor. Bloody quacks, you're all the same. All I need is a good night's sleep. I find it difficult to get to sleep without--' She picked up the framed photograph of Bill that she kept on her dressing table. 'Did you know my husband has left me? Of course you didn't. I've been abandoned, left to fend for myself.' Margot suddenly let out a terrifying scream and hurled the photograph at the mirror, shattering both into hundreds of tiny pieces.

'Do you feel better now?' the doctor asked.

'What do you care?' Margot spat. The doctor moved towards her and put out his hand. 'Don't touch me! And don't pretend you care,' she said, jabbing her finger at him, 'because you don't. No one does.'

'I care, Margot,' Salvatore said. 'Natalie and Anton care and so do George and Betsy – and Bill loves you, you know he does. We all love you.'

'But it isn't easy to love you when you're like this,' the doctor said.

Tears fell from Margot's eyes and rolled down her cheeks. 'Without Bill I have nothing! I am nothing! I'm a square peg in a round hole, the thirteenth guest at dinner – the odd one out.' She buried her head in her hands and wept.

The doctor rested his hand gently on her shoulder while he spoke to Salvatore. 'Margot's missing her husband. He's her anchor, keeps her feet on the ground. He has always been there when she gets home to look after her and to help her unwind and relax. She can do anything if Bill is by her side, but without him she finds it difficult to function. She may be Margot Dudley, West End star, to the public, but I can guarantee that at home without Bill, she's frightened, paranoid and lost. She's on the road to self-destruction, and if she doesn't get help soon…'

'Should we send for Bill?' Salvatore asked.

'No!' Margot jumped up. 'No, please don't tell Bill…'

There was a knock on the door and Bernard Rudman stepped into the room. He told Dr Thurlingham that there was an ambulance outside.

'I'd like you to come to the clinic with me, Margot.' She shook her head violently. The doctor ignored her. 'You can come voluntarily, or I can have you committed.'

Margot looked at Salvatore, her eyes wide and pleading, begging him to help her. 'He can't do that, can he, Salvatore? He can't have me--?'

'Not without Bill's permission--'

Margot closed her eyes and hung her head. 'All right.' She looked up, the pretence and sparkle gone from her eyes. 'I'm tired,' she whispered through shuddering sobs.

Salvatore put her coat around her shoulders and picked up her handbag.

The official line: After a severe bout of flu, Miss Dudley had taken a well-earned holiday. The truth was very different. Margot had been admitted to the Thurlingham Clinic where she was being treated for depression and paranoia, brought on by sleep deprivation, caused through the over use of sleeping pills, pep pills, pain killers and alcohol.

'Is that Bill?'

'Margot? Is something wrong?'

'Why does there have to be something wrong? Can't a wife telephone her husband to see how he is after years of being apart?'

'It's only been a couple of months, Margot, don't exaggerate.'

'It feels like years.' Bill laughed. There was silence for some seconds. Then Margot said, 'I miss you, Bill. Please come home?'

'I am home, Margot.'

Margot held the telephone away from her ear. She scrunched up her face, closed her eyes, and opened her mouth wide. She wanted to scream. Instead she whispered, 'Of course you are.'

'I miss you too, Margot, but--'

'But what?' Margot hissed. 'Sorry! I'm sorry,' she said again, 'but I hate it here. I'm frightened. There are strange people everywhere.'

'There aren't any strange people in the Mews, Margot. Well, no more than there were when you insisted we moved there.'

'I'm not in the Mews, Bill.'

'Not in-- Where are you, the Albert?'

'No.'

'Then where?'

'I don't know. Please come and get me, Bill. The bed's ever so hard and I can't switch the light off. It's so bright it hurts my eyes. And they're trying to poison me. Shush! Someone's coming,' Margot said. 'I shouldn't be in here. I'll be punished if they catch me. Bill, I'm frightened.'

As he entered the consulting room, Dr Thurlingham held out his hand for the telephone.

'Margot, what the hell's going on? Margot! Are you there?'

'Goodbye, Bill,' she said, and she handed the telephone to the doctor.

'Mr Burrell? This is Dr Thurlingham. We've been trying to get hold of you.' Margot moved to the far side of the room and stood in the corner. 'No, your wife hasn't been in an accident. She has had a breakdown and has been admitted to the Thurlingham Clinic with severe nervous exhaustion. There's nothing to be alarmed about, she-- Yes, Harley Street, but there's no need for you to--' The doctor held the telephone away from his ear, and then put it down.

After talking to Margot's doctor, Bill understood more about her condition and was given permission to see her. Rustling behind him in a stiff white uniform, the nurse given the task of accompanying Bill to see Margot could hardly keep up with him. As soon as they reached Margot's room she left, muttering something about visitors turning up out of hours.

Bill tapped the door before entering. Margot, crouched in the corner of the room, looked up. She wiped her hand across her face and scraped her fingers through her hair. 'Bill?' she cried, stumbling to her feet. With tears in her eyes, she ran across the room and threw her arms around her husband's neck. 'Take me home, Bill,' she pleaded, 'take me home.'

Bill held her tightly and whispered, 'Shush sweetheart. Shush…'

'Please, Bill,' she cried. 'I miss you. I want to come home.'

'I miss you too, darling. And I'll take you home as soon as you're better.'

Margot pushed him away and returned to the corner. Sliding down the wall, she hugged her knees and laid her head on them. Bill followed and put his hand on her shoulder, but Margot shrugged it off. 'Leave me alone!' Turning her face to the wall, she began to mumble.

'Margot? Talk to me, love. Come on.' Bill crossed the room to Margot's bed and sat down. This isn't so bad,' he said, bouncing up and down a couple of times. 'And look? Here's your tea. Come and sit with me and have something to eat?'

'You eat it!' she spat, and resumed mumbling.

'If you want to get better and come home, you've got to eat, Margot. And you've got to talk to the doctor. He can't help you unless you do,' Bill said.

Margot looked up. Her eyes roamed round the room. 'Shush!' She put her finger to her lips. 'They're listening,' she whispered, beckoning Bill. Bill went over and knelt beside her. 'They're trying to kill me,' she hissed. 'Do-not-eat-the-jam!' Bill looked around. There wasn't any jam. Margot waved her hand in his face. 'It's in the food,' she said, pointing to the plate of sandwiches. 'Go on, have a look. Open one and smell it, but be careful... They say it's salt and pepper, but everyone knows it's poison.'

'I can't see any poison, Margot.' Bill sniffed the food. 'I can't smell any either. I know,' he said, 'what if I taste it? Take a bite of the sandwich before you eat it. I'll be your personal taster. Like the kings and queens had in the old days,' he laughed.

Margot laughed with him. 'Like in Laurence Olivier's *Henry V*? Like that?'

'Yes, love, like that. Come over here and sit by me, and we'll eat the sandwiches together.'

Smiling for the first time since being admitted to the clinic, Margot rolled over until she was on all fours and pushed herself up. Walking slowly across the room to the bed, she sat down next to her husband. 'Right!' he said, picking up a quarter square of sandwich. 'Let's see.' He took a bite. 'Mm-hum, it tastes good. Everything is as it should be, your Majesty,' he said, offering it to Margot.

She took a bite. 'Not up to my usual standard, but it will suffice,' she giggled.

Bill picked up another quarter, tasted it and nodded. After Margot had eaten the first small square of sandwich she ate the second. 'I was hungry,' she said when she'd eaten them all.

'So will you eat your dinner tonight?'

Margot nodded. 'That's my girl,' Bill said, putting his arms around her. 'And will you talk to Dr Thurlingham?'

'He's a psychiatrist, Bill. Only mad people talk to psychiatrists. I'm not mad, am I?'

'No, you silly goose. Sorry I--' They both laughed. 'Of course you're not mad, Margot. You've become dependent on pills and you've been drinking too much--'

'But I'm not--'

'Shush darling, let me finish. You became dependent on the tablets you were given to stop the pain in your ankle. You weren't able to sleep so you were given sleeping pills by the private quack you went to.'

'I know. Then he gave me pills to get me up in the morning. I told him I didn't want to take more pills, honestly I did.' Bill put his arms around her and rocked her gently. 'I shouldn't have taken all those pills – and I shouldn't have been drinking with them.' Margot looked up into Bill's eyes and took a shuddering breath. 'I'll see the doctor-- psychiatrist. I'll see anyone and do anything not to feel like this,' she cried.

Bill held her until she fell asleep. Then he laid her down, put a blanket over her, and went to see her doctor.

Dr Thurlingham looked from Bill to Margot. 'Do you feel ready to face the outside world, Margot?'

'Yes,' she said, taking Bill's hand.

'I would have liked you to stay with us for another couple of weeks.'

'You told me a couple of weeks when you brought me here and that was two months ago. Besides--' Margot looked up at Bill, her eyes sparkling with excitement.

'Besides what, sweetheart?'

Margot bit her bottom lip. 'Bernard Rudman sent a bouquet and a get well card.' Bill looked around the room. 'They're not here. I knew you wouldn't be happy about it, so I put them in the communal sitting room. He's written to me several times, asking when

I'm coming back. He said my spot at The Talk was waiting for me when I'm ready. And he's asked me to top the bill in cabaret, on Christmas Eve and New Year's Eve.'

A black cloud took Bill's smile and his face turned scarlet. Exasperated, he snatched his hand away from Margot's. 'I should damn well leave you here!' he shouted. 'You're your own worst enemy.'

'It's only once a week for an hour. That's not too much, is it?'

Bill threw his arms up in the air. 'Do as you like, Margot, I'm past caring.' He shook the doctor's hand. 'Thank you for everything you've done for her.' He picked up Margot's suitcase.

'You're welcome, Mr Burrell. And if there's anything I can do in the future, don't hesitate to get in touch. And you, madam,' he said, turning to Margot. 'No more pills and plenty of rest.'

'I will. Bill will make sure of that,' she said. 'We'll see you when I come back for my check-up, won't we--' Margot turned, expecting Bill to be waiting for her, but he had gone. 'Better dash,' she said, shaking the doctor's hand. 'When he realises I'm not with him, he'll worry.'

Margot walked along the main corridor, glancing down narrow passageways, but she couldn't see Bill. In the foyer she spotted him standing outside the main doors. 'I wondered where you'd got to,' she said, taking her small vanity case from him and slipping her hand into his. 'Come on, it's too cold to hang about out here.'

Bill led Margot to a waiting taxi and after stowing the suitcase, sat opposite her. Making herself comfortable on the back seat, she looked out of the window. As the cab pulled into the traffic, she sighed.

There were reminders of the war everywhere. The cab slowed in advance of a sign saying DETOUR and Margot looked up at a badly damaged building that had once been a hotel. It had been shored up, but loomed dangerously above a crater in the road. As the cab sat in traffic, Margot watched an army bomb disposal team lift the bomb out of the hole with a crane. For a moment it hung in the air threatening to fall. Her head began to throb. She crossed the narrow space between the seats and sat next to Bill. With her head on his shoulder, Margot cuddled up to the man she loved.

The following morning, Margot opened her eyes, stretched her legs and sighed contentedly. Tears of happiness spilled onto her pillow. She was home – and she was safe. Soft pastel green wallpaper instead of stark white walls and bedroom furniture instead of a solitary chair, which was all they allowed her in the clinic, met her sleepy gaze. She smiled through her tears. When they first moved into the apartment, Margot dragged Bill all over London looking for pretty bedroom furniture. They had ended up with what she called a boring utility suite. Looking at it now, it was the most beautiful furniture she had ever seen.

Still glowing with love, Margot reached up and pulled Bill's pillow towards her. She buried her head in it and, breathing slowly, rhythmically, closed her eyes. Bill hadn't said a word in the taxi on the way home from the clinic. She could feel his anger. But as soon as they were home, he took Margot to bed and made love to her, pleasuring her, and then waiting for her, so they reached a loving climax together. Exhausted, they had fallen asleep in each other's arms.

Margot felt a stirring in the pit of her stomach. She wanted Bill again. She inhaled deeply, suppressed the need, and slipped from between the sheets. She put on her dressing gown, brushed her hair and thanked God for her life – and for her wonderful husband. Things would be back to normal now Bill was home.

'Bill?' A small fire burned in the grate and the table was laid for breakfast, but Bill wasn't there. Margot touched the teapot. It was still warm. She took a slice of toast from the rack and bit off a corner. 'Bill!' she called again, looking in the kitchen. He wasn't there either. She heard a vehicle enter the Mews and ran to the window. A black cab pulled up beside Bill and his suitcase. She hammered on the window. 'Bill?' He looked up with sad eyes. 'Don't go!' She ran through the apartment and down the stairs. As she opened the door the cab pulled away. 'Bill!' she screamed, running barefoot into the Mews.

Bill looked out of the back window and mouthed, 'I love you.' A second later he had gone, swallowed up in the traffic on Tottenham Court Road. Margot fell to her knees and sobbed. A passer-by helped her up and walked her back to the apartment. Tears coursing down her cheeks, shivering uncontrollably from the bitter winter fog, she stumbled inside and threw herself at the door. It slammed shut. Sobbing, she took hold of the stair-rail and pulled herself up a stair at a time. In a daze she staggered into the bedroom and crawled into bed.

CHAPTER TWENTY-FIVE

Dr Thurlingham thought for a moment before looking again at Margot's notes. 'No, Margot. It's too early to go back to work. You're doing well, but you can't rush these things. It'll soon be Christmas. Use the holiday to relax, recharge your batteries, get to know your husband again without the pressure of having to perform every night. We'll discuss your return to the theatre again in the New Year.'

Assuring the doctor she would take his advice, Margot made an appointment for January 24th 1946, and left the clinic. As soon as she was outside she hailed a cab.

'Where to, Miss?'

'The Prince Albert Theatre on the Strand,' she said, jumping in. 'And put your foot down, I'm late for rehearsal.'

Margot didn't need Dr Thurlingham's permission. She would have liked it, but it was academic, as Bill would have said. She hadn't only accepted Bernard Rudman's offer to do cabaret at The Talk of London every Saturday night, she had been to lunch with Natalie and Anton, and when Anton offered her the role of the Good Fairy to George's Wicked Witch with Betsy as Princess Aurora in *Sleeping Beauty* she had accepted without a second thought. And that night, when she met her friends at the Prince Albert Club to celebrate the three of them working together, Salvatore asked if she would like to do a late-night spot again. Margot said she'd think about it but she knew, as he did, that she would do it.

*

Margot threw herself into work. She was so busy during the day, learning new songs for her cabaret show in addition to rehearsing *Sleeping Beauty* at the theatre, that she was able to put Bill to the back of her mind. And at night, performing at the Albert Club or The Talk of London, she was, as Dr Thurlingham had said, Margot Dudley, star! But afterwards, at home on her own, she swung from missing Bill and loving him to being angry and hating him – depending on how much she'd had to drink. Alone in the apartment she became aware of every sound – outside and inside – and felt vulnerable and frightened. She asked the cab drivers who brought her home at night to wait until she'd checked the flat. When she had put on all the lights and looked in every room, she waved out of the window – only then was she content for the cabbies to leave. She thought she was going mad. She ran downstairs a dozen times to make sure she'd locked the street door, and left the wireless and lights on when she went to bed. If she didn't cry herself to sleep she'd toss and turn with the lyrics of songs running around in her head, or she'd lie for hours pining for Bill. Already becoming paranoid, her mind raced through the gamut of emotions until she became confused and anxious.

As the weeks went by, Margot's workload took its toll. She wasn't sleeping and began to lose focus in rehearsals. She tried to catch up on Sundays, staying in bed until lunchtime. But she needed to work too, so she learned songs and routines in the afternoon – as she had done when she was an usherette – but it didn't always work. When Monday morning came she was often exhausted and had to drag herself out of bed, but she didn't take any pills.

*

Margot opened her eyes as soon as the small hammer on top of the alarm clock hit the bell. Eight o'clock. She sat on the side of the bed for a second and yawned. 'Breakfast,' she said, leaping to her feet. Tea and toast would do but first she stripped the bed and put on clean sheets, in case Bill stayed overnight. She felt the butterflies of excitement in the pit of her stomach. She wanted him, needed him, it had been--. She swept the memory of the last time they had made love from her mind and set about cleaning the apartment. When she had finished she checked each room. She wanted it to look perfect for Bill – and it did.

Breakfast ignored, Margot bathed and, wrapped in a bath towel, went into the bedroom. She took a pair of smart navy-blue slacks from the wardrobe and the powder blue cardigan she'd bought to go with them from the drawer and laid them on the bed. Then from her bedside table she took the three-string necklace of pearls that Bill had sent her. Dropping the towel, she put on the creamy pearls. They looked perfect; just a little deeper in colour than her skin. She then put on her underwear, slacks and cardigan and looked in the mirror. She unbuttoned the two tiny mother-of-pearl discs at the top of the cardigan to show off the necklace. She had opened the small parcel as soon as it arrived and read the card over and over. She picked it up and read it again. "Happy Christmas, darling Margot. Hope to see you soon" and three kisses.

Natalie had invited Bill to watch the show with her and Anton in their box. Margot hoped that meant he would go with them to the first night party. With this in mind, she had bought a simple but beautiful dress with the remainder of her clothes coupons, plus seventeen pounds. The thought of spending all that money on a dress... But if Bill liked it, it would be worth it.

Bill hadn't actually said he was coming to the opening night of *Sleeping Beauty*, he said he'd try, but Margot had convinced herself he'd be there. She looked again at the pearls. They were beautiful. She'd keep them on in case Bill came to the theatre before the show. She was desperate to see him and hoped-- Her thoughts were interrupted by the familiar sound of her taxi arriving. 'Damn.' She ran to the window and waved. The cabbie put up his hand in recognition. Quickly she buttered a couple of rounds of bread and made a cheese sandwich, in case Bill was hungry when he arrived, if he arrived. Before she left she scribbled a note telling him how much she loved and missed him – and how much she was looking forward to seeing him after the show. Coat over her arm, handbag and keys in her hand, she locked the door and jumped into the cab.

'Come in!' Margot said, thinking it was stage management knocking. 'Surely it isn't beginners already-- Bill!' she cried, as her husband entered the dressing room. 'You're here. I don't believe it. I didn't think you were coming,' she said, running to him and holding onto him as if she'd never let him go again.

'I haven't missed an opening night yet, and I don't intend to start now,' he said.

'Beginners, Miss Dudley,' the stage manager called. 'On stage please!'

'I'd better go. See you after the show,' Bill said, kissing Margot before making his way to the door.

'When I blow a kiss into the audience, I shall direct it at you in the Goldmans' box. Oh Bill,' Margot said as he was leaving, 'I do love you.'

'I love you too. Have a wonderful show.'

'I will now,' she said as he closed the door.

Sleeping Beauty was an amazing spectacle. The songs and dances, contrasting characters, costumes and set were magnificent – and as always there was a standing ovation at the curtain.

Bill accompanied Margot to the first night party with Natalie and Anton Goldman. They left after half an hour for The Talk of London, where Margot was in cabaret. Natalie and Anton arrived with George and Betsy as Margot began her last number, the popular American hit, "Moonlight Serenade".

'Thank you for calling in,' she said, joining them at the bar.

'We must go home, Margot,' Natalie said, kissing her on the cheek. 'It has been a long and very exciting day.

'We're off too.' George and Betsy kissed Margot and then Bill. 'See you tomorrow night, Margot,' Anton said, before shaking Bill's hand.

After waving their friends off, Margot pulled Bill onto the dance floor and they danced into the early hours.

For the next week, Margot and Bill spent their mornings making love, followed by a late breakfast. Arms entwined, they walked in the park, only letting go of each other to feed the ducks. At night, walking into the apartment after the show and seeing Bill sitting in the armchair listening to the wireless brought tears to Margot's eyes. Life was perfect.

She came off stage at The Talk of London the following Saturday night and joined Bill at their table. He was looking thoughtful. She held her breath, sensing something was wrong. 'What's the matter, Bill?'

'You are as wonderful in cabaret as you are in a play or a musical, Margot,' he said, looking into her eyes. 'I understand now that performing, singing and dancing is your life. And I shall never ask you to give it up again.'

Margot's eyes glistened with tears of joy. 'Does that mean you'll--?'

'Let me finish. It has been a wonderful week – and there will be others – but--'

'Of course there'll be others – as many as we want.' Margot's voice began to tremble. She searched Bill's face. 'You're not staying with me, are you?' He didn't answer. 'Bill?' A feeling like grief engulfed her. 'Please don't leave me,' she cried.

'Shush,' he said, putting his arms around her and holding her tightly. 'As much as I love you, and you know I do, I'm going back to the Midlands.' Margot began to protest but Bill put his finger on her lips. 'Try to understand, love, that while I don't want to be without you, I don't want to live in London. In the war I had a job to do, a reason for being here. I don't any more.' Margot buried her head in Bill's chest. 'This is your life,' he whispered, 'your career. I have no right to ask you to give it up to live with me in a semi-detached somewhere in the country.' Tears streamed down Margot's face. 'We want different things, Margot,' Bill said, wiping away the tears and then kissing her on each cheek. 'I'm going to give you your freedom.'

'You're not going to divorce me, are you, Bill? I love you.'

'No, you silly goose. I love you too. I've never loved anyone but you, you know that. But I'm going back to the Midlands. I'll look for a house,' he said with a catch in his voice, 'and when you're ready, if you're ever ready, to come home--' Bill broke down in tears.

'Bill, don't cry. Please, Bill.'

'Come on. Let's go home,' he said, helping Margot to her feet. 'I want to catch the early train in the morning.'

Looking through the cards and telegrams on the post table, Margot bit back the tears. 'Has Bill phoned, Stan?'

The stage doorman shook his head. 'Not today, Miss.'

It had been two months since Bill left London – two of the loneliest months of Margot's life. 'Never mind, I wasn't expecting him to ring,' she said, forcing a smile to hide the disappointment she felt. Except for the first time she appeared on stage, when she took over from Goldie, Bill had always sent her a good luck telegram. She swallowed hard and looked over her shoulder. 'He's been working all hours. I don't expect he had time to get to the post office.' She picked up the envelopes with her name on and dropped the rest on the table with a carefree shrug. 'See you later.'

'If-- When the telegram comes, Miss, I'll bring it along,' Stan called after her.

Margot didn't turn. 'Thanks, Stan.' She had asked the same question of Stan every night for weeks and every night the answer had been the same. No card, no telegram, not even a message. Overwhelmed with disappointment she entered the dressing room and began to cry. She kicked the door shut and sobbed.

Looking in the mirror above her dressing table, Margot looked to the left and then to the right. With carefully applied makeup she had an English Rose complexion. The fashionably high waves at the front of her hair accentuated her cheekbones and the roll in the nape of her slender neck was flattering to her jawline. She looked every inch a star. She had achieved fame and stardom. She was topping the bill at The Talk of London and starring in the most popular West End theatre show, so why was she so desperately unhappy? Great pear-shaped tears fell from her eyes. She was tired. She was tired and she was lonely – and she wanted Bill.

Margot reached inside the drawer of her dressing table for her handkerchief and found the pep pills that the private doctor had given her. Turning them over in her hand, she recalled the feelings she experienced after taking them. One stopped her from feeling sad. Two made her feel happy and stopped her thinking about Bill. But three made her paranoid. She would never take three again.

At the sink, she filled a glass with water. Her hands were shaking, so she put the glass down before taking the top off the bottle of pills. She inhaled deeply and caught sight of herself in the mirror above the sink. The beautiful star known as Margot Dudley was looking into the mirror, but the woman who haunted her dreams – the haggard old woman with dull unseeing eyes, the woman dependent on drugs and alcohol – looked back at her.

'No!' Margot screamed, and she threw the bottle and the glass at the wall. Immediately regretting what she'd done, she fell to her knees and crawled around until she'd found every pill, putting two into her mouth before returning the rest to the bottle. She retched as the bitter-tasting pills began to dissolve. Hauling herself to her feet she ran to the sink and spat them out. She turned on the tap and cupped her hands under the running water, scooping it into her mouth, swilling it round and gargling and then spitting it out, but the bitter taste remained. She slid to her knees desperate for something, anything, to take away the vile taste. Brandy! There was a small bottle in the cupboard by the chaise. On all fours she crawled to the cupboard, opened it and took out the brandy. The glass was smashed so she unscrewed the cap and drank from the bottle. She shuddered and shook her head. The strong spirit overpowered the taste of the pills as it burned its way down her throat, but she'd need another drink to make her feel better. She put the bottle to her mouth again and gagged at the smell. Still on the floor, she leant her head against the seat of the settee.

She'd rest for ten minutes; half an hour at most. Then she'd feel better, refreshed. Her eyes felt heavy, so she closed them.

'Margot? Margot, wake up!' George was pulling her, dragging her to her feet. 'Stand up!' she ordered. 'Margot? Can you hear me?'

'Of course I can hear you. What's the matter?'

'Thank God. Are you all right?'

'Yes. Why?' Margot opened her hand. She had fallen asleep holding the bottle of pills.

'How many have you taken?'

'None! I was going to, but I didn't. And I won't. I promise. I'll never take them again. Would you get rid of them for me?' she asked, handing the bottle to George, who was leaning suspiciously close to her. 'And the brandy you can smell was one sip. Honestly,' Margot said, allowing George to take the bottle from her.

All the applause in the world, all the cards and the flowers, couldn't make up for Bill not being there, waiting for her at the stage door, his motorbike helmet in one hand and hers in the other. She had been embarrassed the first time he arrived at the theatre on his motorbike. The boyfriends and husbands of the other dancers called for them in cars. Salvatore sent a car for Nancy, Kat's married politician boyfriend collected her in a chauffeur-driven limousine, and Bill turned up on his motorbike. What she would give now to see her handsome husband waiting for her in his leather overcoat and old motorbike boots.

Margot kicked off her shoes and sat down. 'It's no fun without Bill,' she told her reflection in the dressing table mirror. Her feet ached and her ankle was swollen. 'These shoes are too tight, or I've overdone it again,' she said, rubbing one foot and then the other. 'If Bill was here he'd take me home, give me a gentle ticking off for working too hard, and then put me to bed and rub my feet until I fell asleep.' Margot smiled through a yawn. She was tired; she'd hardly slept since Bill left. She hated going home to the empty apartment and she hated sleeping on her own.

While she took off her show jewellery, Margot looked in the mirror and gurned a couple of facial exercises, twisting her face into grotesque expressions. She looked absurd. Daubing cold cream across her face to remove the stage makeup, she smiled a wide theatrical smile before wiping the cream off with a soft cloth. Her face was clean, but looking closer to see if the cream had removed her eye makeup Margot recoiled. Her eyes were dull with dark shadows beneath them and her skin had blemishes that she hadn't noticed before. Makeup covered up most things, even exhaustion, but without it...

Feeling tearful and irritable, and generally unwell, Margot went to see Dr Thurlingham.

'There doesn't seem to be anything physically wrong,' he said. 'Have you considered that you may be pregnant?'

Margot's mouth fell open. 'No! Do you think I am?'

'It's too early to tell. I'll do some tests. It may just be that you're suffering from exhaustion. Pregnant or not,' he said, looking at Margot gravely, 'unless you want to end up back here, you must take a break. Twelve months,' he said, 'of complete rest.'

Shocked, Margot agreed to take time off once the current show closed. Leaving the doctor's surgery, she could think of nothing else except whether or not she was having a baby. No point in planning anything until the results of the tests came back. In the meantime there were people she needed to see, if she was going to take a year off.

Artists and performers from all over England, as well as London, were in the audience to see Margot Dudley's last West End performance. At the end of each number the audience stood up and applauded. After the last song, Margot was joined on stage by her friends George and Betsy, who had brought their army, navy, and air force caps. Artie played the piano and the Albert Sisters fell into line and sang "Bugle Boy" as they had done in the ENSA concerts.

At the end of the show, as was the tradition, a pageboy entered the stage and gave Margot a bouquet of roses. What wasn't traditional was Anton arriving on stage with not only all the artists, but with Natalie, and the backstage and front of house staff. After thanking her for all the wonderful performances she'd given over the years, Anton told the audience how much everyone at the Prince Albert Theatre was going to miss their leading lady. 'And,' he said to Margot, 'we're keeping your name plate. Stan assures me that it will only take him a minute to put it back on the door of dressing room one.' Everyone applauded and Margot blew Stan a kiss.

She had arranged for food and drink to be brought to her dressing room for theatre staff who weren't able to go onto the Prince Albert Club after the show. They crowded in with gifts and flowers. Looking around the room, Margot smiled and thanked everyone – and then she froze. Bill was standing in the doorway. Hardly able to believe her eyes, she made her way to him. 'Bill!' was all she said before falling into his arms.

Margot and Bill, Natalie and Anton Goldman, and George and Betsy ended the night at the Prince Albert Club as Salvatore's guests. When Margot walked in, customers who were already seated at their tables stood up and applauded her, as did the bandleader – and she promised to sing for them.

'You'll miss all this, you know, back in Lowarth,' Bill said, as they sat down.

'Not as much as I'd miss you if I stayed.'

'You said there was a lot more you wanted to do the last time I was down.'

Margot laughed. 'I've had some of the most wonderful roles in one of the best theatres in the West End, I've topped the bill in cabaret and I've toured with ENSA. What more is there?'

'Not so long ago you wanted to get into movies,' Bill said.

Margot thought for a moment. 'Maybe I don't want to be in movies, if it means being without you.'

'I don't want you to end up resenting me – us – if you give up your dream.'

'I won't.' Margot looked into her husband's eyes. 'What about your dream, Bill? What about what you want?'

'Me?' A look of surprise spread across Bill's face. Both he and Margot had focused on what Margot wanted for so long that he'd forgotten what he wanted.

'Yes.' Margot leant forward and whispered in Bill's ear. 'What about your dream of settling down and starting a family when the war ended?'

'What? Are you saying that we're ... that you're ...?'

'No! Maybe. I don't know... I'll know more next week.'

'Well, I'd better go home and find us somewhere to live, just in case,' Bill laughed.

Margot left her stunned husband. She walked across the dance floor to rapturous applause and spoke to the bandleader. The band began to play the introduction to "They Can't Take That Away from Me". She walked to the microphone. The club was full. Everyone's gaze was fixed on her standing in the spotlight. But Margot couldn't see them. Her audience now was just one: Bill.

THE END

Outlines of the other books in The Dudley Sisters Quartet.

The third book**, China Blue**, is about love and courage – and is Claire Dudley's story. While in the WAAF Claire is seconded to the Royal Air Force's Advanced Air Strike Force and then the SOE. Claire falls in love with Mitchell 'Mitch' McKenzie, an American Airman who is shot down while parachuting into France. At the end of the war, while working in a liberated POW camp in Hamburg she is told that Mitch is still alive. Do miracles happen?

The fourth book, working title, **Bletchley Secret**, is about strength and determination – and is the story of Ena, youngest of the Dudley sisters. Ena works in a local factory. She is one of several young women who build components for machines bound for Bletchley Park during World War 2. The Bletchley secret costs her the love of her life. In the 1960s, a successful hotelier and happily married, Ena encounters someone from her past, leading to shocking consequences.

ABOUT THE AUTHOR

Madalyn Morgan has been an actress for more than thirty years working in repertory theatre, the West End, film and television. She is a radio presenter and journalist, writing articles for newspapers and magazines.

Madalyn was brought up in a busy working class pub in the market town of Lutterworth in Leicestershire. The pub was a great place for an aspiring actress and writer to live. There were so many wonderful characters to study and accents learn. At twenty-four Madalyn gave up a successful hairdressing salon and wig-hire business for a place at E15 Drama College, and a career as an actress.

In 2000, with fewer parts available for older actresses, Madalyn learned to touch type, completed a two-year course with The Writer's Bureau, and began writing. After living in London for thirty-six years, she has returned to her home town of Lutterworth, swapping two window boxes and a mortgage, for a garden and the freedom to write.

Madalyn is currently writing her third novel, China Blue, the third of four books about the lives of four very different sisters during the Second World War. First and second novels, Foxden Acres and Applause, are now available.

Visit Madalyn Morgan online:

The Foxden Acres Website:
https://sites.google.com/site/foxdenacresbymadalynmorgan/home

Non-Fiction Blog:
http://madalynmorgan.blogspot.co.uk/

Fiction Blog:
http://madalynmorgansfiction.blogspot.co.uk/

Actress website:
http://www.madalynmorgan.com/

Made in the USA
Charleston, SC
09 February 2016